with this ring,
i'm confused

with this ring, i'm confused

an
Ashley
Stockingdale
novel

by kristin billerbeck

THOMAS NELSON
Since 1798

NASHVILLE   DALLAS   MEXICO CITY   RIO DE JANEIRO   BEIJING

Published in Nashville, Tennessee, by Thomas Nelson. Thomas Nelson is a trademark of Thomas Nelson, Inc.

Thomas Nelson, Inc., titles may be purchased in bulk for educational, business, fund-raising, or sales promotional use. For information, please e-mail SpecialMarkets@ThomasNelson.com.

Publisher's Note: This novel is a work of fiction. Names, characters, places, and incidents are either products of the author's imagination or used fictitiously. All characters are fictional, and any similarity to people living or dead is purely coincidental.

Library of Congress Cataloging-in-Publication Data

Billerbeck, Kristin.
    With this ring, I'm confused / Kristin Billerbeck.
        p. cm.
    ISBN: 978-1-59554-033-1 (TP)
    ISBN: 978-1-59554-335-6 (repak)
    1. Weddings—Fiction. 2. Georgia—Fiction. I. Title.
PS3602.I44W58 2005
813'.54—dc22   2004028393

Printed in the United States of America
07 08 09 10 RRD 5 4 3 2 1

A hearty thank you to Jeana Ledbetter, my trusted
agent and friend, and Natalie Gillespie and Ami McConnell,
my fabulous editors, for helping me complete this
book when the well had run dry!

To Colleen Coble, Diann Hunt, and Denise Hunter: thanks for
being there during the day when I need a pick-me-up.

And of course, to my family who has to put up with too many
Ashley moments when I'm on deadline.

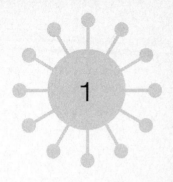

I've imagined my wedding dress since I was a little girl. It's an elegant shantung sheath with cap sleeves, a sweetheart neckline, and tiny seed pearls sewn on the cinched bodice . . . Seed pearls, hah! Now that I'm standing in the bridal boutique, something has snapped. Girlfriend, I want satin, yards and yards of it! I want sequins and crystals and a bum bow the size of Brazil, leg-o'-mutton sleeves, and a train that practically explodes onto the scene. I want something that screams, *I'm the bride!* lost in a snow flurry of white. Bring on winter, baby! Ashley Stockingdale is getting married!

Okay, really I just want to tick off my future sister-in-law. Emily Novak, jobless in Atlanta, is here in Silicon Valley to make sure the wedding day runs smoothly. Granted, she has no experience in this field, but that doesn't seem to stop her at any junction. She is the expert in her own mind, and apparently, that should be good enough credentials for all of us. That, and the copy of the *Wedding Planner* by Martha Stewart is supposed to impress me. Three days I've been searching for the perfect Tussy Mussy. Until three days ago, I didn't even know what this silver piece of hardware was, but it is apparently quite important to "brides in the know" such as my Victorian ancestors and now me. It's a bouquet holder. As in, you hold it in your hands, and no one sees the design anyway. The first rule of good fashion is it should definitely be noticed. Am I right?

I hear Emily clap her hands, and I feel myself cringe at her entrance. "No, no, no. Who brought this gown to you? It's completely wrong. *Hideous!*" She stretches the word to its full three syllables with more than a hint of Southern drawl.

I swivel around. "It has a butt bow."

She sighs extensively. I seem to make her sigh a lot. "Ashley," she says, as though someone has expired. "My brothah has a reputation in Atlanta. His bride will be splashed across every society page in Georgia. This simply will not do."

"But I like it. It says, *Baby got back.* You know what I'm saying?"

"I have no idea what you're sayin'. A Novak bride should be above reproach, and that means, at the very least, elegant style. Classic. Think Jacqueline Kennedy, Princess Diana, Jennifer Aniston."

"Jennifer Aniston?" I ask, hearing that old *Sesame Street* song about how one of these things just doesn't belong.

"The point is, Ashley, you want Keh-vin to gasp at the sight of you, to draw in his breath and never forget the moment. That dress is truly *forgettable*, but don't worry. I've got everything taken care of."

I beg your pardon. This dress is anything but forgettable. Apparently my good hair days have not spoken for me to Emily. I have impeccable taste in clothing. I could easily be a stylist instead of a patent attorney, but Emily is so fun to mess with that I can't help myself. I want to try on the pink gowns, the blue ones, maybe even the golden, shimmery yellow one. I want Emily to imagine me as a satin Easter egg floating down the aisle, stealing her brother from good taste forever. Oh sure, you're thinking I'm immature, but I dare you to waste three days on a bouquet holder and tell me you'd feel any differently. I've had patent processes move quicker than this.

She clings to that Martha Stewart ringed book like it will unlock all the secrets of humanity. She has it tucked inside a Coach leather folder, trying to make me think she comes up with all this brilliance herself, but the truth is she's a paint-by-number wedding planner and Martha holds the color code.

The fact is, I want Brea. My best friend should be here, but I know getting a babysitter for two kids under two is virtually impossible. Especially in the Silicon Valley, where kids are considered dirt with noise. I know Brea would be enjoying my tacky fashion show with vigor and bringing in more for me to try on while we giggled and added sparkle-encrusted tiaras. But Brea is busy, lost in a sea of diapers and spit-up from her babies, and Emily is shockingly free. Go figure. Besides, Kevin is anxious for me to get to know his sister. She doesn't have many friends back home, and gee, isn't that a surprise?

"Ashley! Sorry I'm late." I hear Brea's voice, and I want to run to her and kiss her feet. She takes one gander at my gown, and I see her smile ever so slightly. "That is gorgeous! But I think it needs a few more bows on the sleeves. It doesn't really announce you enough. Let me go look on the racks."

"Stop! I'll go look," Emily shouts and leaves in a huff.

Brea and I fall into a wave of giggles. "Check out my bow." I turn and let her see that not only is my train covered in satin ribbon bows, but also that one special, prominent bow is probably a foot in diameter. "Am I hot or what? Name a man who could resist me." I shake my bonbon with vigor.

"You have to try on one of the pink satins. Did you see that fuchsia number on the clearance rack?"

Do we think alike or what?

"Poor Emily, she's endured enough. I think it's time we got down to business. Besides, I'm annoying Hannah the shop girl. I just had to have my protest moment. I'm fine now. What was I thinking to have my future sister-in-law as my wedding coordinator? Who am I, Jessica Simpson, that I need a coordinator anyway?"

Hannah, the shop's manager, is from my church and is a complete doll, but even she has her breaking point. I almost want to buy this gown to put it out of its misery, like the Charlie Brown Christmas tree.

"The shop is never going to sell that number anyway, even on the clearance rack. You're doing it a favor to try it on." Brea crinkles her nose at my gown. "They probably got it free from an up-and-going designer. Does Emily know you already ordered the Vera Wang and that we're actually here for bridesmaid gowns?"

Tsk. "Sure, bring on the guilt. I was having a perfectly fine day until you had to remind me to grow up. Age is relative, you know."

"You're terrible, and you have to live with this woman forever. You're marrying into her family. The wedding is the least of your issues. You should be thinking about your first wrinkle—or egad, stretch marks, and how they'll fight to hand you the plastic surgery cards. Gosh, they're all like walking ad campaigns for *Extreme Makeovers.*"

"Emily will be back in Atlanta before the weekend's up!" I do a little jig. "I'm going to be good now. I was just entertaining myself until you got here." I slink out of the gown. The black-velvet Elvis painting of wedding wear, if you will.

Kevin, my fiancé, is from big money in the South. His father is a prominent surgeon and attends the proper functions that a good family should. This is why Kevin is in California, hoping to avoid this lifestyle and focus on his first love: medicine. I'm beginning to think the distance to Atlanta is not nearly as wide as I once thought. Perhaps there's a surgical opening in South America.

Emily enters the oversize dressing room with a multitude of boring gowns that say, *I'm elegant and don't have a mind of my own, nor a speck of vision.* Now, I'm a realist, and I've seen my mother's wedding photos. If they taught me anything, it was this: always go classic, never trendsetting. Otherwise, you risk looking like Carol Brady to the next generation.

"Emily," I say softly. "I've actually already ordered a Vera Wang gown. I just wanted to make sure it was the right one today." I yank my suit skirt back on.

"We really should have picked the gown first. And in fact, I did pick the gown—to go with the theme. I was waitin' to show you the style as the grand finale."

"I'm missing something," I say. "I'm the bride, and *you* picked the dress?"

"I had to. To pull off the theme."

"Theme?" I croak. *I'm afraid to ask. I'm having prom flashbacks.*

"Your name is Ashley Wilkes Stockingdale. Your dog is Rhett. Your husband is from Atlanta, the home of the great Margaret Mitchell. Your theme has to be *Gone with the Wind.*"

Um, no, actually it doesn't. "You know, Scarlett and Rhett didn't exactly part on the best of terms. I'm thinking maybe that's not where I want to go with a wedding theme." I'm all smiles. I could be head cheerleader at the moment. "Right?"

"Ashley and Rhett are for*evah* in love, as you and my brothah will be. I'd love to see you walk through raised swords of Confederate soldiers."

"But I'm a Yankee," I say with the utmost seriousness. *I'm a "Yankee"? I'm a patent attorney living in Silicon Valley in the new millennium.* Something about this conversation is making me forget that reality. "I mean, I'm a native Californian. Beach, Hollywood, movie stars." Granted, I live nowhere near these things, but I'm reaching here.

"We won't hold that against you, that you're a Yankee. The Confederate uniforms won't clash with Keh-vin's tuxedo, like a Union soldier's would, aftah all."

Help! I look to Brea. My gaze tells her, *I think she's a crazed lunatic. Help me!*

"I think what Ashley is trying to say is that this is not the wedding she imagines for herself," Brea says. "You understand how a bride dreams of her day, and I've never actually heard of a wedding planner selecting the gown."

"Well, my brothah is the groom. He has some say too." Emily only sounds very Southern when she's getting angry. Look out for the accent.

"Kevin never said anything to me about soldiers at the wedding." I can't imagine my Dr. Kevin Novak, pediatric surgeon at Stanford's

Lucille Packard Children's Hospital, hoping for a Confederate wedding, but then, maybe we haven't known each other long enough.

"Ashley, a weddin' is about mergin' two families together." Emily threads her fingers. "Our family is Southern and proud of its heritage. Just because your family is without history does not mean we should forget our roots. Wouldn't you agree?"

My fists fly to my hips. "Without heritage? I'll have you know, we've had the chicken dance at every one of our weddings. And we start the music with Kool and the Gang's 'Celebration,' like every good American wedding should. I suppose you think the 'Macarena' is tacky?"

I feel Brea's hand on my back. "Ladies, this is serving no good purpose. Let's start the selection of the bridesmaid gowns, shall we? We'll just have to work the theme around Ashley's dress, Emily."

Emily shakes her head. "The dress is the theme. I've found a seamstress for the bridesmaid gowns, a woman who made the reproductions for the Road to Tara Museum. We'll have the traditional tiered skirts, with ruffles and cinched waists."

Brea comes undone. "Listen, I'm not wearing ruffles. I've just had a baby, and I've got enough ruffles of my own. In fact, I'm wearing a shaper to get rid of those ruffles, so I'm certainly not adding any more!"

"Let's not get excited," I say before Brea goes postal. "Maybe it's best that we don't decide this today. Tensions are high, and there's still plenty of time to work around a theme. A different theme," I say.

Now I've got nothing against the South. *Gone with the Wind* is one of my favorite movies, despite my ridiculous moniker, but I'm just not sure I'm ready to recreate the moment at my wedding. In California. With my high-tech friends.

I munch my lip, thinking. "I'm not even sure most of the engineers here have heard of the film. Now if I was going to have a *Lord of the Rings* wedding, I'd be stylin'!" My cell phone rings. "Excuse me," I say, lifting a finger. "Ashley Stockingdale."

"Ash? It's Kevin. How goes the wedding plans?"

"Fine," I offer cheerily, showing teeth just to make it real. They say if you act the part, you believe it.

"Is that my brothah? Let me speak to him." Emily rips the phone out of my hands. "Keh-vin, I came out here to help you, but I really must have creative freedom to plan the weddin'. This will be the social event of the year in Georgia—even though it's in California," she adds with distaste. "I thought we agreed on a Southern theme so that Mothah would be at ease, and your bride is fightin' me at every step." She pauses, tapping her foot and staring me down. "She didn't even want to select a Tussy Mussy."

I've spent my entire thirty-two years wanting to be married. And suddenly, I want to run to the security of my singles group. I want to watch science-fiction movies with engineers and my dog. I want to sketch out patents on my laptop and remind myself that I'm good at something. As I listen to Emily rant about me to my fiancé, the first sting of tears hits. A dream wedding is a myth. A dream wedding would not have Scarlett O'Hara on steroids in it, and it would not include a family that thought purchasing my wedding gown was acceptable. *Boundaries, people!*

"I have to get something," I hear my voice say, and I run out of the shop, down the street—without my cell phone, as Emily is still yelling into it. I've got my coffee card, and that's all that matters at the moment. Jaunting into the coffeehouse, I hand over my card with desperation. "Double shot, on ice."

"Bad day?" Nick, my barista, asks.

"The worst." He pulls the shots, and my mouth starts watering. "I'm beginning to think my brother had the right idea getting married in Vegas. You know, you should just announce to people you don't want to go through the trouble. Vegas it is."

Nick hands me the espresso, which is as thick as sludge. I down it straight.

"Whew, I feel better. Let me have another." I bang the plastic cup on the counter.

Nick's eyes widen. "I don't think so, Ashley. You're hyper enough without caffeine. I'm not going to be responsible for you going over your limit. Weren't you arrested once in that state?"

I slam the cup down on the counter again. "I was arrested for *lack* of caffeine. I had jet lag from Taiwan and no espresso, unless you consider bubble tea strong enough. I don't. And the cop grabbed my Prada!"

He just stares at me, blinking.

"There's a Starbucks on the corner," I threaten.

"I'm cutting you off, Ashley. And I don't think you'd make good on your threat for corporate coffee. I know you too well."

Ack. Foiled again.

Brea walks into the coffee shop, tossing her purse the size of a small African nation over her shoulder. She has my cell phone in her hand. "You've got Kevin worried. Why don't you call him?"

"I'm getting married in Vegas. Southern beauty queens are banned from Vegas, aren't they?"

"Vegas? Now you've got me worried. Did you forget that Seth showed up in Vegas? There are no good memories in that cesspool for you. Call Kevin now."

I've abandoned my future sister-in-law in a bridal boutique. "Brea, maybe I shouldn't be getting married after all. Kevin's family has issues. Major issues, and I've got enough of my own. Think of my kids' gene pool! Do you know, his sister asked me to take the IQ test again for his mother? I mean, what if I didn't pass? What if our kids are stupid, and they blame me? I mean, would it really matter if they were stupid? I'd dress them cute."

"It's impossible that they could be more stupid than asking someone to take an IQ test."

"All right, you've got a point, but that doesn't change this." I look down at my cell phone. "I don't know how I can share any of this with Kevin. What if he thinks I *should* have the right Tussy Mussy?"

"Then isn't it better to know? Kevin works with sick children every day of his life, Ashley. He doesn't care about a bouquet holder any more than you do. You're getting delusional with stress."

Deep down, I know this is true, but Kevin has a hard enough time with his family. I don't want to make things worse. I look back to Brea. "I've got to get back to work. Purvi is going to wonder what's going on with me. She's already bailed me out more than once."

Purvi is my fabulous boss, originally from India. She got fired from Selectech for being a decent mother, and they offered me her job, but I turned it down (along with the immediate ticket to Taiwan). I got a new position at Gainnet as General Counsel. However, I had no idea what I was doing, so they hired Purvi as Executive General Counsel (at my request) and things are back to normal. I'm a grunt patent attorney again. I make enough to live and dress well. What more do I need?

Brea speaks, reminding me I'm not yet in the peaceful place of my familiar chaos: work. "You've got to go back to the boutique, Ashley. Emily is paying for the gloves now, and she's waiting for you. I made an excuse for your rude behavior, but I've got to get home to the boys soon."

I draw in a deep breath and feel my fear. "I don't want to do this."

"Get used to it. Marriage is all about compromise. That's why you have to plan a wedding together first," Brea says. "If you make it through that, you'll be ready for what's to come."

"So you're willing to wear ruffles and a hoopskirt?" I ask with my arms crossed.

"Not on your life. Compromise, Ashley, but don't put me in a tacky bridesmaid gown or I'll have to hurt you, and I won't lend you Miles as ring bearer." She winks. "And please don't have the dog; that's just weird."

Turn the other cheek. That's what being a Christian is all about, but I have to admit, I'd like Emily to get an eyeful of a big satin bow when I do. I slam my hand on the counter and throw my shoulders

9

back. I've handled my brother for years; an unemployed Southern belle from Atlanta has nothing on me. *Bring it on!*

I look down at Kevin's grandmother's ring, and I'm reminded that he's worth an exhaustive search for the perfect Tussy Mussy. In it, I'll place heather to remind me that wishes do come true and red tulips for my everlasting love for Kevin, the man who made me see that pining for someone who doesn't love you isn't really love at all. Love is steadfast and consistent, not filled with courtroomlike drama.

"Ashley?" My future sister-in-law comes into the coffee shop holding a pink bag, which I can only assume is filled with silk gloves.

"I'm sorry, Emily. I had an urge for caffeine." *And room to breathe.*

"Your boss called the bridal shop after you left. Apparently she couldn't get through to you on your cell." Emily looks at my cell in Brea's hand.

"Did she give you a message?" I ask anxiously.

"That unless you're appearin' on the cover of *Bride* this month to get back to work." Emily giggles and looks upward in deep thought. "Oh, and Microsoft . . . hmm . . . wait a minute, I'll remember . . . Microsoft just filed for a patent on your process."

I drop my head in my hands.

Mental note: Mensa membership has no bearing in reality.

"I gotta go!" I leap from the shop and rush back to the office. Lord forbid I fail at everything today.

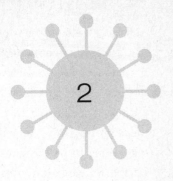

There are no perfect men. There are no perfect men. Well, there is One, but He's more than marriage material. Here on earth, there are no perfect men. I love my fiancé, Dr. Kevin Novak. He's charming, gorgeous, treats me like a princess, and looks like he stepped off the silver screen. Everything a girl could want, right? But he also comes equipped with a textbook-quality dysfunctional family. My ex, Seth: normal family, freaky self. See? Life is all about weighing your options.

Kevin's mother is the plastic-surgery queen, and while she looks great, there's still something "off" about her appearance. Like she's wearing a frightening yet beautiful mask. It makes me want to break into the song "Phantom of the Opera" and maybe a tad afraid to walk under chandeliers.

Kevin's surgeon-father is as cold as his scalpel and just as cutting. He has this fascination with beauty and his narrow definition of it: eerily thin with facial skin pulled taut. I think his dream woman is probably one of those ultrathin actresses like Lara Flynn Boyle *after* liposuction. Dr. Novak's issues will probably be the death of his wife. Age has a way of catching up with all of us eventually. Even Cher one day.

Then there's the daughter, my bridal consultant: Emily. Emily is not thin by her father's standards but borders on anorexic to the rest of us. She's five-foot-nine and maybe weighs 130, blond, with exceptionally dewy Southern skin. She's an overachiever in everything except employment. Kevin says she's had ten jobs in the last four years, but they always end in disaster. She has either dated the boss, taken stock from an elderly stockholder, or once, nearly married a man of fifty-eight years. Additionally, she has been unable to get along with the other employees—which I can only assume means other female employees. In her repertoire, she's been a dental office manager, a doctor's assistant, a front-desk clerk at an elegant hotel, and a radio intern. Her last job was managing a small florist's shop in Alpharetta, Georgia. Currently, she's got the best gig going as my bridal coordinator. She can't marry the boss (her brother), and she can't get fired unless she succeeds in finding a better bride for her brother, which seems to be her priority.

My cell phone rings, and I plug the earpiece in. I'm tooling down the road, anxious to get to work yet understanding my presence will make no difference today other than the fact that Purvi will have someone to yell at about our patent being "stolen." Purvi's yelling has no effect on me any longer. She just gets it out of her system, and we're back on track. I love her, and she loves me. We can handle our lack of communication skills. Though we probably drive those around us crazy.

"Hi, Kev," I say into the phone as I turn my CD off.

"Ashley, what's going on? How come you didn't answer your phone?" His voice sends that surge of fear through me again.

"I'm just not having a stellar day. Thought I'd spare you the angst."

"We're sharing our angst, remember? That's what married people do, share the angst."

Not when my angst has a name and it's your sister. "Right. You're right. Emily went with Brea. They were going to continue to shop. I hope that's okay." *It was either that, or I had to take her out.*

"I don't expect you to babysit her, Ashley, but they're shopping without the bride? Isn't that a bit odd?"

"I told Brea she has free reign over the bridesmaid dress, and they didn't have long because of Brea's kids. She knows what my dress looks like, and I'll get final approval." Here, I pause a minute. "Do you have a thing about Confederate soldiers?"

He laughs. "What?"

"I mean, what would you think if I had period soldiers at our wedding?"

"I'd think you'd gone over the edge, Ashley."

Whew. "Just checking."

"My sister is not trying to have a Southern wedding, is she? We talked about that."

Can't let Emily know I tattled. "I just wondered if you might want to include your heritage in the wedding, that's all." I don't want to tell Kevin his sister is not the dream wedding coordinator. Scarlett's maybe, but definitely not mine.

"Ashley," he says with the utmost patience. "The Confederate flag would not go over big in California. Correct? I don't want my co-workers thinking *skinhead* as you walk down the aisle. "

I start to giggle. "Skinhead. That's funny. I just wanted to make sure. No Confederate flags." I scribble onto scrap paper sticking out from my dashboard. *No Confederate flags.* As though I need a reminder.

"Are you coming to the hospital for dinner?" Kevin asks. I can almost see him staring at his watch, calculating the time window he might squeeze me into.

"You're working again?" I groan.

"It's Friday night. Why do you even have to ask?"

"Because I'm ever-hopeful, Kevin." *A fool, if you will.* Once I had a boyfriend who never had the *motivation* to see me. Now I have a fiancé who never has *time* to see me. Like I said, you pick your battles. "I probably won't be in tonight, Kevin. I need to work too. We lost a key patent today, and I need to let Purvi know I'm committed to getting this right next time. She thinks I'm doing nothing but planning the wedding."

"Well, you're only getting married once. She ought to understand, but it's fine you're working. I'll probably only take half an hour for dinner anyway. I want to get home before Emily goes out. The last thing I need is her falling for another old man at some karaoke bar."

"Some women like older men," I say coyly. Kevin is a year younger than me. While I've grown accustomed to this fact, I'm not exactly comfortable with it. I was raised old-school, I guess: guy is taller and older. Well, we're half there. At least I can wear heels with him.

"Some women know better than going older. You and Demi Moore have something in common. You know how to pluck a piece of fruit from the tree when it's ripe for the taking. Not wait until it's all raisinlike and requires prescription meds."

I know he's trying to make me feel better. But really, when he reminds me of my age, I feel like Mrs. Haversham standing around in my dress . . . waiting.

"You sound exhausted already. I'm thinking delirious. How long have you been working?" I pull into my company parking lot. I'm probably making this conversation last longer than it needs to, but I'm not ready to face Purvi or everything I've done wrong for the day. Emily's coordinating is mistake enough.

"I've been working too long. I've lost count and I'm starting to have Ashley-humor. Meet me for breakfast tomorrow?"

"I'd love to." I feel my stomach surge with excitement. *How does he do that?*

"I can't wait to marry you, Ashley Stockingdale. I'll make you breakfast in bed every Saturday, and I won't have to meet you anywhere. I'll open my eyes, and you'll be there."

"I've tasted your cooking before. Breakfast is not a big draw for me, actually." I know he can hear the smile in my voice, but better to tease than actually think about my future. *What if it doesn't happen this way?* It's all about expectations, and if you don't have any, you can't be disappointed.

"I'll have you know," Kevin says, "there are women out there who would die to have my waffles for dinner."

"I don't doubt that, but it has nothing to do with your waffles. I think it's probably closer to the fact that you look like Hugh Jackman on one of his good days, and skipping dinner to get right to dessert is probably why they want your waffles."

"Whew! Getting hot in here. Definitely getting hot in here. I need to get back to work. I'll pick you up at eight tomorrow. Wear jeans. I miss my woman in jeans. How's that for a sexist comment?"

"It's California lawsuit material."

"So sue me."

"Is eight going to give you enough rest?" I ask, even though my mind is still wandering to Kevin in a robe with coffee.

"It's going to give me enough time away from you. I'll be up at six, regardless. Put me in your Blackberry."

"I'll be ready." As I start to have romantic fantasies, reality strikes. "Is Emily coming to breakfast?"

"She'll probably still be sleeping. But if she's awake, I'll invite her. It's nice to see you getting to be friends. I'll tell her you're hoping she'll come."

"Right."

I hear his name paged in the background. "Love you, gotta run." He clicks off the line.

I turn up my CD and have one last listen to Chris Tomlin at full blast. Anything to pump me up for "losing" another patent. I'm bracing for Hurricane Purvi. Is it my fault that most patent examiners have minimal experience? Or that sometimes the concepts are just difficult for them to grasp? But I'm thinking negatively. Our patent hasn't been denied, and it has to be different from Microsoft's process. I just hope it's different enough to warrant its own patent. I button up my suit coat and square my shoulders. *I am Super Patent Attorney. If anyone can do it, I can. I'm strong to the finish.*

I yank open the door to Gainnet. *I'm ready for anything; just check out the squared shoulders.* I have just survived the Ya Ya wedding coordinator; patents have nothing on me.

Purvi is in the hall, arms crossed over her chest, her foot tapping. She's in Indian dress today. I'm thinking this does not bode well for me.

"The world must stop for you to get married?" Her hands are now flying.

"How long did your wedding last in India?" I shot back, knowing full well an Indian wedding is a much bigger deal. And judging by Purvi's pursed lips, she knows I'm right, which only makes her angrier.

"You are an insolent thing. Just never mind. Did you see the patent pending?" she asks.

Obviously, I haven't been into my office yet, but whatever. "No, I'll get to it right away. Just calm down, Purvi. Yell at me when I know what you're yelling about. It's much more effective that way."

She pounds her fist in her palm. "I want you to go back to engineering, and I want a new process. A better process that outstrips this!"

Yeah, like engineering suddenly works for us. In Silicon Valley, there is the engineering department, and then there are the rest of us "support" systems. Give me a break, I'm going to march in and tell engineering what to do. Right before they consider me the daily entertainment and fire my bum. Deep down, I know Purvi understands this. She's got to be stressed, and judging by the Indian dress, it's not a good day to upset her. When her husband is home, her mother-in-law (who lives with the family) tends to mark her territory and show Purvi who is woman of the house. I once heard that the Chinese symbol for unhappiness is two women under the same roof. If Purvi is any indication . . .

"Just let me take some notes and see where I am, Purvi, okay?"

"Where you are is back in Taiwan. The VP of engineering is there, and I want you to meet with him directly." She claps her hands. "We've got to move on this."

I'm calm. *Ohm. Ohm.* "He'll be back next week. Don't react,

Purvi. Act, don't react. Remember that management training they sent us to?" Now these words coming from me have very little effect, as I am the resident drama queen.

"With fire in his eyes, he'll be back. I want to ward this off and be ready. This time, we're ready," she says in Patton form.

I slink to my desk and look at the paperwork in front of me, and suddenly my eyes widen. "Our patent was filed before this date." Once again, stress for nothing. *Like I need additional cortisol released in my system. Makes you fat, you know?* "They need to review this at the patent office. It's our intellectual property, Purvi." I look through the files quickly.

"You're avoiding the subject. I want you in Taiwan."

I am avoiding the subject. *Ashley Stockingdale, U.S. Patent Attorney.* Look at the nameplate. It says nothing about Taiwan on there, am I right? I lift it off my desk for reassurance. If I'm not mistaken, *U.S.* stands for *United States*; no foreign nations mentioned.

My office phone rings. It's my mother, according to caller ID. "My mom's on the phone," I say. Purvi, even in her excitement, knows a mother takes precedence. Purvi exits my office in a huff, and I kick the door closed gently. "Hi, Mom."

"It's Mei Ling, not your mom. Do you know where she is? I'm at her house, but she's not here." Mei Ling is my sister-in-law and the mother to my mom's only grandchild. Which, of course, gives her priority as my mother's favorite "daughter."

"All I know is Mom couldn't shop today because she had baby Davey. We went to the bridal boutique without her." Trying to keep the pout out of my voice. She is *my* mother!

"Oooh, what did you pick for the dresses? Am I going to be a hot mama?"

Please. "Mei Ling, need I mention you're a size four and I could put you in a gunny sack and you'd be a hot mama?"

"I'm a two, actually."

"Must I hurt you?" I ask.

"I just didn't want you to order me the wrong size," she says in all innocence.

"I should make you wear padding if you're going to stand up next to me."

"As if Kevin will have eyes for anyone else. He's really a guy who has some capacity to love. Very opposite of Seth."

Not going there. "Did you call my mom's cell phone?" I ask, getting back to the point of our conversation.

"I don't know why you bought her that thing. She never carries it. I don't think she even knows how to charge it." Mei Ling pauses a moment. "Yep, here it is on the kitchen counter. Dead."

"Is her car in the driveway?"

Another pause. "Yes."

"Then she's at the neighbor's showing off Davey. Try 1705."

"Thanks, Ashley, I knew you'd know. Somehow a daughter always understands how her mother's mind works."

Purvi's outside my office window, and I can see that her bouncing, jittery self is anxious. I hang up the phone and go out to meet her. "Sometimes you're hard to like, you know that?"

"I'm not here to be liked. I want to book you on Sunday's flight and assure the VP that everything is under control."

For the first time, I realize that marriage is going to impact my career. I'm planning a wedding, but more important, I'm getting married. To a man who spends his life saving sick children. Supposedly I have a dire emergency, and that means going to Taiwan to kiss the feet of an engineering VP. *Please.* If we're going to get into the psychology of the moment, this is about Purvi trying to be above reproach while her husband is home; and I'm caught in the middle with a sixteen-hour plane ride. She'll be over it by the time I'm in the air.

I shake my head. "I'm not going to Taiwan."

"Ashley, it's your job to go to Taiwan." Purvi's face is wrinkled with concern.

Forgive me here, I'm having a moment. A moment when I'm thinking, *I'm getting married to a surgeon. Like I need this stupid job.* But I get attacked immediately with a pang of guilt and the thought of doing my job as unto the Lord.

I look straight into Purvi's brown eyes. Purvi's like an Indian Barbie. She's got this creamy exotic skin that makes you want to run and exfoliate. Plus, she's got long, silky black hair that you can just see the model running her fingers through for a conditioner commercial. All this beauty combined with the intensity of Dick Cheney.

"Let me call Kevin first, all right? I can't just take off to Taiwan without telling my fiancé," I say.

"First, go meet with the new director of software. He's got some processes he wants to speak to you about."

"We have a new director of software?"

"He's pretty good. Has some clean patent ideas already." Purvi nods her head and looks at a piece of scrap paper in her hand. "His name is Seth. Seth Greenwood. We got him from Mitel."

I can't breathe. I just stand here shaking my head. "No," I say aloud.

"No, what?"

I grab the scrap from her hand. *Seth Greenwood.*

Certainly, there are two Seth Greenwoods. There has to be. This one is not my ex-boyfriend. He can't be. That Seth specialized in communications software. We make . . . I feel my eyes fall shut. *We make networks.* You don't just change industries, but as soon as I think it, I know how related the fields are. My head is spinning, and I have lost the ability to swallow. Reality sinks in. There aren't two Seth Greenwoods from Mitel. There's only one. He's bald, blue-eyed, and I once loved him with everything within me. This can't be good.

3

I crumple up the paper in my hand. "Seth can wait, I think."

Purvi tosses her hand in the air. "Ashley, how you prioritize your day is beyond me. If you weren't the best patent attorney out there, you'd be locked away for good. You're like Howard Hughes: functional, business-savvy, but very, very strange." In her up-lilting Indian accent, it sounds like a compliment.

I start to laugh and collect the multitude of files on my desk. "I'm going to go home. Pack for Taiwan," I say with a final grin. "Have Debra book me for Sunday's flight," I say, knowing it's useless to fight fate. I am the girl who goes to Taiwan. I need to just accept my life, as does my future husband.

I stuff the reports into my briefcase. "I'll need time to prepare for the VP of engineering." Which, of course, is a crock. With a sixteen-hour plane flight, I'll have nothing but time. Mostly I just need to get away and think. My mind is overwrought with details. Details of a wedding, a few patents, and now an ex-boyfriend who can't seem to leave my personal space alone. Gainnet is my territory. If I have to mark the hydrant, I will.

Purvi is staring as I'm mumbling to myself. She knows not to mess with me when I act crazy. And I am definitely on the loony fringe today. I think Purvi has accepted my actions as part of my genius. Of course, there is no such genius. I'm just weird, off-center. She shakes her head and walks toward her office.

"We'll have you booked for Sunday. Think patent, not patent leather, all right? The time for shopping has come to an end."

My thoughts wander back to Seth and his unfortunate reappearance in my life. He and his sidekick, Sam, have changed churches because every once in a while, a great cloud comes and captures all the singles, lifts them up, and deposits them at the new, hipper church. I realize they all think this new experience will bring them closer to true spirituality, but really they're just hoping for a better class of date. Granted, they all rotate together, which doesn't allow for much fresh meat in this scenario. Hence, they stay put until the next cloud appears, and their old church goes on as before with people who do the actual work.

My point is that Seth floated away on this singles' cloud, and I haven't seen him since an unfortunate run-in the night I got engaged. As time skims on, I know now that I had no interest in seeing him. *Hello, God, do you hear that? No interest!*

There are two ways I classify ex-boyfriends:

1. The possible missed opportunity. (What if I'd said this? Done that? Was I supposed to bear his children? What if he wasn't waiting for Jennifer Garner's twin?)

2. The Praise-His-Name Ex. You can't say his name, i.e., Seth, without uttering a *Thank you, Jesus! Thank you for sparing me from my own mortal blind spot.*

Seth is definitely the latter. Quality person, decent human being, and yet completely oblivious to the thoughts and needs of others. I think Seth has a kink in the emotional gene . . . as in, he doesn't have one. I imagine him at the birth of his first child: "Great. Great. What's for dinner, honey? Do you need me to take something out of the oven?"

At some point in my life, I found his aloofness sexy and intriguing.

Now I see it for the major issue it is, and rather than intriguing, I would call it something closer to coldhearted and detached. I exhale a deep breath and look toward the software hallway.

Of all the telecom joints in the world, he walks into mine.

I dash out of the office without looking back or confirming my flight. Purvi didn't look right. I probably shouldn't have left, but I drive home and get lost in the music. Oblivious to the wedding planner from the dark side, or the reappearance of Seth, or the fact that Kevin is busy again. I'm going to focus on tomorrow's breakfast with the doctor of my dreams. And my new shoes: Kenneth Cole wedding sandals with a beaded ankle strap. Ah yes, the world fades away at the thought of unworn shoes. They're like a flower of promise; an unhinged bud.

Once on the porch, I drop my briefcase at the door and fumble with the keys. I can hear Rhett, my mini-horse-sized dog, panting on the other side of the door. "Hi, baby, Mommy's home."

As I enter the house, Rhett is barking happily, and his tongue is lapping at my nylons in between yelps. "Shh, Rhett!" I say as I pat his head.

My eye is drawn to a white trail cluttering Kay's perfectly organized house. There's shredded paper everywhere through the living room and down the long hallway. "What did you do?" I pick up a sheet and see that it's tissue paper.

"Rhett!"

I pick up another and follow the path to my new shoe box. My new, now-opened shoe box. Breathing heavily here. I close my eyes to prepare. Lifting my lids and picking up the footwear, I see the wedding sandal covered with dog slobber as tiny crystal beads fall to the hardwood floor. I slump down onto the couch. "Forty pairs of shoes, Rhett. You have to go for the gold every time?"

Okay, the shoes are history. I'm moving on. Anxiety will get me nowhere. I'm going to relish anticipating my date with Kevin tomorrow since that's all I have left. The phone rings, and I run for it while

yanking Rhett out to the backyard to do some time. I grab the vacuum on the way back.

"Hello," I say, kicking the vacuum into an upright position.

"Ashley, it's Emily. Your boss said you went home."

*Oh, right, the other benefit: I also had freedom from the dark side.
Not.*

"Hi, Emily, I brought home my laptop to search patents here.
How did the bridesmaid dress search go?"

"I have something fabulous in mind; I had hoped they'd have
something to do it justice. That shop is awfully tiny, and I just don't
think it's going to do at all. I'll have a sketch for you by the end of the
week, and we can get started with a seamstress. Is my brothah there
by chance?"

"I think he had a surgery this afternoon. Do you need something?" *A lobotomy, perhaps? Bad Ashley.*

"I ran into this guy after you left the coffee shop. He says there's
a get-together tonight in San Carlos at his place. I wanted to see if
I could hitch a ride with Keh-vin."

Emily is a grown woman. She's twenty-five years old, and she
does not need a babysitter. But this thought doesn't have time to register. She obviously needs a babysitter. The way I figure it, if she plans
my wedding and does a good job, she goes home to Atlanta to start
her own business, and I'm free. But if she meets someone, it significantly throws a wrench into my life, as well as into her future plans
of being employable. I consider this a life coach moment. Life coach,
or self-indulgent interloper. You be the judge.

"Where are you, Emily? Did Brea drop you off at Kevin's?"

"She couldn't leave me in town, said you'd hurt her. I don't understand all this talk of violence among friends. It's not civil at all."

She's home safe. Audible sigh of relief here. "Kay and I usually
watch a movie on Friday night. Why don't you come over here
instead?" I shrug, not that she can see me. "Wouldn't that be more fun
than going out with people you don't know?"

"He was really handsome, Ashley."

And your brother will really kill me. "Handsome men are a dime a dozen in Silicon Valley." *Granted, they all have issues and more money than social skills, but we digress.* "I can invite a few guys from the singles group over. I'm sure there's a few you'd consider handsome, and you'd be safe." *Unless you are a video-game controller, they have no trouble keeping their hands off you.*

"Ashley, no offense, but y'all don't drink, and y'all act like you're on *Happy Days.* It's my last weekend in California; I want to party. I don't want to sit around with a bunch of losers who can't get a date. No offense."

"No, of course not." *I'm going to regret this question.* "Is the guy under forty?"

"Ashley Stockingdale, I am a big girl. I know my brothah thinks I am fohteen, but I can assure you I am capable of seeing to myself."

Okay, but you're not.

"It has nothing to do with you being an adult, Emily. This is California. We don't just go to parties of people we don't know. Even on eBay, you check out someone's references, am I right? Safety first?"

"I have no idea what you're talkin' about. I prefer older men, Ashley. Matt is perfectly respectable, and I'm a fine judge of character."

I'm trying to hold this back, but I know it's coming. *Wait for it . . .* "Do you want me to go to the party too?"

"Heavens, no! Whatever would my friend think? I'll just take a cab. You needn't worry over me. I'll extend my Southern hospitality without worry."

Time for some psychology. "A cab? Do we even have cabs in Silicon Valley?"

"Of course you do," Emily says. "Haven't you been to the airport?"

"Granted, I've seen them at the airport. I just never actually knew someone who used one." *Getting my voice of disgust on here.* "Are they, you know . . . dirty?"

"Dirty?"

"Never mind. Just take a moist towelette with you. And I wouldn't wear white."

Long pause.

"I've got my friend's number. Maybe he'll pick me up," Emily says in her chipper voice.

I slap my forehead. Does this girl not get a clue? And how does this translate to Mensa membership, which my fiancé's family seems to worship? Subtle is not going to work. "Emily, you can't go meet some guy in California at his house. People meet in restaurants, coffeehouses, that sort of thing. Personal safety is what I'm worried about. I don't really care who you date." *Although I would prefer someone in Georgia.*

"Y'all aren't very friendly here in California."

"We all don't want to get attacked."

Another long pause. "Can we invite him to your place?"

Choices: I can let my future sister-in-law go to a man's house alone, I can invite this prime suspect into my home, or I can let Kevin worry. "Yeah, he can come."

"Thanks, Ashley, I'm going to call him right now! I'll warn him your friends are nerds."

Stellar.

She hangs up on me, and I settle onto the couch, still gripping my lost wedding shoe and staring at the vacuum, knowing I should get up and do something about the trail of beads.

"The red egg and ginger party!" I shout, and Rhett barks.

My roommate, Kay, comes in just as I say it. "Are you talking to yourself again?"

"I just figured out how to get out of Taiwan."

"You're keeping your job, right? Because I'm trying to find a new roommate before the wedding, but it won't do me any good if you can't pay the mortgage, and employment isn't exactly your strong suit."

"Forget about that. Like I can afford to quit after that tax bill. They're having a red egg and ginger party tomorrow night for my brother's baby. That's why my mom kept Davey all day. It's the excuse I need to stay home and focus on the patents on my desk."

Red egg and ginger parties are held when a baby is one month old and are notoriously expensive. You invite everyone you know and formally name your baby. And you feed people. Lots of people, with lots of great buffet food. Sit-down if you can afford it, but quantity is what seems most important.

"How do you figure red eggs and ginger are going to impress your boss? When's your flight? Can't you just postpone it? It's a party, Ashley, not a three-day ceremony. Are you going to try and convince Purvi this is *Monsoon Wedding* for babies?"

"Don't confuse me with the facts. It's cultural. No human resources department can fight culture in California." I stand up and do a spin. "Purvi will understand, and by the time it's over, the VP of engineering will return and life will go on as planned."

Kay has dropped her keys at her "landing spot," the place at the door where she starts her proper organization. She slips her briefcase into the custom space created for her things. "You seem satisfied with yourself. Since when does it bother you to go to Taiwan?"

"Since I have a wedding to plan and only four months left to do it. I don't even have the chapel yet, and since church meets in a high school, I'm not getting married there."

"I thought Kevin's sister was in charge of all that."

"Sure she is, if I want to give control to the Confederates again."

Kay just shakes her head. "Your life is just not that bad, Ashley. You're marrying a surgeon who could be cast on *ER*. Every family has issues. You're good at cultural awareness. Try and be aware, will you?"

"You don't understand, Kay. She wants to have soldiers with swords!"

"What do you care? The wedding is one day. You get Kevin for the rest of your life. Let Emily send him off in her Southern way.

There's probably a great deal about their background that you don't understand."

"You're kidding, right?"

Kay shrugs. "I just don't think it's a big deal. No one cares anyway, as long as the band and the food are good."

"Go away." I start to walk back to my room, picking up the shreds of paper and beads. Kay doesn't say a thing about the mess.

"I just don't see the big deal about one more trip to Taiwan. You can't spend the next four months doing nothing but planning a wedding. It's pathetic, actually. Since when did you become a mindless bride?"

I open my mouth to defend myself, but you know, it is pathetic. So what am I going to say? I have a patent to defend, my honor to defend with Seth in the office, my dignity to defend with my future in-laws, and I'm worried about a jaunt to Taiwan. *Seems like I have bigger fish to fry.*

Kay starts to pick up the rest of Rhett's bejeweled mess.

"Are you going to be around tonight?" I ask her. "I invited some people over for a movie. I thought you'd have your normal crew, so I took the liberty of—"

"Who did you ask?" She looks at me mortified, as if there is a shred of paper on the floor and she might be seen as the world's worst housekeeper if not given ample time.

I start to straighten the books on the coffee table. "Emily and a friend."

"Emily has a friend in California?" Kay asks.

She does now. "She met someone, actually."

"*Where* did she meet someone?"

"Outside the coffee shop. Near the bridal boutique."

Kay shakes her head. "I'll invite the guys over for protection. We weren't planning anything, but I'll tell them I'm cooking."

Free meal always equals engineers on call.

"You're incredible, Kay. I owe you."

"You *so* owe me. What kind of dress did you decide I'm wearing for your wedding? That was today, right? Am I going to look ridiculous?" She yanks off her Mr. Rogers cardigan and hangs it in the closet. "I'm forty-four now, Ashley. I can't exactly pull off polka dots or pencil skirts."

Kay runs three miles a day. She could pull off whatever she wanted to, but fashion has never been her thing. She'd rather create a gourmet meal and spend her money on granite countertops in our recently redesigned kitchen than spend more than $24 for a pair of shoes. She has the body we would all die for and does nothing with it. Talk about your waste of resources.

"Kay, between you, Brea, and the Southern belle, I don't know how I'll ever make everyone happy. It's one day of your life, you know? If I want a pencil skirt, you can suffer."

"You'll figure out what is best for all of us, Ashley. If there's a fashion crisis to be solved, you'll find the answer. I have no doubt. Why are you home, anyway?"

"Sit down."

"You didn't lose your job again? You said you couldn't afford to. You didn't lose your job, right?"

"Sit down."

She does. Kay worries a lot about me losing my job, because I haven't had the best track record, and hey, I pay half the mortgage. That's reason enough for her to be concerned, but what it's really about is her own insecurity. Did she fail by giving me the chance to purchase half her house?

"If this is about buying you out on the house, I'm working on that, Ash."

I shake my head. "It's nothing like that. We got a new software director today."

She looks away—up toward the ceiling, actually.

"Kay, did you know we got a new software director at Gainnet?"

Kay doesn't look at me. "I gotta call the guys if we're going to have men here tonight. And get dinner started. I have to get dinner started."

"How could you! How could you not tell me Seth was taking the job? That's like Girlhood 101A!"

"I didn't want you to quit. Seth's been looking for something new ever since he came back from India. I sorta told him they were looking at Gainnet."

"Kay! Do you think I want to see my ex every day at work?"

"I didn't think he'd get the job. Besides, he and Arin are together from what I understand."

My stomach lurches, and I slowly descend to the couch. "Arin's not in India?"

Kay just shakes her head. "I really better make those calls." She walks down the hallway.

Arin got her way. Arin, the size-two missionary, who seems more interested in free travel than actual evangelism. She's back, and her name is still associated with Seth's. People move on. I've moved on, so of course I don't expect Seth to sit and pine over me and never go forward. Except, maybe I do just a little bit. Couldn't he grovel for just a bit? There's that whole unrequited love thing that should at least give him pause!

4

I work for a few hours on patent materials, and there's a quiet knock on my bedroom door. I open the door a smidge: the traitor stands there.

"I know you're mad at me," Kay says.

I open the door wider and go plop on my bed.

"You're engaged, top in your field; you have a great home in Palo Alto. Isn't that enough revenge for you? Seth lost his job over that India relocation, and his church so you would comfortable. Don't you think he's paid enough? I felt sorry for him being unemployed. As a Christian, don't you?"

"Hmmm." I shake my head. "No, not really." I smile. "I'm kidding. But you could have warned me. Can you imagine what it was like for me to just hear his name as the new software director?"

She exhales. "Whew. I'm glad to hear you've calmed down. I should have warned you, but I didn't want you to say anything to HR and ruin his chances. He needed a job, Ash. I knew you'd never get in his way, ultimately. You still care about him, I would think." Kay bites on her thumbnail. "I need your help, Ashley."

My eyebrows shoot up. "You need *my* help? Do you have a kitchen patent or something?"

Kay is the epitome of organization. She could star on that HGTV *Mission Organization*, only she'd probably organize the camera crew too and drive everyone nuts. But I can just see her driving up in her car to the black hole of the day, with loads of baskets and plastic bins—plus the labeler. Kay labels everything! I consider myself fortunate that I don't have my name taped across my forehead.

"I need fashion help," Kay blurts.

Well, that goes without saying. "You need fashion help? Why?"

She shifts uncomfortably and looks up toward the ceiling. I'm glad the ceiling is recently painted. It seems to be Kay's favorite focal point lately. "Do you remember I told you about an old wound?" She pauses and takes a deep breath. "A long time ago? Longer than I care to mention."

I am definitely intrigued. Kay and a man. This is the story I've been waiting for. "The one who seemed to swear you off all men for eternity?"

Kay purses her lips but then says, "Yeah, that's the one."

"So you admit it."

"Admit what?"

"That the guy made you swear off men."

"Let's just say he and my father didn't help my situation." Kay is rubbing her hands nervously.

"Kay, women dish! There's nothing wrong with telling someone this. You probably should have done it years ago and freed yourself of the burden. So how is this a fashion emergency anyway?"

"He's coming by soon. I think to ease his guilty conscience." She ponders this statement a moment. "He should have a guilty conscience."

"*The guy* is coming here?" I'm going to meet the man who did this to Kay. With certainty, I realize that I want to hurt him. Badly.

"Listen, it's nothing like you're thinking," Kay says. "There's no romance. The guy's a complete fascist. He's married, he never had any kids because he didn't want to support them, and he used to be a pastor before he became a full-time missionary. He left his church in New Orleans. It's a long, tumultuous story." Kay looks me in the eye.

I look at her in awe. "Still waters run deep."

"He wasn't the last man to break my heart, just the first. But I almost fell away from Jesus then, so this one holds a particularly hard memory. It wasn't romantic, just a letdown from what I expected from fellow Christians."

Wonders never cease. Kay has a history. "So why are you seeing him then? He sounds like the ultimate loser, the kind of guy I picture in a hunting T-shirt who advertises his complete lack of social graces."

"Ashley, are you even here with me?"

"What?" I ask.

"I'm allowing him to come because I want him to see me. That he didn't break me. I want him to see my house, my success, and me. I want to show him I'm not one of his casualties, that Jesus was stronger than what he did, and so am I."

My mouth is agape. "That doesn't sound remotely like you." I abhor my next thought. "It kind of sounds like me, actually."

"I know, but there it is just the same. Will you help me?"

Will I help her? Kay is a blank canvas I've been dying to get my hands on since I met her. "Can we throw away that Michelin down jacket of yours?"

"Let's not get crazy. It's just one night." She walks into my room, toward my closet. "Can you lend me something?"

"Of course I will, but I don't think you recognize the power of a new outfit. It's like spinach to Popeye, the super energy pill for Underdog's ring—"

Kay rolls her eyes. "Can we get on with it?" She thumbs through my clothes and finds the most boring thing in my closet.

I grab it from her. "No. Think red. Scorned woman gets her revenge, only red will do. Remember when Scarlett has to show up at Ashley's party after the—"

"I don't want revenge, Ashley. And I don't want to look like a brazen hussy. I want to look successful. I am successful, but he probably won't see that since I never married."

"You are successful, Kay. Remember, the best revenge is looking good."

"Then you're right. I do want revenge."

We both laugh, and I grab her a Ralph Lauren springy wrap dress in silk, with a fabulous pinkish-red bouquet print. "This is an incredible dress!" The tags are still hanging off it, and I try to hide them so Kay doesn't feel pressure.

"I'm not wearing that, Ashley. Let's be realistic. One doesn't go from Melanie to Scarlett in a day."

"Okay, too froufrou." I grab a Ralph Lauren silk handkerchief skirt in the same fabric. "I couldn't make up my mind. I'm going to take one of them back."

"You had a hard time making a decision on a man too. Maybe you should work on your skills." She pulls the skirt in front of her and sees its length is appropriate for her comfort level. "What would I wear this with?"

"Short-sleeve silk sweater." I pull out one in the same red hue. I put it up to her neck. "Oh, it's your color!" I pause for a minute. "Speaking of color . . ." I finger her hair.

She pulls away in a flinch. "No, I'm not dying my hair."

"Do you want him to see all this gray and how you've aged?" I say as I lift a strand. "Dye is not the enemy, Kay. I can make it look really natural."

Kay pulls away. "I'm not coloring my hair, Ashley. It *is* natural."

I put up a finger. "Wait, I've got the perfect thing." I go into the bathroom, rummage through my closet, and come running back into the bedroom. "Temporary color. No one at work will ever know. We'll wash it out by Monday. I have this from when Brea and I went as blondes for the All Saints' Day party. You'd be a great blonde, Kay."

"Absolutely not."

"Not a platinum blonde, just a nice light ashy-brown color, see?" With a smile, I hold up the box.

Kay's still shaking her head. "I knew this was a mistake."

I'm losing her. She's slipping into the taupe abyss. Must retreat. "No mistake. We'll work on the clothes." *The hair can wait.*

"What do you have that I can wear that doesn't say, *I want to impress?*"

"Hmmm, why would I own *that* piece of clothing?" Then I say, "Kidding. Just kidding." I'm still eyeing her hair and thinking chunky highlights. She picks up an old Shelli Segal Laundry dress. "It's out of style, Kay."

"I don't care about style. I just want something that's more updated than my—"

"Plaid," I finish for her.

She purses her lips. "I do not wear plaid."

Kay does, however, wear the fashion equivalent. "Well, maybe not plaid. But flannel!"

"What's wrong with flannel?"

"If you have to ask, you just need to trust my judgment." I point to the bed. "Go stand over there. I'll find you something." I rifle through my closet looking for the perfect mixture of trendy yet sophisticated. Classic but not too colorful. "I've got it." I pull out a Jones New York dress in red with tiny black polka dots. "This is perfect. It will show off your long legs and toned arms."

Kay backs away from me. "It's too bright."

"Just try it on, no pressure. The black polka dots tone it down," I say reassuringly. I toss the dress at her and go out into the hallway. Unlike normal women, Kay gets all freaky when she undresses in front of other women. She'd never survive a Loehmann's sale.

I head to the bathroom and collect my makeup. I may never get this opportunity again, and in my entire time of knowing Kay, I have somehow resisted the urge to attack her with an eye pencil. "The girl needs eyeliner," I say to myself as I throw it in a basket. And mascara, and just a smidge of lip gloss. I reach for the nail polish but decide not to push my luck.

When I get back into the room, Kay's back in her velour, short-sleeve sweater and black jeans. "What are you doing?"

"It was too bright. I told you, too bright."

I rifle through my closet again and find the drabbest thing I own, an olive-green cargo dress with a cinched waist. I must have been depressed that day. "Okay, try this on."

She takes it and cinches up her nose. "It's too short."

"It will go to your knees. Contrary to what you might think, dresses don't have to be at the ankle anymore." I wink at her. "Even the petticoat can go."

Kay laughs and takes the dress. "Fine, I'll try it on." She stops and looks at me.

"I'm leaving. No wonder you don't belong to the gym. If I had your body, I'd be traipsing around everywhere." I exit and hear the phone ringing. Kay canceled caller ID, so I'm at the mercy of whomever feels the need to dial us up. "Good afternoon, Ashley's Extreme Makeover."

"Ashley?" I hear in a stern Southern tone. *Uh-oh. Is she mad?*

"Hi, Emily. Did you get ahold of your friend?" *Uh, the stalker?*

"He's comin'. Keh-vin called awhile ago. He's goin' to pick me up on his dinner break and drop me there. Matt's comin' to your place at 6:00 p.m."

"Matt?" So the stalker has a name. "What's his last name?"

"Matt Callaway," she says with a heaving sigh. "He's dreamy, Ashley."

"I'll look forward to meeting him," I say with my finger down my throat.

Emily turns on her business voice. "I've been workin' on the bridesmaid gown drawings while I've been here. I'll have something to show you tonight! So I can go back to Atlanta and get the ball rollin'."

Must stop this. "I'm not sure, Emily. My gown is already ordered, as I said—"

"It's completely wrong for the theme. My brothah wouldn't care for that at all. Too sleek and without shape. It's far too sophisticated for a bride your age. You need something that announces your presence to Southern society, that lets you appear younger than your advanced years. You'll look like every othah bride in *that* dress. That's why I canceled the order."

I open my mouth, but nothing comes out. All I can say is that I'm glad she's not here, because at the moment my thoughts are less than Christian. I'm thinking about how I'll have to reorder and avoid whatever hideous thing she's got going. Most important, my future kids have Mei Ling, Brea, and Kay. What on earth do they need Aunt Emily for? I can't think of one single thing. At the moment, anyway.

I'm keeping my voice calm, like I would treat a rogue engineer. "Emily. We'll need to go back down to the shop tomorrow and reorder my dress. That is the dress that I selected, and I am the bride." *Is this stating the obvious or what?* "I don't know what happens in the South, but I'm quite sure it's universal that the bride selects her gown."

"Do you want to make my brothah happy? Or shall I call him at work and tell him we're havin' trouble with the plannin'?"

Unclenching my teeth now. "We're not having trouble, Emily. I am the bride. You are the coordinator. Therefore, I dream. You coordinate," I say, feeling victorious.

"I've already ordered you a new dress. I did it months ago, actually. When my brothah announced your nuptials." She says the last like she bit into a bad olive.

"That's fine, Emily," I say like a preschool teacher. "If you cancel my gown, we can cancel *your* gown before payment is made."

"Actually, I got started on it before I left Atlanta. It was when I had an epiphany about your day and how to make my brothah happy. When he sees you walk down that aisle, he's not goin' to believe his eyes."

That's what scares me.

"You know, we'll just talk about this when you get here. All right?"

"Not a word to my brothah, Ashley. I've never done anything that he was proud of, and he's goin' to be the picture of pride on your weddin' day. Beamin' at both of us. This is the beginning of our sisterhood."

"I've always wanted a sister, Emily, but—"

She hangs up without so much as a good-bye. I guess sisters love each other enough not to need the word *good-bye*. At some less-than-lucid moment I thought this wedding coordinator gig was a good idea. I thought I could focus on patents, and Kevin, and selling my portion of the house. Yet here I am. I'm not focused on patents because I have a new director of software I must avoid. I'm not focused on Kevin because he's finishing his residency and perfecting his role as an absentee fiancé, and I'm not focused on selling the house because Kay doesn't approve of anyone. At this point, I'm so blurry even LASIK wouldn't help.

Kay comes down the hallway, looking like an unmade-up Sarah Jessica Parker. With the same figure! "You look incredible! But you need shoes." I run into the bedroom before she disrobes and grab a pair of Stuart Weitzman strappy sandals. "I got these before Stuart Weitzman was a big deal. They were cheap," I tell her so she doesn't feel bad about slipping into them.

Kay ponders the heel. "I can't walk in those, and cheap to you is a fortune to normal people."

"I'll teach you to walk in them. If you can run downhill at Rancho San Antonio, three inches is nothing."

"I'll be tottering like a Weeble. Do you even remember what a Weeble is? I want to look confident, not like a bad runway model going splat in front of him."

"Hey, Weebles wobble but they don't fall down." I grin at her. She doesn't smile back, not even a hint.

"Okay, wait here." I give in. I run to get some easy slides and run back. "Now let me do your makeup."

Kay sits down at the dining room table and clutches the end of it like she's about to face a torture session. "How long will this take?"

"Have you ever even been to a spa, Kay?"

"No."

"A hair salon?"

"Does Supercuts count?"

"No."

"Then no. I mean, I've gotten haircuts before."

"Kay, how can you call yourself organized with a bad haircut?"

She feels her locks. "You're saying my hair is bad."

"Um, no, I'm not saying it's bad. It could just be better."

I take out my Jane Iredale mineral powder foundation because I figure it's the fastest way to get to my desired result. Which is to see Kay in makeup.

"What's that?"

"Foundation. Just hold still."

I proceed to work my magic, and in a matter of minutes, Kay looks like the real Sarah Jessica Parker. On a good day.

She gets up and walks over to the mirror. She blinks a few times and then starts to giggle. "This would be great if I could get away with this look and still have engineers listen to me." She smiles at me. "I'm going into the bathroom to wash this off, and I'll start dinner."

"Don't wash it off. Just get used to it. One evening at home isn't going to change your life. You're beautiful regardless. I just think it's fun seeing the change."

The doorbell rings, and she looks at me, frozen in fear that someone might see her like this. "Answer the door. I'll go take a shower."

"You answer the door, Kay. It's just the guys from church. It would be good for them to figure out you're a girl."

She shakes her head. "I haven't had the chance to call them."

"I have to get the dog." I proceed to walk outside when I notice Kay open the door. It's not the guys from church but a fabulous-looking man I've never seen before. I watch his eyes take in Kay and a slight smile cross his face.

"Hi," he says, not taking his gaze from her eyes. He puts his hand out. "I'm Matt Callaway . . . Emily's friend."

Kay grasps his hand, and they don't let go. Not for a long time. I wish I could see Kay's face, but I can't. Still, their "time stands still" pause is just how I felt the day I saw Kevin for the first time. It's then that it dawns on me that this is Emily's date! The last thing I need is to have sister-something-wicked-this-way-comes *and* have her be scorned!

I rush to the door. "Hi, Matt, you're early. I'm Ashley, Emily's future sister-in-law. Come on in!"

5

It's 6:20 p.m. No sign of the Southern belle and no sign of the male members of the singles group coming to protect us. (Granted, we never called them, but I thought they had extrasensory perception.) Just the said stalker who I must admit is cute, but he seems wholly interested in the wrong woman! Even Rhett isn't barking at him. What gives?

"How old are you?" I ask Matt Callaway. *If that's really even his name.*

"Forty-five." His espresso-brown eyes widen. "Is that the right answer?"

I cross my arms. "Emily's twenty-five. Did you know that?"

He looks flustered in front of Kay. And why wouldn't he be? I mean, isn't that kind of age difference illegal in some countries? "I didn't realize she was so young."

"Yeah, well, she is." I walk toward the door. "We can tell her you got lost on your way."

"Ashley!" Kay gives me a look. "Since when are you so rude?"

Since he's old enough to be Emily's father, and I've got to answer to Kevin. "I just think when you make a mistake, it's best to correct it as soon as possible." I open the door a little wider. *So I'll just correct it for you.*

Matt stands to leave. "I'm sorry. Ashley's right. I should go." He looks at me with those melting brown eyes, and I have to say, he's like a basset hound, innocent and lovable—not in the least bit frightening. But he shouldn't be here.

"It's the one-year anniversary of my divorce," he continues. "My wife left me. She said if I was going to simply be a wallet, she'd find a bigger wallet. We had no kids, never had time for them. I promised myself I would date one year after the divorce was final. You know, to get back in the game. Emily was nice to me, and I got carried away, it being the anniversary and all." He looks at Kay again, and their gazes linger. "I'm sorry I made a fool out of myself."

Strike up the violins!

"It's Ashley who should be apologizing. This is my home too." Kay in uncharacteristic shrew-mode is staring daggers at me. *I've created a monster with just a little foundation.*

The phone rings, and I breathe a sigh of relief. "Hello."

"Ashley, it's Kevin."

"Kevin, where are you? Your sister's friend is here."

"I'm not having a great day. I have a patient who went into shock, and it gets worse from there."

"I'm sorry." Now I feel guilty.

"Can you pick up Emily and bring her to her date?"

I look at Emily's said date, who has seemingly decided to make another date. He and Kay are walking out the door. "Wait a minute, Kevin." I look toward the new couple. "Where do you think you're going?"

"Out to dinner." Kay looks at Matt. "It doesn't look like Emily's going to make it. We have an anniversary to celebrate. It may not be a happy one, but I don't want Matt alone for it either."

Lord, have mercy! Kay always manages to find the strays. Since she found me when I was homeless, you'd think I'd have more compassion here. But no. I'm not there yet.

"Ashley?" I hear Kevin ask. "You there?"

"I'm here, babe." The sound of his voice makes me forget the mess

I'm in and that the date I'm now supposed to be picking his sister up for just walked out without her. "I wish you were here."

"Tomorrow morning, Ash. I have to run. Give Emily my love, and thanks for all you're doing. I know she's not easy to deal with when she's been abandoned."

You have no idea.

"When I hear your voice, I want to run to Reno tomorrow and marry you. All this planning seems like such a waste when I just want to be with you."

"Charm will get you everywhere," I say.

"Love you, Ash."

"Right back atcha, Kev."

I hang up the phone and look to Rhett. "How do we deal with this one, Rhett?" I look out the window. "And where is the engineering cavalry? What am I going to tell Emily?" I ask Rhett, who pants in answer. "That her date is out with someone more appropriate?" I can't bring Emily here, that's for sure. What if the two of them come back? Over a year of living with Kay, not once has she been out on a date. Now she has to pick Emily's date? *It's my fault. I had to go with the foundation!*

Before I dial the Georgia peach, I call up Brea. She ought to appreciate this. "Hey, Ash," she answers.

"You still have caller ID," I moan. "I miss it! Can you touch the numbers for me? Just run your fingers lightly across the screen so I can live vicariously."

"Shut up. What are you doing?"

"Not much. I finished a little work, gave Kay a makeover, watched her take off with Emily's date. You know, the usual."

"She did not! I meant to call you, but the kids were wild. Your sister-in-law is crazy. Not like cute-crazy, but like she's-a-danger-to-herself-and-the-community crazy."

"She's just high-strung. She wants to please her family. So if we're all wearing hoopskirts at the ceremony, you'll know she succeeded."

"No, Ashley, *you* are high-strung. She's certifiably crazy. Did you know, rather than wear bridesmaids' gowns, she had the idea that we all wear a different Scarlett O'Hara dress? That's just creepy, Ashley, like someone who has trouble differentiating reality from a movie. And it's not like we're in the deep South here, Ashley. I mean, it's almost like we could be a Franklin Mint plate from the wedding photos."

"Don't give her any ideas, all right? Listen, I'm in a bind."

"You're in more than one. Your brother, Dave, is never going to let you live this down if you dress as a Southern belle."

"Listen, first crisis first. I'm serious when I say Kay really did take off with Emily's date. Got any ideas on what I should tell Emily? I'm supposed to pick her up and bring her back to meet a date who just took off with Kay!"

"Yes, tell her they're cloning Rhett Butler from your dog, and she has first dibs when he's in human form."

"Stop it." I giggle. "I'm serious."

"I'm thinking. Give me a minute." I can hear Brea's babies in the background. They are squealing happily, and I admit, I feel a surge of envy. "Okay," Brea continues. "Tell her . . . tell her that he never showed up."

"That's lying. I can't do that."

"Fine, then tell her your roommate took off with him because he wanted to date someone with all her faculties."

"You're no help. I have something else to tell you before your kids notice you're on the phone."

"Oh, is it good?" Brea asks.

"My company got a new software director. It's Seth."

There's a long pause.

"Brea, did you hear me?"

"Stay away from him, Ashley. He's like kryptonite to you!"

I laugh. "Brea, nothing's going to happen with Seth. I'm just telling you he's at my office and how painfully uncomfortable that is."

"And I'm telling you to stay away from him. You've only got four months until the wedding."

"Well, I can't avoid the director of software for four months!"

"Then quit!" Brea admonishes. "Ashley, you are a smart woman. You are a strong woman. Don't make me come over there and pound you. Though I've never quite understood the hold Seth had over you, I rejoiced with the angels when he was history. I know you're over him, but proximity is everything where you're concerned. It has to be, or there's no rational explanation for Seth in your past."

"Are you done?"

"Yes, now call your freak sister-in-law, and tell her she got dumped. Hard."

"Show some mercy! She was excited about this date."

"She was kicked to the curb . . . thrown out like yesterday's trash . . . a victim of natural selection . . . it's not her, it's him . . . they're better off as friends . . . he's not ready for a commitment . . . and the number one way to get dumped tonight? *Emily, you are not in touch with reality, and my plane is just in a different vector right now!*"

"You are wicked-cold!" I accuse, trying not to laugh.

"You mentioned Seth. His name makes me irritable, and I spent the day with Southern Belle Barbie, and now I have two baby boys fighting over a single ball. I'd say I'm done with your crises."

"You used to be so nice before you had kids." I laugh.

"You owe me. I listened to an hour of the history of the Tussy Mussy." She hangs up, and I stare at the phone. There's a pad of paper on the table beside the phone, and I pick it up and start a list. When life gets harrowing, write it down. Some people journal; I list.

THINGS TO DO

1. Reorder wedding dress.
2. Politely fire Emily from her duties.
3. Nicely do Matt's job and let Emily know she's been dumped.
4. Dash into Godiva's since Prozac is by prescription only.
5. Take the chocolate in the beautiful gold box to the spa, and forget all about a wedding.

"Would you like the hot rock massage or the exfoliating back scrub, Miss Stockingdale?"

"Hmmm." Ashley looks up at her spa attendant, a dead ringer for Brad Pitt, and swallows the last bit of her raspberry swirl truffle. "I'll have both, thank you."

"At your service, miss. I'll find your masseuse presently."

Ashley wraps her spa robe tightly around herself and goes to wait in the salt-bath Jacuzzi. "This is the life," she says to herself as she lowers herself into the bubbling water. She's wearing the newest Miraclesuit that cinches her waist and makes her the size she was meant to be. Without liposuction. As the scalding water reaches her neck, Ashley lets out a long, deep sigh.

"You can tell that's a Miraclesuit." Emily suddenly appears from the deep like a swamp thing. "You've got more pooch than that! I think you've eaten way too many of those Godivas. Or are you sure you haven't had children before?"

"What are you doing here? This is my spa dream!" Ashley sits up so fast that the heat makes her dizzy.

"Savin' my brothah from a life underwater with you."

Ashley emerges from the pool. "This is a nightmare. A nightmare, I tell you!"

"You marryin' my brothah is the only nightmare here. Ashley Stockingdale, you give up my brothah! You let him go now, before it's too late."

"I won't!"

"Then I'll have to get the family rifle. Don't worry, we'll bury you in the family crypt. But first, you did pass the Mensa test, didn't you?"

"Agh!" I startle at the sound of the phone. "Hello," I say urgently while I catch my breath.

"Ashley, it's Emily. Are you comin' to get me or not?"

I look around at the empty living room, trying to force the thought of the family rifle away. "Apparently the party's been moved. There's no one here. Just Rhett and me."

"What do you mean, there's no one there? And you want to plan your own weddin'." She laughs a simpering giggle. "You, who can't even throw a simple movie night together. You might be excellent at those law papers, but social graces are a gift of a different sort. In the South, every day of childhood is a finishin' school of sort."

"I never said I wanted to plan my own wedding. I said I wanted my own gown."

"Put Matt on the phone, will you? I'd like to explain to him my absence, and I know you're tryin' to keep him away. He'll understand my brothah had an urgent surgery." She clears her throat.

"Matt isn't here," I say slowly. "He left." *With Kay of all people. Funny story, actually.*

"What did you say to him?"

"Good-bye. And then he left."

"Ashley Stockingdale, what did you say to my date?"

"Au revoir."

Her pause is making me nervous. I know she's collecting steam and is about to blast me with it. "My father always told us intellect was key. Ashley, please explain to me how, when you haven't passed Mensa, you have managed to snare my brothah."

She hangs up on me. Again! What Southern social graces? I would think it is considered rude in the South to hang up without saying good-bye. Finishing school, my eye! Okay, Brea's right. She is a freak. With a capital *F.* To think I was starting to feel sorry for her getting dumped because, hey, he just wasn't that into her. I'd consider Matt Callaway a lucky man. He escaped the wrath of Emily Novak and got a lovely date with someone who will no doubt have his file cabinets reorganized in record time.

6

The day is dawning, and my phone is ringing.

"Hello?" I answer groggily. Looking at the clock, I see that it's 7:00 a.m. A reasonable time for a Saturday morning call. *Not.*

"Ashley, it's Purvi." *My boss.* Sigh.

"A bride needs her beauty sleep," I say. *Throwing out a slight hint there.*

"You're not getting married for months." *And it misses its target!*

"Purvi, you need a social life. Has anyone ever told you that?"

"I was going over these pending patents. We can stop them easily enough."

Sounding oddly familiar, as in, I said that yesterday. "Yes, we can. We have all the documentation we need to do so." *Is that it, my Saturday morning assignment?* "So . . ." *Say it nicely, say it nicely.* "Your point is?"

Rhett gets up and wipes his tongue across my face. *Disgusting.* But he loves me before I've brushed my teeth, so I reward him with a few pats and let him up on the bed.

"Why do you want to go traipsing off to Taiwan?" Purvi asks me.

"I thought—" Okay, rewind. The day I want to go to Taiwan is the day when couture is offered free there.

"I canceled your flight. I called Tracy this morning."

"Already? Purvi, it's just seven."

"It's 10:00 p.m. in Taiwan. Think internationally, Ashley!"

"What time is it in India? Couldn't you call a cousin?" I suggest.

"Don't think because you got me hired, I can't let you go," Purvi threatens.

"Hey, it was just a friendly suggestion. Helping family relations, that's all. Isn't Gainnet concerned with the 'whole' employee?" I say, quoting the latest jargon to hit the bulletin board. New Age with a dash of false concern: *Oh yeah, I'm feeling whole. A whole lotta garbage!*

"I don't expect you to go to Taiwan, but I do expect you to have the documentation on my desk by Monday."

"But I have a red egg and ginger party today."

"Then it's a good thing I woke you up so you can get started." She hangs up, and if Purvi wasn't the best boss I ever had, I'd tell her what she could do with her documentation. I'm not a morning person. Have I mentioned that?

I close my eyes and whisper a silent prayer. I'm not ready for the day, but the day is here, regardless. I feel a surge of delight as I realize it's a Kevin day! It's been nearly a week since I saw him, and I actually ache for him. I need to look into his green eyes and maybe be reminded one more time that he does not want Confederate soldiers at our wedding.

I open my door and smell pancakes and fresh coffee. It's heavenly. I follow my nose to the kitchen and find Kay over crepes with her specialty cream whipper at the ready.

"What are you doing?" I eye her suspiciously.

"I thought you'd be mad at me," Kay says. "I'm trying to make it up to you. Blessed are the peacemakers and all that."

"I'm not angry, Kay. I'm too stressed to be angry. Did it go well last night?"

She nods her head vigorously. "We had a nice time, Ashley. He looked so broken when Emily wasn't here. I just couldn't let him walk out our door like that." She shakes her head. "Wouldn't have been Christian."

"No, you were right." I rub my forehead. "I was rude. I hope you apologized for me. I haven't been myself since Purvi told me I was going to Taiwan and my wedding plans were hijacked. I barely see Kevin as it is, and his sister is making me forget that he's quite normal. What if he has a good bit of Emily down deep, and after we get married it bubbles up like Glenn Close in that bathtub scene?"

"Are you all right? You look pale."

I sit down at the table. "She canceled my wedding dress order, Kay. How basic is that? That a woman knows what she wants to look like on her wedding day?" I look at Kay and feel a tear escape down my cheek. "Marrying Kevin means I'll see these people for the rest of my life, and I just don't want to mess with anything that keeps Emily here in town. If that means buying two dresses, so be it." But I don't have the money for another dress.

Kay lets out a deep sigh and serves me a plate.

I shake my head. "Oh, thanks, Kay, but I'm having breakfast with Kevin."

She pulls the plate away. "Then you'll feel better when you get back. He'll remind you why you're getting married. If you have to wear something off the rack, Kevin will be there, remember? Emily is not Kevin. But I have to say her taste in men is pretty good." A slow, dreamy smile spreads across Kay's face.

Rhett's at my feet, panting for attention. I take his sturdy head in my hands and rub his ears. "You're right. I'm just whiny, I guess because I'm tired."

"It's always something, Ashley."

I pour myself a glass of orange juice. "So tell me about the stalker."

"Stop calling him that!" Kay bangs her plate at the table. "It was wonderful, like I said."

"So what's his real story?"

"He told you his real story, Ashley. He's divorced, as all the men my age are. Either divorced or dangerously narcissistic; take your pick." She puts a tofu sausage down for Rhett, who promptly sniffs and snubs the fake meat. "It was good practice for next weekend when Simon comes back." Then she halts her fork, and a smile lights up her whole face. "I went on a date, Ash! And I didn't fall over in the shoes you gave me. I even wore makeup. I can hardly believe it. I'm a new woman!"

"You looked great. It was a pity none of the guys from church came last night. It would have given them a chance to see what they've been missing. I'd have given anything to see their faces."

Kay bites into her lip. "Oh, I actually forgot to call them last night."

"Kay! You forgot something? You told me last night. Remember? This guy Simon does have you flustered. Matt Callaway could have been a monster."

She's laughing at me.

"He could have!"

She's still laughing.

"I'm leaving." I turn back to face her. "By the way, what does Matt Callaway do for a living?"

"He's a patent attorney. So you're right, he probably *is* a monster." She giggles again, and I have to say, it's good to see Kay giddy. Totally unexpected, but good.

"I'm going to get a cappuccino before breakfast. See ya," I say before closing the door behind me.

I stand on the front path for a time and just feel the sunshine on my face. Its warmth fills me with energy. I could almost forget I have to tell Kevin about Kay stealing his sister's date, and the little conflict we're having over a wedding dress. Just what a pediatric surgeon needs to hear about: a catfight. And it's not even a good catfight like you get on a nighttime soap opera. There are no slinky dresses, no pool to fall into, not even a good wrestling match. Just two women vying for ultimate power over silk—well, really, over Kevin.

I hear a couple of beeps and see Kevin's car parked at the curb. He opens his window, "Hey, hot stuff, going my way?"

"What are you doing here? I thought we were meeting at the restaurant."

"I just got off work, and I couldn't wait."

Be still my heart. "You haven't slept?" I say as I get into the car.

"I slept a bit. On the cot at work."

"That's not sleeping. Don't you know you're going to permanently disrupt your circadian rhythm? Even a light on when you sleep blocks pineal gland stimulation, which can cause a drop in melatonin—and don't even get me started on messing up your body's internal clock!"

Kevin is staring at me, his perfect teeth hidden behind an open mouth. "Have you been watching public television again, Ashley?"

I take a little pride here. "No, I read it in a health magazine at the gym in my office, actually."

He smiles at me, and all my troubles melt away. *I'm in love.* I'm so in love, and you know what they say? Love is blind. But one needs eyes with Kevin. He's so incredibly gorgeous. And I don't say that as his fiancée. If anything, that was a major stumbling block for me. I don't need the pressure of a guy who looks like Hugh Jackman. What woman does? We all know the reality of what we look like in the morning.

He leans over and kisses me gently on the cheek. "How are things going with the wedding planning?" Kevin starts the car and smiles toward me before taking off.

Alrighty then. Do I dive right in and tell him that I'm pondering Vegas and the Starlight Room for our reception? Or that perhaps his sister is better off in an institution rather than planning our wedding? I decide to avoid the subject altogether. We'll get there, but I think we need to take it slow.

"So will you have to work tonight? Or can you come to the red egg and ginger party with me?" He doesn't answer me before my cell phone rings. "I don't have to answer it," I say as I stare at the ringing phone with itchy fingers. I cannot stand to hear a ringing phone. It's ripe with possibilities, isn't it? It could be the patent office, telling me I'm a genius and they've never seen work like mine. It could be my boss saying they've sold off production in Taiwan and I don't ever have to go back. It could be the jeweler saying they gave me the wrong diamond when they sized the ring. Mine is actually twice as big and has a matching Tacori platinum band.

"Answer it, for heaven's sake, before you lose it altogether." Kevin's grinning, so I peer at my phone, but I must admit, seeing it's my brother I'm a little less excited about it.

"Hi, Dave."

"Ashley, I need your help," Dave says, his voice filled with desperation.

"You need *my* help? This ought to be good."

"I need you to go make a deposit for the red egg and ginger party. It's at Ping's in Palo Alto, and . . . well, I just need your help."

"Ping's?" *Pick the most expensive Chinese restaurant in the Bay Area, why don't you?* "What kind of deposit are we talking?"

"Two thousand dollars. I'll pay you back!"

He won't.

"Didn't they need it before today?"

"I bounced the check, okay, Ashley? They're threatening to cancel the whole thing. Does it make you feel good to know that your big brother is a loser?"

Clamping mouth shut now. "Dave, I'm sorry. I just thought—"

"All of Mei Ling's extended family is here. Some of them are even here from China. This party is a really big deal, and it's my chance to prove that she didn't marry down. It's bad enough I'm not from her culture." He pauses. "Are you going to make me beg? Because I'm begging, Ash. If Ping's cancels the party, you might as well cancel me from Mei Ling's family. And that leaves Davey cut off from his Chinese heritage."

If he could, Dave would buy Mei Ling everything her heart desired. Unfortunately, on a bus driver's salary, his hands are tied.

Mei Ling is a saint, and I'd like to say that I see what she saw in my brother. But alas, I'm a little confused there. Mei Ling is dainty and feminine, and Dave? Well, Dave's a bit Neanderthal, with a Dr Pepper and a remote control on his person at all times. Seeing him with Mei Ling and his son, though, reminds you that he has a heart of gold. He'd do anything for them. Even work.

"Dave, I'm not going to make you beg," I say. "You just didn't give me a chance to answer. I'll drop by Ping's after breakfast. Everything will be fine, I promise." But secretly, I think about my checkbook and the flowers I've paid for and the dress I'll have to buy, and I admit I'm a little nervous. The house purchase was more of a stretch than I thought it would be. No one mentioned the nasty tax bill twice a year! Californians seem to have a fetish for taxes and bond measures. It used to only affect my buying power at Bloomingdale's. Now, with a house, it's serious!

"Don't tell Mei Ling, please," Dave implores.

"Don't worry. I've got it covered." I hang up the phone and look at my handsome fiancé. *Two thousand dollars is nothing. That party is going to cost at least five, and that leaves my wedding dress out in the cold,* I think.

"Is everything all right?"

"I just have to run an errand after breakfast. Is that all right?"

"Sure. So you didn't tell me, how are the wedding plans coming?"

"You didn't tell me, are you coming to the party tonight?"

"I want to, Ashley, but I'm going to need a nap. And I promised my sister I'd take her by the florist. She wants to coordinate something. She has drawings for the florist."

I'll bet she does. "I've made the deposit with the florist already. Kevin, I've been meaning to talk to you about that—"

"I'm so thrilled you're letting her do this, Ashley. It's the first time I've ever seen her really excited about a job and finding her niche in life. When she failed the Mensa test, everything just went downhill for her. She—"

"Wait a minute. What did you say?"

Kevin whacks his forehead. "That's a family secret. Emily didn't actually pass the test for membership. Her IQ was too low, but only according to the test. She's very bright."

Uh, yeah! That's what I've been saying. "Why is that such a big deal in your family anyway? I've been in Silicon Valley my whole life. Some of the most intellectual people on earth live here, and I've never heard anyone talk about Mensa before you. Not even the physicists!"

"It's a long story."

"I've got time. Definitely more time than money. There's got to be a road to enlightenment here, because it is odd. I don't think you realize how odd. Not Mensa, but your family's preoccupation with it. What's up with that?"

"You're calling my family *odd*?" He just laughs. He knows full well they're odd.

"Just wondering where the fascination with Mensa comes from." I shrug as if it's no skin off my nose, but *what the heck*?

Kevin pulls the car into the Hobee's parking lot. He looks at me with his deep green eyes, and something about his gaze makes me think I'm not going to like this story. He lets out a long, haggard breath and starts.

"When my dad was in med school, all his fellow doctors were marrying Southern belles from high school and debutante parties. They had all been turned out and raised accordingly. My dad had a bit of disdain for them because he didn't want a trophy wife. He wanted to marry up, but not financially. Intellectually. He sort of 'auditioned' women for the role of his wife. He told them it would be fun to take an IQ test, knowing what the IQ for genius was. Mensa wasn't too active in the States back then. Most of the women failed his criteria, probably because they were starting to see how strange my father's 'good time' was, and shortly after, my dad would break things off. If they hadn't broken up with him first."

"Consider me informed. I don't think I want to know any more."
Because I'm thinking that Kevin is now sporting alien antennae.

"Ashley, I'm not marrying you for your IQ." Kevin takes my
hand. "It's definitely your body I'm after."

We both break into laughter, and I slap his arm. I look into
Kevin's eyes, and I know he is genuine. He is solid and in love with
the Lord. He is a new creation in Christ, but I just can't help worrying about his DNA. How will he parent? Will he send our egghead
kid to college at twelve? Kevin slides his sunglasses on as we get ready
to go the restaurant, and I have this horrifying vision of little Kevin
Jr. wearing coke-bottle glasses taped at the rim.

"Ashley, are you ready?"

I shake off my thoughts. "Yeah, yeah, I'm ready."

"Good. Because I want to talk to you about our house." Kevin
opens the door to the restaurant.

"Our house?"

"Where we're going to live."

"I guess I just assumed we would live at your place until we found
a place of our own. We can't exactly move in with Kay, especially not
with your hours."

"And all the noises we might make."

I think about that and blush rosy red.

Kevin shakes his head and smiles. But this smile has a bit too
much enthusiasm. "Ash, my parents are making a down payment on
a house as a wedding gift."

I feel my head shaking of its own volition. "As in, we pick out a
house and they put the down payment on it?"

"I didn't really ask. I figured it was so generous that—"

"Ask, Kev! I don't mean to be ungrateful, but . . ." *Next thing
you know, they're buying us a triplex, and Emily's on one side and they're
on the other.* "Definitely ask."

"Does it matter where we live?"

Oh heavens, those eyes. "No, it doesn't matter a bit," I say dreamily.

7

Kevin attracts attention just sitting here. Can you imagine what people would think if they knew he was a children's surgeon? I mean, he doesn't walk on water, and of course, we all know he's human, but considering my generation thinks Ben Affleck is the cat's pajamas, I'm naturally a little freaked that the other shoe might drop. That Kevin might see that he and Ashley Stockingdale are as different as Prada and Kmart. *Although I wouldn't be caught dead in anything by Jaclyn Smith,* I think.

Kevin sits across from me in the restaurant and takes my hands in his. This is the one I picked. The one who picked me. We were made by God for each other. *Not bad.* All those years of searching. Had I known it was going to be this good, I would definitely have had more faith.

Of course, I picked him for all the practical reasons too:

WHY DR. KEVIN NOVAK IS PERFECT FOR ME

1. He has a job.
2. He does not "need" me.
3. He is ready to get married and shares my family goals.
4. He understands my shoe fetish.
5. He likes to eat out.

6. He thinks video games are for children.
7. He understands that every new handbag deserves a compliment.
8. He works with children. He doesn't hang out with them.
9. He has an obvious blind spot and loves me!

Currently, I'm ignoring my fears about my future husband's family. Only because I see Kevin as the support system of his family, not part of the chaos, but one never really knows. *Do they?*

Before I make him sound perfect, let me say he's a complete workaholic, and like my boss, Purvi, he will probably have his coffin wired with a T1 line. Even now he's tapping his fingers nervously on the table, not even opening his menu. He can't be bothered with small decisions like what type of meal he'll eat. He generally is at the hospital cafeteria, so the quality of a meal has little bearing on his life. He just wants nourishment set in front of him without his having to make a decision.

"Is there something you need to tell me?" I ask.

He lets out a ragged breath. "How did you know?"

My heart is beating rapidly. Maybe he's about to tell me about his "thing" for women's undergarments (on himself!) or that he's been married three times previously and forgot to mention it. Or maybe he's really handsome because he went on *Extreme Makeover*, and he loves me because he used to be a troll like me. That really he looks like Shrek and without his platform heels, he's only as tall as Farquat. I close my eyes tight. "Hit me with it."

"What?"

"Just say what you have to say. Let's get it over with. How bad could it be?" I ask.

"That depends on your idea for the future."

"2.5 children and a house in the suburbs. Yours?"

He nods. "The same. But are you open as to which suburbs?"

I feel this enormous lump in my throat, like I've just swallowed an olive whole. I want to smile and laugh this off, but he's completely serious. "Like San Francisco suburbs or San Jose suburbs? Is that what you mean? I just assumed since Stanford is right in the middle, we'd—"

He shakes his head. "That's not what I mean." My cell phone starts to trill, but I ignore it with ease this time and just hit Silent. "I mean, wouldn't you enjoy being a lawyer in the city of brotherly love? Philadelphia?"

Philadelphia.

"Home of the Liberty Bell, the design of the American flag—and is there anything else? I can't say I've been to Philly. The cheesesteak! It's also home to the cheesesteak. I knew I was forgetting something."

"The Constitution. You're forgetting the Constitution, the Declaration of Independence, and being a lawyer, I just assumed you'd go there before the cheesesteak."

"Philadelphia has seasons, I'm assuming."

"Most places have seasons, Ashley. You're just living in a bubble being a native Californian. Wouldn't you love to have a little adventure in your life before we settle down with kids?"

"I like my bubble. Lived in my bubble all my life. I like the ocean and the sunshine and the occasional foggy morning when I want to really mix things up. I like that my convertible is a year-round vehicle and that I can get espresso whenever the urge strikes. I like that all the geeks of the world like me are concentrated in one geek-friendly environment. No one cares here if you had a date to the prom, because they didn't either. Oh sure, maybe those sophisticated types who live in San Francisco. But us *real* Silicon Valley types, we're comfortable with the fact that the AV technician was our friend, if not us."

"They have espresso in Philadelphia, and if you joined Mensa, you could probably meet some fellow dweebs," Kevin says, again smiling with a little too much enthusiasm.

"Why the sudden interest in Philadelphia, Kev? I thought you were happy at Stanford."

"This is just a discussion, nothing more at this point. So don't get upset, all right?"

Bracing for impact. "Yes?"

"I got offered a fellowship in pediatric surgery at the children's hospital there. It's the only teaching hospital in the United States that offers fetal surgery as part of the residency program."

The air has left my lungs with a Nike swoosh. I write patents, but my husband-to-be performs life-changing surgery on infants still in their mothers' wombs. Or at least he could. As I sit here, looking into his eyes, I see the future I'd planned quickly evaporating. Slowly, the truth descends upon me like molten lava. You don't marry a pediatric surgeon and merrily go about your business.

"Are you two ready to order?" the granola-girl waitress asks us.

"Could you give us a minute?" Kevin asks.

She looks at Kevin longer than necessary and readily agrees. As most any woman does when he has a request.

"Ashley, are we discussing this? Because I need to know if it's a possibility or not." I look in his eyes, and he's practically begging for my support. It's obvious this is not something he can let go of without regret. Therefore, how can I let go of it?

"You're at one of the finest hospitals in the country, Kevin. I don't understand. Lucille Packard–Stanford Medical School. They sort of have a reputation going on, you know?" But even as I suggest it, I feel sick to my stomach. How do I make the man I love happy without giving up everything I love?

"I'm just a junior resident at Stanford, Ashley. It's my second year in pediatric residency. There's nothing here that makes me stand out when it's time to move on. I'd be chief resident in Philly, and I'd get the opportunity to perform fetal surgery. Not to mention more than thirteen hundred hours at the operating table. It's my dream, Ashley, and the operating time is so limited here in comparison. Do you know what it's like for me to get time in the operating room now? I could do more laparoscopic studies, and I'd have my own secretary to help with the paperwork on research studies."

I nod, hearing everything and yet nothing at all.

"Let's agree to continue the dialogue at least," Kevin says.

Dialogue? Do you hear any dialogue? "When did you find out about this?"

"I applied before we met. I want to do fetal surgery, Ashley. I have ever since I witnessed Michael Harrison perform neonatal surgery years ago in San Francisco. I just knew that was my calling. The intricacy of it just beckoned me."

I nod my head subconsciously. "Of course you do. You need to do this."

"I'm not going without you, Ashley," he says like a martyr.

"I couldn't be an attorney there, Kevin. I'd have to retake the Bar, and the patent Bar, and have to wait for the results to be posted. It could be a year or more before I worked."

"You could work as a law clerk until that happened." He's clearly thought about this.

I look into Kevin's pleading eyes. His light brown hair is tousled from the night's work, and the fine lines on his forehead are deepening. Just in the short time since I've known him, he looks years older. "Kevin, this job already takes everything out of you. Can you do anything more?"

He squeezes my hand tighter. "Please go with me, Ashley. If you won't go, I'll stay here, but—"

"But I'll crush your dream." I throw up my hands. "What is it with me and men moving? I fall in love, and men immediately rush for higher ground. Be it the mission field in India like Seth or home of the Liberty Bell and fetal surgery, I make men move away."

He laughs. "I told you, I won't move without you. I'm committed to us—to our marriage. As committed as Joseph was to Mary."

The waitress comes back. "We'll have two orders of the San Jose Scramble and tea," Kevin says dismissively.

"This job is really yours if you want it?"

"My father and the chief of surgery at Stanford recommended me. The chief agreed that I needed to pursue the fetal surgery. I have a gift for the intricate work."

"When would we have to go?"

"I would go in two months, come back for the wedding, and you'd fly out to meet me and look for our house. That's where my parents' offer for the down payment comes in."

I sit here with my head in my hands, trying to find the words. I want to tell him that I love him, that I'd follow him anywhere, but there's nothing coming out of my mouth. There's only the stark realization that love might take me across the country to a place I've never known, with a man I barely know. Compare that to my life in the Bay Area where I know every nook and cranny. Every ethnic, hole-in-the-wall restaurant. As I gaze into those tired green eyes, I hate that I'm even questioning. *I love him, but do I love him enough?*

"I know you don't care for change, Ashley, but my parents will make sure we have a great place, and you'll have time to explore your new environment. Right now, you just work."

"Change is good," I say, trying to convince myself. "When Bloomingdale's changes its stock for the season, that's good. When I get a new pair of shoes for a change in the weather, that's good. But this . . . this is so big. I'd have to leave Kay and my house and my car. And your parents buying us a place? That doesn't sound so good." Putting it mildly. *His parents in my housing arrangements? Completely not happening.*

"You can bring everything but Kay. Rhett will come with us. We can find a place with a big yard for him, and you can call Brea every day if you need to."

"And while you're working nonstop, I'll have no friends, a flunky job, and I'll have to find a new church." *Is that my voice? Is there any-*

thing worse than hearing aloud how truly selfish you are? And what a whiner! *How, when given the opportunity of a lifetime to be a partner in saving unborn babies' lives, can I be worried about a lack of sunshine, questionable coffee, and a convertible? I suck so bad.*

Kevin exhales loudly. "It's selfish of me to ask. I shouldn't have, and if I didn't want this so badly, I never would have."

I feel the sting of tears prickling my eyes and the burning sensation in my nose. I'm looking at him, and he means it. He genuinely thinks he shouldn't have asked me. His sacrifice tells me everything I need to know. "Just give me some time to get used to the idea. For it to settle in my bones."

He gets up, comes over, and scoots into the chair beside me. He turns my face toward his and looks deep into my eyes. "I've got a good job at one of the best hospitals in the country. Whatever *you* decide, and I mean that." Then he kisses me with firm lips right here in the restaurant.

"Get a room!" I hear a diner say, which breaks me into a giggle.

"I really shouldn't hold your fate in my hands, Kevin. Actually, I probably shouldn't hold the fate of a hamster in my hands. Just ask my dog. If Kay weren't there to feed him, some days I don't know that he'd make it with me traipsing to Taiwan all the time."

"But I trust you completely with my fate, Ashley. I know you think you have this shallow exterior, but I also know who lurks within. The woman who fights for those she loves, holds her own in an engineering meeting, and will have me dressed properly for every function in my future."

"That's your misfortune to trust me with your fate." I laugh as I say it.

"We'll do the right thing. We've got guidance from above." He moves back to his seat, oblivious to the fact that all eyes in the restaurant have just followed him like one of those eerie paintings.

"Maybe this is a sign." I shrug.

"A sign?"

"Another sign, I should say." I take a sip of my water. "Gainnet hired Seth as the new director of software."

Kevin crosses his arms, rocks, and nods his head. "That's interesting."

"Is that all you have to say?"

"You live the most intriguing life, Ashley Stockingdale. Why shouldn't men from your past be pulled in like a superconducting magnet? Stalk you?" He lifts his eyebrows. "I did, and it worked for me."

"Stop it. Seth's not anywhere near me. He's hardly stalking me. From what I hear he's quite content with Arin, and they're a couple. Kay told him about the job at Gainnet!"

He laughs again. "Kay's a good woman. Besides, let him see what he lost. I like the idea."

"You're a bit cocky!"

"I am, but why shouldn't I be? I'm marrying Ashley, and he's most likely having dinner with Sam at his own expense. I don't know what Arin wants in this life, Ashley, but I highly doubt it's Seth. She doesn't want any chains binding her down. Maybe that's the attraction. They probably have the same cell phone service, and calling is free."

"Are you saying Arin could do better?"

"Didn't you?"

"You're incorrigible."

"I am. So tell me about my wedding." Kevin sits back as the waitress puts his meal before him. *Um, ladies first!* He douses his eggs in Tabasco and closes his eyes for prayer. Taking my hand, he leads us and blows me a kiss at the end. He melts me, I'm telling you.

"About the wedding," I say as I oversalt my eggs. "Well, your sister has definite ideas about our ceremony."

"You two are getting along okay, aren't you?"

"Yes, everything's fine. I just was looking for California elegance in the ceremony. You know, sort of Vera Wang meets Colin Cowie." *Not really Southern sweet tea with crackers.*

Kevin swallows his eggs. "In English, Ashley."

"Vera Wang's a bridal designer; Colin Cowie is Oprah's party planner."

"So what's the problem?" Kevin shrugs. "Sounds simple enough. Emily is all about elegance. I know she doesn't have as much shopping experience as you, but I thought you'd help her there."

"Emily does have a certain Southern charm . . ." *That I'm not sure really translates.*

"Is something wrong, Ashley?"

I suck in a deep breath. The time has come to tell him that I can't do this. I can't get married with Emily planning the wedding, but he's thinking about moving to Philadelphia. Do I really want to whimper about his sister's crazy wedding plans?

"Keh-vin!" Speaking of crazy, Emily herself appears at the side of our table, her face twisted into the ugliest scowl I've seen to date. And trust me, I've seen some scowls! "Your fiancée stole my date last night!"

"I, uh . . ." This, of course, is an easy explanation. Although not exactly. Looking at Emily, I think my stalker may turn out to be female.

8

Catfight. I can see by Kevin's stricken face, he definitely doesn't know how to handle a catfight. Kevin pulls a chair over for Emily, but it's obvious she doesn't want to sit. She wants to slit my throat, perhaps, but she doesn't want to do eggs and bacon.

"There's an explanation, Emily. Sit down. What would Ashley do with your date?" He sits up straight. "After all, she couldn't exactly improve on perfection now, could she?" He winks at me across the table.

"She pawned my date off on her spinster roommate!"

Spinster. Now there's a word you don't hear everyday. Kevin hasn't asked for my input yet, and as far as I'm concerned, we can just let this opportunity fly by without comment from *moi.* I shove a bit of egg in my mouth. Now is definitely a good time to eat.

"Calm down, Em. How did you get here, anyway?" Kevin asks.

"I rented a car. I got tired of being at everyone's mercy to leave the house, and I called the rental place. I don't know why I didn't think of it before. Perhaps if I had, I might have salvaged my date last night!" Emily's eyes narrow in my direction, and Kevin finally looks at me.

I widen my eyes in mock innocence. I could start any number of places at this point: *He was forty-five. She picked him up in a coffee bar. She was invited to his place for a party that didn't exist. He's celebrating*

66

his divorce. Worst of all, he's a patent attorney. If that doesn't say everything, well, I got nothing for you.

Emily continues while pointing at me, "She told me Matt left, but Matt really left her house *with Kay*. He had dinner with Kay last night! My date!"

"Is that true, Ashley?" Kevin asks, though I can see he's only asking out of requirement. He could really care less about his sister's dateless night. Maybe if she had more dateless nights, she might have a goal in life. Being too cute is a curse.

"Sort of," I say with a shrug.

He keeps looking at me expectantly. Emily is sitting now, but her fists are on her hips and her foot is tapping. It's not the most comforting pose, as there are knives within reach.

I look right at my future sister-in-law. "I didn't think it was safe for Emily to go out with Matt. She didn't even know him, and he was nearly twice her age," I blurt, like the grown tattletale I am. If I was in junior high, I'd get beaten up for this.

"Is that true, Emily? Did you just meet this older person?"

"What business is it of hers if it's true? Or yours? I'm not twelve, Keh-vin. I'm a grown woman, and I can see who I'd like to see. I know enough about men to know who to trust. She," Emily says, pointing at me, "forced Matt's attentions on her desperate roommate. He had no choice but to go out with her. It's been a year since his divorce, and he needed—"

Kevin drops his fork suddenly, but he says nothing. I can see it in his eyes, though, that he finally gets my drift. "It's my fault about last night, Emily. I was supposed to pick you up, remember? This whole thing is just a misunderstanding, and there's no reason to blame Ashley. Or Kay," Kevin says.

"When you couldn't pick me up, Ashley had an obligation to come around for me. I'm all the way out here for her weddin'." Emily holds up her Coach portfolio. "The least she could do is see that I had some entertainment for my weekend in California. I'm workin' my fingers to the bone for her, and she doesn't even appreciate it." Emily flips her hair like a cartoon character—and pats the portfolio hiding the Martha Stewart fill-in wedding planner.

"I shouldn't have treated you like a child, Emily. I'm sorry," I say. "And you're having a really good hair day," I add, just for fun.

"Sorry? You're sorry? Ever since I got out here it's been like pullin' teeth to get you to do anything for this weddin'. You're a complete snob about the Tussy Mussy, you won't even listen to my plans for the weddin', and now you sabotage the only good time I had scheduled for this weekend."

I look at Kevin. "I was just trying to protect her. You don't go to men's houses here without protection."

"You, dear Ashley, are being ridiculous if you hope to get this weddin' off the ground. I can't believe my brothah thinks so little of himself as to marry you when you have proven yourself to be un-trustworthy and disloyal." Emily slams her hand down on the table and rises. She walks out without another word.

I shouldn't have wasted the good hair comment.

Kevin stands and drops his keys near my plate. "I'd better get her. I'm sorry, Ash. I should have left you out of family problems. I'll call you before the party today. I'll get some rest, and I'll be there if I can, all right?"

So there you go: not only have I just been yelled at in public by Scarlett I-need-some-Prozac O'Hara, but also I have been left alone in a restaurant so the patrons can discuss the "boyfriend napper" publicly. I shove a forkful of eggs in my mouth. A girl needs her protein, regardless.

After I pay the bill for breakfast, I look at my empty wallet with new insight. It's a darling pink Coach wallet, and it has *money* written all over it. Unfortunately, it has no money in it. I've paid out deposits for the dress order that no longer exists, the flowers that are being reworked by Emily, and the swing band that will probably get vetoed. Altogether, there's a rather large hole in my checking account. Getting stiffed for breakfast didn't help either. Kevin ran after psycho sis without even paying the bill!

As I walk out of Hobee's, I smile and wave to the gawking patrons. *See, I wasn't jilted,* I try to communicate silently. I head to Kevin's car, contemplating my finances—or lack thereof. Although my parents are thrilled I'm "finally" getting married, they're not so thrilled that they want to pay for the festivities. Apparently that offer became null and void when I turned thirty and they added on a den. Parents only have so much patience. I look at my check register and see that I have a mere $2,500 in my account. Considering that half of that amount is my mortgage and that I told Dave I'd cover him for $2,000 today, I'd say I'm in dire financial straits. For once in my life, I'm going to rely on credit and I'm not even going to come out with a good pair of Stuart Weitzman's. Which is pathetic, really, when I could tell Kevin I need money.

But there's something inside me that won't let me do that. I'm not marrying Kevin for money, and I don't want to give that impression. I slide into Kevin's car, adjust the rearview mirror, and start heading toward Ping's. As I prepare myself to hand over the last of my money, I'm whispering silent prayers that God will care for my careless self. I remember when I was a bit cocky about my money. Well, pride goeth before the fall, I suppose. I can hear the splat now.

Pulling up to Ping's, I see a man dressed in a white cook's uniform sweeping the front porch like a scene from the Old World. Getting out of my car, I approach him, and he points me inside the restaurant without a word. Once inside, I see a man wearing a full suit. It's only 10:00 a.m., and I wonder if he'll still be around in his full suit for tonight's party. And I thought high-tech involved long hours. He peers at me, head cocked to one side.

"I'm here for Dave and Mei Ling's red egg and ginger party. I want to leave a deposit." Okay, I don't really want to. I suppose the proper words are "have to."

He nods. "You Ashley?"

"Yes," I say as I hand him the check.

I wait while he calls my bank, which thankfully is open until one o'clock today. They tell him the check is good, and then he asks for a credit card if I want to ensure "a buffet aplenty." I assume Dave wants enough food, so I hand over the card, the last vestige of my solvency.

I am officially broke in Silicon Valley. How unique and yet pathetic at the same time. I'd tell my brother Dave, who'd get a great kick out of it, except that he'd think I was rubbing in his own poverty and what he now owes me. The manager runs my credit card through a manual machine and hands it back to me. "Done. See you tonight. We throw best red egg and ginger party in the entire Bay Area."

I clutch my card and put it back in my bag. "Thank you. We're looking forward to it. We're certainly bringing the cutest baby along for the festivities."

As I head for Kevin's car, I'm struck by the fact that most likely, I'll be attending yet another family party without my fiancé. I'm sure my extended family is beginning to think I'm making him up. I look down at Kevin's grandmother's ring. It's very special to me, an art deco platinum ring with a small emerald-cut diamond in the middle. I'm beginning to see that marriage isn't going to solve all my problems. It's only going to create new ones. That's not the most comforting thought.

Let's make a list of the facts:

IMPENDING DOOM IN THE
MARITAL DEPARTMENT

1. Kevin's sister hates me. Maybe *hate* is a strong word, but she's not throwing me any "Welcome to the Family" parties. Frankly, I can't say she's on my list of favorite people either.

2. What about his parents and their four basic life groups: golf, country clubs, taut tummies, and photochemical facials? When I contrast my own parents with their beer bottle collections, family heirlooms from the Avon catalog, and enjoyment of the ever-popular green bean casserole, I wonder if I haven't disrupted some cosmic time continuum. Perhaps this is a cross-cultural marriage not meant to happen: blue blood and blue collar. Bringing these two worlds together is a bit like nuclear chemicals colliding in Stanford's linear accelerator. They don't mix without a cosmic explosion. Our families mesh like the Montagues and Capulets—and my life should be a comedy, not a tragedy. I'm certain of it.

3. I may have to subsist on Philly cheesesteak sandwiches. Philadelphia? No offense to brotherly love and all that, but who in their right mind would give up the California Dream life to move to Philadelphia?

4. No more Spock death scenes at the singles' group's coffeehouse karaoke nights. *Ha! Those memories alone are enough to make me want to head down the aisle—today!*

5. The fact is, I love Kevin, and he loves me. And he loves God and his kooky family. Really, is that such a bad thing? No, but I just don't know if *I* can stomach them for a lifetime.

As I walk in the morning sunlight, I can smell the salty marsh of the Baylands, and I want to run along their path, away from my money problems and wedding woes. I want to relish the complete silence, with only the birdcalls and the wind blowing gently through the reeds interrupting it. And, of course, the ever-present Cessna sounds overhead from the small Palo Alto airport nearby. But I look at Kevin's car, and I know he probably needs it. There could be an emergency at the hospital, or his sister might get called back to Atlanta for a manicure crisis. Life is a series of have-tos that just seem to get worse as I get older.

I accelerate up the frontage road, gaze at the Baylands, and try to remember what peace feels like. I remember when all I wanted was to get married. Okay, and to have a great new Ann Taylor outfit. When I foolishly thought a husband and then a child would complete my circle of life. Unfortunately, there are lions in this scenario, and I feel like they're ripping me limb from limb. And unlike the mountain lions of Palo Alto, no environmental group is coming to my rescue. My mother always said, "Be careful what you wish for." Yeah, yeah, yeah. And she also said, "Love isn't just blind—it's deaf, dumb, and stupid." Does that mean I'm supposed to turn a blind eye and deaf ear to Kevin's family and keep my mouth shut? Or does it mean that I would be completely stupid to hook up with them before God and mankind? Hard to tell for sure.

I speed up on the frontage road before I'm too tempted to stop and bail on my day's responsibilities. How I wish I could go handbag shopping and forget it all. My problems get lost in a Michael Kors signature print or a pebbled leather by Cole Haan. I sigh dreamily. I hate being broke.

Arriving at Kevin's place, I see his sister get into Matt Callaway's Miata and drive off with a distinctive smirk for my benefit. My stomach lurches at the sight as I think about Kay at home, happily dancing through the kitchen after her first date in I don't even know how long. I kick on the emergency brake, grab my Prada (ah, the good old days), and walk up the front steps. Kevin is nowhere in sight, and I let myself in, deciding I can call Kay for a ride home if he's asleep.

Once inside the condo, I see that Emily has definitely left her mark. There are new pictures on the wall, one of Atlanta's red dirt and what must be a painting of his family homestead. I study the picture, and pain washes over me like stabbing prickles under my skin. *What am I doing here?* I'm thinking of giving up my job; my bank account has dwindled to nothing—all for a family that hates everything I'm about. They hate my Christianity, my untouched face, my collagen-free lips. According to Emily, I should have at least done

Botox by now, but just the idea of stabbing botulism near my brain could only do more damage.

Sheesh, I haven't even gotten LASIK. I'm a plastic-surgery virgin and hope to stay that way! I still wear glasses when I work at the computer, like the bucktoothed seventh grader who still lurks in me. Kevin might be pure California gold, but his family is only silicone—and it eventually loses its value—and elasticity, I'm told. *But you're stuck with it for its billion-year half-life. Joy!*

"There's my girl." Kevin leans against the hallway doorjamb. He's in his green scrubs and looks more luscious than a lime Popsicle, but that's just my hormones talking. I have to wait for reality to descend. *You marry the family too.*

"I thought you'd be sleeping," I say to Kevin, whose hair is in tangled disarray.

"My sister and I had it out. I'm too keyed up to sleep now." Kevin shakes his head and looks at the floor. "I don't think I'll ever understand what she wants. I know what she needs, but there's little I can do about that. I worry she's just going to keep fighting, like a fish flopping at the bottom of a boat."

"Look, I'm really sorry about Emily. I didn't help matters." I focus on the new painting. "I'm sorry about the wedding plans and how nothing has gone as it should. This event has turned out to be such a fiasco. I guess we should have expected this. I don't exactly live a charmed life." I focus on Kevin's green eyes, and my heart is pounding, but I have to say it. "Maybe I'm too old to get married. The window of opportunity has passed me by, and we're just trying to force this square peg in a round hole." I tug at the ring on my finger as Kevin comes toward me.

His arms are outstretched. I hold up a hand and walk to the window. "Ashley, don't overreact. If you're looking for an easy ride to the altar, you're not going to get it."

"This isn't anything like I thought it would be. I thought it would be romantic and careless and exciting, but it's really just stressful and frightening. I have an issue with expectations, I suppose. They're always too high; life is always too disappointing."

He surrounds me with his arms, holding me close, and whispers in my ear. "My sister is a walking bit of chaos. It's just her way. As for being too old, you're younger than any of the surgeons I work with— and they're not even thinking of marriage right now. That makes you a spring chicken in my eyes." Kevin pulls back and winks at me, and I'm disarmed momentarily. *How does he do that?*

"It's not your sister. Not really." But it is his sister. His sister, his mother, his father, and his job. It's my age. It's Kay alone in the house. It's my fears. It's a million and one things. It's everything. *Is love enough?*

"I know I've been working too much. But there's this little girl, Ash—" His voice cracks. "She has no mother, and I just hate to leave her alone in the nursery. When her surgeries are completed, they're going to send her into a care home or foster care." He rakes a hand through his hair, and I can feel his stress. "I hate to leave her alone at night in that darkened room all by herself. I'm a terrible surgeon, according to my father, because I can't separate. I want to help, Ash, but I can't help them all the way they need to be helped. So I feel useless."

I put my head against his chest. I can feel his heart beating and smell his clean scent, woodsy with a little antiseptic thrown in. *I want to be here forever.* But I don't want to fail at everything else—and I don't want Kevin to fail either. We're just two completely broken people inside these well-dressed packages. You will never know the extent of people's weaknesses until you get a glimpse inside their souls. What lurks beneath the Gucci is not pretty.

"What's wrong with the little girl?" I ask.

"She was born with enlarged organs. They've had to be compacted surgically." I feel Kevin's arms close tightly around me again.

I look up at him. "Will she be okay?"

"Medically, she'll be fine. But they'll probably put her in a care home soon. She needs round-the-clock care, and that means a facility." Kevin pulls me over and we sit on the couch. "I think I'm in the wrong business. I never saw my father crack over a patient. I don't think he ever did."

"Because you have a heart, you're in the wrong business?"

"I wonder if it goes away. Nothing seems to affect the older surgeons. Maybe I'll become a crusty old ogre like my father without any emotions. Maybe I'll come to believe the world's problems can be solved by surgeons."

"Like that guy on *The Swan*?"

"What?" Kevin looks confused by my reality show reference. And the last thing I want to do is explain the whole makeover scenario and my shallow interest in this train-wreck of a television show.

"Nothing. Listen, maybe older surgeons are just better at hiding their feelings. Or maybe they've come to see they're doing what they can, and that's all you can do."

Kevin looks toward his door. "Look, I'm sorry, my mind is full. And I just have to get some rest. Did you need me for anything, Ash?"

"Everything!" I want to shout. *I need you to make it all better for me, too.* But I just shake my head. "No," I say into his chest, and we just hold each other for a while. "I just wanted to drop off your car."

"By the way, what kind of guy is that my sister left with?"

"He seems innocent enough. A little lost, perhaps, but harmless. Nothing a date with a twenty-five-year-old won't help." I give Kevin a little smile. "He's just trying to rebuild his ego. Your sister will be gone tomorrow, so I doubt much harm will be done. He'll think he's James Bond, and life will go on as before."

"My sister's a wreck, huh?"

"You're helping her, though. You've given her a job, for one thing." *Much to my dismay.*

"Spending *your* money." Kevin smiles. "I'm not sure that's helping. Do you need cash? Has she sucked your account dry yet? My father always complains she has a way of spending other people's money that, if marketed, could be employed by the federal government."

Do I need cash? Mentally, I tick off the reasons for my newfound Silicon Valley poverty:

REASONS I NEED CASH

1. Dog ate wedding shoes (didn't I use that excuse for a missing homework paper?).
2. Wedding dress ordered/canceled—yet oddly, no refund check in my pocket.
3. Reception money. Prawns and bacon-wrapped scallops off my desired menu replaced by veggie dip, perhaps chips and salsa, if things don't change.
4. Costly check gone for a red egg and ginger party, and I'm neither Asian nor a mother.
5. Tax checks sent to help the stellar California school system (again, not a parent!).
6. Down payment to photographer—and I still won't look 105 pounds!
7. Down payment for flowers that will last one day yet cost more than an entire front-yard landscaping project.

I *want* to tell Kevin I need money. I want to tell him to call off the dogs, or in this case, his pit-bull sister—but I don't think he can handle my financial and emotional crises today. Looking into his eyes now, none of that seems important. I tighten my grasp around his neck and snuggle into his chest, and we just quietly sit together on his trashed, college-style sofa.

"Don't worry about it, Kevin. It's not important. We'll get through this." Kevin goes limp in response. As I look up at him, I see he's completely asleep. *Story of my life.*

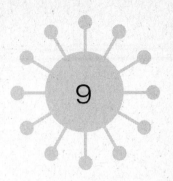

9

Once I peel myself away from my dead-to-the-world fiancé, I head home to get ready for the red egg party. All that, and I'm still in Kevin's car. He needs his sleep for the party, and a small thing like taking his transportation—if that helps my cause? So be it. I'm a woman. I'm not above simple manipulation.

I take the long route home, since seeing Kay is something I dread. I think about keeping my visual of Emily and Matt to myself, but then I'd be no different from Kay and her silence on Seth's hiring. Didn't I just get through giving her the women-stick-together speech? As I approach the house, I ponder the best way to tell her that Mr. Charm was out with Emily. That he had fallen victim to the fleeting beauty that is my sister-in-law-to-be.

It's one of those miserable truths in life that men act pathetic around beautiful women. Case in point? Rich Manhattan men. Now I know they think they're Mr. Big with sexy, teenage fiancées, and they don't care that it looks ridiculous. They must believe the rest of humanity is jealous, I'm assuming. But for us realists, I have to ponder the fiancée's thought process. Granted, she probably sports a twelve-carat diamond. And I'm not immune. I'm the first to admit I could do some pretty insane things for twelve carats.

But marry a man nearly twice my age and live in his tacky gold palace? Um, no. Not for me. It's too close to bringing Stepford into reality, giving up oneself to be someone's bride. There isn't a big enough diamond in the world to substitute for real love.

To love a man like I love Kevin is to forget the size of your diamond. It's to believe I am the luckiest woman alive for the rare five minutes a day (a week!) that I get to see him. I want to look into his eyes and feel utter disbelief that I get to wake up to this man every morning in my future, not wonder what I can buy next with his money. But I digress.

My point here, and I do have one, is that last night Matt Callaway seemed like a fairly intelligent human being. Yet he fell quickly and easily under Emily's spell. That's not completely unexpected. I mean, she's got this luscious strawberry blond hair that falls down her back with youthful sheen and the same green eyes as her brother, with long black eyelashes (I think she had them dyed) and full Angelina Jolie lips—also most likely helped by professionals, but still. Her face has incredible symmetry, everything aligned to PhotoShop perfection. But more than any of those attributes combined, Emily has this feminine, sensual way about her. She moves with intent, like a Siamese cat crossing the room toward a feline hater's leg. She knows who will win, who has the upper hand, and has the uncanny knack for making men feel she's impossible to resist.

Emily appears completely innocent, yet something about her says she isn't—and she manages to give men this message without speaking. Women, naturally, can just sense this type, but it's like a dog whistle to men. They're completely oblivious. These women rarely have a lot of girlfriends, and they don't want them because women are the bloodhounds that sniff them out. I don't know what this "magic" is, but it's a powerful tonic for men: the girl next door with a dash of vixen.

If Emily was born with this "gift" (or "curse," depending on your point of view), she took the time and care to perfect it. She knows how to wrap people around all her fingers, and she is used to getting what she wants. Letting her run off with my wedding is like a free pass to control her brother, me, and in an obscure manner, her parents. I've reached my limit, and this morning's Emily-induced breakfast indigestion crossed my personal boundaries. I'm like a dog. You mess with my meal, you will hear about it.

I pull into my driveway, and Rhett comes bounding out of the house when I exit the car. I walk to the garage and retrieve the big, fake bone I bought him days before but forgot to pass on.

"How's my boy?" He drops the faux bone and continues to lick at my feet.

"Stop it, Rhett. That tickles."

It's the month of May, and Kay is sweeping the front porch to get ready for the approach of summer. Although Kay celebrates each month's holidays with decorations, May is a bit of a quandary for her. Mother's Day is not big here, as she's never been a mother and doesn't think much of the state in general. And Cinco de Mayo, while fun and festive, doesn't have much to do with Kay's German roots; so she ignores that too. Plus, it's over on the fifth, so she feels it's a waste of decorating paraphernalia.

Kay celebrates May with "Spring-Cleaning" month and a break from the festive decorations to organize—as if she needs to do more of that! Pots organized by letter of functionality are strange enough, I should think.

The entire front porch has the pungent odor of Formula 409. "What did you do?" I ask while holding my nose. "Disinfect the entire house? I can smell it with my nose plugged. That can't be healthy. Only you would eat tofu as a food product and then poison yourself with inhalants."

"I washed up the outdoor tables, repainted the house trim, and I'm going to oil the teak chairs next," she says proudly, waving her rag.

"Kay." I steal the rag from her. "The dog won't even follow me up here. I think you're breathing too many of those fumes. You're going to pass out. Why don't you wait, and I'll help you?"

Kay grabs the rag back. "It wouldn't hurt you to spring-clean that room of yours, but I doubt *the bride* has time for disinfectant." She purses her lips like someone's angry mother.

"I prefer to keep what brain cells I have. You can't be too careful."

"Speaking of brain cells, Purvi expects you in the office this morning. She called here looking for you. I guess you didn't have your cell on you." Kay goes back to humming. She's far too happy for someone cleaning. "How was your breakfast?"

"Don't ask. I'm just going to grab my laptop and run into work for a few minutes before the party this afternoon. If Kevin calls here, would you ask him to call me if he needs his car?" I reach for the screen door and I think I'm home-free, but . . .

"Did you see Emily this morning?" Kay asks.

"Yeah," I say as I pull open the screen door and start to step over the threshold.

"Well, what did she say about her date last night? Did you tell her the truth about Matt and me?"

"I didn't really get a chance to speak to her. She was more interested in giving me her two cents."

"What do you mean?"

I shut the screen door with a bang and look at Kay. *Lord, help me be gentle with this one. The last thing I want is to hurt Kay.* "Kay, I have something you might not want to hear."

She starts to scrub with vigor, waiting.

"Emily was leaving the house with Matt this morning. Apparently they made arrangements on the phone." I feel like I'm back in high school, telling Brea that Jim Warden was asking someone else to the prom.

Kay's response? Nothing. She stops scrubbing. No expression, no tears, no mourning. Just stoic Kay and tight, pursed lips. She nods her head a few times and goes back to cleaning.

"I'm sorry, Kay. I never should have allowed that to happen. He's a dog, or he wouldn't have made a date with Emily in the first place. She's a child next to him. He doesn't want a woman. He wants a girl."

"You don't have to try to make me feel better, Ashley. Last night was fun for me. It was good practice, and I feel better about being single. Better than I ever have. When Matt talked about his wife, or ex-wife, he seemed to have no respect for the years they'd spent together. I don't need that kind of stuff in my life." Kay's on her knees, looking up at me with wide eyes. I can tell she's trying to convince herself that she's not crushed. "My life is good. Last night was fantastic confirmation of that. The singles group needs me to organize, and I'm good with that."

"I don't think you need a man, Kay, and far be it from me to say so. But don't you ever want one? It's okay to want one."

She sighs with a rush of air. "Maybe I did, at one time. You know, I had all the little-girl bride-dreams about playing house. But the funny part was, for me, there was never a husband in the dream, only the house. And I've got that already, and it's clean just like I kept my playhouse." She smiles.

I break into an anti-male Alanis Morissette song.

"Very funny. You really don't need to worry about me, Ashley. I'm not desperate to get married like you are." She says it softly, gently, like there's not an arsenal of bullets in that statement.

"What? You think I'm desperate?"

"You know what I mean," Kay says.

"No, I really don't. Do you think I'm desperate to get married?" *Does everyone?*

"*Desperate* is the wrong word. I just think you overemphasize marriage and its effect on your problems." She wipes her forehead with the back of her hand. "You're not riding off into the sunset, you know."

"What problems do I have that I think are getting solved?" I ask, incredulous. "I have a nice house, car, and job, and my walk with the Lord is growing. I've been soloing at church . . . tithing. What problems?" I repeat.

Kay sits up on her knees and blows her bangs up. "I think you don't know how to be alone. You've spent so much time chasing a man that now you don't know what to do with him."

"I never chased a man." *Yeah, that's not really true.* "I never chased Kevin," I amend.

"You never had to." Kay shrugs.

"Look, this isn't about me. If I'm making a mistake, I'll feel the pain. I didn't want to tell you about Emily and Matt. I'm sorry I did, but you don't seem to care much. Most likely, they deserve each other. Two broken people chipping away at what little is left."

"Ashley! I've known you to say some extraordinary things, but that is downright mean. Emily is lost. You know that. Maybe you can't do much, but you can try to love her."

I hold up a palm. "Whatever. If you're not mad, I'll be incensed for you. You talk about me being desperate, but at least I face my fears. You had fun with Matt. How hard is that to admit? Emily is more worried about a piece of property being stolen from her than Matt's feelings."

"Stop!" Kay says as I head into the house. "My fears aren't yours. My fears aren't that I'll never find a man, Ashley."

"Maybe not, but what's wrong with exploring the option? I may be desperate, but you're equally averse to submitting yourself to a relationship. You make Seth look downright anxious to get to the altar."

She follows me in and slams the door shut with a flattened hand. "There's nothing to be mad about with Matt, all right? I had dinner with the man. I had a great time being a girl for a night, and it's over. Now what are *you* really angry about?" Kay asks.

"You really want to know? I've been dragged all over town by a steel magnolia for the week. I've had my wedding dress order canceled for heaven knows what reason. I've spent my mortgage money on a red egg and ginger party, my office just hired my ex-boyfriend, I have a fiancé I never see, and when I do, he falls asleep. My mother doesn't want to play mother-of-the-bride but rather grandma. This week evil became personified for me, and its name is Emily. And if you won't be mad at her for her wiles and finagling, I will! I've tried to be politically correct with Kevin, but the fact is, his sister is hijacking my wedding. And just like the day I discovered that Dave and Mei Ling's wedding wasn't mine, Emily's gonna know whose wedding this is."

Kay exhales deeply, as though I'm a child in need of a spanking. Which may be true, but I'm *so* not in the mood to hear it.

"Whatever you do, don't do it before the shower, Ashley. We'll all be sitting in the living room, and none of us will have a thing to say. Just ask yourself when you're not angry anymore if it's worth it, this power you're giving her. Until then, go to work and play with patents for a while. Because matchmaking is not your skill."

There she is, the voice of reason. *So* not on my agenda today. "I make no promises."

———————

Gainnet's giant, cement-box building with the standard mirrored windows is quiet for a Saturday morning, with only a few cars scattered in the lot. Ever since the dot-com crash, you can tell the difference between a weekday and the weekend. One big advantage to the implosion. Engineers actually learned the definition of Saturday: more time at the Xbox.

"Hey, Jim," I say as I enter the building. I brush my badge through the electronic checkpoint as Jim nods toward me. No *Good morning*, no *Happy to see you*, just the typical security guard nod that tells me he acknowledges my presence, but also that he can take me down if necessary.

As I'm walking to my desk, I stop in my tracks as I see Seth coming toward me in the cubicle hallway. I look around frantically for an escape, but what am I thinking? It's clear he sees me, unless I've suddenly developed the skill to disappear. He stops too, and now we're both standing here like a pair of idiots waiting for the other to make the first move. If I'm going to stand up to Emily, I figure I need the practice. I start walking toward him, my shoulders thrust out like a *Vogue* model for extra confidence.

"Hey, Ash, did you hurt your back?" Seth says with a puzzled expression.

"What? No." I relax my shoulders just a tad. "It's good to see you, Seth. I heard you got the job here. Congratulations." See? Totally professional. No bitter angst, no melancholy, no pathetic I-wanted-to-marry-you tone. But as I look into his blue eyes, I *feel* his presence. My heart still jumps just a little at the sight of his angular face, his smooth bald head, and those tanzanite eyes. I force my vision to the floor. *Focus on the Diesel Sporties,* I tell myself. But all these memories come flooding into my mind: Seth's laugh, his gift of Rhett the puppy. *His clueless, engineering style.* He doesn't begin to tempt me, but I miss his friendship. I wish I could forget that I once loved him. It's like a daily reminder of rejection. I wish there were more than, like, four Christians in Silicon Valley so the opportunity to run into him wasn't so blatant.

Seeing him only reminds me that he dumped me like yesterday's garbage. Oh, I know, *officially* I dropped him. But let's face it, he wasn't going to marry me. What self-respecting woman waits around with futile hope? You either break up or enter the realm of woefully pitiful. Quite frankly, I think I was already there before I finally found the strength to move forward.

"You look good, Ashley," Seth finally says. "Kay tells me you're doing well." He lowers his head to meet my eyes and tries to force my gaze. "Rhett too."

"Thanks. I have been well. Busy. You know how it is." I must look ridiculous nodding my head but not looking him in the eye. I should be able to stare him down, even scare him if necessary, but I am rendered useless. I can't look at him without remembering I got dumped. Hard.

"Purvi tells me you really are getting married."

"August." I nod. *This is good. Talk about Kevin, the man who loves me back.* "Kevin has a short leave from the hospital then, so we can take a honeymoon." It suddenly occurs to me this wasn't the nicest observation on his part. "What do you mean, *really* getting married? Not all men break out into hives when a wedding is mentioned."

Seth rolls his eyes as if to say, *We're not having this discussion.* "Do you have a minute to go over some of the software patents I need?"

My mouth dangles open. "No, I don't have time now. It's Saturday, and I'm here to catch up so I don't have to go to Taiwan. If you want a meeting, see my secretary and get on my calendar, like everyone else has to do! You're not entitled to any favors from me." I plod down the hallway, embarrassed that my professional facade just crumbled like the Berlin Wall.

He whistles. "Still fighting that temper, huh?"

Okay, now I want to hurt him and show him the meaning of temper. I turn around and give him my most fear-inspiring gaze, my forefinger extended a mere inch or two from his rather beady, if beautiful, blue eyes. "You are like gum on the bottom of my shoe, Seth. Why don't you go away? All the high-tech companies in the area, and you had to come here? What is up with that?" I see a newspaper sitting on a desk, and I grab it and thrust it at him. "Here are the classifieds. Maybe there's something out there for you. It sure isn't here."

He smiles. "I missed your fiery speech. You're so cute when you're angry. Does Kevin appreciate that? Because it's pretty hot."

"Watch it. I'm a lawyer, and I wouldn't think twice about suing you for sexual harassment. In fact, it would give me pleasure. You wish you had one-tenth the class Kevin has, and you know it. Empty-headed Arin is exactly what you deserve."

He lifts his palms up. "Now that was below the belt. We're Christians. We share custody of a dog. I should think that's enough to bind us for life in Silicon Valley, and you could take a little ribbing."

"We don't share *anything* except maybe a pathetic history that's just as soon forgotten." I storm down the hallway, and I can feel him on my heels. "What do you want?" I whirl myself around.

85

He grabs my hands and looks me dead in the eye. "I want one more chance, Ashley. I think we're good together, and you don't want to be a rich-boy doctor's wife. You're too beautiful to play second fiddle."

For once in my life, I am utterly speechless. One more chance? Sheesh, his odds were way better than the lottery with the number of chances I gave him. All that opportunity, and he still couldn't manage to utter the words a woman needs to hear. Not just this woman. Any woman. I feel like whispering in his ear the magic words that will enable him to sustain a relationship next time, like *I love you. Will you marry me? Okay, Seth. Practice them with me now!* After all, he's no spring chicken, and without a bank account like Trump's, his opportunities are probably drying up. Even Rogaine isn't going to help refresh them.

"Arrgh!" I untangle myself from his grip and jog to my office, where I slam the door shut with a bang. *Seth: ever-clueless, ever-romantically inept!*

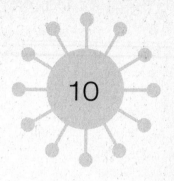

10

B*reathe. Breathe.* I feel like I need a paper bag to restore my respiration faculties. Not because I'm so worked up over Seth wanting me to rush back into his arms. *Give me a break.* Mostly because he still didn't really offer anything. All my emotion and outrage, and he still doesn't get it.

Another chance? Another chance at what? Saturday nights with pizza, his buddies, and science-fiction theater? Or maybe he meant going out to dinner with coupon in hand and coming home for a rousing game of PlayStation 2. Either way, it's not exactly tempting. Yet I feel like he wants me to be grateful for his outburst of emotion. He gave an iota of himself; now I should fall at his feet and hang out for another year.

"Arrgh!" I scream out in frustration.

I glance at my desk, and it's so covered with files and sticky notes that it makes me think Purvi owns stock in 3M. Schematics and folders are everywhere just gasping for my attention, and where am I? Thinking about Seth and being trapped in this office while he holds court over the hallway. I hate my life some days. I want to call Kevin, but he is dealing with shock victims and critical patients. My crises can never compare, and complaining about my paltry excuse for a past now bleeding copiously into my present is hardly a worthy interruption.

I even question Seth's motives. Like, did he make this pitiful attempt at my heart to put us on equal footing in the office? So he can be seen as the victim? Poor, forlorn Seth who was left all alone. My anger starts to swell like a pent-up earthquake on the San Andreas Fault. I'm pacing my office like a rabid dog, and one thing becomes clear: I have to make a list.

Of course. A list will help me clarify my priorities, be the strong woman I am, and hey, maybe God will see these thoughtful words and help me out. Granted, this is probably not a biblical way to go about things, but it works for me at the moment. Since I have no Bible handy, it's going to have to do.

MY VOWS ON HOW TO BE A CONFIDENT WOMAN, AT EASE IN ANY SITUATION

1. I will *not* let my future sister-in-law hijack my wedding, with her bouncy hair and fashion tips from *Victoria*.
2. I will not allow Seth to keep me captive in my office. I am the reason for Gainnet's stock price. I am Patent Guru, and I will act the part. He will be my software slave.
3. I will tell Kay she must get my half of the house sold or rented by my wedding date. (She put up with me. She can certainly find someone to fit her *Clean Sweep* criteria.)
4. I will tell Kevin that Philadelphia is too big of a change with a new marriage. They have winter there, and I'm not anxious to take two more Bar exams. Spring at Stanford Shopping Center is my future.
5. I will tell my brother to pay me back what he owes me and not let him continue his cycle of freeloading. (No, I really won't, but it sounds powerful, doesn't it?)
6. I will tell Kevin his parents will not buy us a house. (I'm thinking mother-in-law unit, and that ain't pretty.) Remember: better a dump without the in-laws than a

mansion paid for by silicone. (I'm sure that's a proverb, isn't it?)

There. I've put my list in my Blackberry, so it's official. I feel my confidence growing by the second. It makes me want to strike a *Vogue* pose and remember this moment. I actually get three patent schematics looked up before there's a soft knock on my door. Peeking through the side window is Seth, my still-present ex. *He's like Pigpen's dust cloud!*

I sigh aloud, take one more look at my list, and shove it in the desk. "Door's open."

Seth has a file in his hand. "Our history aside, I really do need patent help."

You need help, all right. As in, help getting a clue.

"Fine, but on Monday, okay? I have my brother's party to get to today, and Kevin's car is in the lot. He might need it to get to the hospital. You'll soon find out that everyone needs a patent, so you might as well learn now to get in line."

"Kevin's not going to the party with you?"

"Did I say that?" I bark a bit too sharply.

"No, I was just curious," Seth says. "You said he needed his car. Never mind."

Software slave. You are nothing but a software slave. "Leave your file on my desk. I'll get to it first thing Monday, and we can meet in the afternoon. Schedule me in after three."

"Thanks, Ashley. Hey, I'm sorry if I made you uncomfortable."

My lips are pursed tightly. I feel like Kay. "No, you didn't. Nothing to be uncomfortable about. We have a history, it's over, and here we are working in the same claustrophobic industry. No biggie." Suddenly a thought occurs to me as I remember his last plea. "Hey, what about Arin?"

"We're friends," he says cryptically. Probably the same thing he told people after we'd been dating for ten months. He doesn't want to limit his options, you understand.

89

"Uh-huh, well, stunning. I need to get to work. Tell her I said hello." I scan the file he's just dropped in front of me, but I can still feel his presence. He's not leaving. *Just like gum on the shoe, I tell you!*

Seth closes my office door. *Um, you're on the wrong side of the door, buddy.* "I wouldn't have said anything about us, but Kevin went after you with no regard for my presence. I figured he deserved the same."

"Ah, yes, the biblical principle of pummeling the other cheek. I know it well. You've got nothing to be mad at Kevin about anyway. *You* left for India. *You* told me commitment wasn't something you were ready for. Is any of this ringing a bell? Your own mother wondered what was happening."

"I made a mistake. But don't marry the wrong guy because of it."

Oh, trust me, I'm not. I try to laugh here, but it's not coming. "Why do you assume Kevin is the wrong guy? I mean, if you need closure, I understand that, but this is definitely the end. I love Kevin. Maybe you're not buying it, but it doesn't matter. Because it's the truth." Seth's opinion is null and void in my life.

"You're going to do what you want, Ashley. I know better than to try and tell you anything. I just wanted to make sure you were sure. If you change your mind . . ." Seth steps out of my office, and I drop my head to the desk. This is like the never-ending relationship. *So* yesterday. Am I in that movie *Groundhog Day*?

I lift up my head and see the frames filled with babies: my brother's baby, Davey, and Brea's little boys, Miles and Jonathan. I recall a recent article I read about women having too many personal items on their desks. Apparently my career could be fiendishly halted by this ghastly display of human emotion. By all accounts, I should rush to foreign countries and purchase ethnic masks and fertility gods in order to show that I am a worthy candidate to claw my way up the corporate ladder. No estrogen showing here. However, since I begged Gainnet to hire Purvi because I was in over my head, maybe I'm as successful as I want to be. I'm certainly a better patent attorney than a bride.

As I focus on my nephew's big brown eyes and toothless smile, it only reminds me I'm not like normal people. People seem to meet, get married, and have children without incident. With me, just trying to make it to the altar is a lesson in perseverance. Why does everything I touch turn to green Jell-O?

Comparably, Kay's single life boasts a nice granite kitchen and garage organizers and is becoming more appealing with every passing second. By remaining single, I could avoid this confusion. And everything I own would be labeled by Kay for perfect storage opportunities. That's what I need: a labeler, with emotional titles to remind me to avoid toxic people. I'll thrust these labels on their foreheads (with the footnotes, of course):

LABELS

Seth: COMMITMENT-PHOBE
Unless someone else is interested.

Emily: OBSESSIVE-COMPULSIVE STEEL MAGNOLIA
Chaos is us.

Purvi: WIRED WORKAHOLIC
Motto: You handle this stress, instead of me.

Mrs. Novak: TAUT, TONED, AND TERRIFYING
My brain is the only thing left with wrinkles, but it has lots of them!

Kay: CALM, COOL, COLLECTED, AND DISCONNECTED
If Tupperware comes in human form, I'm it—with the airtight lid.

My office phone rings and takes me away from these very important musings. I look up to see it's my private line. Considering how much work I'm getting done, I'm up for a phone call. It's Kevin.

"Hi, Kevin," I say, so relieved to hear his voice. I want to wrap myself up in his words.

"Ashley Stockingdale, did you steal my car?" There's this morning grogginess in his voice, and it's unbearably sexy.

"I *did* steal your car."

"Did you steal it so I'd be forced to attend this red egg and ginger party?"

He knows me too well. "That depends. Did it work?"

He laughs with a sleepy growl. "I told you if I got enough sleep, I wouldn't miss it. And I don't lie. Especially to the woman of my dreams, no matter how manipulative she might be."

"Don't forget you promised the woman of your dreams and your sister that you'd finalize the location for the wedding tomorrow. Leave it up to me, and you could be getting married in the Nordstrom Café for easy shopping access afterwards."

"I thought we decided on the country club."

"No, that was your mom and your sister who decided on that. We can't really afford the country club on our budget, Kevin. I don't want to go into debt for one day of our lives. It's more important that the money go into my gown so I can look good for the pictures. And I want to be able to afford a hairstylist. Sheesh, priorities! Must I constantly remind you? Like I care if these people eat. It's all about me, baby."

Kevin laughs. "Well, be that as it may, you want enough people to see you in your gown to make it worthwhile, don't you?"

"Oooh, you're good."

"We're paying for the wedding together, Ashley. My parents will pay for the location, especially if they want the club. It's nothing to them, and you should buy the dress you want. This is *our* day."

Yeah, tell that to Emily and her fill-in-the-blanks Martha wedding guide.

"But the money is something to me, Kevin. You're marrying into a blue-collar family, and while we may not have a country club membership, we still have a strong work ethic. I want the wedding we can *afford*. I worked hard for my stuff, and I'm proud of my ownership of half a house, even though no one warned me what sinking half a million into a 1920s piece of rubble costs in additional sweat equity. But I do have pride of ownership, and I want to own my wedding day." *And I definitely don't want your parents and Emily to own it.*

"Ashley, I can't believe you're worried about this. I want you to have the wedding day you've dreamed about. What about the fancy shrimp and elegant waiters I've heard about? Blue-collar and your wedding just don't fit."

"A mortgage has cured me of my dreams quick enough." How do I tell him that my current poverty has cured me? "This wedding is going to be affordable chic because I don't want to fret after it over buying a pair of Cole Haan's on sale."

"Ashley Stockingdale, you're sounding positively practical. Cut it out. You're scaring me. I'm not marrying Kay."

But I'm not deterred. The last thing I want is to owe Kevin's family. "Your resident's pay is less than mine, and with both of us having Silicon Valley mortgages now . . . Besides, you have an uncanny knack for getting called away when the bill appears. Beeper, my foot."

"Are you calling me cheap?"

"I'm saying you have impeccable timing. Did your sister get home?" I ask, changing the subject and hoping that Matt the Stalker isn't really one.

"No, but she called. She's having lunch with Matt. They went for a walk this morning, and she's going to attend the party tonight with us."

Peachy.

"That's good," I say with forced enthusiasm. "I need to talk with her about my gown."

"She says it's gorgeous, Ashley. It's due to the dressmaker on Monday. She's been working on it for months, designed it just for you, she says. I haven't seen her really get excited about something before. I think she's found her niche. She won't let me even peek at the drawings. I can't thank you enough for helping her through this. What if this is her true calling?"

I feel my teeth clench. "Funny. She won't let me peek at the dress either. Actually, Kevin, that dress is not my dress. Women generally pick out their own gowns. While I want to keep the wedding affordable, I do want to select—"

"Shoot. My beeper's going off," Kevin says amid a high-pitched beep. "I'll call you right back." Kevin clicks away, and I decide venting is good and continue my conversation without him.

"That's right, Kevin. Actually, my wedding dress is Vera Wang, not Scarlett O'Hara. But the issue here is not really the dress. It's that your sister is running free in society. Emily's a crazed control freak who should probably be checked back into the hospital with pale green walls and extensive lawns. The one where they talk softly and give her many puzzles to assemble."

I'm not liking myself much at this point. One thing I've noticed about living in God's will: just when you think you have something mastered, like how to get along with difficult people, He will test you to the very limits to knock down that pride of yours. He's an expert in pointing out you how far you have to go, not how far you've come. *I hate that.*

With a tinge of depression, I dial Brea. She's not nearly the fun she used to be. Brea and I are like two ships passing in the night lately. She's on a different time schedule with her babies, and my wedding is hardly her priority. I don't blame her, but it's not anyone's priority other than Emily's, and there's something infinitely sad about that fact. It's not personal; it's just that Silicon Valley is not exactly the most connected place on earth. Need something done? Hire out, because your friends have to schedule you in. Heck, my mother has to pencil me in.

"Hello," Brea answers, sounding winded.

"Brea, it's me. Is this a bad time?"

She lets out a long sigh. "Did you know that Duplos clog toilets?"

"No, actually, that's a new one on me. What's a Duplo?"

"Never mind. What's up?" she asks amid lots of squealing and banging in the background.

"Nothing much. Just called to see what's happening. Get a little calm voice of reason."

"You called the wrong place then. I have a clogged toilet, two dogs caged and barking, and a dirty diaper that I'll spare you the details of."

"I won't keep you," I say, but I'm bummed, really bummed. "I just wanted to let you know Emily ordered this wedding gown for me awhile ago. Kevin says the dress shop should have it on Monday. I was wondering if you could use your skills to help me with Hannah at the dress shop. You're better friends with her, and I just have to get rid of that dress! I have to get my own ordered again before it's too late. And I'm afraid I don't really have the money to reorder at the moment."

"Didn't they credit you the first down payment?" Brea asks, her voice perfectly smooth, though the background noise at her house makes it sound like she's watching an old World War II movie.

The credit. Of course, if they canceled my order, I forgot they would have credited the account! Emily couldn't charge on my account. "Brea, you're a genius!"

"I know. Now I'm off to tweezer a Duplo from the toilet. Pray for me."

11

For anyone not familiar with the red egg and ginger party, this is a tradition in which people from the Chinese culture celebrate the birth of a new child, handing out red hard-boiled eggs (red for good luck; egg for the new life) and eating lots of food at the new parents' expense. It's also currently why Mei Ling's hands, waving as she greets the partygoers streaming into Ping's, are tinged red from the dye session. These soirees are a really big deal, costing nearly as much as a wedding. Parents of the newborn invite everyone they've ever met and inundate them with an Asian food spread that makes a casino buffet look light on the choices.

Normally, in a traditional ceremony, the grandparents name the baby. However, that's sort of died in the American culture, and Mei Ling is not from a typical Chinese family—her father is American and not in contact with her. Her mother is in China, and there's a history there of "don't ask, don't tell." Baby Davey's formal name or "milk-name," as Mei Ling calls it, is "Chen Li Stockingdale." Okay, kinda loses a little in the translation, but the name means "great strength." With a moniker like that, he'll need it.

Most families have this party when their baby is a month old, but Davey is now four months old, because even though my brother saved every penny he had for this celebration, it wasn't nearly enough. I wish it had been. I don't care that much about the money I loaned him, it's just that my brother, Dave, has worked so hard to be the perfect husband to Mei Ling. She would have done without the party if she'd known what it had done to him.

To watch Dave hover over her, seeing if she needs anything, is enough to make me forget how he has endlessly teased me for being "bus bait." (As in, a woman over the age of thirty has a better chance of getting hit by a bus than getting married. Ha! Guess I'm showing him.) I really do want Dave to feel good about himself, because he deserves to for trying so hard to give Mei Ling what she wants.

Twinge of guilt here. I imagine that's what Kevin wants for his sister, too. Kevin, always the healer, wants to rescue Emily from herself. She's lived in the lap of luxury for so long. Her sensuality always seems to get in the way of any career because she gets far more attention for her appearance than any accomplishment. I should have such luck.

Speaking of Emily, she's dressed like an '80s diva in an aqua silk suit with big, padded shoulders. She has perfectly coifed hair, and she actually looks beautiful but also like she beamed out of another era, á la *Dynasty*'s Krystle Carrington, whom she is entirely too young to remember. Emily is wearing spiked heels that make her five-foot-nine frame appear gargantuan in a desirable way. She seems dressed for trouble, planning to see Matt after the party, heavy on the cleavage. She walks into the restaurant expecting all eyes to turn her direction, and most of them do. The child in me wants to trip her at this point, but I remember I'm a church girl and force my eyes to the host's stand.

"Ashley doesn't seem to know what she wants for this weddin', Keh-vin. It's a good thing y'all brought me out here," she drawls, taking his arm and batting her eyelashes at her big "brothah."

Can I hurt her? Just a little?

"Ashley's got a lot on her mind. Trust me, she knows what she wants." Kevin winks at me.

Hello, I am standing right here!

"She may know her mind, but gettin' it accomplished is not in her realm of capability. I've been runnin' myself ragged to get things done. I hope she's good at patents, because weddin' plannin' is not her forte." Emily plucks at something invisible on her sleeve.

"I think we just have cultural differences in what we deem important," I say, and Emily looks at me like the snake has slithered out of the bottle and spoken.

She gives a tinkling laugh. "Like good taste is cultural. Oh, Keh-vin, what a delight she is." She turns to him and mutters quietly, "You can't be serious about this, Keh-vin."

I feel my fists tightening. If God is pushing me toward maturity, I'm most definitely not ready.

The maître d' ushers us into a private room where there are tons of people I've never met. Across the room is my family. You can tell the difference, because Mei Ling's distant family is mostly Asian and very conservatively dressed. My extended family feels that this celebration, like all others, deserves sequins and fresh burgundy-red hair dye. I should really invest in Clairol. My family must keep them in business. You know how there's realistic color, and then there's the stuff at the end of the clearance rack at Target? Guess where my family shops?

My conservative mother, who doesn't believe in dye except on the red eggs, is here holding court over Davey. (The purpose of the party is to pass the baby around and show him off, but my mother's not having any part of this tradition, she announces with disgust in her voice.) Her view of the party is that it's for everyone to know who is Davey's grandmother.

"Ashley, you're here." Mei Ling pulls me aside, and she appears distraught as my brother downs a soda next to my father. "Get the baby from your mother, will you? My relatives are ready to meet Chen Li." Mei Ling's mother and father are not here, but she seems to have other relatives coming out of the woodwork. And while my sister-in-law loves and respects my mother, there's obviously a boundary issue here.

"I'll do my best." But looking at my mother and the clutch she's got on Davey, I'm not too hopeful. Being a grandmother seems to be what my mother has been waiting for all this time. And seeing her with Davey, I'm closer to understanding her frustration over my lack of marriage opportunities.

"Ashley," my mother says and pulls the baby closer to imply I'm not getting my hands on him. "Did you get everything done for the wedding yesterday? This is sure turning into quite the ordeal." She bounces Davey on her hip.

"I did. It was a positively lovely day," I lie. "Mom . . ." I say gently.

"No. There's too many germs here. I'm not handing him around to all these strangers."

"He's Mei Ling's and Dave's, Mom, and they want to introduce him to his extended family. That's what the party is about. That's why they gave you the pamphlet on the red egg and ginger tradition."

"A baby shouldn't be around this many people, Ashley. It's just not done."

"If they could do this in ancient China and the babies lived, Davey will survive his red egg and ginger party at Ping's. They'll give him a nice, cleansing bath when he gets home. A baby spa."

"You're not a mother, Ashley. You don't understand."

My regular reminder. "I'm not a mother, but Mei Ling is."

"But she's a new mother. There's a difference."

"Mom."

"All right, but you're responsible if he gets sick."

Me? How exactly am I responsible? Mom's lips flatten, but eventually she hands me the baby. He coos and grins at me, and I smell his fresh-baby scent. Now I don't want to hand him over myself. He's the most beautiful baby, like a porcelain doll, with big brown eyes and straight black hair hanging down over his forehead. He has Mei Ling's beautiful coloring and Dave's chipmunk cheeks. I take in a deep breath and approach my mom on the next subject. "Tomorrow after church, we're finalizing the location of the wedding. Do you think you can come with us?"

"Ashley, we'll still have relatives in from the party, so I doubt it. This wedding of yours is very badly timed for us. It's so good that Kevin's sister is here to help you."

My eyes start to well up as I look into Davey's wide, innocent eyes. "Of course. I'm sorry. I forgot about the relatives."

I kiss the top of Davey's head, hand him to his mother, and walk back toward Kevin. Without explanation, I put my hands around his waist, and my tears start to sting my nose. One falls down my cheek.

"Ashley," I hear him whisper in my ear. "What's wrong?"

The manager of the restaurant approaches us. "You have more people here than planned. It will be $32.95 per person extra. Just want to keep you posted, as your credit card will be charged. Your relatives opened a bar tab as well."

This sends me into a full-blown tearfest, and I didn't wear waterproof makeup.

"Ashley, pull yourself togethah," Emily hisses. At that moment, I just want to forget I'm a Christian. I'm ready for a good *Dynasty* catfight, Alexis versus Krystle in all her well-padded glory. Looking at her scowl, I lose my cool.

"Just stay out of it, Emily. I've had about all I can handle of you, and it's none of your business anyway. If I want to cry, as the old song says, it's my party and I'll cry if I want to!"

"Emily, that's enough," Kevin whispers loudly.

"Enough? Keh-vin, I haven't even begun. This weddin' is barely off the ground, and we've got a long flight ahead of us. If your fiancée is goin' to be cryin' as though she's not the happiest bride in the world, well, I'm just at a loss. We just don't do that in the South."

I close my eyes, willing all of this to go away. When Kevin and I were just dating, none of these nightmares plagued us. I've always known the fact that my family is strange. The difficulty now lies in adjusting to a whole new kind of weird.

"Emily, we'll discuss it tomorrow."

She opens the portfolio for her brother's full approval. "Let's see.

Tomorrow we'll be finalizin' the location. Keh-vin, I must be certain this is what you want before the big deposits go out." She runs her manicured finger down the Martha book, and something in me snaps.

I rip the Coach portfolio Emily is carrying out of her hands and shake it right in her face. "Why do you carry this everywhere? To taunt me that I'm too inane to plan my own day? This isn't your wedding, Emily. It's mine. Oh, I may not be Mensa material, but I can pick out my own wedding gown, and at least it won't be a fashion flashback. It will be classic, not some, some—"

"Ashley!" Kevin says, his eyes wide and incredulous.

I'm not proud of this moment. It's not one of my better ones. I look at him, my eyes still pooling. "Yes, Kevin." I'm breathing so heavily I'm about to explode.

With my attention diverted, Emily grabs for the notebook in my hand. As I clutch it tighter, everything happens in slow motion. I see the waiter come in, his tray full of pork buns and short ribs, and I hear myself say, "Noooo!" like Luke in *Star Wars*. But it's too late.

The Coach portfolio collides with the tray, and when time starts again, there are little mounds of pork buns making a polka-dot design on the carpet. Emily looks victorious with the Coach portfolio back in her clutches, and I drop my face into my hands. "I don't even want to think what that's going to cost me."

"Ashley Wilkes Stockingdale," my mother shouts as she marches across the room. *Oh sure, let's make my joy complete here.* "*What* do you think you're doing? This is your brother's party, and you're fighting like a common street hoodlum?"

"I'll handle this, Mom," Dave says. "Stay here!" He pushes Kevin in the chest and yanks me out onto the restaurant's front porch. "What the heck? Are you all right? That was hardly my respectable lawyer sister in there. You want to explain why you've suddenly decided to lose it at Davey's party?"

How does one explain acting completely freaky? It's not like I can make everyone understand. If I was at Nordstrom's Half-Yearly

Sale clutching the last pink cashmere sweater, people might understand, but attacking a Chinese waiter with a Coach leather folder? Not so much.

I'm really crying now over what a mess I've made of things, but I'm more angry than sad. "I'm sorry, Dave. I'm not handling in-laws-to-be very well."

"I guess," he says.

"I shouldn't have even come. I knew there was *disaster* written on this night as soon as I saw Emily's football-player-sized shoulder pads. She's like Mommie Dearest come to life."

"Ashley, Mei Ling acted just like this when we were planning our wedding. You're just stressed."

"She attacked somebody?" I sob.

"Maybe not just like this." Dave laughs.

I try to smile through my tears, but I know it's more of a grimace. "I'm not just stressed. I'm mad. Really mad. That woman thinks this is *her* wedding!"

"Grandma always said dogs get mad; people get angry."

"Grandma never met Emily Ann Novak."

"Can you imagine? Grandma would have told her to get the bee out of her bonnet." Dave laughs. "Why does she get to you, anyway? I would think if you could live with Kay, someone like Emily would be like a fly you swat away."

"I don't know why she gets to me. That's part of the frustration, I suppose. I don't like that I react to her, even when I know that's what she wants."

"Well, you've got a choice to make, I suppose. Kevin's a package deal."

"Emily is one gift-with-purchase you can keep! She's like a bad lipstick color in the Estée Lauder set. Completely useless to me."

"Come on, let's go back in. Davey wants his auntie. There wouldn't be a red egg party without you, even without your credit card." He puts his arms around me. "What could be so bad about your fancy lawyer life? The TT giving you trouble? Plumbing problems at home?"

"Getting married is more mental stress than I thought it would be. Maybe getting married is not for me."

He pulls away. "What?"

"You just said I had a choice to make. Kevin's family is a bit psycho."

Dave starts to laugh. "I got news for you, Ash. Our family is psycho too. It's all a matter of degrees. Comparing whose family is more psycho doesn't really start until after you're married. That's when the real fireworks begin. You love this guy, right?"

"What's not to love? But Mom doesn't even want to help me plan the wedding, and—" I try to finish, but my emotion gets the best of me. "I feel like Mom is saying, in her own way, that she doesn't think I'll go through with this. She doesn't want to get her hopes up like she did with Seth."

"Then ask Mei Ling to help with the wedding. She'd love to help you, and you know she sews better than any fashion designer on your list. Did you see what Davey is wearing tonight?"

"I did. He's darling. Mei Ling is a miracle worker—just being married to you proves that."

He slaps my arm. "I resemble that remark."

"Anyway, how can you be sticking up for Kevin's family? The only time you met them, they put your wife down for plastic surgery and you for a job dragging their golf clubs around the course."

"Because before you first met Mei Ling, you asked me if I met her at the immigration department. Do you remember that?"

I cringe here. Yeah, I did say that. Definitely not one of my brighter moments.

"People say stupid things when change is brewing. People don't like change, and they don't understand differences." He takes a swig from his Dr Pepper. "Every family is different, even if you grew up on the same block. Consider this your own personal Tower of Babel."

"You're a bus driver. What do you know?"

"See, it's comments like that, Ashley, that I will generously ignore because it's your ignorance speaking." He laughs. "I've met people from more countries on that bus than you'll ever dream about seeing on your business trips, and I understand them better too. You have to give the prom queen a break. Emily's been around people just like her for her entire life. How do you expect her to act? In her world, women aspire to being in *Southern Living* magazine. Or to be Miss Peachtree or something."

"I expect her to act like that in Georgia where she belongs, fanning herself and drinking sweet tea at the country club."

Dave and I look at each other, and we both laugh. "You're wicked-cruel."

"Aren't we all?"

"No, but if it makes you feel better, Ashley, you go ahead and justify your bad behavior. On Monday, you'll call Mei Ling about the wedding plans and quit dropping pork buns all over expensive Chinese restaurants."

"Mei Ling's busy with the baby, Dave. Just like Brea, she doesn't have time to do petty wedding stuff. Emily has nothing but time."

"You're just using that as an excuse. You're whining! You want to know what I think?" Dave asks.

"Not really. Let's just agree to end this conversation. The last thing I need is advice from my little brother."

Dave shrugs. "No skin off my nose, but I have to say that for years you preached at me about a loving and forgiving God. Now go back into that restaurant and do some penance, will you? Prove to me it wasn't all jawing? She's just Kevin's harmless little sister."

The idea of showing an ounce of grace toward Emily is more than I can bear, which doesn't make me warm to myself. I pray for God's filling, because I tell you, if given the choice, I'd go for the *Dynasty* brawl here. But my brother is walking with the Lord. His wife has helped him along, and they're bringing up their baby in the Lord. I have so much to be grateful for, and yet there's Emily . . . I always focus on the negative.

As I start to enter the restaurant, Emily and Kevin come walking out. I just noticed Emily has bits of BBQ pork on her shoulder pad, and I'm embarrassed at the small thrill this gives me. *Offer to pay for her dry cleaning, Ashley!*

"Where are you going?" I ask as gently as my heart will allow.

"I know you are a bride," Emily says. "And from my experience, brides do not act in their normal realm of maturity. So I am goin' to give you the benefit of the doubt. Keh-vin's takin' me home. I shall see you tomorrow for location scoutin', and we shall forget this ever happened." She marches toward the car. "I'll wait for you in the car, big brothah," she says over her shoulder pad.

Forget it happened? I was just wishing it was on videotape so I could watch the BBQ pork splatter on that big shoulder pad. Ugh. *Forgive me, Lord.*

Kevin looks at me, his eyebrows arched. "You're certifiable, you know that?"

"I don't have my Mensa membership yet. Do you want to translate?"

"Crazy, Ashley, but I love you." Kevin kisses me on the lips. "I'll be happy when the two women I love are on opposite sides of the country again."

Trust me, can't happen soon enough. He kisses me again, and I'm lost in the moment. "You make all this worthwhile, you know," I say dreamily.

"If I can't overcome my own family, I figure I'm not ready to get married."

I try to laugh. "I'll see you tomorrow. I love you too, and don't forget, Monday night we have another marriage class at Brea and John's."

"Marriage class." Kevin shakes his head. "If there's a class that tells a man how to be married to you, I definitely need it. A master's in loving Ashley Wilkes Stockingdale, now there's a degree I can get into."

"You're all Southern charm; don't think I'm not on to you," I say threateningly, but it's scary how much I love this man. His sister is nothing next to the notion of spending every day of my life with Kevin. But marrying into the Southern Golf Mafia still seems like an awfully big hurdle I have to overcome.

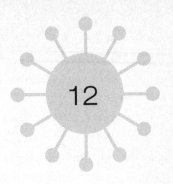

12

After signing off on my credit card for nearly $3,000, I go home to a "Reasons" party at the house. The Reasons consist of our church singles group, most of them over thirty-five, with various reasons why they haven't gotten, or can't get, married.

They're here with their feet on the coffee table watching *Shrek 2*. Maybe this getting married stuff isn't so hard. Clearly, my options aren't as wide as I remembered.

"Hi," Kay says from the couch. "Are you hungry?" Kay is in her glory tonight. The house is clean. The friends are here to eat. Life just doesn't get any better than when she's in complete control.

"I'm not hungry, thanks. Hey, Tim, Jake, Jim . . . Sam," I say like Newman on *Seinfeld*. Sam is Seth's sidekick. You know how the AV guys always traveled in pairs? Well, here they are in living grown-up color. Sam always seems to be present where there's free food and a sofa spot. Silicon Valley is home to the extremely ambitious, so Sam sticks out like a sore thumb. I think he's sort of become the Reasons' mascot, like if everyone takes a little responsibility for Sam, the job will get done. I know I sound heartless, but I got in the way of Sam's sofa spot at Seth's, and I have no idea what he did to get rid of me. I don't trust him as far as I could throw him. Which wouldn't be far. Maybe I'm paranoid, but the coincidences are uncanny.

"Ashley, where ya been?" Sam asks. "We thought after Seth dumped you, you'd be around more."

"I'd rather not talk about Seth if you don't mind." Said extremely casually, mind you.

"I just figured it's been long enough you could laugh at it, ya know?"

It's only been since this afternoon that I've seen Seth, so I'm not exactly ready to break out the stand-up at my expense. Am I touchy because we split up? Absolutely not. Because he won't disappear from my radar screen? Absolutely.

"Seth's working at Gainnet, so it hasn't been quite as long as you think."

I start to walk up the hallway when I hear Kay come after me.

"You know Sam. He doesn't mean anything by it. I think seeing Seth upset made Sam realize you meant more to him than just a standard girl."

"So now he knows I'm the Yoko Ono of Seth's life. What a coup. It sure would be nice if I could move forward at some point. I feel like everywhere I turn reminders of Seth are taunting me. By the way, do we charge Sam room and board for the chips he goes through?"

"Ashley. Don't take this out on Sam. You'd think you still cared about Seth."

"I don't!" I scream, practically stomping my foot. *What is it with ex-boyfriends in the church?* I cradle my head in my hands. "Kay, I've had the worst day. I'm sorry I let Sam get to me. He's your guest." *Though why, I'll never understand.* "I keep trying to move forward, and you know me, I just have no ability whatsoever to make matters better. I just screw things up to enormous capacity, everyone gets mad, then I usually lose my job and my home. I'm like the American Arafat. Only he kept his job."

"You're not losing your home as long as I'm around, and you got your boss your job, so I'd say you're exaggerating this one. You do have a habit of doing that, you know. I believe 'drama queen' has been used to describe you more than once before, Ashley."

"I know Sam is your friend, but I'm just not ready to strike up the band for his presence, okay? I feel like because my fiancé is not part of the singles group, neither am I. Since my fiancé is lost at work and spending time with his visiting sister, who also keeps me on the defensive, I just am not exactly giddy. Brea's busy with kids, my mom's busy with Davey, you're busy with the singles group—"

"I thought that's what you wanted, Ashley. To be getting married, leaving these Saturday night movie nights in your history." Kay shows her frustration by shaking her head and tightening her ever-pursed lips into an even thinner line.

"Why does everyone have to take Seth's side? Emily's side? Isn't it possible they're wrong?"

"No one's taking Seth's side. He's not here. Considering I ran off with Emily's date last night, I'm certainly not taking her side. I don't understand why you think the world's against you, Ashley." Kay bends over, picks up a doggy squeaky toy, and hands it to me.

"Let me slow down. You got Seth a job, Kay, at my office. Purvi seems to think he's brilliant, and I can't exactly move on when I'm mired in the past here. You've got his best friend sitting on my couch! I feel like Seth is everywhere, looming like a gray ghost. He wouldn't stick around when I wanted him to, and now he won't go away when I need him to."

"It's your imagination," she says as she lifts Seth's jacket off the hall tree.

"Where did that come from?"

"He was just here for a little while, Ashley."

"Ugh!" I lift my hands to the ceiling. "So *not* my imagination."

"The dog's in your room. He doesn't seem to care for Sam."

"My shoes!" I rush down the hall to open my door. As I do, several designer, I-paid-for-each-of-those-individually beads come bouncing out toward me. "Rhett!" Gingerly, I bend down and start picking up beads—again. With my financial status, I'm going to be sewing these back on by hand. It was too early to buy shoes without the dress anyway. What was I thinking?

My answering machine is blinking, and I can't say I'm ecstatic to answer the red flashing light. Perhaps it's Kevin trying to cancel our plans for tomorrow or Seth hoping I'll meet him at the soup house for a late-night apology session. Closing my eyes, I press the button.

"Ashley, it's Purvi." *Super.* "We missed a filing deadline because you're too childish to talk to the new director of software. What is going on? There's just no excuse for this. Your work is getting shoddy. This is not like you—*Beeep!*" My machine cuts her off, and I'm wishing I had something built-in so I could just turn off everyone around me at will.

"Now that would be a nice feature," I say to Rhett, and we tumble onto the bed.

"You're about the only one I didn't tick off today, Rhett, although you ticked me off royally with your latest shoe feast. How does it feel to be the one person on my fan list? Okay, the one dog on my fan list?"

Rhett gives me a wet nose on the chin, and the phone rings.

"Hello."

"Ashley, it's Kevin." *Be still, my heart.* His voice still makes me tingle, but here it comes. He's thought about my behavior or gotten an earful from Emily. The lecture I deserve about not acting like a Christian or basically being a grown-up in general must be on its way. But when someone messes with the wedding dress you've drawn since high school, there's some serious angst wrapped up in the moment.

"Hi, Kevin. How's your sister?"

"She left with Matt. They were going to see the *Rocky Horror Picture Show.* It's showing at the retro theater."

"Please tell me she didn't dress up."

"Ashley, she has no idea what she's in for, and I think the costumes will come as a surprise. She thinks she's going to a scary movie."

"And in many ways, she'd be right. Not nearly as scary as the clientele, but won't she be in for a shock?" The idea of seeing Emily catch her first glimpse of Tim Curry in drag makes me want to throw on my Steve Maddens and run for the real show: the Southern belle unraveling.

"Emily didn't even know why Matt had toast in his hands." Kevin laughs at one of the many inside jokes of the movie, which is even before my time, but lots of the lunatic fringe in high school went. *This, I wish I could see.* "If she thinks the engineers and *Lord of the Rings* are odd, she's in for a night of surprises. She's going to find out dating someone from a different generation has its drawbacks."

"Why didn't you warn her?" I ask. I mean, even I would have warned her. "The *Rocky Horror Picture Show?* Is *he* in some sort of time warp?"

"Oh, I did try to explain. I told her it was a modern-day melo-drama, a cult artwork, if you will. She left thinking they were in for a cultural experience from yesteryear. Performance art of another era. At least, that's what I thought when she shouted, 'Keh-vin, I'm quite adept at understanding artistic endeavors.' She took a couple of art classes before deciding college wasn't for her."

"Did you at least tell her she's younger than the movie itself?"

"Emily's a lot like you. You can't tell her anything as she enters the cave of doom. She likened it to being able to enjoy *Casablanca.* Well, she'll have to figure it out." He pauses. "You did, eventually. You're marrying me, right?"

I must say, I'm thrilled his offer is still good after my own per-formance art this evening. "I'm sorry tonight went so badly. My mind was in a million different places, and seeing that Coach portfolio . . . Well, there's no excuse. I snapped." *To think of a quality leather designer product having such a negative effect. I'm telling you, the girl is hurting my psyche.*

"Don't feel too bad. Emily will forget all about it by tomorrow when you meet."

"You mean, when *we* meet? As in, you, me, and her?"

He sighs.

"Kevin?"

"Remember the patient I was telling you about?"

"The little girl," I venture.

"Holly is her name."

It's here that I realize that I, myself, am toast. I can't compete with an ill child, and Lord knows, I wouldn't want to. I want Holly to have the expertise of Dr. Kevin Novak. "Emily and I will handle everything, Kevin. You just worry about Holly. I'll be praying for her."

"Thanks, sweetheart. I'll make it up to you."

"Did you talk to your parents about the house? And that we appreciate the offer, but . . ."

He's silent for a moment. "We haven't really talked about that yet. There's Philadelphia to consider too."

"I checked on the Internet. I'd definitely have to take the two Bar exams again, Kevin. Basically, start from scratch. And I'd have no friends while you worked, ostensibly even more." Not that I'm brimming to the top with friends at present. But all the more reason I can't afford to give up what I do have and try for new ones. "Think how long it would take me to train a new barista to have my coffee ready for me when I enter."

"That's certainly going to enter into my equation." He laughs. "I'll come over tomorrow night after dropping Emily at the airport, all right? We'll hash this all out, and there will be no more questions. You'll be in control, at the helm, once again. Deal?"

"No, because I don't want you looking at me with those green eyes when we talk about moving. That Hugh Jackman smile of yours, and my actual thoughts will be history. No thanks."

"You're always saying that. Who on earth is Hugh Jackman?"

"An actor who looks just like you and gets better-looking women than you do. So just you never mind."

"Impossible."

"No, he really does look like you."

"That he gets better-looking women, Ashley. That's what's impossible."

"Why? Do you have a nurse on the side?"

"Trust me, you're all I can handle. You're the one who might consider multiple husbands: one to shop with, one to support that spending habit, and one to live with until death. I'll be the last guy."

I start to giggle. "There's a reason I'm marrying you."

"I hope there's more than one."

My fears lift away on an invisible cloud. "There's more. Your narcolepsy not being one of them. At some point, it will definitely hurt my carefully constructed emotional balance if you're always falling asleep on me."

"Speaking of which, I'm going to sleep now. I'll see you tomorrow night."

"I have to go anyway. The Reasons are here, and I want to let Rhett loose to do his business. He's been locked up all night, and we both deserve a little fun," I say and laugh. "I'm kidding, although I would be willing to clean up any accidents Rhett might have."

As I exit my room, the scent of orange soda and BBQ potato chips assaults my nostrils. This house smells like a bad eighth-grade slumber party. I have the sudden urge to put shaving cream in someone's palm and tickle their nose. As I venture into the living room, I have to admit my intentions are not good. I turn around before I do something I'll regret.

"Ashley?" Kay calls after me. "You can come out. The movie's over, though."

"That's okay. I've seen *Shrek 2*." I dated Seth, remember? *He's obsessed with all things green and alien.*

Sam picks up my copy of *Bride* from the coffee table and thumbs through my sticky notes. "Going to the chapel, Ashley?"

I rip it from his sausagelike fingers. What is it about Sam that pushes my buttons?

"Ashley's date is fast approaching." Kay sounds overly cheery to avoid the fact that Sam and I have a distinct personality conflict.

"Date with what? Destiny?"

"Her wedding, silly. To Kevin?" Kay says, and I watch Sam's expression fall.

"You didn't know I was getting married?" I ask. *Avoid Cheshire cat smile,* I tell myself.

Jim, Tim, and Jake all stand. "We'd better go," says Tim.

"Late night," offers Jake.

"Don't leave!" I implore. "I'm going to my room." *After all, why shouldn't Sam feel more comfortable in my house than I do?* "I'm sure Kay's got her wonderful midnight snack prepared, and she's had to smell Fritos all night. It's the least you can do to eat something healthy she prepared." I grin, and the men all sit back down. With the exception of Sam, who never thought of leaving in the first place.

Sam follows me down the hallway. "You're really getting married? To the pretty-boy doctor?"

"News flash. There isn't a thing pretty about Kevin. He's tough, intellectual, he saves children every day, and he has manners. Not a bad gig if you can get it."

Sam steps closer so the guys don't hear him. "But what about Seth?"

"Seth is my ex-boyfriend, Sam. Note the *ex* in that phrase. People date. People decide they're not right for each other. Even Christians."

"But Seth likes you." Sam nods his head in a figure-eight motion. "He might even love you."

Pass the homeroom note. "I'm thirty-two this year, Sam. It's not enough, really, that he likes me." Need I mention I'm in love with another man and wearing his ring?

"You can't marry Kevin." It's the first time I've heard any authority in his voice. Okay, except maybe when he orders at Applebee's.

"Come August 21, I will marry Kevin. I'm finalizing the location tomorrow. The dress is ordered. Well, that's a long story, but where have you been, Sam? Didn't Seth tell you? What do you talk about every night when *Star Trek: Voyager* is over?"

He walks in front of me and stops me. "No, I mean you can't marry Kevin. You and Seth have been an item for what, three years or something?"

"Ten months, actually. It just *felt* like three years."

"He had a crush on you long before that, and now that Arin's dating that Indian guy, he's going to be left with nothing."

Arin and what Indian guy? Anyway, cry me a river. "I don't know what to tell you, Sam. I'm getting married." I cross my arms in front of me. "Besides, what do you care? You've always made your opinion of me quite well known."

"I have a good opinion of you, Ashley. I think you're funny and well dressed, and you really do sing like an angel. I just wanted you to know when you did marry Seth that I would be a fixture for movie nights and stuff. I didn't want you two to break up. I just didn't want my buddy and me broken up."

Sadly, I'm feeling sorry for him. I didn't know the emotion was possible with Sam, but there you go. "I appreciate that, Sam. I think Seth is a great guy. I really do. He's just not the great guy for me. There's a certain amount of time you devote to something before you give it over to God. And I gave it over, and then Kevin came into my life. He's the answer to a lot of prayer."

I believe . . . I believe I need a list. I say good night to Sam, head into my room, settle in on the floor against my bed, and start writing:

MOVING FORWARD IN LIFE

1. Strive for the perfect wedding day by getting along with my future sister-in-law.
2. Embrace my new family with a godliness worthy of a good, Christian girl. No more *Dynasty* or *Melrose Place*

catfight fantasies (or realities, for that matter.) No more restaurant soap operas!

3. Tell Seth with sweetness that I'm thankful for our time together, but we must not beat this dead horse anymore. Be so sweet and grateful that he accepts defeat and looks for a new job, a new girlfriend, and doesn't live the fantasy of his make-believe angelic Ashley. (Bad cycle for Christian men, to believe they lost "the one." Powerful excuse for avoiding future commitment.)

4. Start actively looking for Kay's new roommate/co-owner. Explain the benefits of five fruit and vegetable servings prepared each day. Not to mention biweekly cleaning with the HEPA filter—very good for allergic people. (Search for someone with hives.)

5. Find a house for Kevin and me to live in together before his parents plop down a down payment in Philly. (Remember, good real estate and a good handbag are always the answer.)

6. Ignore said financial crisis, and trust that God will provide. Granted, maybe not designer footwear, but we'll get past that. *Okay, probably not.*

I peruse my list and feel Rhett's tongue slide up my cheek. "I know! It's a good list, don't you think?" I'm so ready for tomorrow. Bring on church. Bring on the Reasons. Bring on my psycho sister-in-law-to-be. "I am Ashley Stockingdale, ready and able. Outta my way, world, I'm moving forward!"

13

It's Sunday morning, and let's just say the empowered mood I felt when I made my list last night has evaporated like the morning fog. Right now, I'm feeling less than Christian. Yesterday was not one of my better runs as a godly girl. In fact, it was pretty pitiful. My attitude toward Emily has come back to haunt me this morning, and I pray for forgiveness. The funny thing is, I mean it!

"I promise I'll be good, Lord." Granted, He's heard that from me before, hundreds of times, and if ever there was a reason to question my good intentions, it's a day spent with Emily. With that little prayer offered up, I feel better. Call me an optimist, but I'm hopeful for the day. I put on my Seven jeans, some magnificent heels, and a Boucle jacket I got on sale at Bloomingdale's. My look says I am fashion-savvy, completely capable of making solid, en vogue decisions. I am not in need of a wedding dress selector. I *am* a confident woman, moving forward!

I'm a confident woman who's a little late as I hustle into the back row of the high school auditorium where my church is held. The music is loud and washes over me like a steady heartbeat, bringing me into a connection with Jesus. A connection I need so desperately this morning. I let it rain over me and soak in the reminders of His sacrifice for my pettiness. It's overwhelming, actually. Saved by grace. If that miracle wasn't created for me, well, I can't imagine a more perfect candidate.

After a sermon on loving others as myself, I am ready to face Emily Novak. I pull up to Kevin's doorstep with my shoulders straightened and my personality tamped down like fine espresso. I visualize myself as Mother Teresa and ring the doorbell. There she is, my Calcutta street urchin: Emily.

"Is that what you're wearing?" Emily asks with a tinge of disapproval.

Good morning to you too, Emily. How are you this fine morning? Only it doesn't come out quite that way. "Is that what *you're* wearing?" I retort, looking at her springtime dress straight out of a matinee showing of *Grease.* The skirt is only missing the poodle. I want to turn around and show her my Seven label. I want her to get a good look at the Marc Jacobs stilettos. *This is fashion, girlfriend. Get out your pork-bun-covered notepad!*

"You're wearing jeans to hit some of the area's nicest hotels?" Emily's brow wrinkles in disgust.

"I'm wearing Sevens," I correct as I turn around and thumb the label. "This is California," I explain. "We like to dress our jeans up, but we're the casual state, second only to Hawaii or maybe Florida," I say in an upbeat weather forecaster voice. I even sweep my hand across the sky like it's a blue screen.

She puts her palms on her chest. "I am dressed casually as well. But my dress says that I care about appearances and that these meetings are very important to me and my marital future."

Peachy. "Okay, well, you're not the one getting married, and I'm not changing. Let's go, shall we?" I say, avoiding any further discussion. *One small step for Ashley Stockingdale, one giant step for false, behind-the-back womanhood.*

We get into my convertible, and I have the top down because it is a gorgeous California day. I can tell this is not going over well with Emily and her hair-sprayed, beribboned ponytail. Without even a comment, I lift the top and slowly latch it closed. *Taking the high road! Are you noticing, Lord?*

"My brothah passed on your feelings about the country club, so we're heading to the Fairmont Hotel first," Emily announces while looking at the slightly stained notebook and showing me the blank line next to "Location." "We have a meeting with the director of catering."

"I'd really prefer to decide on the wedding's location first. San Jose is awfully far for most people, and I'm not sure I'm a Fairmont kind of gal."

"What's wrong with the Fairmont?"

"Well, nothing, but I'd like to get married outdoors, not in a hotel, since we don't really have access to the church." The idea of getting married in the high school auditorium with gum under the seats and teen-angst graffiti is not something I'd find romantic, even if that is my "church."

"Y'all can get married by the pool there at the Fairmont. It's on the foh-th floor and overlooks the park across the street."

"Can people swim while we're getting married, or will they close it off?"

"Well, they have to keep the pool open for guests, I would think."

I shake my head. "Not liking that idea. What if some kid comes and does a cannonball in the middle of the ceremony? Or worse yet, if Pamela Anderson takes a dip while your brother tries not to be too distracted to say, 'I do'?"

She scratches out the Fairmont name, putting way too much pressure on her pad. "There, you happy now? You have such a fatalistic attitude, Ashley. How is anyone supposed to make you happy?"

Can you disappear? Bad Ashley. Sorry, Lord, really trying here. "What's next?"

"The Duck Pond in Palo Alto," she says excitedly.

"Have you been there?" I ask tentatively.

"No, but I saw it on the map and it sounds just perfect, right by the Bay, and—"

"It's next to the sewage plant, and about four times as many ducks live there than is humane. It smells like something died, and you can barely walk from all the . . . Well, you get the picture."

Emily harrumphs and again scratches her pen with virulence. "So where would you like to go, Ashley? It seems to me you have the perfect weddin' in your head, yet you don't offer anyone suggestions as to what that is. Would you care to share your infinite knowledge?"

"Well, it's hard because there isn't that much locally. But I want to keep it local because of the people Kevin works with." I gnaw on my lip, thinking. Churches aren't a big commodity in the Bay Area unless they're universalist, or transcendentalist, or something else that allows people to be "spiritual" but have no real relationship or accountability.

"We're burnin' daylight, Ashley. Where should we go? My plane leaves at seven."

I can't help a glance at my watch. Eight more hours. *I can certainly do eight more hours.*

"If I have to exchange my ticket, I won't be very happy. I do have a life back in Atlanta, you realize. I've been out here workin' tirelessly, but I really must get back to—" She stops here. *Yeah, kinda hard to come up with an excuse when you're unemployed.*

"No, no, you don't have to exchange your ticket," I assure her. "We'll be done in plenty of time. I'm quite decisive. It's what makes me good at what I do. No dillydallying and all that."

"So where to?" Emily asks. "I'll need to call and cancel all these appointments." She takes out a cell phone, and I keep driving. I see I'm frustrating the daylights out of her, and at this juncture, she's got good reason to be annoyed.

"I've got it!" I twist the car around and head to Stanford. "Stanford Chapel. How could I dream of anything else? The painted dome ceiling, the historic architecture, plus Stanford is where we met!" The Fountain Creamery, where I looked at Kevin and drooled like an oversized mastiff. *Who would have ever thought he'd have this incredible blind spot for a valedictorian geek?* "That's it; I'm settled. Let's go make the arrangements. See? I told you I was decisive. I just needed the right motivation."

"Stanford's on my list, Ashley, but accordin' to their coordinator, whom I called from Georgia, there's a two-year waitin' list to get married in that chapel. I doubt my brothah is willin' to wait that long. I know my parents aren't. They're hopin' for grandchildren by then."

I shake my head. "Stanford. August 21," I say with conviction, and I mean it. I'm visualizing myself as a bride on the raised altar straight out of classic design, backed by stained-glass windows. Everything to make you believe you're in Europe being married in one of the oldest churches. *It's perfect.*

We drive in silence as she ponders the two-year dilemma, and I blissfully ignore the facts and concentrate on how to make it happen. We reach the palm-tree-lined street that ends in the magnificent chapel. It's like being in the middle of Rome, and it's so odd that you can see something every week of your life and not really see it, or its incomparable beauty, until it matters.

"It's a bit easier if you're Catholic." Emily chooses now to be the voice of reason.

"Well, I'm not converting for the ceremony." I laugh. "We should pick the reception hall. I'm thinking the Stanford Park Hotel."

"Ashley, you can't pick the reception hall without a place to get married."

"I told you. I'm getting married at Stanford Memorial Chapel."

"I'm your weddin' coordinator, and I can hardly allow you to disregard the facts surroundin' the availability of certain venues."

"Sure you can. We just have to make the venue happen." *A wedding coordinator's job.* I look ahead at the exquisitely painted church in the distance. "You haven't known me very long, Emily, but I'm pretty persistent when I'm determined. I feel in my stomach that this is it. This is just like going after a patent. You find a way."

"You must be persistent if my brothah is marryin' you. I didn't think he was the marryin' type, and I certainly never thought he'd marry a Yankee."

I choose to ignore this. *Good Ashley!*

Emily waves a paper in my face, which I push out of the way to keep my eyes on the road. "Look, it says right here in my notes that the chapel doesn't consider postgraduate work to meet the full-time student criteria. Which makes Keh-vin ineligible to marry there." She stuffs the paper back in the notebook. "Since you didn't go to Stanford, I'd say that lets you out completely."

"Where there's a will, there's a way. Do you know how much I've spent at Stanford Shopping Center over the years? That has to let me into some kind of club." ·

Emily proceeds to rattle on about my spoiled, immature self for the next few minutes. She sounds like the Charlie Brown teacher. *Wah wah wah, wah wah wah, wahhh.* "It's just ridiculous," I tune back in to hear her finish.

"I agree, but I see myself here," I say, looking toward the grand, painted facade. "You want an extravagant Southern wedding. I want the California version, and I can't afford the Olympic Club in San Francisco, so this is the next best thing. Besides," I add dreamily, "this is where I met your brother. That day was like magic." Except for the part where I found out he was dating someone else. *That sucked.*

"I find it odd your parents aren't payin' for this weddin'." Emily crosses her arms and waits momentarily for a response before launching into the rest of her attack. "Your budget borders on paltry. I know you're under this illusion that you have good taste, Ashley, but, my dear—"

"Lots of people pay for their own weddings when they get married a little, um, older," I falter. "I think my parents gave up hope on me, and they have a beautiful den that they enjoy every day. My dad watches football on a television so large that it makes you want to attach the speaker to your car's window. I'm happy for them."

"I can see why they gave up hope," Emily mumbles under her breath.

I park the car, and we get out and walk into the Spanish-style courtyard below the Stanford Chapel. Just being here makes me feel like dancing, and I skip across the cobblestones. "The hills are alive!" I sing in falsetto.

Emily is mortified and retreats to the car lest anyone thinks she's with me.

"With the sound of muuu-sic . . ." I continue, sort of chasing after her and trying to grab her hands. She covers her face with her hands. She slinks back into the car, and I run to the window. "Emily, you're in California! There's nothing to be embarrassed about. It's not like we're driving a domestic car or something really humiliating. Get out and sing with me! This is a town that has a makeshift memorial to a mountain lion. The poor mountain lion that shut down three schools! Do you think they're going to notice us singing?"

"We have work to do. I'm going to call my brother and tell him you're not working with me."

"Brother? Not brothah?" I clarify.

She taps her fingers on the ledge of the window. "Ashley, get in the car."

I smirk at her but come around to the driver's seat. "I am getting married here," I say as I slide into the seat.

"Of course you are, darlin'." Emily opens her notebook. "The Stanford Park Hotel. Your meeting with them isn't until tomorrow. I didn't think it was really a possibility."

I start the car. "Emily, I appreciate that you're trying to help, but we're not going to get anything accomplished if we pretend nothing is wrong. You don't want me to marry your brother. I can appreciate that, but it's not your decision to make. You're going to have objections to whomever he picks, so just give it up to the Lord that you can't change things, and accept me."

"I'm doin' my very best," she says through gritted teeth.

Well, that's something, anyway. I drive away from my dream wedding scene. "Will you call the chapel, or shall I?"

"I'll call them, but, Ashley, what you're askin'—"

"It's my wedding. Humor me. If they say no, we'll go to plan B, okay? If we end up at the Duck Pond, we'll just go tea length."

We get to the hotel. We're way early for the appointment, like by a day. And it's Sunday. Need I say more? They look at us like we stepped off the red planet, thrust a business card toward us, and send us on our way.

"That was productive," I say as we get back into the car.

"This is why I took care of things on the weddin' gown, Ashley. I wanted to know your dreams were settled. Your schedule, traipsin' off for unknown countries, hardly helps. I've never worked with a bride who had such an impossible schedule."

I could mention she's never worked for a bride before or that her short tenure in a floral shop does not a wedding coordinator make, but I hold my tongue.

"Go back to that last part. My dreams? Emily, I don't even know what this dress looks like, and how many brides have ever *not* selected their own gown? That's just . . . well, it's a little odd, Emily. I can't believe they do that in the South. I may be naive on Southern customs, but I think I can take a leap on this one."

"I was goin' to surprise you, but I think it's time you saw the reason I've canceled your gown order. I know you'll be pleased."

I scan her expression, trying to see if she really has tried to make me happy or if it's just another one of her ploys to show her air of superiority toward me. I can't tell. My heart is pounding. "You're going to let me see it?" *You do realize this does not mean I'm wearing it,* I add silently.

"You've seen it before," she says like Willy Wonka, bursting with enthusiasm. *Am I going to get an Everlasting Gobstopper?*

My breathing lengthens, and I close my eyes like I'm about to witness morgue pictures or the like. "I'm ready."

She thrusts a full-color photo at me. At first, I'm just speechless. I open my mouth, but I'm like a beater car. There's nothing, just sputtering. I blink a few times to see if the image changes. No such luck. The gown is . . . it's huge! I think three of me could fit into it. Carefully weighing my "out-loud" options here.

"Do you recognize it?" Emily asks. "It's the weddin' gown that Scarlett O'Hara wore to marry Charles Hamilton! An exact replica I had created especially for you. The moment my brothah announced your nuptials, I had him get me your size. Of course, we'll have the seamstress at the wedding shop fit it to you perfectly."

I'm still looking at her, waiting for words to come.

"I'm havin' fresh magnolias, peonies, and blue hydrangeas—the hallmark of a good Southern bouquet. We'll have parasols for the bridesmaids, invitations with tea-stained papers, white doves. It's going to be perfect, Ashley!"

"For whom? Perfect for whom? And why is the gown yellow?"

"It's not yellow, Ashley. It's tea-stained French satin. Thirty-one yards of it, not counting the handmade silk leaves."

"It has leaves," I say, looking closer.

"Aren't they gorgeous?"

"I don't know what to say. I can't afford this, Emily, and I wouldn't want to. It couldn't be less my style. Maybe you'll save it for your wedding." I hand it back to her. "Besides, Charles Hamilton died. I can't think that's a very good omen for a wedding."

"Charles Hamilton wasn't real."

"News flash! Neither was Scarlett O'Hara." *That was apparently not the thing to say.*

She grabs the page and tucks it back in her notebook. "This entire exercise is futile. Take me home. You're an impossible bride to work with, and I shall nevah do this job again. I've put countless hours into y'all's weddin', and all I've heard is your ungrateful heart lashin' out at me. I know my brothah, Ashley. He loves the South. He loves his heritage, and the least you could do is allow him to have the weddin' we've talked about all these years. You're impossible!"

"Scarlett wasn't exactly sweetness and light," I say to lift the mood. *Um, no. Not working.*

"You have your first fittin' tomorrah at the weddin' shop. If you choose not to go, I'll tell my brothah that I wipe my hands of this entire fiasco."

"Really?" I ask a little too enthusiastically.

"Take me home, Ashley Stockingdale." Uh-oh. Emily actually has tears running down her cheeks. I see in her face that perhaps she honestly thought I would appreciate this help. Maybe her upbringing allows her to believe that all women want to be Scarlett O'Hara—that we all thrive for the red dirt of Tara to fill us. I don't know.

"Emily, you don't mean that. I'm sorry. We have a lot of work to do. Your brother loves me. I love him. We just don't want to get married like we're living in 1861." I crinkle my nose. "That *is* when the war started, right?"

She sighs. "It's like he's completely forgettin' his roots. For California, of all places!"

Roots. I'm not thinking Southern slave owners with that term. "Surely, not all Southerners have a *Gone with the Wind* theme. There has to be some reason you see this as the perfect wedding."

"Ashley, I've told you before. We're from Atlanta, your name is Ashley Wilkes Stockingdale, and your dog is Rhett. It's written in the stars, don't you see? This allows my family to be a part of your day. To see that they've raised their son with a heritage he loves and honors."

I stick my head out the window, look up at the sunshine, then gaze back at her. "I don't see it in the stars," I joke. "Kevin and I are Christians first. We want a godly ceremony in an ungodly place. We don't want to be laughingstocks. He's a surgeon. I'm a lawyer. We have reputations to maintain, and I'm afraid dressing in costume is just not going to go over well with our colleagues."

"Reputation? You were singin' and flyin' through Stanford's courtyard. What could I possibly do to you that's more humiliating?" Emily asks.

I take a deep breath and proceed to tell her, "I want to have my own dress at the ceremony. I don't want a fancy string quartet with gentle pluckings in the background. I'd like a swing band with lots of Glenn Miller. Maybe I have more of a World War II background in mind than the Civil War."

"I suppose it doesn't matter what I want!" Emily rants.

Bingo!

"I want both families to be comfortable and happy at the ceremony, Emily. You have to believe that."

Something changes in Emily's expression, and it turns dark as a thundercloud. "We're not goin' to be happy, Ashley Stockingdale. That would be impossible. Because we aren't marryin' at the trailer park with lots of glittery cleavage showing, which would seem to please your aunts!"

Oooh, that was below the belt. I'm literally so stunned that someone would make such an ugly accusation publicly, I can't even answer. Granted, I don't want people talking behind my back, but if they're going to say this, I guess I do. *Please, talk behind my back!*

We drive in silence for a long time. I can hear Emily sniffling, but I can't think of anything to make her feel better. I mean, giving in will only strengthen her power over me. Over us, and I can't do that. Because if I do it now, I do it for a lifetime. I pull up to Kevin's house, and Emily gives one last sniffle.

"Tomorrow is your fittin'. If you're not goin', I suggest you call Hannah and explain yourself." She slams the door and turns around once again. "And you tell your roommate to stay away from Matt Callaway. He's mine!" She stomps up the steps and slams the door.

I hope Kevin wasn't sleeping.

"I'm not going after her," I yell up to God. "I tried to be good. I've said everything I can say to her."

But there it is, the guilt. Okay, Lord. I drag myself out of the car, walk up to the door, and knock. Emily opens the door, visibly shaken. "What's this about, Emily? Are you willing to give me the same freedom to plan your wedding? Carte blanche and all that?"

"Keh-vin should be marryin' Amy, and he knows it." Emily slams the door in my face, and I'm standing on the porch wondering where I go from here. *Amy?* Now there's a name I haven't heard mentioned before. Maybe Amy is this fabulously gorgeous Southern belle who knows how to drink sweet tea and eat fried chicken with dainty fingers. Amy. Arin. Ashley. Hmm. I'm seeing a theme with my fiancé, and it is not A-OK with me. I turn and slowly head back to my car, deciding that I will definitely deal with the subject of Amy tomorrow when Emily is long gone. After all, tomorrow is another day!

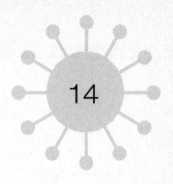

14

It's officially another day, and Purvi isn't in yet as I enter Gainnet on this fine Monday morning. At least I don't see her, but she's usually like a horror movie villain, popping out and scaring you when you least expect it. I look around the halls like Elmer Fudd looking for that wascally wabbit and sneak into my office, but Purvi and my admin, Tracy, follow me into my office and close the door.

"How do you do that?" I ask Purvi.

"We see you get out of the car, Ashley. Relax, I don't have eyes in the back of my head. Yet." Purvi laughs.

"What's this I hear about you and the new software guy?" Tracy asks.

I shuffle the papers on my desk. "It's quite scandalous, actually," I whisper. "We were really close friends for a long time, and we share custody of a dog. I feed the dog, clean up after it, and sleep with his furry, snoring self on my floor, and he . . . he . . ." I shrug. "Well, he does nothing. I guess you could say I have full custody with no visitation and definitely no puppy support."

"This is the bald guy, right?" She points behind her with her thumb, still hoping for gory details that do not exist.

"I was talking about the dog," I say.

You know, there are moments when I think I'm just not right in the head. I want to tell them this great story, the one where Seth stood across from me at the altar. One glance, and he ran screaming from the church. He was committed to the institution a few days later. I have this brief fantasy of Seth in a straitjacket. I look at Tracy and Purvi's peering eyes and fantasize that I could open my mouth and tell them that Seth and I were scheduled to be married, but he had another pregnant girlfriend, and I found out in front of the preacher. Then there was much weeping and gnashing of teeth.

This is all completely fabricated, of course, but it's so much more interesting than the fact that we dated for a year, but he couldn't commit and left for India, then went back to a life of video games and pizza nights with his buddies. I can't even get dumped with intrigue.

"Okay, yeah, the bald guy," I answer.

"You know what they say about bald men!" Tracy winks and clucks her tongue.

"Actually, I don't." I raise my palms. "But you know, I don't think I want to either."

She sits down and rubs her hands together. "So tell me why you broke up."

"Is this going to interfere with your working with him?" Purvi asks.

I put some files into the drawer. "He moved to India. That's why we broke up."

"Come on, Ashley, really," Purvi says.

"Really. He moved to India for a job. He was going to set up an Indian base. I guess it didn't work out."

Tracy looks disappointed. "That's it?"

I'm a thirty-two-year-old virgin. How much excitement is she expecting here?

"That's it."

She gets up slowly and smirks at Purvi. "That's no big deal. I hear 'ex-boyfriend,' and I think, finally, my Ashley has a secret social life. Something that makes her about more than patents." Tracy drops her chin to her chest. "You've disappointed me, Ashley."

"I'm sorry to hear that," I answer.

She pops back up. "He's got great eyes. Have you ever noticed that?"

Saw them on my future children at one time. "I have. Seth has great eyes," I agree.

"He's coming in for a meeting in five minutes," Purvi says as she rises. "Clear your calendar until you have the details of his patent. If you're not going to prioritize for yourself, Ashley, I'm going to do it for you." Purvi exits and shuts the door behind her.

Tracy settles back into the chair. "I'll take notes."

I cross my arms. "I don't need you to take notes, but thank you."

She grunts at me. "You really are no fun. I want to see if he still has feelings for you. I'm really good at reading that. Like, I'm psycho!"

I laugh aloud, but I can't bear to explain this to her.

"Trust me, you'll be nothing but bored as we discuss the intricacies of software processes."

"I don't care what you say to each other. I want to see the sparks fly."

I lift up my left hand. "These are the only sparks in my office, and they belong to Kevin's grandmother's diamond."

"Yes, but I haven't met Kevin. I'm sure he's dreamy, but I love the idea of your ex working here. It's so *Days of Our Lives*, and nothing good ever happens here. I mean, the men don't even date. It's like working with a bunch of robots with no social skills. The Stepford men." She crosses her legs. "You know, that would be a great reality show. They should cross *Queer Eye for the Straight Guy* with *The Bachelor* and give the women in Silicon Valley some hope."

"As interesting as these musings are, don't you have something to do for Purvi?"

Tracy shrugs. "Not a thing. Why?" There's a knock at the door. "He's here!" she sings, like my date has arrived. She opens the door wide to give all the admins a good look at my expression. "Seth, welcome to Ashley's office. She's all ready for your meeting. Would you like some coffee?" *Coffee? Tracy normally wouldn't get coffee for any-one else even if she was on her way to Starbucks with eight cupholders.*

"Thanks, Tracy," I say with my eyebrows lifted. She grabs a notepad and sits back down. "It's okay; I've got it from here. If I need you for notes, I'll buzz." I take the notepad from her hand, and she mouths at me, *You're no fun!*

Seth sits down in my office and looks around at the photos. He sees Brea's kids, my nephew, and he flinches at Kevin's picture. I think he did, anyway, but maybe it's my overactive ego working. A girl needs her ego in Silicon Valley.

"Ashley, you're looking good this morning. Or is that sexual harassment to say that?" He winks at me.

"It might be harassment, considering everyone knows you're my ex. Do you mind telling me how that came about?"

"In the interest of full disclosure, I told HR before they hired me." *Full disclosure or indecent exposure?* "Stellar. Is that my paperwork?"

"Listen, what I said the other day—"

"Don't worry, Seth, I'm quite aware you spoke out of turn when you were heading toward a committal statement." I scan the paper-work in front of me, flashing my engagement ring for him to witness. "What makes this process special? Give me the high points."

"It's a new user interface for the Sunflower project. Reduces the number of mouse clicks to one."

"One?" I say with disbelief.

He shoves the file in front of me. "One. You have a software engi-neer with talent and drive. No one listened to him before now." Seth looks at me, narrowing his tanzanite eyes.

I get a little defensive here. "If his director doesn't report it to me, I'm hardly responsible for creating patents out of the blue. That's why your predecessor isn't here any longer and you have the job." *Sheesh. Make me responsible for world famine and WMDs while you're at it.*

Seth leans over my desk, his hands spanning its width. "Touchy,

touchy. You were awfully busy following that foreign boss of yours to Taiwan last year. How do I know you didn't blow off the last software guy like you tried to do with me on Saturday?"

"Seth." I grit my teeth in frustration and roll my chair backwards. "Never mind. I'll have this looked up and compared by the end of the day. If I can get you a process patent, I will. Either way you'll know by the end of the day what my plans are."

Seth's expression softens, and the gentle man I've known comes back. I wish I could take back the years and erase the pain for both of us. But I can't. It's not my problem. *Thank heavens!*

As I gaze into those eyes that once melted my heart, I don't think he'll ever get married. He'll be so worried about doing it perfectly that it won't ever happen. Engineering is a perfect place for him. Seth can constantly achieve the next realm of technology, and he doesn't have to have much human contact. Of course, it's his loss, and that makes me sad. I still care about the guy. Not in *that* way, but in the way that makes you want your friends to succeed in life.

"I know you think I'm nuts, and maybe I've acted that way," Seth says. "But I'm worried about you, Ash. You've wanted to get married for so long, and I just think Kevin is not right for you. He's from a different world. For one thing, he hasn't been a Christian very long. How do you even know he's grounded?"

I tap the paper edges on the desk to straighten them. "Let's agree not to discuss this, okay? Let's avoid the marriage topic. Sort of like when we were dating."

"I'd have married you if that's what you really wanted."

I can't help it; I laugh here. "Seth, as romantic as that is, you would not have! You'd have some great crisis that took you to India or the mission field in the Philippines. I appreciate your concern, but I'm not as desperate to get married as you think I am. And you were never as eager as you think. But I do appreciate the sacrificial thought. You're a good friend."

I think he breathes a sigh of relief here. It's silent but deep.

"The Sunflower project." He looks to the desk. "We'll get it done."

"We will," I agree. And Seth backs out of my office on the same sorry horse he rode in on.

Tracy sticks her head in my office. "Purvi left for the day."

"Why?" Purvi comes in when she's back from China on jet lag.

"She didn't say. Something to do with her husband."

"Her husband in India?"

"He's back."

I don't know why, but I feel a chill run through me. "Very well. She has some patents on her desk that need to be signed by the higher-ups. Did she leave any other instructions?"

"No. Hannah from the bridal shop is on line one," Tracy adds.

I pick up the phone, and I can hear Hannah humming. "Ashley Stockingdale here."

"Ashley, it's Hannah. FedEx just came, and your wedding dress is here!" She pauses to let me take this information in. "When can we do a fitting? It's incredible. I can't wait to see it on you!"

I'm shaking my head. "That's not my wedding dress. I ordered a Vera Wang, remember? You helped me pick it out."

"Your bridal coordinator canceled that. Emily assured me this is what you wanted, and she offered to pay for it. Your deposit will go to the veil unless you protest. I can issue a refund check in a week." Hannah sounds nervous. I'm not blaming her. Emily is very persistent, and Hannah had about as much chance of changing her mind as that of an aircraft carrier turning on a dime.

I'm actually calm here. *I'm floating away on an espresso crema cloud. Up, up, and away.* "Yes, I realize she canceled it," I say softly. "What's so great about the new gown?"

"Well," she says, tentatively now.

"If you weren't having a costume party wedding, would you wear it?"

"It's very finely made, Ashley. I think you should come look at it. The stitching is incredible."

"I'll look at it, but only to be polite. How long will it take to order my Vera Wang again?"

"At least three months to allow for proper tailoring. Six is ideal."

I've lost a month, maybe two. But money can speed up anything. Too bad I have none left. "I'll be right over."

Even as I say it, I know I'm going to pay for this jaunt. I have the Sunflower project to do ASAP, an upset boss, and an ex who will be happy to report I have left the building, like Elvis. But Ashley Stockingdale in Scarlett O'Hara's wedding gown? It's just not natural. It qualifies as a wedding emergency! I have kept myself in couture despite being surrounded by techs in T-shirts and jeans everyday. I can hardly set an example dressed like an 1860s version of hoop dreams, now, can I?

"I'm running an errand," I say quickly as I pass Tracy's desk, trying to act like it's desperately important. Of course, she knows I was just talking to the wedding shop, but I've got seniority on my side, especially with Purvi out for the rest of the day.

"Your mom called while you were on the phone. She said the candy-coated almonds are in for you to wrap in tulle."

"Candy-coated almonds?" *This is what my mother chose to contribute to my wedding? Maybe she could include ribbon-wrapped Twinkies while she's at it.* "It's four months until the wedding. Ick."

"You have to buy the tulle." Tracy's reading her notes, which I'm sure my mother dictated slowly and methodically. "She didn't know if you wanted pink or green. There's either at the dollar store, so you just have to make up your mind."

The dollar store. Now that ought to go over big with Emily. "Thanks, Tracy. I'll be back before lunch." I look back at my office, wondering if I should take the Sunflower project with me, but I'll be back.

Driving across town, my cell phone rings. Hallelujah, it's Kevin.

"Kevin, hi." I soften as I begin talking to him. Melt is more like it. He's worth his sister's Scarlett O'Hara fetish.

"Hi, sweetie. Remember me? You survived my sister? She's worried about you."

"Emily's worried about me?"

"She said you were dancing and singing by yourself at Stanford. She thought the stress might be getting to you, and perhaps we might want to do a psych evaluation before the wedding." Kevin laughs.

"Let's see. Well, honey, you have missed most of the Great American Wedding Saga, so let me get you up to speed. I have no dress. We have no cake. We have nowhere to get married or have the reception. I'm living in one of the most populated cities in the country, and my wedding coordinator is in Atlanta. No, honey, I'm not the least bit stressed, or I would have been doing Tai Chi in the courtyard, not singing."

"Of course, that's just what I told her." Kevin laughs. "She said you wanted to get married at Stanford's chapel. Is that true? It's a beautiful venue, but I think rather impossible to get into."

"Not impossible, just more difficult than most. You think I'm willing to settle like the common folk?" I laugh. "Where do you want to get married?"

"We could get married in my backyard for all I care. I'm really more into the honeymoon."

"Kevin!" I chastise. "We can't get married in your backyard. Your condo doesn't even have one! And mine is riddled with dog excrement. I was thinking more along the lines of honeysuckle scent or maybe jasmine candles."

"Your yard is beautiful, Ashley. You live with Kay, and you expect me to believe she lets Rhett do his thing without consequences? How naive do you think I am?"

I let out a little whimper. There's something happening here. Some strange wind of darkness swirling about that keeps me from actually settling anything.

"I am the world's worst bride," I finally say. "I used to be good at decisions and reality, but I'm off my game."

"You are *not* the world's worst bride. Why did you think you'd be above the fray in the stress department? I'm off work this weekend. You plan for whatever we need: cake, tuxes, china, the honeymoon suite for the wedding night. I'm game to select it all."

"You have a one-track mind, Kevin. We have to get married first, you know."

"I'm a guy with a gorgeous fiancée. Like I'm thinking about the stupid cake."

"Am I ever going to see you?" I ask. "I feel like I'm completely alone, like I'm doing all this planning to marry a groom who doesn't exist. You are real, aren't you? I mean, people say the romance dies after the wedding, so things aren't looking great here."

"That's why Emily came out to help. She knew I'd be busy with my workload during the residency. Once we get married, it won't be so hectic. I'll be coming home to you every night."

"In a galaxy far, far away. In the meantime, I'm in a perpetual state of invisible monogamy. Not really single anymore. Not married yet. Just one big interim blob," I say as I hear his beeper. "I know, you have to go."

"I love you! If we have to go to Reno, I'm marrying you August 21. I don't care about where or how. I don't care about any of that, all right? Just let Emily handle it. She'll make sure we have what we need."

Yeah, that's gonna happen.

"I'll call you tonight." He hangs up just as I'm pulling up to the bridal shop.

The boutique is very exclusive looking, and Hannah has been a long-standing fixture in our singles group. So I feel very comfortable as I walk in, and the little bell tinkles, signaling my arrival. I'm lost in all the tulle and satin, and something about the pure white calms me. *I'm getting married!* It's not a figment of my overactive imagination. Inside that cell phone lurks a fantastic man, and he wants to marry me!

As I walk toward the desk, I see it: my dress. There's no mistaking it. It's the color of a French yellow cabinet from another era. It boasts tiny leaves sticking off the skirt like silk barbwire in a swirled pattern. And the leg-o-mutton sleeves . . . they look like a lamb with major thigh issues. A lamb that needs liposuction! *This is not happening.*

"Isn't it exquisite?" Hannah comes out from the back and reverently touches the gown.

I drop my jaw and shake my head, still trying to find the words.

"Look at the stitching on this, Ashley. It's incredible. The detail work is so finely done. It's pure genius. Your sister-in-law must really care about you."

"How tall was Scarlett?" I say, scanning the dress.

Hannah shrugs.

"She was tiny if I remember correctly. I will look like the giant Stay Puft Marshmallow Man in *Ghostbusters* in that thing."

Hannah's countenance falls, making me feel like the shallow girl I am. "You have to at least try it on, Ashley. I think you're going to be pleasantly surprised."

Tentatively, I walk around the dress. It's like a spider hanging from its web in the center of the room. "It's just not my style, Hannah. It's beautiful, but I'm thirty-two, not eighteen. This is a dress for an eighteen-year-old bride with an eighteen-inch waist with stays."

"It's so much nicer than what you ordered, Ashley. The quality is impeccable. Your sister-in-law went beyond the call of duty. I wish you'd give it a chance."

"How can you be on her side? She canceled my wedding dress! That cost you money. It cost Vera Wang money!"

"I can appreciate true artistry. This gown is unforgettable, Ashley. No one will ever forget you in it."

"That's exactly what I'm afraid of."

Hannah takes it down. "Just try it on."

We walk into the dressing room, and there's my favorite: the three-way mirror. *Yeah, I need to see this in 3-D.* I slough off the black bow dress I got at the last great Bloomingdale's sale and kick off my heels. I step into the dress, and Hannah brings it up around me.

She doesn't even get it buttoned. "It's . . . it's . . . hideous. I look like one of my aunt's toilet paper creations at the wedding showers. There's just fabric everywhere!"

Hannah stands back and surveys me. Her forefinger comes to her chin, as if she's thinking about how to say, *Yes, it is hideous, actually.* "Well, perhaps it's not right on you. But the dress itself is impeccable. I could sell this easily for a mint."

"How much?" I ask eagerly.

"You know, if you took in the sleeves a bit—"

"It would still look ridiculous. How much do you think you can get for it?"

"I don't know, Ashley, but it's all paid for. Your sister-in-law had it completed in Atlanta. I only have to do the fitting."

"Can I take it with me?"

"I want to show it to my boss, and she hasn't catalogued it, so I can't really let it go yet. The work is exquisite, and we might use this seamstress for some of the custom gowns. We can make it work for you, Ashley."

"Can I pick it up after work?"

Hannah sighs at me. "I have a date tonight. Why do you need it tonight?"

"I just have an idea. Please, Hannah."

"I'll get you a key. But no trouble, all right? You'll bring it back tomorrow so Carol can see it, and we'll order you a new one."

I lift up my fingers. "Scout's honor."

"Were you ever a Girl Scout, Ashley?"

"Um, no. But I wanted to be."

Hannah nods. "I'm sure I'll regret this, but technically, it is your dress."

"You won't regret this. Who's your date with?"

"Malcolm Waterhouse. You know him?"

I shake my head.

"He's new. Just got a job maintaining Web sites for Sun. He looks about twelve, but he's really thirty-four. Sort of balding."

"Where'd he come from? Did another singles group implode?" She shakes her head. "Atlanta."

"Run!"

She laughs. "Are you ready to change? You look beautiful. I really think you should wear this one. Kevin dressed as Rhett would be amazing. Like Hugh Jackman in that movie—what was it called? The one with Meg Ryan?"

"Kate and Leopold." This stops us cold for a moment while we pay tribute to Hugh Jackman in Victorian attire. "Do you have any copies of the dress I chose? I don't think I can afford the original anymore."

"*You* are asking for a copy? What's the world coming to?"

"Hey, I'm a practical girl . . . when I have to be."

"If you were practical, you'd wear this one."

I scan the gown again. I'm completely unable to recognize its beauty. "Okay, I'm not that practical."

"I'll get you some gowns to try on. Did you want to call your maid of honor? Or your mother?"

Ah yes, more rejection. I need that in my life. "No, I'm good." Just as she exits, I see a vase of sunflowers, and it reminds me the Sunflower project is waiting, haunting me like Purvi herself.

"On second thought, I'll come back tomorrow. I need to get back to work, but tomorrow we need to order the gown!"

I used to love sunflowers. They were the first flowers I received from Kevin. Now they are the bane of my existence.

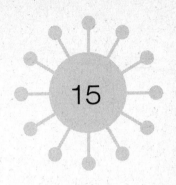

15

I look down the hallways of Gainnet before creeping back to my office. I feel like a night prowler.

"Hey!"

"Ahh!" I scream as I turn around and see Tracy.

"What are you sneaking around for?" she asks.

"I'm not sneaking," I say as I try to gather my bearings. My heart's racing like the NASCAR leader. "What are you doing hunting the hallways like a bad spy movie? Sheesh, next thing you know, you're dropping from a line in the ceiling."

"You're only saying that because you're guilty. How was your wedding dress?" she asks with her arms crossed.

"Ghastly. Thanks for asking."

"Purvi called while you were gone. To make sure you are working on the Sunflower project, I suppose."

"What did you tell her?" Now I don't want anyone lying for me, but I haven't exactly been the pillar of employees lately either. I could use a slight fib.

"That you asked not to be disturbed. Which was partially true because you weren't exactly here to bother."

I exhale. "I'm going to get fired by a boss I got hired. All because I went to pretend I was a Southern belle. This ought to be

141

interesting. But if anyone can succeed at total failure, my money's on me this week."

"Purvi's in no mind to care about your wedding. She's like the walking wounded. She barely had the will to ask about patents. When she asked about the Sunflower project, it was almost like she didn't know what it was."

"What do you mean?"

"Come in your office." Tracy drags me in and shuts the door. "Purvi's husband, Sagar, is here. He wants to take their son back to India."

I gasp. "That boy means everything to Purvi. He can't take him back."

Tracy laughs. "He wants Purvi to go too. She's his wife. He's tired of living without his family, and he's decided he doesn't want to live here. He says it's time to leave America behind for now so their son will know his culture. Their son can come back for college."

I let this information wash over me. "How did you get all that out of Purvi?" She's not exactly the personal life-sharing type.

"I talked to her mother-in-law when I called back to ask about a patent. I didn't think she spoke English. But she does. Quite well, in fact."

"Well, Purvi is not going to India," I insist, but I know she probably is going. I know that Purvi loves this man we've never seen and that she misses her family back in India. His family, I should say. Purvi left hers when the marriage was arranged. It's so hard for me to understand this part of her culture. Purvi is the most intellectually stimulating woman I know. She runs her law department like everything is of White House importance, and her command is gold. So it's so hard for me to picture this complete submission she has to a man across the world.

Yet who am I to judge? The arranged marriage statistics are a lot better than our American ones. Sadly, even our Christian marriages. Purvi is a woman of principle. She'll do what she must. And maybe that's what it's about, being committed to commitment. When I think about Philadelphia and the relatively small sacrifice on my part, I cringe. When a non-Christian is better able to sacrifice than me, who's been given everything, it doesn't do much for my spiritual ego.

Tracy starts to straighten up my office. "So be prepared. Purvi's going to be all business until this gets settled. You might do that prayer thing you do."

I pull a picture out of my purse, unwilling to face another work change. Avoidance is always best in these situations. "This is my true gown. I'm going to see if my sister-in-law, Mei Ling, can make it before I reorder it tomorrow."

Tracy looks at the photo and oohs and ahhs appropriately. "I thought you just went to see your wedding gown."

I shake my head. "That's the imposter. I have plans for that one tonight." Sinister thoughts enter my head. *I'm going to get rid of that one tonight.* I am not wearing that overblown yellow balloon. I'll look like a stuffed sofa from *That '70s Show.* The last thing a bride wants is to be mistaken for retro furniture. And not even good retro. No, it's the era that brought us black lacquer and brass.

My phone rings, and Tracy, being the consummate professional and completely nosy, picks it up. "Ashley Stockingdale's office. This is Tracy." She slowly moves the phone away from her ear. "Charming," Tracy says with lifted brows. "It's Emily from Atlanta." She hands me the phone while she mouths an obscenity.

"Ashley, did you go to your fittin'?"

"I did, and the handwork is just beautiful," I say in my best bipartisan voice. I've learned in negotiating to throw in a positive before dropping the explosive. "But, Emily, that dress is not for me. It's incredibly made, and I so appreciate that you've gone to the effort, but I look like the Michelin Man in it. I'd like to do a sleeker gown for my special day."

"You have time to lose weight before the weddin'. Do you have a gym membership? Can Keh-vin arrange for you to work out at the hospital? Perhaps I can find you a Pilates instructor online."

I'm squeezing my fists to avoid saying something I'll regret.

"Perhaps a personal trainer?" she suggests. "Would you recover from a tummy tuck in time?"

"My weight is not the issue," I say through clenched teeth. Now I'm no lanky model, but I'm not ever going to be—even if I starved myself. And dealing with Emily, the chances of me doing without chocolate are slim to none (or not so slim, as the case may be), so I'd say my weight is what it is. "You know how Scarlett wanted her eighteen-and-a-half-inch waist again? I have never had an eighteen-inch waist, at least not since I was four, and I just think this gown would be gorgeous on a younger, more anorexic bride." *Shouldn't have added that last part.*

Emily takes on my college psychology professor's voice. "Listen, it's all right with me if you want to be in denial, but the mirror doesn't lie, even if my brothah does. You'll have to live with the pictures telling that truth for a lifetime, and they'll be plastered all over the society pages here. I don't mean to be harsh, Ashley; I just wanted you to know. I'd be horrified if someone didn't tell me."

"Is there something you called about, Emily? I really need to get back to work."

"Yes, your weddin' schedule is goin' to have to be strictly adhered to if we're to get everything done in time. You have an appointment next month at Stanford Park Hotel, July 2 at 11:00 a.m., for a sample meal. I'm hopin' Mothah and I can get there, and you should certainly invite your mothah. I wouldn't count on Keh-vin with his schedule. Next Saturday, I've arranged for you and him to select weddin' gifts at Bloomingdale's at ten, and I'm workin' on the chapel. When selectin' gifts, please be sure to provide as many gift options as there are invitations. You'll need bed linens, table linens, china, crystal, proper cutlery, silver . . . I've told the sales representative everything. She'll provide you with a checklist so you will understand and be able to have a proper weddin' registry. You'll need to decide if you're hyphenatin' your name for monogramming or if you'll be takin' Keh-vin's last name. I advise the latter for Southern entertainin'. I'm faxin' your schedule. Should you have any questions, get back to me as soon as possible."

Sure enough, the fax machine starts to beep, and I see this endless list of useless things, the kitchen equivalent of the Tussy Mussy, rolling off the machine. I read the first few things on the registry.

Coffeemaker options. Um, walking down the street to the nearest espresso shop. There's your coffeemaker options.

Flatware options. Um, silverware. Maybe a nice set of chopsticks for eating Chinese out of the box.

Linen essentials. Duvet cover. It rarely hits below 50 degrees here. No duck should have to die for my bedspread.

Crystal stemware. If these don't go in the dishwasher, they don't go in my kitchen.

Sushi plates for Japanese/seafood entertaining. Four sushi restaurants in walking distance. Count them. I'm sure they've already purchased the fish plates.

"Emily, I'm looking over this list, and we've had our own places for some time now. I hardly think we need all this. My mom never uses her china, and what will I do with crystal without Kay? I'd rather just have good day stuff."

"Ashley, you'll be a surgeon's wife. You're goin' to be entertainin' on a regular basis. You can hardly bring out the paper plates and plastic forks for the chief of surgery and his wife. My mothah was always ready for a drop-in guest, and I would hope you'd do the same for our darlin' Keh-vin. Being a surgeon's wife is a job of its own. I do hope you understand this."

The fax machine is still spitting out lists. The funny thing is, I like lists, and I like shopping. You'd think I would enjoy this part. Somehow, Emily takes the fun out of it.

"Kevin and I both work ridiculous hours. I'm just not the type to polish silver, Emily. I don't think that's why he's marrying me." *If it is, Lord have mercy!*

"Then you'll hire someone. My mothah says your new house will have a maid's quarters."

"A maid's quarters?" Hello, like I really want some cute young thing who can clean better than me living in my house. "We don't have a house. We haven't even started looking, and I should think I'll know if it will have a maid's quarters. It won't, by the way."

Tracy's eyebrows knit together, and I can see she's dying to know what Emily is saying.

"See page three of your agenda, Ashley."

It says, "House Hunt," with three addresses and a realtor's name. "Has your brother told you he's considering Philadelphia?" *Now I'm not considering Philadelphia, but if it gets me out of the in-law real estate tour, bring on the cheesesteak.*

"My fathah is ready to go into escrow on one of these three housing options. Philadelphia is not on his list of sites. This will have to be something to add to your agenda if it's a priority."

"Let me study this schedule, and I'll get back to you with changes, Emily."

"No, no, no, no, no. No changes. This is the schedule we must adhere to if we're goin' to pull off a weddin' of any caliber. Invitations must be mailed in July, which means you need your chapel, your reception information, and your gift registry filed and ready for people to send gifts."

Bridezilla has nothing on the Coordinator.

Seth comes into my office, ignoring the small fact that I'm on the phone. "Did you look up the comps yet, Ashley?"

I just can't help myself. I start to scream, and both Tracy and Seth look at me like I'm crazy.

Emily is still barking orders.

"I have to go." I hang up on her without another word. Seth and Tracy are both looking at me with intrigue. "What?"

"You screamed," Seth says.

"Did I?"

"You did," Tracy agrees.

"I feel like screaming again. 'Get out of my office' comes to mind."

Seth grins that disarming smile of his. "Let's go get some coffee."

"I don't want coffee. I want to work."

My office phone rings again, and I pick it up and shoo the odd couple out. "Ashley Stockingdale."

"Ashley, it's your mother."

Joy. "Hi, Mom."

"Aunt Babe wants to throw you a shower before she leaves for Las Vegas on vacation. She's got this great idea of having a lingerie party! I have to admit, it wasn't my first choice, but I think it will be fun after she described it."

That's all this day needs, the idea of my great-aunts providing me with a thong selection. "Mom, I don't think that's especially appropriate. We barely know Kevin's family, and they might think their son is getting a loose woman with that sort of shower. Underwear is sort of a personal shopping experience." *Or it should be.*

"Nonsense. It will be funny. Someday you'll look back and laugh about it. The day when you can't get a leg into it, you'll just roll."

I think not. You know, call me naive, but I'm hoping that I'll be able to get my leg in a honeymoon-something for a lifetime. "What does Mei Ling think of the idea?"

"She doesn't like it either. I'll admit it's not traditional, but I thought you young girls were more hip than that."

"Apparently not. Mom, I can't believe this would be something you'd approve of. You wouldn't let me wear a George Michael shirt in high school because he sang that song about sex, and this is akin to the family knowing my underwear choices."

My mom clears her throat. "I'm sure it will be very tasteful, Ashley. You'll be married. It's not like they're contributing to your delinquency. You're lucky to have your great-aunts around to care about you so much."

"Mom, Aunt Babe thinks home shopping for cubic zirconia is tasteful. What if I get a bunch of marabou feathers and colored lace?" *I hate colored lace.*

"You needn't be snotty, Ashley. It's nice that the aunts want to do this for you. As they say, don't look a gift rabbit in the face."

"Gift horse, Mom. The rabbit was in that weird English movie you like."

She starts to laugh. "Oh right, *The Holy Grail.* Well, you understand my meaning."

"I do, and that's what scares me."

"So does the weekend of August 7 work for you?"

"The weekend works for me. The lingerie, not so much. What if Kevin thinks he married some hoochie mama?"

"Ashley, receiving a gift doesn't mean you have to put it on. Just put a pleasant smile on your face and say thank you. Think of it as a white elephant party with underwear. You can always pass it on."

"Ya think? Mom, Kevin's family is all worried that I have the right china and monogramming for the towels. I'm afraid this invitation to a lingerie party might upset them."

"I can tell you something, Ashley. Lingerie will do more for your marriage than china."

Ewwww! "Never mind, Mom. I got the idea. The seventh is fine for the shower." *After all, I can't wait to see what my sparkly aunts think is sexy.* "And Kevin's family will be across the country. I assume that's best."

"Be sure and invite some people from work, Ashley. It will be nice to share you personal side with them."

"Mom, I'm not inviting people at work to buy me underwear. It's just not professional. We don't need to get that personal." Besides, the idea of Tracy walking into Victoria's Secret for me scares me, to say the least.

"Well, okay. You certainly know best in that arena. You've done very well in your career. I can help you this weekend if you're ready to make the candy almond favors."

"I think it's too soon. The candy is going to get stale."

"No one eats it anyway. It's not really for consumption."

"I eat it! Mom, thanks for your help and the shower information. I have to get back to work." *Dang, I sound ungrateful.* "You're the best, Mom!"

"All right, sweetheart. Give Seth—I mean Kevin—I always forget the boy's name. Give Kevin a kiss for us."

It's dark by the time I get out of work, but the Sunflower project is well on its way to Patentville. I drive up to the wedding shop, and it's completely dark. There's a Starbucks on the corner, but it's half a block away, and its green glow only makes the wedding shop look darker. I peek in the window, catching my second glimpse of the Scarlett gown hanging there: a neon, tea-stained beacon of historical fashion. It's taunting me from its central location in the store. I breathe heavily with anticipation. I can't wait to get the gown in my hands. To show Kevin why it won't work to have his sister as our coordinator. Physical proof that I am neither crazy nor living in a time warp and that the Coach portfolio contains Emily's dream wedding, not my own.

I clutch the picture of my true wedding gown in my pocket. "Vera Wang, Mei Ling style," I say aloud. When Mei Ling sees my gown, she'll see it for the fashion emergency it is. Her sewing machine will become alive with fervor. Besides, I bought Mei Ling's red Chinese wedding gown for her reception. She owes me.

I take the key out of my pocket. It glistens under the green glow of the Starbucks sign. The key slides in easily, and I turn on the lights as I enter. I'm like a kid in a candy store: *veils and garters and gowns, oh my!* The only place I'd rather be at night is in the New

York diamond district with my pick of the platinum, putting my careful knowledge of the four Cs into action!

So I won't get Hannah into trouble, I lock the door behind me and go straight for my gown. Okay, I'll finally admit it really is lovely, but it reminds me of something a little girl would play dress-up in, not something a bride would actually wear. Still . . . Hannah said the detail work was exquisite, and there's something stirring within that says maybe I should give it one more chance when I don't have such an attentive audience.

I pull it into the dressing room and try it on. The three-way mirror isn't nearly as bad when you don't have anyone staring. I can't loop the buttons, so I pull the neckline closed with my hand. I stare for a time, then I notice flashing red lights. "What the heck?" I say aloud as I go toward the front of the store. There's a policeman on his radio. Good thing I'm in here. The last thing I need is to be in the middle of a police action.

I go back to the mirror when I hear the pounding. "*Police! Open up!*"

"Gosh, they are close." I venture another look out the window.

"You, the bride! Open this door."

My heart is in my throat. "Me?" I say with my hand on my chest.

"You, princess. Open the door."

I am wearing a Scarlett O'Hara gown. It's like I've been awakened from a dream world, only it's really much more of a nightmare because I'm dressed most inappropriately. I pride myself on being dressed appropriately for all occasions. But answering to a cop, I'm not sure of the proper dress.

"Open this door!" he shouts again.

I shuffle the gown toward the door and unlatch the deadbolt. The police officer takes a look at the dress and fights a battle with laughter. Finally, it bursts forth. He covers his face with his hand. He's handsome, albeit short, and his mustache is twitching. His laughing isn't doing anything to endear him to me.

150

"What's so funny?" I ask with a hand on my hip. *Like I've got any space for an attitude.*

"Nothing. Can I ask what you're doing in here after hours? Dressed like—like that?"

I swish the skirt around and straighten my shoulders, trying to maintain a sense of dignity. "I'm picking up my wedding gown. It was flown in from Atlanta today," I say with false pride and authority. "See? I have a key." But the key is momentarily missing. "Just a minute. I'll find it."

"You may have a key, missy, but you set off the silent alarm. Unless you have the code to turn it off, you're going to have to come with me."

"Just call the owner. I'm sure this is all very easily solved. See, Hannah had a date tonight, and—"

"Gee, her number isn't in my PDA." He's got his arms crossed.

"Sarcasm in a police officer is not a positive trait," I chastise. Of course I don't have the owner's number. I don't even have Hannah's cell, and she's out on a date. This is not good.

"I'm waiting."

"This is all a slight misunderstanding. My girlfriend Hannah works here. She lent me her key, and—"

"I'm sure your story is true, because I can't believe anyone would break in for dress-up in that gown, but I still have to take you to the station. They'll check out your story, and I can get back on the street fighting the real bad guys."

"The station? No, no. I can't go to the station. Think of all the paperwork you'll have. I was arrested last year for assaulting an officer with my Prada, and I'm a lawyer, and—" His jaw has dropped. "I'm not helping my case here, am I?"

"You have the right to remain silent. Anything you say can be used against you in a court of law."

"No, this is not a court case. It's just a misunderstanding. Look, here's the key! Hannah must not have told her boss."

"Good. Breaking and entering will be left off the charges." He swipes the key from my hand. "I'll take that, thank you."

"I'll take the dress off. Just give me a minute—" As I start to wander towards the dressing room in a dizzying fog, he shakes his head and pulls me back by the elbow.

"You have the right to an attorney present now and during any future questioning. If you cannot afford an attorney—"

"Stop the Miranda Rights. I'm a lawyer. Why would I break into a wedding shop?"

"Maybe it's some fantasy you've developed. Who knows what fetishes people have? I've seen them all." He grabs me by the elbow and escorts me to the flashing red lights. The people on the sidewalk outside of Starbucks are having quite the laugh. "Fine, I won't arrest you until we check out your story, but you're still coming with me."

"Hey, look! Princess Fiona is getting arrested," I hear one of them shout.

I am going to the police station. In custody. Dressed like Scarlett O'Hara. And I was worried about a lingerie shower. I'd take a private marabou teddy moment over this any day.

16

I've been hiking back and forth in the cell for an hour, lest I sit down and destroy this very expensive, albeit enormous gown. Kay is sure taking her sweet time about getting here. At first, the cops couldn't verify my story because Hannah was unreachable on her date, and the owner was not answering her phone. But they all got their laugh for the evening. Clearly, they weren't worried about my hardened-criminal background when they invited other inmates in to share the laugh. *They are certainly easily entertained.*

I've been informed there was a break-in at the shop a year ago, and they're not taking any chances. I could, after all, be the bridal shop bandit. I'd be free right now if it weren't for my record. But that arrest wasn't my fault. I was drunk with jet lag. Duh. You try working straight through for days in Taiwan and then flying back eighteen hours at the end of it. Can anyone really sleep on a plane? Who would be coherent?

Kay comes in, and she stifles back a chuckle. "I see now why you didn't call Kevin."

"Did you post bail?"

"You don't need bail. They know where you live, and you're not under arrest, just here for questioning. They got hold of Hannah, who verified your story. So you can go; you just need an escort back to your car—and your own clothes. Whose dress is that, anyway?"

"Vivien Leigh's."

"I think the police just wanted their entertainment for the night. I'll have to admit, I got mine."

I gather up my stuff, sign a few things, and we're on our way. I think the officers are going to miss me.

It's now that I notice Kay is not dressed like her normal self. She's wearing a darling dress with a swingy, colorful skirt and actual heels. My dress, actually. I nod toward her. "What's this about?"

"Saturday night is my big reunion, remember? I was trying on dresses when you called."

"Seems as if both of us were having a fashion show with other people's clothes."

"Except I actually had free access to your clothes without breaking and entering."

"I did not break and enter. Just take me back to the shop to put this monstrosity back on the hanger and get my car." I take the crumpled picture out of my bag. "This is the dress I'm actually wearing. I'm hoping Mei Ling can make it for me."

Kay peruses the gown and hands back the paper. "It's beautiful."

"That's it? That's all you're going to say?"

"Forgive me. All I could hear in my head was 'Jailhouse Rock.' It threw me off, I suppose." Now Kay does throw her head back and laugh. "What should I say, Ashley? Guide me."

"It's much easier to get hauled into the police station than I thought when in law school. You know, you watch *Cops*, and you think it's all about shirtless men and living in drive-up motels. But it's really a lot easier than they show you."

Kay rolls her eyes. "No, it really isn't, Ashley. You live a charmed life there, I guess. Getting hauled in might be your specialty. An interesting opportunity for a young female Christian, I must say." Kay pulls into the parking lot of the bridal shop. Thankfully, the curious Starbucks crowd has dispersed.

"All right, Kay, you stand outside the door and be my witness that

I am putting this dress back, *not* stealing anything," I say as I start to unlock the door again with Hannah's key.

It's then that my life drops a few notches. Kevin is standing in the parking lot and gets a full view of me as Scarlett O'Hara.

"Ashley?"

"Kevin, what are you doing here?" I feel naked. No, naked would be an improvement.

"Kay paged me. The message said, 'A needs moral support. Come to wedding shop.' I was going to take thirty minutes to eat anyway, so here I am. The better question is what are you doing here, wearing that? Is that your dress?" Kevin's striking green eyes are focused on the gown, his fears obvious.

"This is the gown your sister had made for me." *Can we agree on a structured program for her now?*

A flicker of understanding dawns in his eyes. "You know what, honey? I have to go. Love you!" He comes toward me, kisses my cheek, and looks me over from head to toe, shaking his head and stifling a chuckle. But his eyes are tender. He loves me; he really loves me. "I'll take care of it, Ash," he says gently, my own Leopold. Then he's gone, like the invisible wind on which he blew into my life.

"Why don't you just buy another dress?" Kay interrupts my romantic reverie. "I've never known you to avoid buying anything you thought would make you feel better."

"I'm not sure I'll have time. Plus, I'm a little short this week. Those bookshelves we put into the living room set me back, then we had the taxes, and there's all the wedding things I've bought." I turn the knob, hurry into the shop, and change back into my black bow dress with a major sigh of relief. I hang the Civil War–era creation back in its web and head back out the door.

"Why don't you get wedding sponsors?" Kay asks as I step outside.

"I beg your pardon?"

"I saw on television this couple had businesses sponsor their wedding, and they got everything paid for. Even their honeymoon," Kay says with raised eyebrows.

My mouth falls open. "It's my wedding. It's not a commercial endeavor. I'm thinking *no* on that."

Kay shrugs. "Just an idea. It's a better one than you not paying half the mortgage. But I probably think that's personal on my part. You could ask Kevin."

"I'll get the money, Kay."

"Why can't you just ask Kevin for the money? What good is it to marry rich if you pretend you're poor?"

"Kevin doesn't have any money, and that means the money would come from his parents. Neither of us wants anything from them. Not to mention announcing my poverty to Emily is beyond what my fragile ego can take at the moment."

"Then you're going to have to decide what's more important: a wedding at Stanford Chapel with all the trimmings or doing it yourself. This is one place you can't have your cake and eat it too. Safeway makes a nice wedding cake."

As we step into our cars, I look down at my hands and Kevin's ring. "Safeway?"

"See, you're a snob," she says through the window. "You either want to get married or you want to put on a show. No one would know it came from Safeway."

I would! We both pull out of the parking lot and head for home, but I know we're not through with this conversation. Sure enough, my cell rings. It's Kay.

"There you have it: you're a snob."

"Maybe I am," I say as I adjust my earpiece so I can drive with both hands on the wheel. "I'm poor. I *so* hate being poor. It's not in my genetic makeup to be poor. When God cast me in this role, I just know He said nothing about poverty."

"Poverty? Oh please, you could sell your half of the house and live in a mansion anywhere else in the country. Besides, there are worse things than being poor, Ashley."

"Name one."

"Being sick."

"Name two."

"Not marrying the man of your dreams and spending your days alone. With me and the Reasons, as you call us."

"You never married. I thought you said it was a good life."

"I never met the man of my dreams. Besides, I'm not talking about me. I'm talking about you, my beloved, man-crazy roommate. I think you'd die of emotional starvation without a boyfriend."

"Man-crazy? Granted, I don't like being alone, but that's because I feel without direction. You're such an anomaly to me, Kay. You're beautiful. You have a body to die for . . . and you can cook. Your being single doesn't make any sense to me, I have to admit."

"Because you see being single as failure. I don't."

She's got a point. Her life is unacceptable to me, and I can't imagine where I got this opinion. Maybe it was too many days of Barbie play. Maybe I'm Elaine Novak in my own way, and when I have that scary, surprised skeleton face from too many brow lifts, I'll finally have clarity. *Ohhhh, I see, you mean it wasn't about taut skin and good shoes? Joke's on me.*

"Didn't you ever want to have kids?" I ask her. I figure if Kay's going to open up, I'm going to pry the doors as wide as possible. How often do I get this opportunity?

I can hear Kay mulling this over across the satellite waves. "I don't know about kids. I can't remember ever wanting them. I guess I always thought I would have them, but once the time passed, it didn't seem that big of a deal not having them. Life is full of twists and turns. We can't plot our course. We only think we can, and eventually you become content with what God gives you, or you screw it up further."

"That's good, though, Kay. You have no regrets. Every day my life is filled with remorse because I second-guess everything. Which is why I can't seem to plan this wedding for the life of me. Why I fall victim to Emily's pushing. She just seems so sure of herself."

"Oh, I have regrets. I made a lot of mistakes I would take back if I had it to do over again. But of course, I can't, so you move on."

"Really? Like what do you regret? Granite instead of Corian in the kitchen? What would you change?"

She goes deathly quiet for a minute, then says seriously, "I wouldn't have let Simon ruin me."

I squirm uncomfortably. Hearing Kay's true emotions gets to me. "Simon didn't ruin you, Kay. Look at your success, not to mention how you care for everyone around you. You're the singles group mother."

"I make fun of you being man-hungry, but you know what you want, Ashley. Maybe you're confused on how to get there, but you do know what you want. When Seth wouldn't marry you, you were brave enough to move on and start again. I have to admire that even if I can't duplicate it."

"Like I had options, Kay. Move to Punjab, India, with no wedding ring or commitment, or stay behind and see if he'd come running back. Is that a choice to you?"

"You had options. You could have sworn off men altogether, like I did."

"You regret that?" I can't hide my shock here.

"Don't get me wrong. I don't regret being single. I like my life. I like being in control of my destiny and my house, but I'm always filled with 'What if?' What if I'd not let that harden me? What if my heart was still soft and pliable, and not cold and closed? What if I allowed myself to get hurt again? Would it have happened and crushed me? Or would I have survived and been bigger for the experience? Did God protect me from something worse? Or did I not give Him the opportunity? It's just something I'll never know."

"So why see Simon again? I can't say running into Seth at work every day is doing me any favors."

"Because facing him is facing the fear. That's an important part of moving on."

"I hope he's bald," I say and break into a giggle. "And has hair growing out of his ears. Oh, and back hair. He should definitely have a full rug of back hair."

"Ashley, you really ought to work on allowing the thoughts to fester before they come blubbering out. Is there downtime between the idea and the actual speech for you?"

"Not much, no. That's why litigation is out for me."

"I don't know if he'll have back hair or not. I'm not planning on him being shirtless."

"All the better. You can just imagine that matty carpet o' hair on his back. Oh yeah, just try and take him seriously now."

"You are so mentally deranged."

"I just got taken downtown for dressing like Scarlett O'Hara. What part of deranged were you missing?" I think about Kevin's quick appearance and quicker exit. I'm glad Kay paged him and that he showed up, but where did he dash off to?

"Before you moved in with me," Kay says, and I focus on her again, "I would have thought you were much closer to the edge than you really are. But I see now that your mind works as quickly as your mouth, and therefore what most of us keep to ourselves, you share. Generously. You're not nearly as crazy as you are open. God should have provided you with a Ziploc closure."

"Why'd you let me move in, anyway? We were never exactly close in singles group, and we were clearly polar opposites in life strategies. I mean, remember the clipboard? It was your life, Kay. You took it everywhere, consulted it before you spoke. You were like Linus with a hard baby blanket. Worse yet, Emily with her Coach portfolio."

Another silence. Finally, she speaks. "I didn't want you to move in. I thought you were immature, sloppy, self-absorbed—"

"Um, Kay. Never mind. I don't think my ego is up for this conversation. I did just get out of jail."

"I was going to say no, but I prayed about it, and God clearly told me that if I didn't let my sister in when she needed a place to stay, I was a clanging gong. A mere symbol of a Christian, not a real, loving version. That, and Seth begged me to let you come. When you brought that mutt home, and I started tripping over your shoes and cleaning up dishes in the sink, I knew I'd made a big mistake."

Now Kay starts to giggle.

"You needed me, Kay. Otherwise you might have had that clipboard for decades, until you were organizing the senior group. And by then, you might have a microchip version implanted in your wrist. Oh yeah, I saved you." I sit back in my seat as Kay continues to laugh through the phone.

"Frankly, Ashley, you moving in has been one of the best things that could have happened to me, because it forced me to stretch my wings, to love annoying people when they get on my nerves. And maybe their dogs too."

"I'm annoying?" This shocks me.

"Deathly so."

"Really? I like to think of myself as intense and intellectual. You know, the kind of person who enters a room and stirs conversation."

"Intellectuals don't really watch that much reality TV, Ashley."

"How do you know? Even intellectuals need to come down off the cerebral high once in a while. Who's to say they don't sit down in front of a good *Joe Schmo* episode now and again."

"Sure they do, Ashley."

"I bet you'd be surprised."

"Uh-huh." We turn right, and I recognize the glowing sign just up ahead.

"Hey, you look great, Kay. Let's celebrate my being out of jail and Simon's thatch of back hair. We never do anything single girls should do. Let's live on the wild side."

"Wasn't a trip to jail wild enough?"

"Ha-ha. I was thinking more like the Dana Street Roasting

Company. It's right in front of us, and I'm in the mood for a heaping iced mocha with real whipped cream. Not that fake stuff the cheesy coffee shops use, but the full-frontal fat assault."

Kay looks over at me while we sit at the stoplight and shrugs. "Sure. How much trouble could you get into at a coffeehouse?"

"I agree. What's Ashley on a double-espresso anyway?" I ask.

"On second thought." Kay waves and hangs up as she turns and heads for home.

So much for Kay the party girl. Doused before we even got started. Where's that clipboard?

17

Since the small police incident, my week has been relatively quiet. Purvi hasn't come in much, so many Post-it notes have been spared an early death. Seth had to go to Taiwan—and since he enjoys fresh (killed instantly and slapped on the table) seafood, I can only assume this is good for both of us. Either that, or the calm before the storm.

I haven't seen my fiancé since the mad dash from the parking lot. This is typical, growing ever more so as time passes. I'm wondering if I will be this lonely in the future. I used to live by myself, but now I realize how codependent I've become having Kay as my roommate. I mean, there was that time I left for yoga and had my pants on inside-out with the tag fluttering in the back like a short, white tail. Who would have been there to save me from gym humiliation, were it not for Kay? Certainly Rhett would have tried, but it's not the same. Kevin's always so bleary-eyed for sleep—even if he is home, would he notice?

Kay is sitting on the sofa this fine Saturday morning. Let me repeat that. Kay is sitting on the sofa. All is not right in the State of California.

"Kay?" She doesn't move. "Kay?" I say louder.

"Yeah?" she says without inflection, still resting her chin on her balled-up fists.

"What's going on? Why are you just sitting here? Doesn't something need to be disinfected?"

"It can wait."

"What?" I rush over to the chair and shake her. "Snap out of it. What's the matter?"

"I don't need to see Simon."

"No, you don't. That's true. But the back rug? Aren't you remotely interested?"

She doesn't catch my joke, and not so much as the slightest smile makes its way onto her face. "What if he doesn't want to apologize for what he did, Ashley? I've forgiven him and moved on, but if I have to open that wound again and he doesn't apologize, I don't know if I'll ever forgive him. He's never claimed to be at any fault, actually pointed the blame at my mother! Once again, it will be my burden."

"What did he do, Kay?" She's freaking me out here. Seriously. Kay is not the maudlin type, and I'm not exactly sure why she agreed to this meeting.

"You don't want to know. I've prayed about it. I don't want to see him, but I'm getting this nudge. I can't tell if it's from God or not, but maybe I shouldn't see him."

Looking at her face, stark white with a lack of emotion, I'm thinking this is not a good thing. "Give me his number. I'll call him and cancel. There's no sense in making yourself miserable."

Kay doesn't even look at me. "It's on my cell. He called the other day and left a message. I thought I was over this. What is wrong with me? Christians forgive, and they move on."

"In theory, yes. But sometimes moving on is moving away. What's his last name?"

"Jameston. It's a New Orleans number. 504 area code."

I find his number and call. "Simon Jameston. How can I bless you today?" he answers. Funny, he doesn't sound frightening. If anything, he sounds weak-willed, milquetoast. I'm picturing Matthew Broderick. You might think I couldn't possibly tell all this from the guy's one sentence, but trust me, it was a very weak-willed sentence.

"Simon, you don't know me, but I'm Kay Harding's friend. She won't be able to meet with you this evening after all." I'm pure business, no emotion lest he think Kay might change her mind.

He lets out a ragged breath. "She won't see us?"

"Is there a reason she should?" I probe.

"Is she there? May I talk with her?"

I look at Kay, and she's still ashen. I can't help the lie that comes out of my mouth. "No." Well, it's really only a lie if he thinks I'm answering the first question. Clearly, I'm answering the second.

"Will you tell her something for me?"

"I will." *If I like it.*

"I'm a pastor, going on television with my ministry. I wanted to warn her in case she saw me that she's involved in my testimony of how the ministry came to be. Not by name, of course. But she's there, and she'll know it's her, so I wanted to tell her up front before she heard it in the wrong place. It will be on the *Bless You* show two weeks from tomorrow at 4:00 p.m. eastern."

"Thank you. If she has any questions, she'll call you." I've got to admit, I can't imagine Kay has deep water. Especially if it's not one part white vinegar for a cleaning solution.

"Would you also pass on that Ruth is so sorry this has had such a harsh effect on Kay? We had no idea she would be so sensitive to our actions back then. Ruth will be beside me on television. Thank you," he adds before hanging up.

Kay has lived her entire life trying to control her environment. Clearly, this is something she was unable to control. I see her safety bubble in definite jeopardy, and I want to protect it for all it's worth. Television? Of course no one will know it's her. Milquetoast Backhair assured me of that, but Kay will know. She's looking straight ahead at the blackened television screen. I have my Saturday agenda in hand, starting with the wedding registry, but I toss it on the coffee table.

"He's a pastor still."

Kay just nods. "I know that. He's been doing a speaking ministry for years. People actually listen to him." She lets out a halfhearted laugh.

"He's going on television to talk about his life, his testimony."

Kay's eyes go wide and round.

"He won't mention you by name."

"He won't need to, Ashley." She gets up and starts straightening the books on the coffee table. *Like they were crooked to begin with.* "Ministry. If he cared about ministry, he'd—" She stops her sentence and goes quiet again.

"I have a theory," I say, because it's awkward silence, and I want to fill it with my irrational thoughts. Anything is better than Kay's silence at the moment.

"When do you *not* have a theory, Ashley? And in case you haven't noticed, your life is not exactly the model of perfect behavior. Keep a job for a year if you want to dole out advice, okay? Or better yet, let a year pass without getting arrested for some fashion crisis." She rolls her eyes. "Hitting a police officer with a Prada. Puh-lease."

A little brutal. Certainly not the Kay I know and love. "No, this theory is good, Kay. I've used it before. When we keep our sin quiet, the Enemy uses it. When we come clean, God uses it. You may have forgiven this guy, but it doesn't seem to me as if you've moved on."

"And he has? Finding speaking engagements where he can talk about his fabulous ministry until he's blue in the face?"

"So you fell victim years ago to your . . . to your yearnings? It was a mistake; it's over."

"I'm not talking about it, Ashley. Please don't try to fill in the blanks. You couldn't be more off base. It's not as easy as you'd like to think, so let's move on. I'll go back to what you like to call my OCD life, and you'll get married and move forward. See? Everybody's happy."

"I just don't see how this history can be that dark and desolate,

Kay. First off, it's you, so I'm not expecting extreme drama. Second, there is nothing new under the sun, so why do you think you're so different from the rest of us? I imagine God counts you as a sinner too. Just like the rest of us mere mortals."

"Drop it. Go shopping, Ashley. You've got to have a registry before the first shower, so please just go. You should have taken care of this already. I'm fine. I don't have to see Simon, and that's a good thing. You took care of it, and I appreciate that."

"I'm not leaving you like this. Just tell me and get it off your chest, will you? You're not made of steel. Why do you have to act like it? This is just a form of narcissism. Pride in its worst form, because you think you're too good to sin." *Oooh, that was good. I have to remember that one.*

"That's ridiculous. You don't even know how ridiculous." She gets up, and I'm assuming she's off to clean something.

"Then get it off your chest, for crying out loud!" I yell after her.

The phone rings, and I go to it while Kay fumbles with her words. *Sheesh, I should have such trouble getting things off my chest.*

"Hello," I answer.

"Ashley?"

Oh, the horror. It's Emily.

"Off to do my shopping for the registry," I say cheerily.

"I'm callin' with a new name to add to the guest list. Amy Carmichael is goin' to be in the area! She's an old friend of Keh-vin's, and I think he'll just be so surprised. Let me give it to you."

Amy. No doubt the Amy whom I distinctly remember Emily mentioning that Kevin should be marrying. So, um, no. She'll get on the wedding list when I ask Seth to walk me down the aisle.

Emily rattles off this girl's address, and like a pathetic lemming, I scribble it down. Did I expect Kevin to be history-free? No. I have mentioned he looks like Hugh Jackman, have I not? I already knew he and size-two Arin had a brief but twisted romance, but Amy . . . can't say I'm overly fond of Amy entering the picture. Mostly because

I don't know her story, and hearing her name from Emily doesn't bring warm fuzzies for me.

"Who was that?" Kay asks, still lost under a mask of parchment-colored skin.

"Emily calling with one of Kevin's ex's addresses for the wedding. I suppose I should be happy. She could have been my new maid of honor, complete with a lavender parasol. Maybe she'll don a secret veil like Leah and Rachel in the Bible and be packing a crowbar in her garter."

Kay just nods indiscriminately. "That'll be nice."

"I think you should come with us, Kay. I don't know anything about kitchen gadgets anyway. Kevin's got a million things on his mind with all his work. Come do this for us. I mean with us."

Rhett is following her everywhere. He senses something isn't right too. "No. You and Kevin haven't spent any time together. This is an important day, and what's the worst that could happen? You pick out the wrong salad spinner."

Salad spinner? "Is there really such a thing?"

She sighs. "Yes, Ashley, there is a Santa Claus and a salad spinner."

"I don't mean to be naive, but what's it do?"

"It spins lettuce leaves so they dry out when you're making a salad."

I shrug. "Isn't that what paper towels are for? Or better yet, the salad bar at Whole Foods?"

"It also can dry a cashmere sweater without harming it."

"Hey, I might be able to use that!"

"Ashley, go shopping."

I haven't told Kay the part about Ruth, who I can only assume is Simon's wife. Something tells me now's not the time. Simon said two weeks from tomorrow. I have two weeks to wait until Kay rolls back into a good mood. Perhaps the singles group will need a flowchart, and she'll be back in the game.

"You're sure you're all right?" I ask.

"Ashley!"

"I'm leaving. I just want to cheer you up."

"At the moment, you have about as much chance of cheering me up as I have of providing a closet big enough for your shoe collection."

I step out onto the porch, and with a rush of air, Kay slams the door behind me. "Don't let the door hit me in the butt on the way out!" I yell through the door.

"Go away!" Kay yells back.

As I gaze out onto the sycamores that shade the street, I see Kevin's car at the curb and my heart plummets. I march down the stairs and knock firmly on the window, which startles him awake.

"Have you been home at all?" I ask.

He turns on the car and rolls down the window. "Beg your pardon?"

"Have you been home? Have you slept?"

"I just had a great nap. I've been out here since seven." He smiles.

"That's not even three hours, Kevin."

"We're picking out plates. I'm not performing surgery. I'll be fine."

"Residency is legalized abuse. You realize that? No, wait, residency combined with workaholism is a masochistic existence."

"Don't be mad at me. You haven't seen me all week. I miss your smile. I don't miss this naggy part all that much." He laughs to himself, gets out of the car, and comes around to open my door. He stands over me, and my stomach warms at his proximity. "Do you have a kiss for your fiancé?"

I cross my arms in front of me. I want to be mad, but one good whiff of his clean, antiseptic smell softens me like butter in the microwave. We fall into an embrace and a heart-stopping kiss that makes me tingle all over. *Life is good.*

"How's Holly?" I ask as I get in and buckle my seat belt.

"She's doing better, which is good news and bad. She'll be leaving the hospital soon."

"I'm sorry."

"I know."

A girl dreams about her wedding registry. There's such a romantic air to picking out your first things together. But at the moment, Kevin looks like the walking dead. After my conversation with Kay, this just puts me in a worse mood. "Remember this moment," I warn. "It might never come again. I do not want to shop right now."

"Even when it's your chance to show me how it's done and spend other people's money?"

"Did you even take a shower? Your hands smell like hospital soap," I accuse, though secretly I've developed quite an attraction to this scent. I'll be the only woman on earth to walk into a hospital and have a Pavlovian response to clean people.

He puts his arms around me before he starts to drive. "I don't need a shower. That's pheromones talking to you. Kind of sexy, no?"

"No!" I wiggle free.

"All right. A shower will make you happy? I've got clean clothes in the trunk. Let me run in and take a shower. Is Kay home? I don't want to scare the poor woman."

"You can't go in there. Kay's home, and if you don't want the *Psycho* shower scene coming to life, I suggest you steer clear."

Kevin kisses my cheek, and my anger slowly dissipates.

"Stop that." I punch my fist into my hand. "I want to be mad at you."

"No, you don't. Tell me law school was easier than my residency. This is just part of my learning curve, Ashley, and I'm slower than you."

"You're not going to charm me today."

"Ashley, you're shopping. All day. You get to buy stuff that you're not going to have to pay for. Why are you in a bad mood?"

Expectations. It's those nasty expectations again. "I thought you'd be more excited about this, that you'd actually be awake and showered for the event."

"Ashley, we're picking out tablecloths. If we were picking out stereo systems or flat-screen televisions, I might have more enthusi-asm." He sneaks a kiss onto my lips. "Got you. You're slippery today. Let's go shop for junk I'll never use."

"Who's Amy Carmichael?"

Well, there's a conversation killer. Kevin doesn't exactly sound as chatty as he did a minute ago.

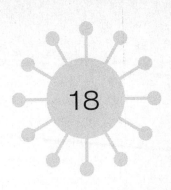

18

I don't want to say that Kevin avoided my Amy question, but he did get easily sidetracked as we headed for the mall. As I look at his tired frame, I can tell he's only recently discarded his scrubs. He's pulled on the jeans and wrinkled shirt he keeps in his locker for those rare occasions when he actually needs real clothes and not the jade-colored uniforms he normally wears.

As I look over at my gorgeous, albeit exhausted fiancé, I realize what a warped place I live in, because his movie-star looks are not all that sought-after here. This is probably the only place in the world where men five-foot-six and under are actually a hot commodity. The geekier they appear, the more band instruments they played in high school, the higher up they were on the AV staff, the hotter their dating résumé is. That's because their geek pursuits often led to wildly successful careers here in Silicon Valley, where Erector set and Lego mentality lead to fabulous engineering minds and big stock options.

I know men who couldn't get a date in high school who have become the most eligible bachelors in town. But let me tell you the downside of most of these stock jockeys: money doesn't change them. They were cheap when they were mere engineers, and they're cheap when they become millionaires. Granted, you might live in a mansion because that's tax deductible, but heaven help you if you want to buy something unreasonable like an umbrella for the rain. If you didn't buy it at their perceived value or under, it's going back to the store.

I've seen bosses who owned $8 million homes take back pancake mix to Costco because their beloved didn't get it for the best price per ounce. As they say, cheap runs deep. Unless it's tax deductible, of course. Then the sky's the limit.

My point is that I've learned to speak engineer. I can learn to speak Southern. *Fried okra, sweet tea, tomato sandwiches, Keh-vin.* See, I've learned already. And I am heading for Bloomingdale's hand in hand with my fiancé and armed with the knowledge that the salad spinner is my friend.

"What are you thinking about, Ashley?"

"Tomato sandwiches and your groom's cake."

"I'm having a groom's cake?"

"You sound surprised, but this is one Southern tradition I think is fabulous. It was once said if you took a piece home and ate it, you'd dream of your future groom." I pause for a minute. "How cool is that? Maybe if I'd had it at twenty, I wouldn't have been so anxious to be married. I know it's going to be great for the singles group. I'm going to tell the tradition at the wedding and send all the engineers into commitment-phobe insomnia that night."

Kevin raises one eyebrow.

"Going back to the Stanford Shopping Center is so appropriate for us. This is where we first met. Do you remember?"

"I do. I was being politically correct at the time. Trying to rid myself of Arin and date her friend. You know, I broke the guy code for you. If that ain't love, well—"

"Why would you do that?" I've heard his explanation, of course, but I'll ask him when I'm eighty, because I get all warm and tingly when he tells me.

"Because when I saw your face, I realized what I was looking for all along: a woman I could bring home to my family. Granted, you may have stumbled over those first words a bit, but I knew the spark was there. I'd seen you sing, you know, and your voice touched me in a way I still can't explain."

"Did you know that they say women have a symmetry to their faces that makes men find them beautiful? The better the symmetry, the more beautiful they're considered?"

"Where do you get this stuff? Can I go back to being romantic now? Because I want to tell you that when you looked at me, it was as if you looked right inside. I'd never seen eyes like that. They actually made me feel something. Just with a look, and it wasn't long. You wouldn't look at me much."

I giggle. "I remember thinking it was like staring directly into the sun, looking into your smile. Every time I look at you, Kevin, I feel completely unworthy and know that God must truly love me to bring you to me."

He nods. "That day, I'd just had a dentist friend try out whitener on my teeth. They were pretty bright."

I lift up my head. "You did not."

"I did."

"You mean all this time I thought I fell for you, and I was really blinded by peroxide?"

"There are lesser things marriages have been built upon."

"True."

"Hey, did you get your real dress? I had a discussion with my sister. She knows you will not be dressing as Scarlett. I wish you'd come to me earlier. How goes the rest?"

"Well, I've found the photographer. Your sister picked out the invitations, and you know the chapel I want. I just have to get confirmation. I was going to ask Mei Ling to make my wedding dress, but I think I might try something off the rack in San Francisco's warehouse district."

"Did you just say 'off the rack' for your wedding dress? All right, what's going on?"

Here it is. This is the moment when I have to tell him I have no money.

"Emily has distinct ideas about our wedding, and Southern weddings in general. She canceled my gown order in order to present me with what we'll call the Scarlett Fiasco. I'm having to scramble to get something else."

Kevin closes his eyes and processes all this. One thing I've noticed about Kevin is that he's not that quick on the draw when it comes to people. He always looks for the best in people, which is a good quality. I mean, he's marrying me, right? It's only an annoying trait when he's more gentle as a dove than wise as a serpent. There's supposed to be a balance. I suppose this is why we're a good couple. A positive and a negative charge binding together.

"My sister canceled your wedding dress order?" he repeats slowly.

"Yes."

"Why?" He drawls this out so I really hear the Southern gentleman in him.

"Because she had the other gown designed for me."

He crosses his arms. "When I left so quickly the other night, I had a talk with Emily after seeing you in that dress. I knew something wasn't right. But, Ashley, why didn't you tell me what was going on?"

"I don't know if you noticed, but that's an exact replica of Scarlett O'Hara's gown from her wedding to Charles Hamilton in the film."

Kevin raises his eyebrow again. When I nod to say it's true, he starts to bubble over with laughter until he's literally cracking up. "My sister thought you would dress like Scarlett? I knew she had something to do with that dress."

"It's a beautiful gown," I say in Emily's defense. "It's just not really for me."

"No, I wouldn't think it's your dress, Ashley."

"What's that supposed to mean?"

"Do you *want* to look like the type to wear Scarlett's dress, Ashley? Is this one of those 'Does my butt look big in this?' questions, because I'm not very good at those. Humor me until I learn the code, all right?"

"I don't want to wear it, but I don't want you to think I don't look good in it either."

"You looked fabulous in it. It just looked like a costume. I imagine that would mean Emily imagined me as Rhett Butler?"

I shrug. "You'd have to ask her, but most likely yes, you'd have to be Rhett Butler." *You and the dog.*

"I lived my whole young life in Atlanta, and I never knew anyone to have a *Gone with the Wind* wedding. While I'm sure it happens, most likely it's not native Atlantans doing the deed. It's probably tourists who come down with a false notion of how we live."

I breathe a sigh of relief. "So I'm a little behind schedule on a few things, and that's why. Emily wants to make you happy, Kevin. That's the important thing to remember. She thought this would make you proud."

"My mother would have a conniption if her friends showed up for a wedding like that. It would be humiliating at best." A look of understanding crosses Kevin's face, and he lets out a rush of air. "I think I figured out our little belle's motive."

Now I feel bad. Emily was trying to impress her family, and now I have guilt. I know it's not warranted, but there it is. As Kevin speeds into the parking lot, we're right on time for our 10:00 a.m. appointment at the department store. We hold hands and walk down the outdoor walk of stores. I catch Kevin giving a look of contrition to the store, as though he's sorry for having to break the "non-shopping" guy code, but this must be done.

"It won't take long," I say enthusiastically.

"It will take forever. I've done this before."

I stop at the door. "You've what?"

Kevin's green eyes cloud, and he focuses on the water fountain running in the middle of the mall. "I was engaged once."

"Hello? Pertinent information! When were you planning to tell me, and are there any other dark secrets before I tackle the most intimate task of selecting china with you?"

"I was nineteen, Ashley. It was before I went off to college. I think in California you'd have called it a fling, but with my Southern roots, I was ready to get married. I *loved* her!" He says with Broadway drama and drops to his knees, which of course makes me laugh.

"Get up. So that's who the mysterious Amy Carmichael is?"

"What? No, Amy is a friend of Emily's. She always had that big brother crush on me. She's just a little confused and thinks we are meant to be together. Sort of like you were about George Michael. I have a feeling she'll come to the wedding hoping for some romantic reunion. She's watched too many Meg Ryan movies."

"Where do you find these people?"

"Have you met my family, Ashley? We seem to attract a different sort. Mentally incapacitated? Please, come sit by us. Besides, you've got nothing to worry about. Amy couldn't pass the Mensa test if it was multiple choice with one bubble."

"I know that's supposed to be a joke, but you're creeping me out, Kevin. Remember when you were this nice, mannerly gentleman who took me out to fancy dinners?"

Kevin puts his hand on the small of my back and tries to lead me into Bloomingdale's. "Courtin's over, babe. I got you now. I can use me real manners now." He winks at me, then stops and holds my gaze, suddenly serious. "Do you trust me, Ashley?"

I do trust him. I look back at him, nod, and my stomach swirls.

"I was engaged for two months when I was nineteen. When her father got wind of it, that was it. Turns out she was seventeen. She just graduated high school early."

"So you're saying the Mensa requirement started early?"

"She went off to Yale, and I never saw her again."

"I'm getting all weepy. It sounds like a Nicholas Sparks book. Or a movie of the week. Where are the tissues when you need them?"

"Get in here." He shoves me in the door, and our conversation about his brief engagement and Amy Carmichael is over.

Kevin puts his arm around my waist as we walk into Bloomingdale's and through the makeup section, the shoes to my right, the gowns to my left. I feel this very strong tractor beam pulling me in multiple directions. You know, you can have the fancy boutiques. I'm a department store girl. I'm like a kid at Disneyland. I can't decide where to look first. *Should I go for the shoes? Start with the outfit? A handbag? Oooh, lipstick, lipstick!* I was just like this at my brother's wedding in Las Vegas. I'm not a gambler, but I couldn't resist all the lights and bells. It appeals to my love of shiny, blinking things.

"Can't we just look around a little?" I ask with a tinge of whine in my voice.

I feel his hand push harder. "Go."

"Victorian women had it easy. They got to shop for a trousseau. They left it up to their mothers to buy plates and linens. I think I need a trousseau. I'm bound to get a lot more use out of it than plates. You know my favorite restaurants already have plates."

"I think that Scarlett dress is having an effect." He taps lightly on my forehead. "Bring back Ashley!"

Jocelyn meets us at the top of the escalator. *My, she's efficient.* "You must be Kevin and Ashley. Welcome to Bloomingdale's." Jocelyn is drop-dead gorgeous, with dark straight hair and a shiny, model face. How do they get that? Is there some great beauty secret that gives you that plastic-perfect Barbie skin? Because I want it. I'd ask her for the procedure name, but exchanging plastic surgery information in front of one's fiancé in Bloomingdale's is probably frowned upon.

"We *are* Kevin and Ashley!" I say with too much enthusiasm. So much that Kevin looks at me as if to say, *Down, girl.*

Jocelyn claps her perfectly manicured hands together. "We're going to have such an interesting day together. Since most of your list is complete, we'll start with linens."

How is it that her salary at Bloomingdale's pays enough to look like that? I'm in the wrong business.

"Wait a minute. What did you say?"

"Your registry. Since most of it is filled, we'll begin with linens and pots."

"But we haven't registered for anything yet."

Jocelyn looks confused—well, as confused as her shiny face allows. I think Botox probably prevents big shows of expression. "Your wedding coordinator faxed your list, and I've put the items into our computer." She pulls out a long computer printout from her portfolio. "Right here. We can start with your platinum dishes."

"Platinum?" I ask.

"Right here." Jocelyn leads us to the plainest plate I've ever seen. It is white china with a silver ring around it. *Period, as in nothing else. Zip, zero, nada.* Oh, wait. It's a *platinum* ring, judging by its name. How very déclassé of me.

"Yeah?" I say expectantly. "That's a nice plate." *For my grandmother!* "But I'd like to see something with a little more color. You know, a little more contemporary."

"This is the plate on your registry." She picks it up so I can examine it more closely. But it's not like I need an intricate examination of the design. *Platinum. Circle. Got it.*

I look around to the Kate Spade hot-pink plates and the Vera Wang collection that seems to shout at me, *Ashley, come get us. You love color. We make a statement! Leave the mundane to the engineers.*

I thrust the plate away gently. "It's beautiful, but it's not what I'd pick. And I think you can throw that registry away. I didn't pick anything yet. Can we see something with a little more . . . personality?"

"It's what your wedding coordinator faxed in. You want to change it? It's not a problem. I just want to make sure I'm understanding you, because she's got quite a bit to go with this theme."

I look at Kevin, who's staring at the lighting fixtures on the ceiling. "Kevin? We want to change it, correct?"

"That was my mother's china, I think." Kevin squints his eyes and looks closely.

"Great, then we can borrow hers if you get lonely for it." I start to tap my foot.

"Emily helped with my last registry. Maybe she had the information somewhere."

"Let me process this. Not only am I preregistered, but it's someone else's registry? I'm getting a second-hand registry? Why don't we just register at the Salvation Army?"

Jocelyn clears her throat. "Well, I'll leave you two to discuss our next step."

"Ashley?" Kevin says gently, which breaks me out of my horrible thoughts. I think I need to read less Poe.

As I stare at Kevin's guilt-ridden expression, I have the sudden urge to go home and label something like Kay. Maybe my underwear drawer:

> Big White Underpants
> Minimizers
> Shapers

Do you get my drift? I need some control. If it has to come in the form of ultrastrength Lycra, I'm good with that.

"Throw the registry away," Kevin says to Jocelyn. "We'll be starting from scratch."

I rush to him and bound into his arms. "And here I thought you weren't even paying attention," I say gleefully. "Have I told you lately that I love you?"

"Let's see the Kate Spade plates," he says, and I know I'm *so* in love. He knows Kate Spade! He is my missing puzzle piece. My soul mate, my window into the future.

"Oh, can we see the Sheridan bed linens too?"

"Anything your heart desires, Ashley."

I squeeze him tight. "I have everything my heart desires." And I do. *Now bring me that Oneida collection!*

19

It's Tuesday, and Purvi is out again, so I sneak out of work early (if you call 6:00 p.m. early!) and rush to get to the pedicure I booked. As I sit back in the chair and let the attendant go to work, I think back to last weekend's blissful registry shopping experience. (Kevin even let me throw in an Ann Taylor "going away" outfit, once he saw me in it.) Then I remember Jocelyn's face when we ditched Emily's whole registry selection.

One thing I've learned is that if I'm going to get married, it's not going to be a blasé affair that happens with simple phone calls and gentle catalog searches. It's going to be an all-out brawl, like the final two gals on *The Bachelor* who pretend to be friends but would scratch the other's eyes out if given the opportunity. Simply put, my life is complicated. And while God won't give you more than you can bear, with Emily in the picture, I think there was some miscommunication about just how much I could bear. Perhaps I look more muscular from above.

So I sit here in the vibrating pedicure chair as this young girl who doesn't speak a lick of English massages peppermint salt rub into my legs and feet. Here's a girl who gave up everything she knew to come to this country and wash feet for a living. She smiles up at me, and there's a quiet glimmer in her eye, a tad sinister in nature. Maybe she's glad she can't speak to me. I've tried talking to her a multitude of times, but I just make her nervous because she can't answer. So now I sit reading a patent schematic, ignoring her and giving a big tip at the end, hoping she might be better for it.

The experience does provide perspective that whining about the right plate on my wedding registry is ridiculous. Kevin seemed such a dream to me when I met him. I remember hearing power ballads when he walked into a room. He was the kind of man one didn't actually date but looked on with awe from afar. Then God brought him close, and I see that no matter what someone's appearance, everyone has their Achilles' heel. Kevin's is his family and his insecurities because of them. Yes, he's a magnificent surgeon, but nothing's ever good enough for him.

Rather than coming home filled with joy that he's saved a life, he has fears that he might not be able to save one the next day. I think he picked me because I expected so little of him.

"Ka la?" The girl wakes me from my reverie as she rinses off the gritty film o' peppermint.

I shake my head. *What on earth?*

"Ka la? Pik ka la?"

"Color," I say with recognition. "Yes, right here," I say as I hand her a pearly pink. She looks me straight in the eye and takes the color with that look of disapproval. I think it's the only thing that gives pedicurists a sense of power, being disgusted by the color you select.

Life is not fair. I don't know why people think life is fair. It should be, I'll grant you that. If you commit a crime, you should do the time, not be "saved" by a superstar attorney who couldn't care less if you're guilty or not, since he just wants to show off his fancy legal maneuvering and make a few million. But here again, life is not fair. I could have been a manicurist answering to the nail hawker at the door, instead of a lawyer answering to Purvi.

I could take the bus (heaven forbid with my brother driving) instead of driving my Audi. I could be marrying a garbageman instead of a surgeon. In most ways, I really come out with the long end of the stick in life.

My phone trills, and it's my best friend. "Hi, Brea."

"What are you doing?"

"Getting a pedicure and wondering if I am supposed to marry a garbageman."

"You're so weird. Listen, your mom's calling me about a lingerie shower?" Brea has a distinct, questioning lilt, crossed with a dash of disgust.

"I'm sorry, Brea. I told my mom no lingerie shower."

"She *so* needs to get a grip, Ash. Can you see your aunts showing up with—never mind, I can't even go there. So what do you want me to say to her? They think they're rescuing you from a life of divorce statistics with this shower. You do realize that?"

"Let's tell her that I went with Arin to the wilds of Costa Rica and was eaten by the South American crocodile, may I rest in peace, and don't you dare put 'She never got married' on my tombstone."

"Are you done?" Brea pauses. "Do they have crocodiles in Costa Rica?"

"I don't know. What am I, *National Geographic*? Ouch!" I look down at my foot, which has a touch of blood oozing from the big toe. "I've had a pedicure incident! There's blood." The pedicure is not going well. The gal is frantically trying to pat my toe and pretend it didn't happen, all while wearing gloves for her own safety. *What a world we live in.*

"They'll clean it up," Brea says without concern. "Quit being such a baby. Your mother said that all brides have this type of shower now, and she made the mistake once with Mei Ling and wouldn't do it with you."

"Dave." I just drop my head. "I told her it wasn't appropriate, so there's only one answer to this equation."

"That's what I was thinking too," Brea confirms. "Your brother's sense of humor has not expanded since the second grade, Ashley!"

Now my brother is a Christian. He is a fabulous husband and father, but he loves a good practical joke. I can just see him in all seriousness, telling my mother the great-aunts are correct. Ashley *should* have, *must* have a lingerie shower. That it simply isn't done to get married without virtual strangers buying intimate apparel. Considering my mom chose a den over financing my wedding, I figure she probably sees it as a way to make it up to me. Ugh.

"I'll put it to bed once and for all, Brea. Excuse the bad pun."

"That's not the only reason I called, though I have to admit, your family is far too interested in your underwear choices. I just had to explain why most lingerie today has thongs. Explaining thongs to another generation is just not right. I should tell them about the big ol' granny pants you do wear. Sheesh, you're worse than my mother. You could iron those things like a sheet."

"I like comfortable underwear," I say, and the pedicurist looks up at me. *Clearly, she understood that.* "I'm getting married," I add in a whisper. Like this is related to my underwear talk.

"I'm actually calling because I got a call from Emily."

"*My* Emily?"

"Please don't take credit for her. She's a freak of nature; let her remain unclaimed. Or as part of the O'Hara clan, shall we?"

"What did she want?"

"She's coming back into town next month, thinks you need more help. And she's bringing me a prototype for the maid of honor's dress. The dress I think you distinctly told her I was not wearing. You *did* tell her that?"

"I did. Really! Right before I stole the Scarlett gown."

"Does Kay know she's being expected to wear ruffles? Because I can't see Kay in a dress, much less ruffles."

"No one is wearing ruffles. I'll handle it."

"Like you handled the patent for Purvi the other day? By shopping and downing an espresso double shot? Or getting thrown in the slammer for handling the wedding gown problem? And what about making your best friend explain the growth of the thong's popularity to your mother? Manic Ashley is not going to fix this problem."

"I'll handle it," I say in a clipped tone and shut my phone.

"You gettin' mawried?" the pedicurist asks.

"I am."

"You old to get mawried."

"Thank you." *Kiss your tip good-bye.*

"He old too?"

"Ancient."

She finishes painting my toes, and I get out cash. I leave her a hefty tip, even though I could have done without the reminder that I'm old to get married. Which by all American statistics, I am not. But tell that to my mother.

My cell phone trills again. "You popla," the manicurist says, and all of them laugh at me while I exit.

"Hello, darlin'." Kevin's voice fills my senses.

"Is it true Emily is coming back into town in three weeks?" I ask, trying to keep my tone nonchalant.

"That's what I called about. She's coming in, and I'm going out."

"Out where?"

"Out of town. I'm going to interview for the Philly job. I know we didn't get a chance to discuss it, but I just want to get it out of my system. Confirmation that I'm in the right place here at Stanford."

"Kevin!"

"I'm just talking to them, that's all. I'll spend as much time with you as I can until then. Then you'll be busy with my mom and Emily while I'm gone. You have the practice meal and cake testing."

"Your mom?"

"She'll be in town too. She's coming with Emily. I told her your mom hasn't been that involved, and I think she wanted to help."

"Of course she did."

"Don't worry. They're staying at my place, and they have plenty

185

to work on. They're looking for a quartet, I guess. And they've set up our cake tastings."

"*Our* cake tastings. Can you taste from Philadelphia?"

"It's sugar and flour, Ashley. How different can they taste? I'm assuming you'll choose chocolate regardless of my thought process on this."

"Do you even want to get married, Kevin?"

"More than you know. Maybe we should have waited until the residency was finished, but, Ashley, I want to be married, not engaged."

It's what I want too, but we sure are going about it oddly.

"We didn't really discuss Philly, Kevin. And I'm not getting a quartet. I'm not Marie Antoinette."

"Ashley, you can have whatever your heart desires. Just tell my mother and Emily. I've talked to Emily and told her your feelings on the theme, and she'll be much more amenable now. When I saw you in that Scarlett dress, I knew I had to do something. I want to see the package I'm getting on my wedding day, not volumes of antique-looking fabric." He laughs at this.

"I just got off the phone with Brea whining about ruffles! Your sister will be amenable when she's forced down and hog-tied!"

"Ashley, my love, you're so funny."

"No, really, I'm not."

"I'll back you in everything with my family. Just tell them what you want, Ashley. Since when do you wait around for someone to run your life? I've got to get this out of my system. What if God wants me to do neonatal surgery, and I don't follow that directive?"

I sigh aloud. "Tell them. That's your answer. You act like they will actually listen, your mother and sister. Do they listen to you?"

He's silent for a moment. "No."

"So you think they'll listen to me because?"

"You're a lawyer. You should know how to talk to people. If you can deal with Seth Greenwood reasonably, my sister has nothing on you."

"Kevin."

"I'll make it up to you, I promise."

"What if I wanted to move to Taiwan?"

"I'd know you'd been drinking. You hate Taiwan."

"I don't drink."

"Ashley, you're being difficult."

"I'm not leaving you with in-laws and going on a nice hiatus from work and wedding stress. What if I told you you'd be here for a week with *my* mother?"

"It's in three weeks, Ash. And I'm going to supervise a neonatal surgery. It's not a walk in the park."

"Oh sure, how do I fight that? Bring on the guilt, why don't you? That's playing fair, to bring on the sick baby issue."

"I know you don't want to go to Philadelphia, and I don't want to move either. Don't you think I'll miss the weather and the culture here? But I want this senior residence position in neonatal work with all my soul. And I won't shake it by denying the desire is there. We've got to at least consider the option for our future, don't you agree?"

"So what you're telling me is let me eat cake." *With your sister, who will probably throw it up when she's finished.*

"I'm not skipping town or expecting you to follow me without your input. I'm checking out a possible future that I can't afford to ignore. That doesn't mean that I will make this decision alone— without God's and your input. Oh, and I told my dad to hold off on the house. We'd let him know where we're going."

"Why do you always have to say the right thing? Can't you just be a jerk for five minutes? A jerk who wants to move where it snows. It snows there, right?"

"Look at the good side. You'll get to add to that huge coat collection of yours, and they'll actually be necessary. I'll even throw a cashmere scarf into the deal."

"Please." But I'll admit, this gives me a feeling of warmth in my tummy. I love coats!

"Hire the swing band you want. Buy the cake. Take care of all the stuff that matters to you, all right?"

"All right," I say with the pout apparent in my voice. "The Southern belles will receive Southern hospitality, sir. Minus grits."

"That's my girl. I love you, and we have a lifetime together, correct? What's one weekend?"

I open my mouth to give the litany of reasons, but I'm silenced by the thought of a baby in the womb having surgery. *Face it, I've got nothing on that.*

"Look in your car's ashtray."

"What?" I say as I unlock the door.

"The ashtray."

I open the compartment, which is filled with loose change, and see a tiny box. Opening it, there's a pair of diamond earrings, ideal cut. "Kevin, what did you do?"

"It's my peace offering to make up for my mom and sister. I got them at Gleim Jewelers while you were finishing up on dish towels Saturday. I hoped you'd find them by accident."

Looking into the sparkling gems, my words betray me. "I'd move to Alaska for you."

"They have terrible shopping there. See, I'm not asking you to sacrifice everything."

Looking at the earrings, my heart fills with love. I don't deserve Kevin. Emily, I probably do deserve, but I'm counting on God to help me through that one. "I love you, Kev. Call me later."

"Bye, Ashley."

20

Okay, I've spent two weeks hiding behind my desk, trying to concentrate on patent schematics and squeeze in a little time with Kevin, and mostly dreading the reappearance of Emily, this time with Elaine in tow, next week. So I've made a list.

REASONS MY FUTURE MOTHER-IN-LAW WILL LOVE ME

1. I am smart. Sometimes. I was valedictorian. That counts, right?
2. I am Botox-free at thirty-two and counting! No botulism brain here! (Although that may be a negative in this family.)
3. I let her daughter coordinate my wedding! (Sort of. And before I knew about the mental condition.)
4. I'm not going to make her purchase my home. (Will fight it tooth and nail actually, but think of the $$$ saved.)
5. I can make spaghetti, and I do not need a cook to help me! (Emeril would be proud. Bam! A little garlic to kick it up a notch!)

"There." I show Rhett my list. "This is to bolster my confidence scale. Remember my 'I am a confident woman' list?"

The dog whines and sets his chin on my lap. My legs are folded up in yoga position when the doorbell rings. "We've got company, Rhett."

I jump up to answer the door, thinking perhaps my book order has arrived, or maybe a wedding gift! But it's Saturday, and my hopes quickly fade with the thought of a door-to-door cult evangelist.

Opening the door, I see a short man, nearly bald, with Santa Claus sideburns and puffy, ruddy cheeks. A nondescript woman is standing next to him. "Hello." He clears his throat. "I'm Simon Jameston, and this is my wife, Ruth."

A thousand thoughts rush into my mind. This is the man who 'ruined Kay's life,' according to her. But this man doesn't look like he could ruin a kitten's life. He's stocky and genuine looking. His wife is mousy and smiles when she speaks. They look like they just stepped off the Bible bus.

"Please excuse us for interrupting you, but my husband and I need to see Kay Harding. Perhaps she doesn't want to see us, but it's important she does. We love her and want to tell her again."

This is a couple who looks like they're running the church flea market. There's nothing in them that says I should be fearful, and I feel the Holy Spirit around them. Something tells me they're just good people, but I know Kay is not the hysterical type. That title would be reserved for me. My hackles raise as I think about Kay's struggle to create a perfect life for herself. And these people, no matter how they seem, are at the root of that issue.

"I'm sorry to be rude, but Kay doesn't want to see you. I think it's important we respect her wishes. And I really have no power to make her do otherwise." I start to close the door, even though I'm dying to know the truth. I no longer think Kay could have had some torrid affair with this guy. He's like your grandpa. And *ewww*.

"Please," Ruth pleads, and I'll admit I'm an easy mark. "We won't take up much of her time."

"She isn't here."

"Do you know when she'll be back?"

"I really don't. I'll be happy to give her a message." *Now run along.*

They both nod and turn toward their Buick parked out front. Not a nice Buick, an old dilapidated model with ripped seats from the extensive sun in the back window. *No garage,* I think to myself. There's dog slime all over the inside of the windows, and a small black dog rising and falling in the passenger window with a chirpy bark every time he appears.

I feel like dirt turning them away, but I do shut the door slowly and watch them walk down the front path. Sometimes being a friend is a hard business. Besides not wanting to see these people, we'd have to deal with the distinct fact that they showed up without an appointment. A genuine no-no for Kay, who likes everything just so when guests arrive. She always has gourmet snacks and refreshing drinks at the ready. Sometimes when I think how hard others are on her, I know it's nothing next to her own demons. She's her own worst critic.

Rhett's at my side, and it's at this moment that I realize he never barked once while the strangers were at the door. "Some watchdog you are."

Now he barks.

I crumple up the list of why my future MIL will love me. She'll hate me. I'm not a debutante. I'm not a Confederate. I'm not even capable of throwing a quaint dinner party. Well, not without Kay cooking for it, anyway.

The doorbell rings again, and I huff. *These people do not take no for an answer!* I walk to the door and get ready to let the nice little couple in the Buick have it, when I see it's Matt. What is this: "I've wronged Kay" day? It's a national holiday or something. I know she has no decorative tchotchkes for this occasion.

"Emily went back to Atlanta," I tell him without greeting, and Rhett growls fiercely. *Good dog.*

"I'm here to see Kay."

"Get in line. She's not here. And you don't have a cell phone? What's with the personal visit? Kay hates that."

"I didn't think she'd take my call."

"And you'd probably be right. You should try your luck on *Jeopardy* with that kind of extrasensory perception."

"Look, I know I am not your favorite person, but that's not of the utmost important to me. Kay and I really clicked. I'd like to speak with her again, and since you're not her keeper—"

"Even if you knew my future sister-in-law was coming back into town next week? Would you still want to see Kay?"

He pauses. For too long, quite frankly.

"I'd still want to see Kay. How about if we let her make up her own mind about me?"

How about if we don't and say we did?

"I'd like to take her out for her birthday."

Shoot. "It's her birthday?" Good one, narcissistic Ashley; you forgot your roommate's birthday.

"Just tell her, will you?"

I shrug. "No skin off my nose. I'll leave her a message," I say as I slam the door. *Sheesh, and I thought I was only going to get your run-of-the-mill cult salesman.* Now I have to shop and get a present. Not just any present, a perfect present for my roommate who thrives on perfection.

I walk into my bedroom with Rhett on my heels and take out my bridal book. I look at all the items on the to-do list to see if there's anything I can do while out shopping for Kay. I'm disgusted with myself that I haven't planned nearly what I should have by now. According to the checklist, I should be reserving rooms for out-of-town guests. I don't even know who those guests are, and if I don't get a move on, they'll be camping out under my dad's beer bottle collection on the family futon.

The doorbell rings again, and this time, I am ready to give the Kay brigade a piece of my mind. I stomp up the hardwood floor hallway and open the door to—Kevin. With a bouquet of peach-hued roses.

"Kevin!" I fall into his arms, rather too swiftly, and nearly topple us both. I thought he was on his way to Philly. My hand traces his jaw to make sure he's real.

"I have a present for you before I catch my flight," he says.

"More than the diamonds?" I narrow my eyes, teasing. "I thought you said the courting was over." I'm refusing to let him go, clutching him like Miles clutches his baby Gloworm. Kevin is like the sweetest apparition come to glorious life. "I have my present," I say as I squeeze him tighter.

"No, this is better."

I take the flowers from him. "Come on, let's go inside. It's been Grand Central Station here all day. I'll put these in water." I look around to his other hand. "Did you get me See's truffles too?"

"No, greedy, I didn't."

"It was worth a try. So what's my surprise?"

"What do you want more than anything in this world?"

"The Vera Wang gown I picked out originally?"

"I'm not Houdini, Ashley. You sure don't make this easy on a guy."

"I want to marry the man I love," I gush.

"In . . ." he trails off.

"Stanford Memorial Chapel."

"Ta-da!" He hands me a card. It's engraved, and it has our wedding date on it!

"What's this?" *Oh boy, oh boy, oh boy!*

"It's our reservation for the church."

"You didn't!"

"I did. The chief of surgery attends services there and agreed to vouch for us. We're in, Ashley."

"Oh, Kevin!" I squeeze him again.

"Now will you trust me that I'm coming back from Philly in time to spare you from a whole week with my family, and unless you say so, we're not moving?"

"I trust you." And I really do.

"So now that you trust me, who was that guy leaving your house?"

I blank for a moment. "Oh, that was Matt. Your sister's psuedo-date while she was here. I guess her absence has sparked a rekindled interest in Kay."

"Good. I know Kay can handle herself. I'm not sure about Emily."

I shake my head. "I'm not sure about that, Kevin. You know, last week she told me this old pastor had ruined her life. Today, the man and his wife came here, and it's not that I don't think pastors are capable of sin and all that; but the guy looked like Santa Claus, and his wife was a dead ringer for Mrs. Cunningham without makeup."

"Looks can be deceiving."

"I know that. I'm with you, aren't I? But something tells me Kay has a lot of anger that needs to go. These people seem to want to bury it."

"Kay?"

"I wouldn't think so either, but the whole thing just smells of mystery." I pose with a fake gun pointed, my arms straight out in aim. "You won't be sorry I'm on the case, Charlie."

"Good work, Angel. They'd have gotten away with it too, if it weren't for you meddling kids!" We break into laughter, and I realize that inside this gorgeous creature is a true inner geek. Just like me. Isn't God good?

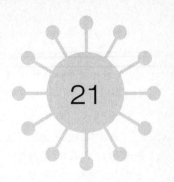

21

Sunday morning has taken on new meaning since I've become engaged. I am no longer "one of them" in the singles group, and I'm treated like a leper of biblical proportion. Gazes are avoided. Conversations verboten. I am the plague, come to life in the form of a woman-over-thirty getting married. You might think there would be rejoicing and excitement. But no, not gonna happen. This is Silicon Valley, and the only thing better than one succeeding is watching the other guy go down in a ball of flames.

I represent fear and trembling for the men, because I "caught" one, and if Kevin was here, he'd be the flopping fish on the hook while the others watched with trembling gills. I am dangerous, dark, and I possess hidden talents they must not see. I am that something shiny in the water that looks so good. Perhaps I might ensnare them too, ripping them from a life of freedom and video games.

To the women I am nothing more than average, and they can't for the life of them see what Dr. Kevin Novak would see in me. I should be prettier (because I certainly couldn't be better dressed). So they avoid me, as is the easiest route, which surprises me, actually. I would think they'd be looking for tips. Not that I have any, but still.

"He could have had anyone," I hear someone whisper, lest you think I'm just paranoid.

"He could have had Arin," I hear in a male tone.

Is it any wonder we women are rife with insecurity? One cannot turn on the television without seeing how deflated we are, how our waist has expanded to unnatural, non-Barbie-like proportions. I mean, if we believed everything on TV, women would have no hips. We would look like nine-year-old boys with overfilled water balloons on our fronts, so out of proportion that any moment we might topple forward, popping the silicone protuberancies. And our lips would take up half our faces, always in a seductive pout.

Naturally, we'd all be competing for the attention of one man, to give the impression that he's Bond. James Bond. Our womanly communication would be subversive, as life is one big game played by keeping emotions close to your heart—until it is time for the close-up. Then bring on the tears. We are pent-up wineskins of emotion spurting forth when the time is right.

Now, to be fair, I wasn't the most popular woman here before I got engaged. Apparently I have too many opinions for popularity.

"Ashley, what are you doing here?" *Not your typical church welcome.* Pastor Max has always relied more on his charm than communication skills. He's extremely good looking, still convinced that his high school quarterback position makes him a lifetime leader, and he's married to a head cheerleader type who doesn't question his many boasts or authority. She just gazes admiringly at him while he entrances others. In his defense, he has about one-tenth the education of most people here in Silicon Valley, so being cool is his upper hand. His power over the geeks is still going strong. Pastors have a thankless job in Silicon Valley, where the average admin makes more than they do and actually has some respect. *Church? God? How could you be so unenlightened?*

"I'm not married yet, Pastor Max. Kevin's out of town, so I thought I'd see how the singles group was faring without me." *Like I'm such a big loss.* "Good to see nothing's changed. I've been coming to church but haven't made the time to get back to group. Did you miss me?"

"Well, it's been relatively quiet here. No call for thank-you notes," he says, in reference to my one outburst for Kay, who wasn't appreciated at Thanksgiving. I just asked the group to do the decent thing and send thank-you notes. They complied, but I think I got a feminist reputation. "Isn't Kay here with you?" He looks around me, hoping to find my roommate, who softens my edges, behind me.

"She went to see her mother last night and left a message that she was staying over."

I've never fit in with this group, which is probably not a bad thing. I've always been on the lunatic fringe. Now, as I scan the room, I wonder if anyone truly fits in. This is a fairly antisocial group. Not because they're Christians, but mostly because Silicon Valley is an anti-social place. Heaven forbid you make a connection with some-one in person, rather than text-messaging or e-mailing. Face-to-face conversation is known around these parts as *intimacy*, and it's a thing to be feared. I remember back on the prayer times within the group, careful little slices of true emotions offered up as a small sacrifice, so as not to embarrass ourselves, or worse yet, be transparent.

I don't feel smug because I'm getting married and they're not. They don't want to get married. More importantly, they don't want to change anything for anyone. Their lives are completely in control. Not fun, but within their limitations. I feel sorry for them that they don't know the joy of living without trepidation and careful planning. It's such an awakening when you realize you can't control life. I won-der if some of them will ever come to it. I wonder if Kay will realize it before she owns every piece that Organized Living sells.

Besides, making a fool of oneself is half the fun of life. Getting arrested in a wedding dress is probably too ambitious for most, but I just wish they could know true enjoyment. Maybe that's my calling. To show joy to the severe. *I'm going to try it.*

There's a Christian song we sing about whether your limbs truly dance free in your joy. I wonder if taking that to heart would make a difference. I look toward the pastor as he shuffles his papers on the music stand.

"You know that song, Pastor Max, about your limbs truly dancing free?"

"Yes, Ashley. The one Kevin Marks wrote. He's a member of the Highway Community now. Are you going to sing it for us?" he asks with trepidation.

"No, I was hoping we might sing that today. You know," I say with a little swaying movement, "part of praise and worship."

"Thank you for the suggestion." *Now go away,* I'd swear he added silently. "Ahem." He calls the class to order with his fake cough. "Let me start with announcements. Kay is not here this morning, but she's planned a wonderful summer potluck and game day at Rinconada Park."

Potluck. Okay, that would assume someone besides Kay would be bringing something to eat, and that's beyond optimistic.

"Kay's left a sign-up sheet." I see him lift the clipboard. *Ack! The clipboard lives. I thought I got rid of it once and for all! She's hiding it from me to get her organizational fix!* "Please feel free to pass it around." *So you can all get a clear view of its empty lines that Kay will have to fill.*

"Let's have our time of worship. Ashley Stockingdale has requested we sing an old favorite." He grabs his guitar, truly a man for all seasons, and starts to pluck the familiar cords.

The slow dirge begins.

"Joy, people!" I shout with a few claps, and I start to sing with vigor. There are a few people helping me, bless their hearts, but the song is quickly becoming a solo, which was not in my plans. But I'm game. I got the decent voice instead of Jennifer Garner's body.

"Child, dance with me . . . You are my soul's delight.

Here there is no more pain . . . There is no more night.

You know I died for you, but do your limbs truly dance free?"

Like a bad music video, I feel my body move to the rhythm. I'm skipping through the pathway of the room, and some are clapping with me, but some have just assumed I've ingested too much caffeine. Is emotionless praise, praise? Maybe it is in Silicon Valley. I'm not certain. I raise my arms to the ceiling, feeling His presence with my whole being.

"Set aside your fears, they have no place with Me."

The room is spinning. No, wait, that's me. To my shock, Pastor Max stops the song, and the entire room is looking at me. Solo is one thing. A cappella, hey, everyone has their limits.

"Do your limbs truly dance free?" I ask meekly, without the assistance of music. *Okay. Clearly not. Am I hearing crickets?*

"Ahem." Pastor Max clears that persistent frog again. "Ashley is very enthusiastic now that she's getting married. And why wouldn't she be?"

I think I'm offended.

Uncomfortable rumble of laughter here, but Jake, one of the older singles, comes beside me and puts an arm around me.

"I know we don't understand Ashley's method, perhaps," Max says, "but we certainly admire her enthusiasm. And perhaps God does too."

Crickets again.

"You know what they say about the prophet in his hometown." I walk toward the door. "I'm sorry if I offended. Jake, thanks."

This singles group makes me crazy. They're more concerned with their own comfort level than other people going to hell. Well, I wish them the best, but I think it's time I moved on.

"As for me and my house, we will serve the Lord," I mumble as I walk out the door.

I think there's applause as I leave the room. Good thing I'm not taking it personally.

Add "Find new church" to my list.

"Ashley?" Kay is walking up the hallway toward me. "What are you doing in the singles room?"

"I'm not married yet." I let my eyes pierce hers. "Don't think I didn't see the clipboard."

She blows her bangs toward the heavens. "Why are you leaving early?"

"You know, I came around to say my good-byes." I nod my head. "I said them. Sang a little. My work is done here."

She focuses a narrowed gaze at me. "What did you do?"

"Nothing. I sang a song." I shrug. "A solo. Said good-bye, that's all."

"Ashley, I know you better. You even look guilty."

"You had some visitors yesterday. Happy birthday, by the way!" I say to avoid the subject at hand. Special lawyer trick.

"Thanks. Are they going to be talking about you when I walk in?"

"How would I know? I mean, maybe, if they didn't like my singing. The arts are so subjective, you know? What is one person's Shakespeare is another's dark and stormy night."

Kay purses her lips. "Who came to see me?"

"Who didn't is a better question. There was a visit from Santa and Mrs. Claus. Oh, and Matt Callaway."

"Excuse me?"

"Simon and his wife came by to see you. They really seemed desperate to talk with you."

"Did you say Matt came to see me?"

I think Kay actually blushed. Is that possible? When she said Matt's name, she softened like warm butter. But must I remind her, Matt isn't a believer? I don't even think he's officially available, but I could be wrong. And our feelings aren't our actions, right? Right.

"He wanted to take you out for your birthday and didn't want to take the chance on just calling."

She's stifling a giggle. *Kay Harding is stifling a giggle.* That's not on her clipboard, and I'm baffled. She's smarter than this, and while Matt is handsome, he's also smarmy. He went out with her, then dumped her. Why does this not register when she's holding an apparent grudge from 1977 or thereabouts?

Kay straightens her mouth. "I'll have to check my appointment book, but a birthday dinner sounds agreeable."

"After what he did to you with Emily?" I say with outrage.

Kay clicks her tongue. "Ashley, don't be ridiculous. He wanted to feel masculine again, and she is a ridiculous creature. I'm sure her girl-ishness appealed to him. It appeals to most men before they realize what it is they want."

"And when the next girl comes along? And I do mean *girl*."

"Ashley, I do wish you'd try to be more tolerant of others. Some-times you can be so judgmental. You don't even know Matt."

"I know enough. The Bible says not to be caught up with the unbeliever, unequally yoked, and all that. Forget all that, that's too spiritual for this situation. Let's just focus on the fact that he's a dog. Is that good enough for you?"

"I'm not in need of a sermon, Ashley."

"Sorry. I didn't mean to preach."

"What did Matt say when he came by?" she asks while practi-cally salivating for the answer.

"That he wanted to take you out to dinner." *Did we miss that?*

"Did he look like he meant a date-date, or a friendship date?"

"You're asking me?"

"You read people well, Ashley. You seemed to understand that dress would work for me that night."

I give up. "It seemed like a date-date," I answer reluctantly. "Are you coming home after church? I have your gift put up high so that Rhett won't destroy it, and I'm looking forward to giving it to you."

"You bought me a present?" Kay gushes.

"Of course I did. You're my roommate and one of my closest friends, are you not?"

"My mom didn't even buy me a present." Kay has a tear in her eye, but of course, she doesn't wear mascara, so no worries on the makeup front. "Did Simon say he'd be back?"

"I told them you didn't want to see them. I hope he listened. He seemed like a reasonable person."

"I thought so too, once. I know better now."

"What's the worst they could do to you now? Apologize?"

"You don't understand, Ashley. I don't expect you to, and be happy that you aren't ever going to be in that situation. That's all I'll say about the matter. I just hate to be a hostage in my own home."

"Seems to me it's better to just get it over with."

"Why don't you come back to singles with me?"

I start to giggle and shake my head. "Trust me on this one." I lift my arms up and start to skip down the hallway, *"Child, dance with me. You are my soul's delight. Here there is no more pain. There is no more night."*

I hear the exasperated gasps and smile as I continue my rendition. Why did it take my getting engaged to wake up that group? *Hello?* I clearly missed that obvious-path gene. God was leading me out a long time ago. Like Moses in the desert, I just chose to walk around in a circle.

22

Patent work is like living in a pressure cooker. (Not that I've ever used a pressure cooker—I remember my mother's ominous warnings, and I don't think steaming artichokes warrants a risk to personal safety.) In the high-tech patent arena, everything is treated like it's of international spy importance. Maybe it's the way engineers liken themselves to 007. I don't know, but after a few years of the same game, it starts to feel hilarious. Like you're whispering, *Trust no one.*

It's as if we're all rushing around trying to stop the world from blowing up, when we're really just creating a new software patent to make some gadget boy's life easier. The worst that could happen is that someone else could get our process and make our money. Which will happen when we ship it to China to be built anyway, and send our stock price diving. But we act like the H-bomb looms with every new patent opportunity. Rather than admit to one another how stupid we look, we all play our parts.

I've finished Seth's patent, and it's in the pipeline, which should be enough for him, should it not? Must I actually have contact with him? He greets me at the door of Gainnet, and I'm half-expecting him to adjust a CIA earpiece.

"How long until we know something?" he whispers desperately. "About the patent," he clarifies as though I'm slow.

"I know *something* right now. The Half-Yearly Sale at Nordstrom is coming up," I say quietly. "Oh, and *I* stole the cookie from the cookie jar."

He gets that confused engineer look. "Ashley, do you realize how often you make absolutely no sense?"

"No secret code, Seth; it was just a joke. For you engineers, that's a process of comical importance that produces laughter."

He's looking at me like I'm slow again.

"The examiner's office will get back to us when *they* know something. Don't hold your breath, Seth. Just know I've checked every process related to ours, and you're safe to manufacture the product. You were right. It's an unknown process. Feel better?"

"Do I have your assurance?" he asks, like a soap doctor saying, "Has she awakened from her coma?"

"You do have my assurance," I say with a salute.

"I heard you visited the singles group yesterday."

"Yes, I did." Word travels fast, does it not?

"You danced." Poor Seth, he will forever be tainted for dating the off-color Ashley.

"I did, just like King David. Are you going to give me the Queen Michal speech about being undignified?" I cross my arms, and he just blinks. *I guess he* was *going to give me that speech.* Don't you just hate it when someone sucks the wind from your sails? Tee-hee.

"Now I'm going to dance to my office and see what Purvi has up her sleeve today. Nice to see you, Seth!" I hum all the way to my desk, drawing the attention of many yet the surprise of none. *It's great to be weird, isn't it?* People don't even bat an eye anymore.

As I get to my office, I see there are boxes lining the wall. Tracy has a look of abject terror, and she's flitting about like a hyper hummingbird. The phone is ringing, but she doesn't answer it.

"What's going on?"

She just shakes her head and walks away, still ignoring the phones. I pick one up: "Gainnet, General Counsel's office."

"I need Purvi. Get her in here pronto." I assume this is the CEO by his obvious rudeness.

"I'm not sure she's in the office, but I'll get the message to her right away." I slam down the phone, not allowing for orders that I can't fill anyway. I'm a lawyer, not an admin or a secretary. You want decent phone help? Avoid voice-mail systems doing the bulk of your customer service.

I look into Purvi's office, and the cardboard boxes are in even greater supply. Purvi is once again wearing her Indian salwar and buzzing about her office, riffling through paper like it's parade confetti. This is nothing like Purvi, who usually just reverts to a little vocal exercise (yelling at me) when she needs to accomplish more.

"What are you doing?" I ask her.

"I'm packing. I'm going back to India." She slams a book on her desk. "Where did I put that file?"

"Shut up. What are you really doing?"

She looks up, obviously wondering if I just said what she thinks I did. "My husband is ready for us to go back. I'm getting as much done as possible, and I'm going to be interviewing and training your new boss before I leave. But you may have an extra load for a time. I'm sorry about that." She pulls her hair away from her face with both hands. "Right before your wedding too. I'm sorry, Ashley."

"An extra load? Purvi, I won't be here. Remember my honeymoon? You can't go anywhere. You just came on. I'm terrible at your job, remember? That's the reason they hired you."

"Ashley, what can I tell you? I'm leaving. You'll figure it out. You're much brighter than you give yourself credit for. Under that power-shopping facade, there's a brain. Put it to good use."

"You can't leave. If I did your job well, you wouldn't be here. I'm a grunt patent attorney. They know better than to have me do management's job."

"It will only be for a short time. You are not bad at it. You're just too social and don't like what the hours entail. If you spent more time in the office and less time in your convertible on the way to shopping sprees and stress-relieving spa treatments, you'd be fine."

She has a point.

"Do you *want* to go back?" I can't help it. I feel abandoned. Everyone I care about seems to flee to India. Which I guess makes sense, as India is definitely an Ashley-free zone. Taiwan, on the other hand . . . but I digress. Purvi is the only boss I've ever loved, even through the yelling. "Stop kidding me, Purvi. I'll stop with the wedding plans. You've made your point."

"Ashley, this isn't a joke. I'm leaving."

"You can't leave, Purvi. You thrive on Silicon Valley's pace. What will you possibly do in India?"

Purvi settles down into her chair. "I'm going to tell you something. You're not going to like it, but someday you'll say to yourself, *Purvi was right all along.* On that day, Ashley, you will appreciate me."

"I doubt that, not if you're still leaving me. I tend to hold grudges."

"Marriage is not about a perpetual reign as princess. Marriage is about sacrifice. Sometimes it's your turn. Sometimes it's his turn. But you know what? It's always someone's turn. What unites you is that you don't ever want it to be your *child's* turn. So you go back and forth through life, taking turns. Or you end up in divorce court, and everybody loses."

I ask her about India, and the marriage sermon is from where? I've never known Purvi to talk on such a personal level. I know it's bothering her, but she'll probably never admit it. She's a martyr through and through. When Seth asked me to go to India, I think I considered it for two seconds. What if we had been married? That leave-and-cleave business the Bible talks about definitely would have gotten in my way.

"So are you mad you're leaving? Sad? What?" I ask.

"Life is not all about feelings. Americans think everything should be determined by how they *feel.* The rest of the world doesn't have that luxury. I'm open to what lies ahead. It's my turn. Sagar's been paying the price for two years now without his family. A boy needs his father, and it's time we went back. We want Pushpan educated in India before he forgets his culture." She goes about filing papers, ignoring me but still speaking. "It's all about compromise."

Whose? My own dilemma rises before me like a ghost. "So if Sagar wanted you to go to Philadelphia because he had a great job offer, would you go? Knowing you couldn't work there with your degrees, and you might be watching *Jerry Springer* all day long?"

Her hands still, and Purvi looks me in the eye. "If it were the right decision for our family, as India is the right decision for us now, you can be sure I would go to Philadelphia. However, I can assure you I would not waste my time with *Jerry Springer*. That's an American misfortune."

This causes me pause. Not *Jerry Springer*, but her willingness to go. How can someone just give of themselves so completely and not question God's will for her life? Where does it end? She's already given up sleep and tons of free time. Now what? "Will you even be able to work there, Purvi?"

"I will not work for some time. Other than helping my husband with his business. I shall like the break."

Break? Purvi wouldn't know how to have a break if it came in the form of a shattered femur.

"You can't be serious. You love this job, Purvi. I don't believe you're just going to abandon us." I cross my arms.

"You don't have a family, Ashley. You don't understand."

"What does a family have to do with abandoning your dreams?"

She laughs. "It has everything to do with it. There will be time for my dreams, Ashley. But I'll never get another chance to raise my son in India, as his father wishes. You have to live with your choices, and this is one I wouldn't get back. Pushpan's childhood."

"What if it's the wrong choice?"

"Then I make the best of it, Ashley."

"Let me know if there's anything I can do, Purvi." I walk back to my office with my head hung low. Tracy is still buzzing about, and there's a mourning look that passes between us. It's official. I am a jinx. Just when I think my life is completely in order, I watch everyone around me fall apart or exit the building. Let's look at the evidence:

EVIDENCE THAT PROVES I AM A JINX

1. Cool-hearted Kay afraid to talk to Santa Claus.
2. Feminist-minded Kay willing to date sorry-doof who is Emily's reject.
3. Purvi packing to go back to a foreign country for a husband I've still never seen any evidence of.
4. Seth, now *not* afraid of me yet still just as annoying.
5. Future SIL hijacking my wedding while I sit by idly.
6. Fiancé off interviewing in a town I've never visited. Heck, a *state* I've never visited.
7. My dream wedding turning into a battle tantamount to the Civil War.
8. My first wedding shower becoming a perverted peep show.

All these things only have one common denominator: Ashley Wilkes Stockingdale. I'm like a human Swiffer, picking up all the dust and junk accumulating in the world and wearing it proudly. I most definitely need to shop. I'm craving an Origins, with all its natural oils and scrubs. *When I get home, I'll exfoliate all my troubles away—with a soothing, scented candle,* I muse as I stare, unblinking, at the piles on my desk.

"Ashley." Tracy sticks her head in my office. "Heather at the bridal shop is on the phone."

"You mean Hannah?"

Tracy whacks her head. "Yeah, that's it."

I pick up the line, certain that there's something else to add to my "sky is falling" list. "Ashley Stockingdale, Disaster Attractor."

"Oh, Ashley, that's funny. It's Hannah. Hey, I have a wedding gown here for you."

"I'm not wearing Scarlett O'Hara's gown, Hannah. Being arrested in it was quite enough wear for me."

"Yeah, I'm sorry about that. I forgot about the alarm. Listen, it's not that dress. It's the Vera Wang gown. The order we canceled. I don't know where it came from, but it's here with your name on it."

Suddenly, the sun has appeared from behind some very dark clouds. "The dress I ordered is there?"

"Paid for and straight from Vera Wang's studios. There's no card or explanation, just the gown."

Now if I were Nancy Drew, I'd go looking for the sender. But I never did have much interest in mysteries. I always wondered about the girls who went inside those dark places, looking for clues. *Hello? Just shut the door and walk away. There's good shopping to be had up the street.*

Vera Wang shantung silk . . . I just don't see the need for questions at this point. Suddenly, my mood has drastically improved.

23

Obviously, work ran late today. The boxes piled in the hallway told me that much before I started anything. Although Purvi's departure is still a week away, I can already feel work ramping up. The invisible rubber band pulling me back, stretching to full capacity, before it snaps and I fly uncontrollably into the seat of Purvi's job.

On a happier note, I worked late enough to realize the bridal shop was closed. Wait, here's the learning-curve part that puts me in the top of the bell. I understood that this rule applied to me as well as the rest of the consuming public. So I only drove by and peeked in the window for a glimpse before heading home, gownless for now, but understanding there is silk at the end of the tunnel. Vera Wang and I will be together at last.

As I walk into the house, Kay is preparing for the month of July and bringing out the summer festives. We've got silk flowers, picnic tables in ceramic, and don't forget the sunflower salt 'n' pepper shakers. Then there's all the flag memorabilia that makes us look like we're preparing for a national political convetion. Rhett is following her around whimpering, hoping to get his teeth around the silk dahlia stalks.

"Hi," Kay says to me as she arranges the silk flowers. "Don't put your briefcase there." She points at the basket where I'm usually allowed to place a small remnant of proof that I actually exist. "I've reworked the landing spot. We'll be putting our things for the door-way in this new cabinet." She comes over and opens it like one of Bob's Beauties on *The Price Is Right*. "Ashley's side," she says with a flourish of the hand. "Kay's side."

"I think you should be looking for another loan rather than another roommate," I suggest. "Are you thinking someone is going to want to buy half this house, and they're going to understand the *landing spot process*? Or the steak knife sharpener versus the cooking knife sharpener? I don't think you give me nearly enough credit for putting up with you."

"Me? Living organized is what most people in Silicon Valley do, Ashley. We're grown-ups. You're the anomaly here."

"I refuse to believe I'm the weirdo. I do not spend time buttoning my shirts on the hanger so the hanger will feel good about itself, you know?"

"I think if someone came in and saw the way I live versus that pigsty you call a closet, we'd have little questions as to who has the issues."

"Oh no, they'd see your Michelin Man down jacket, and I am home-free. That thing should have been thrown out in 1979, all the while apologizing profusely to the ducks. You need another example? I have shoes for all occasions, which means you can invite me to dinner and I'll wear proper attire. You have shoes for different outdoor functions. Period. And we don't live in Seattle, Kay. We barely have rain, but you've got a super hiking boot for any type of Gore-Tex moment. And running shoes that are grass green? Your combined *vintage* clothing is probably worth seventy-five cents on eBay."

"What about the Adam Ant CDs?" Kay lifts an eyebrow and shoots back, "Don't think I haven't heard you dancing in your room like a bad, early MTV video."

Okay, she's got me there. I definitely don't want to own up to the '80s fetish. But girls just wanna have fun. Am I right? Then it dawns on me, and I point at her. "Ambrosia albums. I've heard you croon 'You're the Biggest Part of Me' more times than I can count on one hand."

"At least it's from my era, and I didn't have to steal someone else's. Adam Ant?"

"It was just a few years before my era, okay? So I was mature. Shoot me."

"You're not mature for anyone's era, Ashley."

"Jimmy Buffet!" I strike again. Rhett starts to bark.

"You're upsetting the dog," Kay accuses.

"He just thought we were going to have to hear 'Margaritaville' again, and Rhett knows when to protect us, don'tcha, baby?" I say, patting his head.

"Is there a reason you're in such an interesting mood?"

"Yes, actually. Purvi quit today. I'll be taking over her job in a week, and right now I'm not fit to take over Rhett's job. But my gown is here. My real and true Vera Wang gown. So I'm up and down, like a roller coaster, really. It depends on the moment."

"Need I remind you that you already did Purvi's job once? Badly."

"Oh, and my in-laws are coming into town in a few days to finalize heaven knows what on the wedding."

"Well, Kevin will handle them, right? You just have to worry about Purvi."

"Wrong. Kevin is in Philadelphia on a job interview."

Kay shakes her head and sticks the last silk flower into the Styrofoam. "You must wear a Kick Me sign. Is it true, by the way, that you danced in the singles group before I got there?"

"Can someone please tell me why that's so scandalous? I danced. I didn't strip, for crying out loud. *Y'all* need to lighten up, as my crazed sister-in-law would say."

"It's because the singles group has always run a certain way, and you're always trying to pull everyone out of their comfort zone. They like that zone, Ashley. Can't you respect that? We respect that you dance to the beat of a different drummer."

"No, I guess I can't. They're like a bad happy hour without the booze. Eating and sitting."

"You're judgmental."

"Maybe I am, but I'm not saying anything that the rest of the world isn't thinking. Since when did church become about sitting on your duff waiting for the next cool experience to come along?"

"Ashley, you're hardly the great church historian, you know? Your systematic theology is lacking here. Just give it a rest."

"What's this?" I pick up a vellum envelope from the new entry table.

"It's an invitation to your shower. A real wedding shower, no lingerie deal."

"Where'd it come from?"

"Brea talked to your aunts. It's all set. You'll be a bride with actual kitchen goods. Though you'd probably get more use out of the lingerie with your culinary skills."

"You're so not helping here!"

"I'm just saying." Kay lifts her hands in innocent form.

"Didn't your mom ever tell you if you didn't have something nice to say . . ."

"My mom told me to take 'protection' on my dates, so no, she forgot that one about saying nice things. She was more concerned I didn't make her a grandmother early on. Not because she saw dishonor in my being a single mother, but because it made her old before her time."

"Speaking of your mom, did you call that guy Simon back?"

"I told you. I have nothing to say to him," Kay snaps.

"I thought, at first, maybe the woman was your daughter, but when I saw her, I knew she had to be his wife. Did you have an affair with him?"

"Ashley! You have a filthy mind."

"What? You're saying it's this deep, dark secret. I assume it's ugly, or it wouldn't be such a big deal. I watched *90210;* I'm not completely naive."

She stills her hands and sits down. "You thought I had a daughter? Out of wedlock?"

"It crossed my mind," I admit. "I mean, the guy seemed so nice. I have to say I couldn't imagine it after I met him, but you were so freaked out about it. And him going on television frightened the heck out of you. So what else could it be? Had to be something ugly, so I let my mind take a little walk through the possibilities."

Kay's mouth is still dangling. Apparently I've really shocked her. But am I alone here? I doubt it. The world thinks the worst. We've lived through a decade of *Friends*, after all, where friends sleep with each other's boyfriends, and everyone's all hunky-dory with it. *Yeah, that can happen.*

"It's nothing like that! Did you tell anyone what you thought?"

"Of course not. I just prayed you'd work it out with him and get over it. You might as well tell me. I can watch it on television if I want."

She stares at me for a long time, and I think it's about to come out. But no, Kay silences herself and plops a ceramic hot dog on the foyer shelf. People are so strange about their sins. I mean, let it go, you know. It's not like whatever happened is a way of life for her. She's confessed it. She's moved on . . . Well, maybe she hasn't, but she should.

"I'm taking Rhett for a walk. You know, it might be something more sinister than I'm thinking. What if you murdered his first wife and buried her under the house?" I wink at her while I grab Rhett's leash. "Or what if you were once a nurse and checked his wife into an institution, then overmedicated her with laudanum?"

"Ashley!"

See? By the time I get through with her, Kay will forgive herself for whatever horrendous thing she did at fourteen. Sheesh, talk about a leash. More like a ball and chain. It was thirty years ago. I hadn't even put skirts on my head and belted out Donna Summer songs in the mirror yet. Could anything possibly be worse than that?

24

Today's the day my in-laws arrive. *Future in-laws.* My Scarlett wedding gown is in the closet. It's next to the gown that I'm actually wearing, but I think none of this needs to be mentioned. If Emily's deluded enough to think I'm dressing like a nineteenth-century belle, that's her issue, ya know? I focus on the road and Kevin's old-man mobile, the Dodge. Why he suddenly has to get a conscience and drive a sedan is beyond me, but maybe I'll mature one day too. Stranger things have happened. I can pick up Emily and Elaine Novak at the airport without borrowing my mother's Buick, so life is good. Except that I'm lamenting his really garbage stereo system. David Crowder sounds tinny, and that just ain't right. To me, it's almost blasphemous.

The airport is packed, as it usually is, and I know I have to schlep to baggage claim, since meeting your future mother-in-law at the curb isn't exactly proper manners. Even in California. And we've taken casual to a new level. I believe most states still call it rudeness.

When I arrive, Mrs. Novak and Emily are sitting on two designer bags. I'll admit, I was expecting a trunk or two. (You know that scene in *Titanic* on the English docks?) Mrs. Novak is truly a beautiful woman with bobbed blonde hair and big blue eyes. Her skin is nearly flawless, without any lines or years of anguish apparent.

In contrast, my mother looks like a mother: gray hair she doesn't dye, gentle lines around her eyes and mouth from laughing, and naturally, that wrinkle line in the forehead (from my brother, Dave, of course.) Kevin's mother looks like an aged beauty queen grown up—like the Grandma Barbie. She and Emily look so much alike, but the tension between them is obvious. This is not a love match.

"Ashley, dear." Mrs. Novak comes forward, looking as though she's going to give me a hug, but she stops short. "Slacks? We're having our sample meal today, aren't we, Emily?" She looks toward her daughter. I'm thinking, *What exactly would they have me do now that I'm in slacks, which she finds ill-appropriate? Am I supposed to run home and change to please her? Or smack her with the facts: I could show up in jeans and not a waiter would bat his eye.*

"We're scheduled for noon, so we should get movin'." Emily looks at her watch and pulls her suitcase behind her. I go for Mrs. Novak's bag, and she doesn't make a move to stop me, so I roll it and lead them to the car. Elaine shakes her head at the sight of Kevin's vehicle. Apparently she hasn't gotten over the fact that he's gone domestic. *Ick, something we agree on.*

"How was your flight?" I ask, ignoring the slacks conversation. I mean, Shelli Segal, ladies! Have some respect! I could have worn the low-rise jean, thong-sticking-out style. So I'd say they should count their blessings. Not really, but sheesh! This is the twenty-first century. Dresses are optional last time I checked. Same with corsets.

"The flight was fine for commercial. Now, Ashley, dear, Emily has spoken to me about the *Gone with the Wind* theme, and I must say, it seems . . . well, it seems a little hokey, darling. I know many of you Yankees have elaborate images of our Southern lifestyle, but a Scarlett gown seems over the top, if you don't mind my saying so." Elaine is not getting into the car but is looking me straight in the eye. "I just want to save you unnecessary embarrassment. And, dear, Vivien Leigh was a very small woman." She glances at my waist and raises her eyebrows, which causes the most peculiar movement of her face. I stare, fascinated, for a moment. I can't help it. It's like her entire face is attached to her eyebrows, and she can't move one section at a time. "I'll support you, if that's what you truly want. But I don't think it is." *Translation: If you want to make a complete idiot of yourself, that's your business. But you will not involve my family, you petty, white-trash vermin.*

My eyes are like quarters, and I have to remind myself to blink. Looking at Emily, I can see that she has, indeed, led her mother to believe I am to blame for the Confederate theme. Judging by Emily's lack of ability to look at me, I'd say Mrs. Novak is also inclined to believe she'll be expected to wear a hoop skirt. But here's the thing: Emily is terrified. Her hands are actually shaking. I look back at Mrs. Novak, and she's gaily chattering on like I am gathering her words of wisdom for the pearls they are.

The car is suddenly feeling very small. I can't corner Emily in front of her mother, though quite frankly, I'm very tempted. I mean, how many times am I supposed to hear that I'd look like a cow in Scarlett's dress?

"The luncheon is in Palo Alto, Ashley. Will we make it on time?" Emily asks.

"We've got plenty of time, Emily. Why don't you tell your mother about all my Southern wedding plans while we're driving?" Now that wasn't nice.

"How is it you're off work today, Ashley?" Emily asks, ignoring me.

"How is it I have a job at all?" would be a better question. "I'm going in late after we're finished, and I started at five this morning."

"I never will understand people working themselves to the bone. With my husband, it was one thing. He was saving lives, but women should know their places, Ashley. You should be taking accounting lessons and learning how to manage a household."

I start to giggle. "I can't even manage my closet!" *Okay, wrong thing to say.*

Mental note: Allow Mrs. Novak's domestic dreams for me to give her comfort. Like a strong cup of Earl Grey for her tender palate. Hide the double-espresso power for now.

Mrs. Novak is still rambling, and I pick up her conversation midstream. "There is plenty of time for more worldly efforts when your children are raised. Golf, travel—"

"The pursuit of the perfect Michael Kors bag," I add.

"You have a hearty sense of humor, my dear. I'm sure that's one of the things Kevin finds attractive about you, but coming home to a messy house will not bring him laughter in the future. A wife should take pride in her home."

"I work; therefore, I hire out." *Again. Not the point to insert humor. I'm a slow learner.* "I didn't take you for the housewife type, Mrs. Novak." This blissful domesticity thing throws me. After all, the golf course and scrubbing toilets do not mesh for me.

"A home manager is not a housewife, Ashley. She is someone who manages the business of home and the social calendar so that her husband can be more successful at his profession. That makes you a team, and it bonds a marriage, besides making you a sought-after guest at all Junior League functions."

I'm sure this is true on some level, but I am *so* not going to be vacuuming in my pearls, okay? Kevin's house is covered in models: airplane models, boat models, space models. I'm thinking home organization for him would be about carefully dusting and arranging his hobby, maybe? Or perhaps she means I should add the ceiling fan with a propeller for his personal enjoyment. Not sure if I should clarify. Oh, why not?

"Emily, did you approve of the cake design we made?" I ask, thinking if she says one thing negative, her cover on the Southern thing is over!

"It was a lovely choice, Ashley."

"What type of cake did you order? And a groom's cake? There will be one, true?"

"Mother, we're Southern. Of course I took care of it. No groom's cake? I declare. Ashley just picked the style. We'll be tryin' samples of the different cakes today."

I have been with these women for five minutes, and I am completely exhausted. No one says what they actually mean. Everything is like a big matrix waiting to trap you in its lair if the wrong words escape. I see why these people need Mensa. It's to translate what they're actually saying to one another.

My phone trills, and yeah, I'm thankful for it. "Hello, Ashley Stockingdale."

"Hey, baby, did you show my mom the earrings? Let's skip this wedding and go straight for the honeymoon. What do you say?"

"Yes, your mother is right here, and so is your sister. Their flight was right on time."

"Did you ask them to put all their efforts into the honeymoon suite? Sprinkle some rose petals, and get out." Kevin growls.

"Yes, you shouldn't worry. We've got the groom's cake all taken care of. I know how important that is to you."

"Isn't he sweet to worry about that?" Mrs. Novak says to Emily.

"Are you going to pop out of this groom's cake?"

"Kevin!"

He starts to laugh. "I'm sorry. I just thought since you are spending quality time with the Novak family, why couldn't I play too? I mean, letting you have all the fun is hardly fair."

"How's Philadelphia?"

"I haven't seen much of it, actually. The hospital is nice."

"But does their cafeteria serve espresso? Is there a even a Starbucks nearby?"

"My parents said they'd buy us a place here instead. They were actually happy, because real estate is cheaper. My dad said it was a solid, growing real-estate market."

"No, thank you," I say politely through my teeth. What I want to say, of course, is *If you let your parents lay down one cent for our home, I will crush you like an aluminum can after a picnic.* But I think

I'm Southern after all, or at least on my way to becoming a Novak? Scary thought. Maybe I should keep my name. "I'd rather discuss that in person after we talk about the job."

"She says, 'Before seeing what we can actually afford on our own.'"

"We're a doctor and a lawyer."

"Correction: a resident, and if you join me here, an un-employed California lawyer in Pennsylvania jurisdiction. That trans-lates into a bad, one-bedroom apartment in the hood with a filthy bathroom that I will force you to scrub for denying me my parents' money. Scrubbing bubbles, Ash. I've endured a lot for this down payment, baby, and you're going to get a taste of it today. Take the money and run."

"Are you just trying to depress me?"

"There's way fewer golf courses here, so my parents would have less reason to visit."

He's throwing me a bone. A very small bone. "Is there a Junior League?"

"You know, I bet there is!" Kevin says, overly enthusiastic. "And if you choose what's behind box number three, there's probably a debutante ball for our future daughter too." He laughs. "If I find you a home within walking distance of a Starbucks, are you willing to talk about this? I'm sure there'll be a real roasting company too."

When he says 'talk,' my stomach just does a double axel. I am the luckiest woman in the world, and I know it. And something about making sacrifices in marriage comes back to haunt me. Now where did I hear that? "We'll talk," I agree. *Sheesh, take me by the hair back to your cave.*

"I gotta run. The chief of surgery is back. Grin and bear it with my Novak homies. If you get tripped up, remember, yes, you are the normal one. I'm praying."

"Okay."

"Oh, and Ashley?"

"Yeah."

"I love you with a passion I can't begin to describe." Click.

How does he do that? He makes his mother worth it, does he not?

"I'll have to speak with my son about calling on cell phones in the midst of other important conversations," Mrs. Novak says. For a brief moment, I hear Mother screech at Norman Bates, but I'm back now.

"We're here," I say without inflection. Elaine Novak gracefully exits the car, ankles together like Lady Di. I'm expecting the princess wave for the doorman.

"I'll just run in and powder my nose." Mrs. Novak enters the elegant lobby and disappears, and Emily exhales.

"Thank you for not tellin' her." She places a palm on the wall to steady herself.

"Why did you have that dress made? You knew no one would approve. Least of all me, and since it gives *y'all* countless opportunities to describe me as gargantuan, I'm beginning to think you take pleasure in tearing me down."

Emily stares at the ladies' room door. "I wanted my parents to be the laughingstock of Atlanta. I knew Kevin wouldn't mind, his friends would think it hilarious, and I thought you loved all things *Gone with the Wind*, so I thought I'd get away with it. I didn't know you were going to get into this Vera Wang thing."

Remember that poem: "If a child lives with hostility, they learn to fight"?

Granted, I'd change it to "They learn to exhibit passive-aggressive behaviors rather than fight," but DSM-IV criteria doesn't really lend itself to poetry.

"You would have ruined my wedding to get back at your mother?" I'm a little incredulous. "*Revenge is mine*, sayeth the Lord, and all that."

"It would have been nice, Ashley. Just not my mother's version of nice."

It's at this moment that I notice that Emily is wearing pants. Her mother's diss to my slacks was most likely aimed at Emily too.

"The ruffles? The ruffles aren't anyone's idea of nice, Emily. I'm telling you right now, if you do anything more to thwart this wedding or tell me how I'm fat or dumb or not a Southerner, I will tell your mother this was all your doing, and Kevin will back me up. Got it?"

"Maybe I went a little overboard. I watched *Gone with the Wind* again and got that idea. With the parasols. I thought it might be a little soap-operish, but over the top doesn't usually seem to bothah you. You have a flair for the dramatic."

I point at her chest. "You are banned from watching that movie, do you understand me? Or you'll be eating barbecue at Twelve Oaks on the day of my wedding."

Emily nods. "My brothah already talked to me about it. No *Gone with the Wind.* I understand."

Mrs. Novak opens the ladies' room door. "Emily, you didn't tell them we were here yet?"

"We were talking, Mrs. Novak. I'll let them know," I say.

"We have an appointment. Novaks keep their appointments."

"*Most* people keep their appointments, Elaine. We're just a few minutes late. They'll understand." *Chill.*

I see her lips press together at my utter defiance. But dang, she is a piece of work.

"Emily, announce us." Mrs. Novak tugs at her suit jacket. Once again, it's a St. John knit. I have never seen her in anything else. Variety is apparently not the spice of the country club life.

Emily scampers off to find the catering manager, and I'm just stunned by Mrs. Novak's sharp tones and her icy gaze toward her daughter.

"Emily has done a wonderful job with the wedding. She's left no stone unturned. Even helped find my wedding gown."

"It's time she did something. She's twenty-five years old, un-married, underemployed, and pretending to be in the wedding business for someone inept at doing for herself." Elaine catches her-self. "No offense, dear."

If my jaw dropped down any farther, I would drool on myself. "I'm not inept, Elaine, just busy, actually."

"It's clear you were raised to do for yourself. She was raised to do for other people, Ashley, and though she tries, it's painful at times."

Painful like this conversation, maybe? Sheesh, by the end of this day, I'm going to need a Starbucks in my bedroom.

25

I'm not big on wedding buffets. No matter how elegant the spread, it always comes down to a giant gathering at the pig trough for guests. Plus, buffets are always served on diminutive plates, so guests have to limp back like Oliver Twist: "May I have s'more, please?"

"A buffet is a perfectly acceptable choice for weddings," Elaine is carping as she daintily sips her soup. "It hardly seems reasonable to ask for all the extra waitstaff necessary for a sit-down meal. In the South, this is reserved for very formal occasions."

Um, like your only son's wedding, perhaps?

"It seems a *bit* reasonable, Mother. Ashley wants it." Emily leaps to my defense, and gee, isn't that heartwarming, considering she was planning on using my wedding for her *Carrie* prom moment until her brother got wind of it? My negativity is definitely getting the best of me on this fine occasion. I sip my soup without so much as a slurp.

"A million things can go wrong with a sit-down meal," Elaine continues. "You'll have inexperienced staff who will inevitably serve from the wrong side. You'll have guests who don't know which fork to use at the proper time, or worse yet, which bread plate to use, which sends everyone to the wrong side of the table setting. Before you know it, there's a lone bread plate and a person without it on the opposite side of the table. Chaos. It's utter chaos. Whereas, when the knife and fork come wrapped in a linen cloth with their plate, there's no explanation necessary." She says this last part like, *Call today. There's no obligation!*

Now I live in Silicon Valley. We're considered a millionaire collective, and I'm thinking that if we can handle stock options underwater, we can certainly handle silverware options. Correct me if I'm wrong, but if the guy across from me is missing his plate, I can pass it to him, right? We're just that accommodating.

"But isn't this lovely?" I say as the next course is set before us. "Mmm. Grilled portobellos. Look, you have your own plate set before you." I include a Vanna White sweep of the hand. "You can just eat your bread off *this* plate if you're confused. Plus, I have a good friend in a wheelchair, and I'd rather she be served."

Elaine's mouth snaps shut.

"I think this is lovely, Ashley," Emily says.

At this point, I'm not sure if I prefer Emily's support to her hostility. The fact is, you can't trust her. She always seems to have some invisible motivator, and it leaves me constantly maneuvering to figure her out. As for the food, if I choose buffet, Mrs. Novak will argue for the sit-down. Since I chose a vegan plate for my vegetarian friends, I feel like she'll offer conversion classes at the door on the benefits of being a carnivore.

"I've chosen the menu for the wedding, and so far, everything is delectable. Don't you agree?" I ask. "My mother will be here before the main course. She had my nephew Davey this morning."

Elaine and Emily leave the mushrooms untouched. Apparently, high-end fungus is not a delicacy for them. We're served a grapefruit-tasting sorbet to cleanse our palates, and my mother comes in wearing her "World's Best Grandma" sweatshirt and sets her stained canvas bag on the floor. My mother has never carried a purse. No cows have met their demise for her shoe or bag collection. Rather, Coleman had to nix a few tents to make her Keds and her shopping mall logo bag. And it's not even for a decent mall.

My mom looks at me and then at Emily and Elaine in their

expensive knit. "Oh dear, it looks like I underdressed. But, Elaine, you'll understand. I had my grandbaby all morning, and that child is like a touch of heaven here on earth. Just a cherubic smile, and black hair that sticks straight into the air. I'm telling you, the smartest baby you'll ever meet. He's nearly talking at not even six months, gurgles for what he wants. He's just brilliant."

Thankfully, Elaine is only critical of *my* every move. My mother appears exempt. "Mary, I'm so glad you could join us. We were just saying how you belonged here with us, weren't we, Ashley?"

Huh? "Uh, yeah, Mom. Thanks for coming."

"We've been enjoying an interesting meal, but I want to hear all about your opinion on sit-down meals at weddings." Elaine pats my mother's hand. "It seems so dreadfully formal."

My mom looks at me. "Ashley doesn't like buffets, Elaine. Didn't she tell you that?" She laughs. "I suppose it's from me spoiling her. I served her breakfast, lunch, and dinner every day of her life until she left for college. Being served is what she expects. Why, I wonder how she ever learned to do her own laundry. You do know how to do your own laundry, don't you, Ashley?"

Not helping, Mom. I shove a spoonful of grapefruit ice in my mouth.

"Of course we want the wedding to be elegant, but we want your guests to feel at home too," Elaine says softly, which translated into casual English means, *We're afraid of your trailer trash relatives mixing formally with our high-society guests and stealing their bread plates.* I honestly think if she could have her guests in one room and ours in another, that would suit her just fine. Segregation, Novak style.

"We're not complete hicks, Elaine!" *Did that just come out?* I'm looking around at the aghast faces, and yes, apparently, it did.

"Ashley, Mrs. Novak is just trying to help. Calm down," my mother says, then turns her gentle voice to Elaine. "Ashley's always known what she wanted. I doubt you'll have much luck convincing her of something else when her heart is set. We tried to talk her into a practical car too. You can see how far we got with that. And those handbags she carries. She could feed a third world country." My mom laughs. "You'd think we lived in the Arctic Circle with her coat collection."

"She'll have to rid herself of that convertible when she moves to Philadelphia. It won't be practical."

My eyes pop open wide. "How do you know about Philadelphia?" I ask.

"Ashley, Kevin is our son, and he needed his father's word to get that interview. Philadelphia is a lovely city, and since he called us earlier this week to say how much he loves the hospital, we took the liberty of finding the perfect home for you."

"A home? My home is in Palo Alto. I haven't even discussed this with Kevin."

Mrs. Novak touches my hand lightly. "It's always hard until they get their practice started, Ashley. But then you'll spend the day with charity work, and you'll forget all about your initial arguments."

"No, I mean we've really not decided on moving. Kevin and I don't know what our future holds right now."

"It holds a four-bedroom, two-and-a-half-bathroom colonial on half an acre in Philly." She pulls out a picture of the ugliest house I've ever seen.

"That is *so* not a colonial." Think bad tract house with a sagging roof.

"That might be true, but it is yours. Dr. Novak's offer was accepted right away, and it will be in escrow soon. It's in one of the finest neighborhoods. You can always redesign the house. It will be good for you while Kevin is at work."

I push my plate away. "No. There's no house, no escrow. Kevin and I have hardly discussed Pennsylvania."

"We're buying you a home as a wedding present, Ashley. I do expect some gratitude."

"You've got to be kidding me!" I hear my high-pitched voice

squeak at my future mother-in-law. *Lord, just stop me now!* "I'm not living your life, Mrs. Novak. No offense to your choices, but they were yours. I will make my own. My own wedding decisions, and my own living decisions—"

"Ashley, it is my son's wedding too, and his future. You can't possibly believe your patent work is more important than my son's career. Seeing as how Kevin isn't here, I'm acting in the best interest of my son and his upbringing. And these wedding decisions don't feel *warm* to me."

Stand closer to the candle!

"I think my decisions on my wedding are very warm," I say as the sorbet is lifted away. "The church is overwhelmingly ornate, I'll give you that, but our attachment to Stanford for Kevin and me is important. We met there. We fell in love against the odds, if you will. The romance of it all makes up for what you might deem as too formal. Besides that, the Stanford campus itself is warm. Wrapped in redwoods and eucalyptus trees, it's like a big, open spa scent that calms the senses. You can almost feel the hot rock massage coming!" Okay, now I'm standing and nearly shouting. *Not sounding all that Zen, actually.*

"Kevin has an important future ahead of him. It's your decision if you choose to go along."

"That's right. It is my decision. Actually, it's our decision. Mine and Kevin's. Not yours." I stand up, livid that this woman thinks she can hijack not only my wedding, but also my whole life. Not to mention livid at my wonderful fiancé for abandoning me and telling me nothing about this house.

"Ashley!" My mother barks. "Sit down. You're making a scene."

I grab my handbag. "I don't want to sit down, and I don't want to plan this wedding anymore. No one cares what Kevin and I want. I feel like I'm in a bad reality TV show, and you think we're just playing parts where you insert us at the necessary camera shot. I don't know what I was thinking when I said I wanted to get married. I don't want to get married. Mom, I'm sorry." I walk out, leaving her there with the Southern, coldhearted queen bee of Atlanta and her worker bee offspring.

My head falls into my hands as I realize I don't have a car or transportation back to work. I have to leave Kevin's car with all the luggage in it for the Novaks. Let them pay to get it out of valet.

I can't stand my fiancé's family. I'm in love with Kevin, but if I marry him, I'll spend the rest of my life living in complete turmoil whenever we see his family. I look up to the blue summer sky, and I feel tears roll down my temples.

"Just once, can't You give me something I want without attaching a great big black ball and chain to it?" I moan. My cell phone rings, and it's Brea. "Hello," I say with an added sniffle.

"John said he'd come home if you still want me at the luncheon."

"The luncheon's over, Brea. And there's no cake testing. I'm not getting married."

"You are so getting married. What's the drama about this time?" Brea sighs loudly.

Sympathy would be good here! "His family's crazy, Brea."

"So I suppose you believe you're the epitome of normal?"

"They want to have a buffet, not a sit-down dinner."

"Oh my goodness, Ashley, they're like, evil! A buffet? Next thing you know, they'll be marking your guests with the number of the beast!"

Brea just makes me cry more. It's not funny, and it's not simple like she makes it out to be. Maybe I am overly dramatic, but the thought of my life being one big power struggle between the Novaks and me over Kevin scares the daylights out of me.

"They bought us a house, Brea. In Philadelphia. We don't even know if Kevin will get the job!"

"Ashley, they bought you a house?"

"Just never mind, okay? You don't understand. I don't expect you to. I don't even care if you do. Just let me have my own feelings, all right?" I slip off my heels and start to walk up the El Camino toward work in my stocking-clad feet. My new fishnets will be toast by the time I get there, but life goes on.

"Where are you, Ashley?"

"I'm on the El Camino," I shout over the roar of Beamers and Mercedes. "Across from the mall."

"I'm coming to get you."

"No. I'm going to work, then I'm going home to Rhett where I belong. The one male in the world without excess baggage."

"You know, marriage is not a simple, romantic walk down the aisle. You have to fight every step of the way for your marriage. This is God preparing you. Why do you think you should enjoy a conflict-free existence? Who are you to be free of struggles?"

"Leave me alone, Brea."

"No, I won't leave you alone. With Seth, I left you alone, because he was a dork, but Kevin loves you. And you love him. But if that's all you have, that's not gonna go far, I'll tell you that right now. If you're not committed to marriage, it's good you're walking now, because you won't make it past the first year. Marriage gets ugly, so stick with your dog. I didn't think you were such a wimp!"

Click.

She hung up on me. Brea hung up on me.

I can see Stanford Shopping Center across the wide part of El Camino. For once in my life, I feel like a new pair of shoes can't solve this. Although right now, a pair of DKNY sneakers would come in extremely handy.

26

My office is a bevy of busywork, with only casual glances at my shoeless state and what's left of my eighteen-dollar fishnets. So much about working in Silicon Valley is busyness. I wonder what all these people actually do, all giving the appearance of constant robotic motion, a continual death grip on the computer mouse.

Once in the ladies' room, I shimmy out of my hose, slide my slacks back on, and slip back into my heels. I stare into the mirror for a while, anxious to avoid my office and questions about the "sample" lunch. If this was just a sample, I don't even want to know what the real battle is going to be like.

Purvi is leaving, and I can't bear to think about going back to the general counsel position. I'm a terrible general counsel. It's too political, and I have my hands full searching for patent documents. Apparently I'm not much of a multitasker. Add to that the fact that office politics will include dealing with my ex-boyfriend as director of software, and you have an international incident in the making.

Exiting the bathroom, I garner the stares of a few admins. This time they don't look away; their eyes follow me. Tracy comes up behind me, uncomfortably close, and pushes me into my office.

"What are you doing?" I ask her, and I watch as she yanks my disposed-of fishnets out of my waistline. Apparently I was a tad too anxious to get back to my desk and should have actually checked that the nylons made it to the trash can. "Did I just walk through the office with those hanging there?"

She nods.

"Perfect finish to my afternoon. Maybe I should go grab some toilet paper and stick it to my shoe. Have it trailing behind me for the next meeting."

"No time for that. Purvi is leaving today, Ashley!"

"No, the end of next week," I correct her and grab my calendar and show it written in red. "See, PURVI LEAVING."

"They're starting Pushpan in school, so they're going early to give him time to adjust."

My mouth just drops as my heart starts to pound. In my Silicon Valley tenure, I've seen a lot of people leave work *that* very day, but it's never their idea. What can I possibly say? Not two hours ago, I was a fiancée and a successful patent attorney with too many possible dwelling places. This afternoon, my fiancée status is questionable once Kevin talks to his family. And my job? Well, where once there was success, there is now impending failure. Did I mention that I'm a terrible general counsel? But I should look at the bright side. At least I won't be planning a huge wedding in the process of trying to do the job I'm terrible at doing. Right?

"Ashley, did you hear me?" Tracy asks.

"I heard you, Tracy. I need a moment." Purvi taught me this business. She was the kind of manager who allowed me to do my job because she was doing hers. She didn't micromanage me or get in my way. She allowed me to flourish. Granted, she did it while yelling at me a great deal, but to me, that was just her communication style. I never took it personally. Part of me is angry at her for leaving, and part of me envies her for getting out of the rat race that we call Silicon Valley. Although I'm not sure India's a great alternative, but that's just me.

"Ashley." Purvi pokes her head in the door. "You heard?"

"I heard. You're leaving me already. Purvi, I'm terrible at your job. I won't last a month. When I lose my job, Kay will probably come to India hunting for you because I can't make the mortgage."

Purvi laughs. "You did it for nine months; you will be fine. You know what you did wrong now. You are not one to make the same mistakes. You just needed me to give you a jump start, and that's what I did."

I'm still shaking my head. "No. No jump starts. This career means everything to you."

Purvi shakes her head and comes in my office, motioning Tracy to leave as she shuts the door. "My *family* means everything to me. You are spoiled in America. Most of you have your families and your jobs close by. It's not always that way for us. Besides, you get to be my age, and tell me your career means everything. If it does, it's time to shuffle your priorities."

"It's not always easy for Americans either. I know too many people who go to China and Taiwan, practically with the tide."

She just stares at me.

"I'm glad for you, Purvi, if this is what you want. I wish I had your firm convictions. I have something for you." I pull out a wrapped package from under my desk. "I bought it that last time you sent me to Taiwan. It made me think of you."

Purvi looks at the package, and I swear there's some emotion in her eyes. Here I thought she was just another robot. "Ashley, you shouldn't be worrying about me. Not with that big wedding to plan." She unwraps the box and finds a Seiko clock with two separate dials for two time zones.

"I thought this way you'd always know what time it was here." I smile knowingly.

"It's perfect, Ashley. Now I'll always know the correct time to wake you up on a Saturday morning. I'll never have to guess again." She laughs. "Thank you."

"You're welcome. I'll miss you, Purvi."

"You'll never think about me. You'll marry this handsome doctor

I hear so much about. He sounds perfect for you. Driven, ambitious, and unavailable most of the time. A match made in heaven."

I shake my head. "His family is questionable. I still can't believe you're abandoning this life and leaving me in charge!"

"You'll do fine if you don't give in to emotion. These engineers will walk all over you if you let them. I figure you've handled Seth in other circumstances. You can handle him here. So software shouldn't be an issue. But hardware rules the roost, so be prepared for them. When they come in, they'll expect you to drop everything. The secret is making it look like you're doing just that."

"Are they looking for your replacement yet?" I ask with a small, tentative voice.

Purvi shakes her head. "It's you, Ashley. You're my replacement. You're good at this job, and no one is better trained. You just need to focus your energy and be nicer to the VPs." She raises her palms and shakes them. "Such an issue you have with authority!"

"I'm fine with authority. Generally speaking. As long as it's mine," I quip.

"Well, it's going to be yours, but remember that with authority comes responsibility; and when a patent doesn't get issued, it will be on your head, not mine."

"I figure I can blame you for another six months. There's that whole lag thing going on."

Purvi laughs at this. "I'm sure you do. But I'm hoping you'll last a long time in this job now that you're prepared."

I want to hug her, but of course, this is Silicon Valley and this is Purvi. As wonderful as Purvi is, she's not the warmest chick in the incubator.

"So I'll e-mail you when I get to India, and you can ask me any questions you have."

Purvi comes toward me, her hand extended. "I've enjoyed working with you. You are priceless, Ashley. I wish I could be here for your wedding, but my thoughts will be with you." She shakes my hand and scrambles out of the office.

So I guess that's it. I'm the boss again.

"Ashley?" Seth pokes his bald head in my door. Something in me just wants to slam his scrawny neck in it, but my Christian love wins out, and I repent of my thoughts most rapidly.

"Yeah?"

"Congratulations. I hear you're officially general counsel again."

"Yep." *And wasn't that the most intellectual answer?*

"I have to talk to you about something before you hear it from someone else."

His brows are knit together as one, like Bert's. Of *Sesame Street*'s Ernie and Bert. "Is this something I should sit for?"

He nods, and I feel my stomach tie into knots. He has no power over me, I remind myself, and yet I dread what's coming. I know Seth. I know he's not the demonstrative type, and if he thinks I should sit? I should probably be calling for the defibrillator.

"You and I have been friends a long time."

"Years," I say.

"So you know me. You know my nature and my moral standards."

Right. *Those would be the morals that refuse marriage because going steady and a lack of true intimacy are so much more fun.*

"Yes, I think I'm quite aware of your personality." *Or lack thereof. Ack! Bad Ashley.*

"Arin and I are getting married," he blurts.

Not sure my eyebrows could rise this high, but yeah, I'm like one big brow-lift "after" picture at the moment.

He hasn't sat down but is still pacing the five feet of my office. I stand up and swallow. "I thought you were just 'friends,' that she was dating someone else from India," I venture.

He nods for a moment, pulling his hands together behind his back. You know, I realize now that I'm completely over him. I don't care if he gets married, but Arin doesn't love him, and I feel this in my veins. She'll pull him around like a monkey on her string. Seth's whole life will be keeping up with his high-maintenance wife wherever her whims lead her. So far it's been Costa Rica and India, but who's to say where her shallow breeze will take her next? I know it's awful to think this way of a missionary. But there are bad missionaries just like there are bad patent attorneys, and I'm sorry, but Arin is a bad missionary.

Forgive me. "Why would you marry *her*, Seth? Because she's beautiful? Beautiful women are a dime a dozen. You can do better than her. I don't like the way she leads men on, and I don't like the way her mission trips seem to coincide with where she wants to vacation. I don't like how she doesn't stick with anything. Marriage is a commitment; she can't commit to a country of residence."

Seth holds his hand up. "Stop right there, Ashley. I don't need to hear anymore. Arin is pregnant."

Okay, my eyebrows can, in fact, go higher. I feel for my chair behind me. "She's pregnant," I repeat as I steadily find my seat.

"The baby's not mine. I don't want you thinking I had anything to do with this. She got pregnant by the guy she was dating, but his family doesn't approve of her."

"She's pregnant." *And he's going to marry her.* Seth loved me and he wouldn't marry me, but he's going to marry her carrying someone else's baby. *Bad B-movie here, people. Or an episode of* Dynasty. I try to digest this information, but my mouth is still running. "You're going to marry Arin?"

"I am."

"When?"

"We're going to Tahoe this weekend."

My stomach drops. "Seth, not even a church wedding?" I knew this day would come, when Seth would finally give in to commitment. I just thought it would be for love. That, I could deal with.

"What church is going to marry us, Ashley? She's pregnant. It's not my baby. She's thirteen years younger than me. We're not exactly ready to be on staff for Campus Crusade, if you know what I'm saying."

"Why are you doing this?"

"Ashley, I have to. Arin wants her baby, and I want her baby to have a future."

"What if the father comes back and wants the baby too? What then?"

"He won't."

"How do you know?"

"She wouldn't lie to me."

"Seth, she's been a missionary for the last year. She's been living a lie. Does she love you? Why you?"

"My faith means nothing to me if I don't stand up and do what's right," Seth answers with squared shoulders and the attitude of Superman.

"What does that mean to you, doing what's right? Seth, please explain this to me so I can understand it. Because I don't understand it!"

"You, Ashley, will be fine. You always will be fine, and I knew that. I knew you never needed the likes of me. I knew you loved me, but I never thought it would be enough. You're too strong-minded, too set in your ways, and too in love with life to settle for the world I'd give you."

"Do you really believe that? That's how you justified dumping me publicly? You were doing me a favor? How heroic that makes you seem, wouldn't you agree?"

"Would you be happy with me, Ashley? Could I give you what you wanted? The truth now."

I look away. "Seth, I'm not saying we were meant to be together. Now that I'm with Kevin, I understand that. But because I understand it, I don't want you to settle."

"That's funny, because I see it as the first stand-up thing I've done in a long time. I'll be a good father to this baby. I think I'll be a good husband to Arin."

"Have you talked to Pastor Max?"

Seth nods. "He's coming with us to witness the marriage in Tahoe. He's counseled us on what we're getting ourselves into and will continue to counsel us after the wedding."

"I don't know what to say to you." I catch a glimpse of those tanzanite eyes, and I think how sad it is that Arin won't have them on her child. I know women get pregnant. I know sex outside marriage is a fact of life, but it feels different when your ex falls victim to its consequences.

"When's she due?"

"December. She'll start to show soon, so we're going to make this quick."

"What can I do?"

"Just wish me luck. And prayers would be good." Seth slaps his thighs and reaches for the doorknob.

"I pray this marriage is perfect in the eyes of the Lord." *Because it sure reeks in my book.*

"Keep this between us, all right?"

I nod and watch him walk away. I've become accustomed to Seth's back, but this time I feel like shouting, "Dead man walking!"

27

Rather than think about the pathetic remnants of my life, I work until 9:00 p.m. Patents have a beautiful cadence to them, a rhythm, if you will: the hint of an idea comes like a dewy whisper to an engineer's ear, the fruit of his nectar brought to my office for the collection of research. Then there is the budding flower of the patent application visited by the hummingbird of the U.S. Patent Office.

Clearly, I have been working too long. I'm writing bad patent poetry in my warped, caffeine-laced mind. I know I've gone over the edge as I think about publishing it. Engineer poetry is not exactly on the New York Times *best-seller list, now is it?*

"Are you ever going home?" Tracy is at my door. She looks beat and isn't wearing any makeup, which for her is like being naked. Remember, she is the scarlet lipstick queen. "Even Purvi didn't work this late."

"What are you doing here?" I ask. "Have you been here the whole time?"

"No, I'm back for the international shift to answer phones." She slaps her cheeks. "I'm giving my skin a breather. I didn't think anyone but security would be here. Did you eat something?"

I have to think about this. "I've had a lot of coffee, and if you count nondairy creamer as food, then yes, I've eaten."

"What are you doing here so late?"

"Right now? Writing bad patent poetry."

"I'm not even going to ask."

"Yeah, that's probably best."

"I heard about Seth." Tracy stares at me as if hoping for some reaction.

"Heard what about him?"

"He got some girl knocked up, and he's marrying her."

"He did not get some girl—" But I stop here. Of course he doesn't want people knowing this isn't his baby. *Duh.* Pregnancy, people will understand. This situation with Seth, not at all. "Seth will make a good father. Hopefully, a good husband too."

"Yeah. Whatever. It sort of surprised me. He doesn't come off as the kind who could get a date. You, I understood. You like the smart ones, but a young thing sleeping with him? Weird." She shakes her head. It's amazing how much the admins actually *see* in the office. "Do you want me to get you something to eat?"

"No, I'm leaving." I grab my sweater and slip into my heels, but my cell phone rings, and I see it's Kevin. *For the first time, I'm not sure I want to talk to Kevin,* I think as my anger returns. *Help me, Lord!*

Tracy stares at me. "Aren't you going to answer that?"

"Yeah." I answer the phone, but I don't say anything into the receiver.

"Ashley? Are you there?" Kevin asks.

"I'm here."

"Where are you, at work?"

"Yes. I had Tracy cancel with the pastor. We were supposed to start our premarital counseling tonight. Remember?"

"Ashley," he sighs. "I'm so sorry. I completely forgot, and I guess being across the country, I wouldn't have been much help anyway." He mumbles something to someone at the other end of the line. Doctor words I don't understand. "I heard the luncheon with my mom didn't go well."

"You could say that." *Or you could say that* Wife Swap *is something your mother is hoping for, before our marriage takes place.*

"Tell me what happened."

"No. Tell me about Philadelphia and our new house. Is Starbucks down the street?" Kevin misses—or ignores—my tone and my sarcasm.

"Ash, it's fabulous! The program is better than I imagined. This is everything I want. It's the training I just know was designed for me. Ordained by God. Every piece of information I received today only confirmed more that this is where I'm being called."

"Great." And it is great. I want Kevin to be happy, but where I stand in the midst of all this is a mystery. Would I ever see him if we move across the country for a job? Or would I be sitting in a Starbucks, drinking corporate espresso, alone on my wireless Internet, getting into political arguments with complete strangers for lack of a job? "Purvi left today. They're not hiring another general counsel. I'm it."

"Ash, that's great! See, you're so good they promote you even when you fight it."

Kevin, you're missing the obvious.

"I don't like being general counsel, actually. Too much politics, not enough patents. Besides, if you're seriously considering Philly, and it sounds by your father's real-estate ventures that you are—"

"I know you don't like general counsel," Kevin says, avoiding the hot house topic. "But that's because it stretches you. It's good to stretch, Ashley. You don't want to be caught in a rut like the Reasons, do you?"

"Speaking of which, you should probably know that Seth and Arin are getting married."

Silence.

"Did you hear me? I don't think Seth wants it announced as public fodder, but I figured since it was your ex-girlfriend, my ex-boyfriend, and you and I are now engaged, all in one happy, dysfunctional *Friends*-like arrangement, you might want to know."

"Well, that's shocking. Any reason behind this odd engagement? I have to say, I didn't think Seth had it in him to get married. I considered it a definite plus as I tried to steal away the woman I wanted from right under his nose."

I was stolen?

"They're getting married this weekend," I announce.

"This weekend? What's the rush?"

"True love can't wait," I say facetiously.

"Isn't there a book called *True Love Waits?*"

"Well, it's not waiting past this weekend for Seth and Arin."

"Ashley, forget about them. What happened with my mother today? Can't you just work on being nice? For me?"

Hey, I was nice. I didn't hurt her! And what about the house here, buddy! "She wants a certain kind of meal. Served a certain kind of way, but oh, wait a minute! It's my wedding. So I protested. Albeit, maybe a little too much, because it cost me a pair of eighteen-dollar fishnets."

"It's *our* wedding, and I would think you'd be grateful to my mom and sister for all they've done. Think about how much they've spent on airfare alone trying to help us out!"

They could own controlling stock in Southwest for all I care. "I don't want a buffet, Kevin," I say in clipped tones. "How will Eve get her food?" I ask, referring to our friend with MS.

"I'll get it for her, Ashley. John or Brea will get it for her. We shouldn't be designing our wedding around one guest."

"We're not designing around a guest. We're designing it the way I want it. I thought you told me I had free rein. Now that your mother has spoken, apparently you didn't really mean that. I don't want to be standing around in my wedding gown and trying to pick at buffet food, waiting for buffalo wing sauce to stain my Vera Wang. A meal should be placed before me, like the princess I am for the day. I get dizzy when I don't eat, and I'll be too nervous to pick the right food. Since when did you start caring about the wedding details anyway? Free rein, you said," I repeat, none too gently.

"I care since you're upsetting my mom and sister with the your-way-or-the-highway routine."

"My way? Your sister canceled my wedding dress! She'd have Confederate flag-waving skinheads with swords if I let her. Your mother is telling me what to serve for dinner and insinuated my slacks were inappropriate. She's been in a St. John knit every time I've ever seen her. Do I reproach her on overall lack of wardrobe creativity? No, because I believe in personal choice. And as the bride, I believe in personal choice for *moi* on my wedding day."

"Ashley, my mother has thrown society parties for my dad's colleagues her whole adult life. Surely you can handle some advice. It's not like you're Kay in the kitchen."

I gasp. "Did you just say what I think you did?"

"Are you going to deny it?"

"So what are you saying? I should learn how to be barefoot and pregnant? Maybe cook a four-course meal wearing pearls? In my dumpy fixer-upper in Philly? Are you all part of this evil plan?"

"Now you're just being nasty. A Bridezilla, as my sister called it."

"Bridezilla? How dare you run off to another state, leave me here to deal with your control-freak family, tell me I have free rein, and then renege on that completely when they tell you what they want. I am not going to live my entire life answering to your mother and your sister. This is apparently what will happen, because you swore you'd back me up."

"You've been a fine sport, but it's getting down to the wire now. You're overburdened at work, and you just don't want to give up any of the control here. I'm saying both our lives would be easier if you'd let someone else handle something."

"So you want me to show up dressed like Scarlett? Because that's what will happen. And I hope you look good in Rhett tails, because you'll be dressed like a Civil War dandy! You should be thanking me for standing up for us, because you would look like a grown-up Ken doll dressed by your little sister if it weren't for me! Rhett Butler Barbie."

"You're not yourself. We'll talk about this when I get home. Do you think you can get through the floral arrangements without drawing blood?"

"Are you moving to Philadelphia?"

"I don't know yet. I figured we'd discuss it when I came home."

"Discuss it like here's what you are doing, and I can choose to come along? Or discuss it like you actually might stay here, and we'll have the life we planned? You doctor. Me lawyer. In California."

"The latter, Ashley. This is *our* decision now. But, Ashley, this job is perfect for me. You can always get your license to practice here."

"I've lived here my whole life, Kevin. I don't know how to live anywhere else."

"Maybe it's time for a change."

"I'm general counsel," I say emphatically. "Isn't that change enough?"

"You just said you hated that job."

"But I'm important, and what was all that about being stretched? I'm a regular Gumby now."

Kevin laughs. "You're important whatever you do, Ash, and it would stretch you to move too. Think about it, home of the Constitution. Ashley Stockingdale, patent attorney at large."

"Kevin, your parents bought us a house. For a job you don't even have yet—"

"Actually, I do. They said the job was mine if I wanted it."

The wind rushes from my lungs. "So what are you saying?"

"I'm just giving you options, Ashley."

"Like your father gave us on this ugly house? Those kinds of options? Where you really have none. Someone else lays out the path of your life, and you just follow it. Those kinds of options?"

"My father's gift has nothing to do with this. We can rent it out.

Hire a real wedding coordinator. Will that make you happy? To have my family completely pushed out of the way?"

Hire a coordinator? Is it just me, or did that sound decidedly like Elaine Novak? "I can't hire a coordinator."

"Why not?"

Deep breath. "I'm broke, actually. When I bought half the house from Kay, I wasn't aware of the tax bills that come twice a year. Outrageous, disgusting, California real-estate tax bills! Then I loaned someone some money that I probably won't see again. I put money down for the photographer and for the swing band before you changed your mind, and a deposit for the catering, and well, it turns out that I'm broke, Kevin. The dress fairy dropped my gown out of nowhere at the wedding shop, or I wouldn't even have a dress to get married in. Doesn't all that sound like some kind of omen to you?"

"It sounds like small bumps in the highway. Typical for what any Christian marriage might have to go through. Do you want to get married or not?" Kevin's normally calm voice is sounding agitated.

"I thought I did. But being married doesn't just mean being married anymore. Now it means giving up everything I know to be married."

"I'll be home tomorrow. Don't do anything rash. You tend to react, and we're in no position for you to react."

"Kevin, your mother doesn't like me." *And I'm not necessarily fond of her either.* "Your sister was basically trying to sabotage our wedding by turning me into a modern-day Scarlett O'Hara, and where have you been through all this? Okay, saving babies is a good excuse, but is this a battle I'll have alone my entire life? I'm not sure I'm up for that."

"Can't you just put these meal decisions off until I get home? I haven't had time to think about any of that."

"This isn't about a meal. Or even a house, Kevin. This is about your family and their very strong opinions about things that are our business. Is this my future?"

"If my mother's objections were about your character or your faith, I might listen. But there's history here. She just wants to make sure she's respected for what she does well. And she plans parties well. You must understand, my mother and father have set up a life for themselves that works. They basically see themselves as perfect and all others as inferior. Everything they do is to prove their superiority."

And we are supposed to support them in this? So not soothing me.

"Okay, so if I was a psychologist, I'd have a great case study. But I'm a patent attorney, and I don't want to play these games for the rest of my life. You're not answering my question, and it's a legitimate question. Is this woman going to rule my future?"

"You're a Christian. Act like it, Ashley. Suppress your anger, and learn to get along. I'll see you tomorrow, and this will all blow over. You're making a mountain out of a molehill."

I gasp again. "You think standing up for myself is not being a Christian? Why don't you just stamp 'Welcome' across my forehead for the doormat *y'all* seem to want me to be. Don't you see your whole family has insinuated themselves into our plans?"

"So would you rather live with Kay the rest of your days and see your Tupperware numbered? Where a big Saturday night is playing Xbox with other engineers in another dateless soiree? Is that what you want? To end this?"

No, I want you, I think to myself, as much as I hate to admit it at this moment. *But if I don't measure up to your family, what then?*

"Do you love me, Ashley?" His gravelly voice, always tired and stressed, has such emotional depth. I'm drawn in, unable to withstand the pull.

"I do love you, Kevin. So much. But this is really hard." I'm so confused. Is love enough? *With Christ, I can do all things, but Kevin's family! That's asking me to stretch a little far, isn't it Lord? I'm not made of elastic.*

"The chief of surgery is waiting for me."

"You always have to go. Every time I have to deal with some wedding crisis, or life crisis, you're off to a call." I feel guilty immediately. He's saving babies. I'm fighting with his mother over portobello mushrooms.

"I'll be home tomorrow," he repeats.

"I'll finish the flowers tomorrow with your sister before you get here. But I won't like it." *One more day. I can handle one more day of meowing and keeping my claws bared.* "We'll talk when you get home."

"You're my fiancée still?" Kevin asks.

"I love you, Kevin. If they lock us up, let's be in the same padded cell." After I get off the phone, I scream a good scream. Worthy of any mental health ward.

28

I trudge into my house after 11:00 p.m. on this endless day, and Rhett greets me at the door. He's all slobber and love. "Hey, Rhett, I wish everyone felt that way about me today," I say as I toss my keys on the designated "landing spot."

"Where have you been?" Kay comes out of the kitchen like an angry housewife. *Why is she even still up? A pot or pan out of place? Down, Ashley.*

"At work." There's a tinge of *duh!* in my voice. But my patience is up and gone by now.

"Kevin called here. Did he find you?"

"I talked to him. So are you still mad at me too?"

"I just don't know why you need to be in everybody's business." She wipes her hands on a towel and folds it. "If I want to see Matt, I will. If I want to hold a grudge against Simon, it's my choice. It seems to me you have enough trouble of your own to worry about."

"Did you have to come out of the kitchen for this?"

"I've got a lot on my mind." Kay takes a swig of a disgusting green concoction she's made.

"I just think living with this secret for twenty years has to be harder than saying it out loud." I pat Rhett's head. "I was wrong. Sue me. I don't even want to know anymore. I don't have the bandwidth."

248

"No, I've decided to tell you, because I know you'll watch television just to find out what it is."

K. She's got me there.

"Do I need to sit for this? Because I have had enough of sit-down-type conversations for the day. If it's deep, can we skim the waters?"

Then, without warning, she launches into confession-speak. Apparently I look like Maury Povich tonight, and she's ready for the DNA test. They say confession is good for the soul, but mine can't take any more today. Jesus' shoulders are so much bigger than mine. I pick up her conversation at "Then, when I turned nine—"

"Chapter one. I am born," I say, quoting Dickens and, of course, *Gone with the Wind*.

"Ashley, do you want to hear this or not?"

"At the moment, no." I bury my head in my hands. "I'm sorry, Kay. Consider me a terrible friend, but it's been such a day." I want to break into my own sob story about inheriting a promotion I don't want, ticking off my would-be-mother-in-law from the dark side, getting the ugliest house alive as a gift in a state I don't want to live in, and of course, hearing that my ex-boyfriend is marrying his damsel in distress. But I keep quiet.

"It's always a day for you, Ashley. Sit down. I'm telling you my story," Kay announces.

I plunk down on the couch and put on my best Oprah listening expression. Rhett hops on the sofa next to me, and we prepare for the story that has held Kay captive in her controlled world for years. Just by her strained look, I can tell even reciting the story is difficult for her. I just don't get Kay. She could plan a singles retreat for three hundred people without so much as an anxious moment, but this issue that might hold the reason for her carefully planned world can't be spoken.

"So after my mother's third marriage, when I was fourteen, we moved to Louisiana. There was a store owner there who gave me a lagniappe when my mother bought a drying rack for dishes. I think he could tell we were dirt-poor, because my shoes were too small, and I was walking on the heels because my feet didn't fit into them anymore." She laughs at this memory. "The lagniappe was worth more than the rack. I do remember that."

"Wait a minute, stop the story. What did he give you?"

"A lagniappe, it's a gift-with-purchase, sort of. Like you get when you buy all that makeup at Bloomingdale's."

"Gotcha. Go on."

"On this gift was the name of a church. My mother took us there, thinking they might be able to find us another single-parent family to live with. When we got to the church, Simon was the pastor. It was a grimy church in the midst of squalor off the French Quarter. There were boxes everywhere because it was a church that fed people and took donations from the community. So there were boxes of rice and beans, things people could take home and feed their families."

"Okay, I'm trying to mentally picture you in the French Quarter, and it's just not a visual that's coming up for me. I would have thought you were raised at Yale or something."

"Just listen, will you?" Kay stares at me hard. "So my mom ends up working at the church, boxing the food into groupings that make sense. You know, rice here, so add a protein and a can of vegetables, that kind of thing."

"Where'd you sleep?"

"We got paid in room and board, and we slept in the church attic. It was dirty. I did my best, but to this day I still feel crawly thinking about the dust." Out of nowhere, Kay sneezes.

"I can't imagine you in an attic, let alone a dirty one. Wow, Kay!" *That explains a lot of the cleanliness fetish.*

"So anyway, Simon lived in a great little house with his wife, but they never had kids. We were living in the attic for about three weeks when my mother met some guy who came to get red beans for his family. They took off together."

"Who took off?"

"My mom and this guy."

"I thought he was there for his family."

"Would you let me finish? So Simon didn't know what to do with me because my mom hadn't said if she was coming back. I was too young to live in the attic by myself, and it wasn't the best neighborhood. So he and his wife brought me home with them for a time. Home to this perfect, clean little house on the right side of town." Kay sighs wistfully.

"Your mom left you there? With people she didn't know?"

"My mom always thought Prince Charming was right around the corner. She left me a note that she'd found her soul mate, and off they went. She couldn't help it, Ashley. That was just her genetic makeup, to look for the man who completed her. Simon and Ruth were all in a tizzy because they were scheduled to leave on a mission trip to Slovenia, and now they had me."

"So what did Simon do?" I'll admit; I'm expecting the worst. I clasp my eyes shut tightly for the tale of woe that is sure to come.

"He and Ruth put me in foster care so they could go on the trip."

"Then what happened?" I open my eyes.

"My mom came back after about a year and got me out of foster care."

Maybe I've read too many child abuse books, but this isn't sounding all that damaging to the average psyche. "Were you abused in foster care?"

"No, I stayed with a really nice family. Clean house, organized kitchen—"

"So what does Simon think you're going to do to his TV ministry? It was then that you encountered your first clean house?"

"He doesn't want me to talk about my abandonment and put him in a bad light. Remember, he left for Slovenia and tossed me over to the authorities."

"The abandonment by your mother, you mean?"

"No, by them. *They* abandoned me."

"They weren't your mother! How could people who knew you for three weeks abandon you?"

"My mother left me in their care."

"Without asking!"

"The point is she left me in Christian hands."

I am hearing Twilight Zone *music again.* Kay's mother abandons her. Leaves her to live in squalor over a mission church, and she's mad at the pastor. *For twenty years!* This is a bad Montel Williams show.

"Kay, if this anger you have toward Simon seems justified to you, I have one word for you: therapy. You've been mad at the wrong person for twenty years! I'll admit that wasn't the most Christian thing they could have done, but, Kay, *your mother left you with people she didn't know. For a guy!*"

"My mother did the best she could!"

"Uh, no, she didn't! The best she could do would have been to stay with her child."

"Can you imagine what it's like for me to see Pastor Simon up on that stage talking about his life in missions work when he abandoned the mission?"

I'm dumbfounded. Kay seems to think she's been keeping righteous anger where it belonged. "And forgiveness? Where does this factor in for you? The Bible does say to forgive."

"Forgiveness is one thing. Protecting others is my duty."

"Kay, I've seen the guy. He looks like Santa Claus after a night's work. You cannot possibly believe he's dangerous for going on a mission to Slovenia."

"I had nowhere to live!"

"That was your mother's fault."

Kay stomps down the hallway and slams her bedroom door with the strength of a javelin thrower.

I just look up at my ceiling. "Lord, help me out here, will Ya?" You just never know what moves people, do you? I mean, there are children who survive the worst abusers and become prominent members of society, driven by their survival instinct. Then there are seemingly tough people like Kay who live their entire lives around one moment, feeling that someone else's actions are responsible. Go figure. I can hear Kay in her bedroom. I'm sure she's frantically searching for something to organize, but I'll admit I just don't have it in me to finish this tonight.

I enter my own room with Rhett hot on my heels. I swear he's giving me doggie guilt, but I give him the expression that says I'll fix it later with Kay. I listen to the message that has the red light blinking. "Hey, Ash, it's me, Mei Ling. Good news on your dress! I wonder where it came from! But mine would have been prettier than Vera Wang's. I'm calling about your shower, to tell you that everything is set. Your mother and sister-in-law are coming. They were at your mother's house tonight. So I'll talk with you soon. Oh, and I tried to tell the aunties no lingerie, but be prepared just in case." *Beep.*

I look at the pictures of me in the gown, taped up on my mirror. The thrill of having Kevin as my husband rushes through my stomach. Maybe I've been trying too hard with his family. Maybe I just need to relax. The wedding is one day of my life. I'll have Kevin for a lifetime. I can live with a buffet. Right?

29

It's 8:00 a.m., and Emily is frantically ringing my doorbell. Again and again, like a kid asking to play on Saturday morning. I'll admit, I take my sweet time getting to the door, especially after seeing the Coach portfolio now wiped clean of pork stains. Rhett is barking ferociously like he's a starved, rabid pit bull. Reluctantly, I tell him to stop and open the metal peep door. Rhett stops, but Emily and Mrs. Novak are lost in their own conversation.

"She can't control that dog either," Mrs. Novak says to Emily on the other side of the door. *Um, hello, people, see me through this little grate here? I can hear you.*

"Mama, we have to do something," Emily repeats.

Mama, we have to do something? Wasn't Emily just telling me about how she wanted to get back at her mother? This doesn't sound like maternal revenge to me. This sounds like they're pretty much on the same team. *Maybe I'm just getting paranoid.* I mean, what's not to like about me? I'm educated, well dressed, gainfully employed. Granted, I can't cook, but I can hire people who can. Besides, I love Kevin. Doesn't that count for anything? I wish he were here right now and I could block his mother's image from my mind. I finger the expensive earrings he gave me, and while they're fabulous, I don't want a gift every time as a substitute for his presence. *Although that would make for a lot of presents!*

I open the door, and their conversation halts. "Good morning," I say with a strained smile on my face. "Listen, I'm sorry about yesterday. I'm just getting a tad stressed over all the details, and with Kevin being gone, I just want to get things right for him."

"Does that mean you're willing to go with me on the buffet? I think you'll be so much happier with the variety you can provide your guests, rather than a simplistic serving situation," Elaine says.

Grrr.

"A buffet sounds peachy."

"Will your mother be joinin' us today?" Emily asks.

"No. She's allergic to most flowers. Asked me to get her something without a scent for her corsage." I watch as Mrs. Novak rolls her eyes, and Emily shakes her head in agreement. I don't know if these women think I'm deaf, dumb, and stupid. Or if they really just don't care what I think. *I'm right here!*

At this most inopportune moment, Kay comes out, stomping down the hallway. She looks at me, her arms crossed, but she says nothing and stalks off to the kitchen. Lucky for me, Emily thinks it's about her. "The date stealer is angry?"

"Let's go." I push them out of the house and push Rhett's snout back in the house as I shut the door.

I have decided that men are so much easier to deal with. Rhett's the perfect example. Even my brother, Dave. When he was going to mess with you, you knew it. You prepared for the onslaught. You didn't question his motives. Or what his current mood was, because it was simply to get the better of you. With guys, and my brother in particular, it's all about the attack. With Dave, you got the wedgie, or the backwashed drink, and you knew the game was over when he laughed.

In contrast, with Emily and Elaine I feel locked into a continual game of Risk, where the motives of the attacker are not always apparent, and their moves are underhanded and sly. These women won't be happy until their red flags are all over my game board and I have submitted to complete powerlessness in my wedding, and perhaps my entire future. Therefore, defeat is not an option here. As we near the car, they turn to face me.

"Ashley, we've arranged to have a Southern floral arrangement sent for your special day. The florist here will work directly with our photos of a typical Southern arrangement, and we'll have the hydrangeas and peonies brought from Atlanta to ensure authenticity. This will take care of your something blue, not to mention remind the guests of our beloved city. She'll be sending the columns, with directions for the local florist." Emily looks intently at me, clearly hoping for a reaction, but I won't let her plant the next red flag.

"Columns?"

"Traditional columns with floral decoration. They'll serve as the backdrop at the church on the altar," she says in the same tone that one would say, "Duh!"

Columns sound good. I can live with columns. "It sounds like you have everything under control. Is there a reason I need to come to this meeting?" I ask jokingly.

The two women look at each other. "Not necessarily. Would you like us to handle it?"

"Sounds like you already did."

Emily smiles at me. Falsely, I might add. "We'll handle everything, Ashley. You shouldn't worry your lawyer head about it."

"See you next visit, at the shower," Elaine says. "Ta-ta now!"

They skip down the front steps. Part of me hates myself for not fighting. But I'm so sick of the battle. Look how I fought for Seth, and he was a lamb to the slaughter when the right woman wanted him. I watch them go, and I feel completely stupid, like I offered them my white flag, and they grabbed it without looking back.

Lord, how do I know when the battle is worth the fight? How do I know when to submit and let what I truly want go?

I open the door to Rhett's whimpering. "I know just how you feel."

I walk into the kitchen to make myself an Americano, and Kay is sitting at the table. Kay has the oddest morning ritual. She prepares herself a high-carb breakfast of bagels or granola that would make most of us weigh four hundred pounds, but she'll run five miles and keep that washboard stomach of hers, while you question if a bagel is worth that kind of effort. Especially with that disgusting soy spread she puts on top of it. *Can you say, "Nasty"?*

While Kay shovels granola and bagel into her mouth in precise, alternating bites, she reads the paper in a particular order. If you come in and take one of the sections from her "to-be-read" pile, you will completely alter the course of her universe. Sometime I do this, just to keep her on her toes. Today, I wisely take from the already scanned pile. After the newspaper, she goes to her Bible, reads her passage for the day, and meditates and prays at the table. Needless to say, we don't usually talk much in the morning, as her routine makes me crazy.

I turn on the espresso machine and wait for it to warm up by leaning against the counter. I cross my ankles and stare at Kay.

"Do you have to just stand there and look at me?" Kay asks with the trademark pursed lips and one eyebrow raised.

"No."

"So don't."

"You're still mad at me?"

"You are so judgmental, Ashley. You don't know my mother from Adam, and yet you feel completely comfortable disparaging her up-bringing of me."

"I'm no therapist, and you talk about me like I'm crazy. Maybe I am, but, Kay, your need for control is not healthy. Being unable to read the paper out of order: front page, Business, Peninsula. It's not healthy." *It's weird, actually.*

"Most people read the paper in order, Ashley."

"That's true," I say, pointing at her. "I'll give you that, but most people's entire day is not ruined when there's a section missing. They will not call the delivery boy, who speaks not a lick of English, looking for it. They will not pull the paperboy's automatic tip from the Visa bill."

"Listen, I allow you to read my newspaper for free. If you want to mess with it before I've read it, buy your own copy."

"What happened to Matt Callaway?"

"He said he was busy with a project right now, but, Ashley, he's having a midlife crisis. I don't have time or the inclination to deal with that."

"You don't have the inclination to deal with anything that isn't on your clipboard and completely planned. Deal with it. Put an end to letting him think you're still an option. Wouldn't that feel good? Controlled?"

"You let people walk all over you, Ashley. You let Seth do it for nearly a year. You are letting the Southern belles ambush your wedding, and you're just sitting here drowning your sorrows in espresso. Is that the life you want for me? Well, no thanks. I'll take my clipboard and my power."

"You can push this back on me all you want. You have to deal with your mother issue, and denial is not working for you anymore. She was not a good mother. She may have done the best she could, but it was still crappy. You owe Simon and Ruth an apology if you want to know what I think."

"I owe them an apology? How dare you belittle my mother like that?"

"You live in fear, Kay. Your whole life is about how you can control chaos so you never get touched, but that's not realistic. It doesn't allow for healthy relationships, and I happen to think you're a great catch. I would like to see you enjoy your life more, not spend it planning things for others to enjoy. Did you ever think about how you enable this singles group by doing everything for them? I mean, sheesh, Kay. It's almost a wonder you don't bib them before you feed them every Saturday night."

"Quit turning this back on me. This is about you not having any say in your own wedding. It's pathetic, Ashley, just like you waiting around for Seth to get his act together. He left you for India. Are you going to let Kevin walk out too because you can't speak your mind?"

"If Kevin wants to, yes, I am. Wouldn't it be better that he walk out on me now than after the wedding? See, I learned something in my relationship with Seth. Maybe I was a slow learner, but I did learn. I didn't wall myself off to make sure I never got hurt again."

"You're setting Kevin up to do just that. Fight for him, Ashley. Show him he means something to you! Show him now that you're not going to take his mother's garbage, or you'll spend your whole life being her victim. It's going to make him mad, sure. Who wants to be thrust into that conflict? But you mark my words. If you don't make him do it now, he never will!"

At this moment, Kay and I stare at each other, our eyes narrowed, our backs curved like cats with our claws at the ready. Soon, we start to giggle. "Other people's problems are so easy to solve, aren't they?"

"I'll make you a promise, Ashley. I'll forgive Simon and tell him so, if you tell that mother-in-law of yours to take a long hike off a short pier. This is *your* wedding, and you'll be having the kind of ceremony you want. You stop being a doormat, and I'll stop wiping my feet on Simon."

"And if Kevin blows a gasket, and there is no wedding?"

"Then, like you said, better to find out before the ceremony."

I thrust out my hand. "You've got yourself a deal." I hardly think apologizing to Simon is going to be the end for Kay, but it's a start. Maybe the starting gate is all that's necessary for the full run to take place.

There's a text message beeping on my cell phone. It's from Kevin.

Luv u.
Sorry.
B Hm soon.

"I'll fight for him, all right!"

30

My wedding shower fills me with mixed emotions. I mean, I love to get presents. Who doesn't? But I have to act excited over kitchenware, and that fills me with trepidation. "Oooh, yea! An egg poacher!" I practice into the mirror with a plastered-on smile. Kay appears behind me in the reflection.

"I'm glad I didn't get you the egg poacher. You're not very convincing."

"An egg poacher assumes I'm going to make eggs Benedict, which assumes I'm going to learn how to make a reduction sauce. And I'm not going to learn any of these things, so an egg poacher is simply the symbol of failure to me. I will fail at this. Gee, thanks for highlighting my weaknesses."

"You talk about me being obsessive. At least I'm obsessive about things that matter. Hollandaise is easy. It just takes time and the right temperature. And if you get a double boiler today, you'll be all set."

"You didn't buy me a double boiler, did you?" I ask, crinkling my nose in distaste.

"Ashley, I live with you. If I bought you something for the kitchen, it would have to do with coffee, as that's the only time I ever see you in there."

"Good girl, Kay. I've taught you well."

"Are you ready to go? If that's as good as you can do on your fake thank-yous, we should get this over with."

"How's my outfit?" I twist and turn. "Kevin bought it for me when we shopped for our registry." I model the pink pencil skirt like I'm Doris Day. "It makes me want gloves."

"It's lovely, but it would be nice to see him once in a while."

"From your mouth to God's ears. He comes home tonight, but with the shower, I won't see him until at least tomorrow."

"But after all, tomorrow is—"

"Yeah, funny. Let's go."

"Is your sister-in-law going to be here today? Should I dress better?"

"You should dress better, regardless of Emily, but yeah, she's coming. And my mother-in-law. *To be*, my in-laws-to-be. Heaven knows I'm not claiming them until I have no choice."

"Okay, Ashley, remember," she says like a quarterback in a huddle, "if they get out of hand, you need to deal with it now, or it's going to get significantly worse after marriage."

"I got it. Break! Did you put Rhett out already?" I ask.

"He's happy as a clam. New chew toy and everything. The yard is his oyster."

Brea is hosting the shower, which drives Kay crazy. Kay is the consummate entertainer. Brea will probably have beanie-weenies and Sprite with sherbet floating in the middle of it. If we're lucky, maybe some chips and store-bought dip. Brea is my oldest and dearest friend, and I know she's thrilled I am finally making the leap to marriage. In her excitement, she has failed to remember that she's a terrible organizer and entertainer, and that calling on Kay might not have been a bad idea. It's not that I care what's served at the shower, only that my two best friends are satisfied with the outcome. I can fake enthusiasm over a salad spinner anywhere.

When we get to Brea's, she's got a grouping of green and pink helium balloons out front. I hear Kay groan, but she does her best to recover. "Brea could have at least allowed me to bring something. What's her theme? Lilly Pulitzer?"

"Brea wanted to do this, Kay. It's been hard for us since she got married. We barely see each other since Miles and Jonathan came along. This is her way of going out of her comfort zone."

"Just so you know, Ashley. If I ever get married? Hire a caterer. I won't be offended that you didn't try it yourself."

"Done. But if Kevin's mother has her way, I'll turn into the Stepford Betty Crocker soon and whip up your hollandaise in my pearls."

"No one is that powerful. Not even Kevin's mother."

"You know, I just don't see what the big deal is about cooking. I think it's great that you're a fabulous cook, Kay. I wish I had it in me, but you can literally go to the store and buy ready-made salads, premarinated meats. What's the big deal about doing it yourself?"

"It tastes better that way, Ashley. Premarinated and probably chock full of preservatives. Not to mention, it costs more. Your problem is you don't have refined taste buds."

"Maybe not, but my credit card wrist is about as evolved as they come."

We enter the shower and all the women yell, "Surprise!"

Since it wasn't a surprise, not sure what to do with this, but I smile gleefully, I hope. *This is my official wedding shower! I am the bride!* I did not have to purchase a set of beach towels (my normal shower gift) for someone else. Now I really do look gleeful.

Mrs. Novak comes toward me wearing—surprise!—a St. John knit suit. "Ashley, Emily and I are so happy we could be here today."

"Thank you."

My mom comes toward me with baby Davey in her arms. "Can you believe it's here? You're almost wed, and here I never thought I'd live to see the day." She snuggles up the baby's face, suddenly switching to baby talk. "Did we, my precious little Davey-Wavey? Never thought we'd see the day." Mom pats my cheek briefly, then turns her attention back to her grandson, where it belongs.

Mei Ling comes and kisses me on the cheek. "I have a surprise for you. Come into the bedroom with me."

I say hello to my aunts and make all the possible niceties before disappearing into the front bedroom. Brea has every toy imaginable stuffed in here. It looks like a Toys "R" Us suffered a major earthquake and their shelves were emptied. The floor is completely invisible. "Wow, Brea cleaned up."

Mei Ling is giddy with excitement. "Sit down."

"What's going on?"

"I made you something. Since you got your dress already."

"Did you and Dave get me the dress?"

"Us? Ashley, we're having trouble buying Ikea furniture for our place. We don't have the cash to buy you a dress, but I would have made you one if someone else hadn't done that. You know that."

"Who did it? Do you know?"

"I don't know." Mei Ling opens the closet door and brings out a garment bag. "I know you were trying to decide on this, but I think this will be perfect. And I really wanted to do something for you. I know all about the red egg and ginger party, Ashley. Your brother has a heart of gold and a wallet of tin. Thank you for doing that for us and for keeping it quiet. He was quite the hit with my family."

"How'd you know I did it?"

"Wives know everything. You'll see." She giggles. "Actually, Ping's sent a copy of the credit card receipt." Mei Ling hands me a scrap of paper. "It had your name on it, and I put two and two together." Mei Ling unzips the garment bag she's brought and pulls out a bridal veil.

"Mei Ling, what did you do?" It's the most beautiful veil I've ever seen. It has a platinum leaf-chain design on a tiara, dotted with Austrian crystals with more crystals rising out of the center in a flower style. The flowing tulle of the veil is anchored by more crystals and seed pearls. I'm utterly speechless as she holds it out.

"Do you like it?"

I grasp the veil and walk toward the mirror. "I don't know what to say, Mei Ling. It's the most beautiful thing I've ever seen."

"Kay let me into your closet. It matches your gown perfectly. I checked before I made it."

"Mei Ling, that you would spend time to make it for me is amazing. My brother doesn't deserve you." I hug her in a tight embrace, and I can feel the tears well up. "You're ruining my makeup."

"I'm just glad you like it. I wanted to do something for you because you've always been there for us. I know your mother is really into being a grandmother. I also know what it's like to get married without my mother, so I'm sorry for that. I feel a bit responsible, and I wanted you to know we'll do everything to make you feel like the spoiled bride."

I laugh. "Mei Ling, my mother is a better grandmother than a wedding planner anyway. She's been hanging on to the coated almonds for a while now. And there's still eight weeks to go!"

We both giggle and hug one more time. We zip the veil back up and enter into the world of the wedding shower. The toilet paper stands in pyramids awaiting the obligatory wedding dress game, and there are pink and green decorations everywhere.

"Brea, everything looks great!" I say.

"You think? I made hummus sandwiches. Do you think everyone will eat them?"

Um, no. "Sure they will. Who doesn't like mashed garbanzos?"

"You're right. I'm worrying over nothing. This was just so stressful, and John had to get the babies out on his own. I thought he might go crazy just loading all the stuff he needed to get out of here."

Since my friend Brea has become a mother, her dietary habits have changed significantly. Five years ago, if I'd told her she'd be serving hummus sandwiches at my wedding shower, she would have laughed me off the face of the planet. But the complete dissolution of hydrogenated oil products has forever changed her. And I fear the loss of some of her taste abilities is the final result.

After a meal of bean sandwiches and fruit punch, we play the games no one wants to play and then get to the gifts. My aunts are here, in full sparkly regalia as always. They won the wedding dress contest like they always do. Toilet paper is their medium.

My first gift is from Mei Ling. "Mei Ling, you already got me something."

"That was just a thank-you present. This is for your wedding."

I unwrap the silver paper and find a small picture of Kevin and me in a silver heart frame. "It's beautiful, Mei Ling." Gazing into the picture, I'm reminded just how long it's been since I've seen my beloved. All while seeing Seth every day.

"Maybe it's not that practical," Mei Ling says. "But I'll tell you, when your brother drives me crazy, and I look at a photo where I'm beaming at him, I remember all the reasons I married him. I want you to remember that always too. Because some days it's easy to forget."

"It's perfect, thank you."

Next.

A myriad of gifts until the final tally reads like this:

ASHLEY WILKES STOCKINGDALE'S
FIRST WEDDING SHOWER GIFTS

2 crock pots
1 double boiler
1 salad spinner
1 teak salad set
Too much silverware
8 bath towels
3 serving platters (none of them matching my dishware)

1 down comforter and expensive sheets from my mother

4 gaudy glass frames

3 Frederick's of Hollywood outfits (and I use the term loosely— as most *outfits* do not come with a thong—from my aunts, naturally). *Thank you?*

The doorbell rings, and I feel the plastered smile on my face relax for a moment. A break.

My Aunt Babe thrusts underwear toward me. "It's a comfort thong!"

Not even gonna ask.

"Smile, Ashley, and just say thank you," my mother hisses through clenched teeth.

Okay, but I imagine everyone is getting a mental image of me in this costume, and that's just not right. Lingerie should be Italian, certainly not colored lace from third-world countries. There's a separation between sexy and sleazy, and I'm certain my aunts have led their entire lives not understanding this fine division.

"Ashley, it's Kevin!" Brea shouts.

I look up and see my fiancé for the first time in a week. He's like a wavy mirage, a miracle. I forget about appearances completely and rush to his arms, clutching him like if I let go, he'll disappear. He smells the same, minus the hospital antiseptic smell, and his perfect teeth smile down upon me like a Crest commercial. I squeeze a bit harder. "You're here."

"I heard the lingerie party was here," he whispers into my ear.

"Thanks to my aunts, it is," I say, biting my lip.

"Even better; it will be naughty."

"Stop! Does this mean you're finally here for premarital counseling?"

He looks down at my aunt, who's dangling the thong publicly. "We need more than that to get ready for marriage?"

"Oddly, yes, we do." I pull him down closer so I can get to his ear. "And if you think I'm wearing that, you've been in surgery for far too long."

He snaps his fingers. "Let's get out of here," he growls. "I haven't kissed my woman for ages."

"Kevin!" I say aloud. "Did you see your mom and sister . . . and everyone else here?"

He turns back to my ear, "Actually, I was still thinking underwear. Are we married yet?"

I slap the side of his arm. "Kevin went to Philly to interview for neonatal surgery, everyone!"

A polite round of applause goes up.

"Want a hummus sandwich, Kev? You must be hungry from traveling." Brea holds out a tray, and I shake my head ever so slightly.

"No thanks. I had some pretzels on the plane."

His mother steps up and lifts her chin. "Aren't you going to say hello, Kevin?"

"Hello, Mother." Kevin kisses Elaine's cheek coldly.

"Did you see the new house in Philadelphia?" she asks, and the entire room waits for his answer.

"Can we talk about this later, Mom?"

"It makes me want to get married," Emily spouts. "A new house! You're so lucky, Kevin."

My mother's jaw drops. "You bought them a house?"

"His dad just bought a new investment, Mom," I say, trying not to make my family feel like the poor relations.

"Well, they'll need a place to live in Pennsylvania," Elaine says, fiddling with her diamond tennis bracelet.

"Ashley," my mother says. "What is she talking about?"

"Open our gift," Emily says excitedly.

Slowly and gingerly, I open their present. I pull out a fluffy bathrobe with the name of a country club plastered on an embroidered emblem. "A bathrobe!" I say, faux excitedly.

"Look underneath it!" Emily cheers.

"It's a golf outfit." *Not even a cute one, mind you. Lilly Pulitzer makes golf wear. Tommy Bahama even! This is straight out of the Lacoste collection. Let's forget the fact I don't actually golf.*

Suddenly, everyone makes their excuses and dissipates like Jell-O in hot water. Mrs. Novak takes me aside roughly. "You'll notice the certificates are in the name of Mrs. Kevin Novak."

"I plan to take his name," I say, hoping to refute the feminist argument. "I think that's wonderful."

"Kevin, if you only knew the mistakes I made when I was young. I'd like to spare Ashley those awful days."

Here's the part where I'm supposed to believe Elaine wants the best for me. I'll buy that right after a Birkin bag goes on sale for $100.

Emily's got a sly smile on her face, so I'm bracing.

"The certificates are the best part of the gift, Ashley. I'd like to send you to finishing school before the wedding. To acquaint you with Southern hospitality." Elaine is oblivious to all the guests, which—as my aunts are still talking about thongs—might be a gift from above. "There's a fabulous finishing school that specializes in training wives of executives."

Finishing school? *Oh, trust me, I'm finished.* "Actually, I *am* an executive, Elaine. Maybe this is for Kevin?" I try to pass this off with laughter.

"Mom, Ashley's brilliant. She—"

"I never implied she was anything but, Kevin. However, this is about learning to entertain at the level that will be expected of her."

At this point, Brea can sense my "brilliance" about to reach out and touch someone, so she comes up behind me. "Excuse us, Ashley needs to say good-bye to her guests."

"That woman is nuts," I mumble. "St. John, Brea. She wears couture that's so 1970s, I'm surprised she didn't get me an apron for my shower."

"She's just posturing, Ashley. It's what mother-in-laws do to let you know they still own their sons. You play the game, get married, and then show them who has the keys to the kingdom. It's the cirrrcle, the circle of life!" she sings from *The Lion King.*

"Okay, Mom, we'll discuss it," I hear Kevin say. "In the meantime, can you be more supportive of Ash, please?"

A flat-lipped smile from Mrs. Novak. *I didn't even know she could flatten those collagen-injected lips!* She collects her handbag and turns with Emily at her side. I start to pick up some of the gifts when she catches my chin with her finger and says quietly, "I don't know what hold you have over Kevin when he should be readying for his new job, not traipsing down the aisle, but I feel it my duty to warn you that destroying his future for the sake of your own is hardly the Christian thing to do."

"What hold she has?" Brea dangles my new lingerie. "Kevin hasn't seen her in this yet." Brea winks at my future mother-in-law, and I go from wanting to seriously deck her to holding back guffaws. *Hah, see if they teach me that in finishing school!*

I start to put the gifts in my trunk, and Kevin follows after me. "So are you willing to talk about a new house in Philly? Moving to Philly? Or even finishing school?" He puts the new comforter in my trunk, but it won't fit, so he pulls it back out. "This is nice."

I nod. "It's from my mom. You're kidding about finishing school, right?" But I'm not seeing a lot of humor in his eyes. "Isn't that for English orphans or something?"

"It's a small thing my mom is asking. She just wants to know you respect her, the life that she's lived."

"Then she needs to respect me, Kevin. I'm a lawyer. My life's goal is not to graduate from trophy wife school."

"It will be a couple weekends here and there. For me?"

"Maybe I'm not worthy of the Novak name, and you shouldn't bother to lower yourself into my world."

Kevin's jaw locks. "Maybe I shouldn't."

"Well, it will be no skin off your nose, because the wedding gift is addressed to whomever you marry. I'll be sure and forward her the

Scarlett O'Hara gown too so you can still have the wedding of your sister's dreams!"

"Ashley, you're being childish. We haven't seen each other in a week, and you're just thinking of all the bad stuff."

"I'm being childish? I'm not the one so concerned about my mommy." I climb into my car. "Tell Brea I'll get the rest of my gifts later." I hit the accelerator and speed off, leaving the man I love standing in the street with a comforter in his arms. A comforter in the arms where I belong, and if I had any sense of humility, I'd turn my car around and beg his forgiveness. But I can't stand to think of his mommy winning another round. So I don't. *Forgive me, Lord. I'm such a mess.*

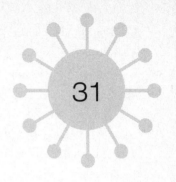

31

Churchless, fiancé-less, but determined not to be shoeless, I spend Sunday morning sewing the beads back on my wedding shoes. Granted, I didn't know the first place to start, but Kay helped me with a needle and directions before she left for church. The beads are bumpy and the rows are no longer straight, but no one's examining my shoes that day either. I gaze into the crystal beads looking through the prism of color and wonder if they'll ever really see the light of my wedding day. Will they ever catch the glimmer of sunlight? Or walk beside my father down an aisle? These questions remain as I sew. It's 1:00 p.m. when the doorbell finally rings. Rhett begins to bark, and I put the project down. "Please let it be Kevin." This isn't so much a prayer as a desperate cry for an end to my confusion. *Am I getting married or not?*

I can't help but wonder if Kevin's allegiance is aligned with his mother and sister. Call me crazy, but this is something I need to know now, as I have no intention of spending my life in Elaine and Emily Novak's skeletal shadows. But being alone doesn't sound all that great at the moment either.

Going to the door, I see that it's not Kevin. It's Matt Callaway. *Make my disappointment complete.* Matt's dressed in a button-up shirt and a tie. A tacky one, but hey, he's got a tie on. Not something you see every day anymore.

"Emily's not here. She's at her brother's." I start to slam the door.

He steps in and shuts the door behind him, "Nice to see you too. I'm here for my date with Kay. Would you let her know I've arrived?"

Kay? I just feel a wave of rage roll through my frame. *Why can't Kay see who this guy is?* "Sure. I'll just send Jeeves to the north wing and announce you. Please have a seat in the library." I roll my eyes and head down the hallway, muttering to myself. I rap on Kay's door, and she opens the door, still dressed from church and now wearing makeup. Granted, not well, but she's wearing it nonetheless. I'd fix her, but . . . nah, I gotta fix her. "Get back in here. You have lip pencil on your nose."

Kay grabs her nose and backs into her room. "Before you say a thing, I'm doing what you told me. I'm facing my fears. I apologized to Simon, prayed about this, and, Ashley, I'm going to do this. We're just going out to dinner. All right?"

"Do what you want. You're a grown woman. I'm not going to tell you what to do, just my opinion of it." I let a smile slip.

"How about we make a deal? If I kiss Matt, I don't tell you the gory details. And if you have an opinion on the matter, you'll keep it to yourself?"

"Deal." I brush the lip pencil off her nose, pound some powdered foundation in its place, and spread it around. "There, a nice even coverage. Now you'll look incredible, and guys will fall at your feet. Then you'll see you don't need to settle for the likes of Matt Callaway."

Kay clutches her neck dramatically. "Matt comes in closer, his lips puckered neatly as he leans toward my face . . ."

"*Stop!* That's just inhumane! Go on your date. I'll say no more."

She bounds down the hallway, my floral skirt flowing behind her. *How come it looks so much cuter on her?* Probably because she jogs five miles a day while I drain mochas. They aren't even out the door when the doorbell rings again.

"Ashley, I think you'd better come out here," Kay calls.

I walk to the front door, and Kevin is standing there. Dressed like

Captain Rhett Butler. He has a black tux on, with a gray ascot and white shirt. Even a top hat. He bows deeply when he sees me.

"Kevin? What are you doing? It's a little early for Halloween, isn't it?" He looks like a dream, and I have to say I'm beside myself with joy at the sight of him. "You're really here."

"Get your Scarlett dress on, Ashley," he says in his sexiest Southern drawl.

"What are you doing?"

"Get your Scarlett gown. We're going courtin' and we have a social visit to make."

"In our Scarlett-and-Rhett wear?" I ask him in disbelief. *What happened to my sober pediatric surgeon? Why is he dressed like a fictional movie icon? Is there such a thing as jet lag from Philadelphia to California?*

"Go on, I'll wait." Kevin says with a sweep of his top hat to his chest.

Kay and Matt are standing beside him, eyes wide.

"Pleased to meet you," Kevin says and thrusts out a hand toward Matt. "Kevin Novak at your service."

"Novak?" Matt coughs. The guilt is like phlegm in his throat, and I can tell he's wondering if he should expose his name. "Matt Callaway," he says through a cough. Nice to meet you."

"I'm not getting dressed until you tell me where we're going," I announce with my fist to my hip. "I don't exactly look like Gisele in this dress."

"Again, no idea what a gazelle is, except some kind of African deer. I hope you don't look like that," Kevin says, and how can you not love that? "I'm taking you home to Tara, Ashley Wilkes Stockingdale. Go get dressed."

"I can't get into that contraption without help."

"Even better—"

"I'll help," Kay quickly says. "This I gotta see. It lost something with the jail-cell background."

I notice the glimmer of fear on Matt's face as realization strikes that he'll be left alone with Emily's brother. *Payback is so fun to watch. Sue me.* It's that whole "Vengeance is mine" thing. Usually God doesn't give you the pleasure of watching it unfold. I'd give anything to just sit right here and watch it happen, but Kay yanks me.

We skip to my room. Kay and I giggle as we take the dress out of its bag. "That thing is hideous." Kay throws her head back in laughter. It dawns on me that I bet I could count the times I've seen her truly laugh like that on one hand. Even if I was missing three fingers. "Where on earth do you think he's going to take you dressed like this?" Kay asks. We look at the hoop, and both our eyes go wide. *No on the hoop.* I don't even have to say it aloud. Kay nods in agreement.

"Maybe we're going to one of those old-time picture studios." I shrug.

"Wouldn't that be fun?" Kay says and starts on the litany of buttons.

"What if I have to go to the bathroom?"

"You'd better hope you have a strong bladder."

"How utterly reassuring."

We get the dress cinched up, and Kay asks, "Where's the veil?"

"No veil. Am I not ridiculous enough?"

"You have to have the veil, Ashley. Kevin's wearing a top hat. Marriage is all about sharing. You'd let him have that humiliation alone?"

"Um, yeah."

She grabs the veil from the bag and tries to figure out how to attach the yellowed lace.

"I'll do it. Are you in on this?"

"I have no idea what he's doing. I'm completely naive."

I tug at my dress and try to appear sophisticated as I walk down the hallway dressed like an 1860s prom queen. When I get to the door, I can't look at Kevin. I feel completely exposed in this inane getup. Kevin sinks to his knees, and my stomach tingles. I thought I loved Seth, but I only loved the idea of Seth. With Kevin, I know it's real. No more immature outbursts or running away from conflict. I'm in this for the long haul.

"Ashley Wilkes Stockingdale, you are truly a Southern belle." He kisses my hand and stands up, cupping his arm through mine.

"What did they do to you in Philly? You didn't get into the drugs, did you?"

He kisses my cheek. "Philadelphia, followed by your wedding shower, gave me a new set of priorities, and you and I are going to test-drive them. Right now."

We walk down the path together, garnering the attention of all my neighbors. I'd like to say this is not the kind of attention I'd hoped for in my life, but after having had these same stares while getting put into the backseat of a police car, I'm okay with it, actually.

Kevin helps me into the car and goes around to the driver's side. He looks at me for a long time, and sparks fly. My stomach remembers all the reasons I'm marrying this man. Love alone may not be enough, but add some major chemistry to it, and I'll tell you something, it's a good start. We drive for a while until we come to his condo.

"What are we doing here?" Seeing the rental car out front, I'll admit, my hopes fade.

"We are paying a social call, Ashley Wilkes Stockingdale."

"Dressed like this? And would you stop calling me that?"

"It's the best way. My family thrives on secrets and quiet conversations. And this is one we're going to have out loud. Can you think of a better way to announce ourselves?"

"Yes, actually. This seems like a DKNY moment to me. Maybe Hugo Boss for you. Perhaps it's a couture moment, Chloe maybe. But it is definitely not a Civil War reenactment moment."

"Then it's a good thing I'm not asking for your opinion, isn't it?"

I slough off the wedding shoes, deciding I definitely need a Birkenstock equivalent before the big day.

"You're going in there barefoot?"

"Look at me, Kevin. Least of my problems."

We head up the walkway, which seems incredibly short all of a sudden, and Kevin rings his own doorbell and then pushes the door open, gently guiding me in first. "No way!" I shuffle behind him. "I'm not being the human shield. Gentleman first in this case."

He walks in the front door. "Mom! Emily!"

I stand behind him. My heart is beating out of my chest. The simple fact is these women scare me. Mrs. Novak is the first to come out. For once, I see she's not in a St. John knit. She's wearing a silk running suit that just makes me think, *Static cling!* She's donning invisible-line glasses, which she slides slowly down her nose and to her side.

"Kevin?" she says sternly.

"Mother."

Emily comes in next, and she has on a pair of swanky jeans. Sevens by the looks of them. Now I can't help wondering if she doesn't have the obligatory tattoo on her lower back. But I'm dressed like Holiday Barbie, so who am I to judge?

"Emily," Kevin says in Alex Trebek baritone.

"Are you two going to a costume ball?" Emily giggles nervously.

"No, we're doing a dress rehearsal in the wedding gear you bought us."

Elaine gasps.

"I have a date." Emily grabs her purse.

"Your date is out with Kay tonight. Sit down," Kevin orders.

Both Elaine and Emily slowly take a seat on the couch. By the looks on their faces, they're not sure if we might have some murderous plots on our mind. Can you imagine the headline: "Scarlett Harlot and Treacherous Rhett Kill Southern Heritage."

Kevin interrupts my *Court TV* fantasies. "I've been doing a little digging this week. I've turned into quite the investigative journalist. My fiancée was a bit upset over the phone because apparently, quite a few things about our wedding had been changed without her knowledge. Including her own wedding dress. See Exhibit A." Kevin points at me. He begins to pace the room with his hands behind his back. "I called Amy Carmichael." He faces Emily. "I'd like to state my other sources, but for obvious reasons, I didn't need any."

Emily sits up to bolt for the door, but Kevin puts his hand up, and she sits back down.

Elaine rises. "This is a family discussion. And as such, we shall have it as a family."

"Sit down, Mother. We are a family. This is my betrothed. Ashley, curtsey to your future mother-in-law, will you?"

I bow and stretch my skirt out extensively. *I could get into this.* I bet you'd have to eat a lot of truffles and frappuccinos before it caught up with you in one of these. You'd just keep cinching that corset until the whalebone wouldn't move anymore. Think of the freedom they had. Carbs were virtually unknown, let alone counted.

Kevin's voice booms again. "It turns out, Mother, that my baby sister, the wedding coordinator, went to the Lenox Square Bloomingdale's with Amy posing as my bride. They picked out virtually everything for our registry, which forced Ashley and me to do it all over again. This was much more difficult than starting from scratch."

"As I said, Kevin"—Elaine's threatening glare mixes with the cold steel in her voice—"this is family business, and as a family, we will discuss it."

Kevin's face goes a shade of red I've not seen before. "*This!*" He points at me. "*This* is my family. Ashley will be my wife. I love her. You either accept that, or we're done. Both of you will stop trying to control my life by sabotaging it. Do you hear me?"

His mother gasps. "I did not raise you up to speak to me this way. And all for a woman dressed like a cartoon character."

Okay, I'm really wishing my mommy and her candied almonds with tulle circles were here. Lord, I will never make fun of the Dollar Store again. Thank you, Jesus, for my mother and her tuna casserole and her Jell-O pudding pies! Normal mothers are a gift from God!

Kevin's face is getting redder. "Mother, Emily, do you remember that scene where Rhett sweeps Scarlett upstairs?"

Both women are looking horrified at the shared memory.

"I'll take that as a yes." Kevin swoops me off the floor, the dress catches on a lamp, and it goes tumbling to the floor. "I always hated that lamp. Mother, Emily"—and then he looks straight at me with his dark green eyes—"this is where I close the door on the old ways."

"We were just trying to protect you, Kevin!" Elaine cries, sobbing into her hands, then peeking out to see if it's working. "How on earth do you expect to host the chief of surgery with a lawyer as your wife?" Elaine says "lawyer" like "prostitute," but whatever.

"I don't need your protection anymore. I'm a grown man, and it's time I acted like it. Now if you'll excuse us, Scarlett and I are going courting. If you plan to be at my wedding, I'll send you details the Friday before. Emily, consider yourself fired. Mother, Ashley isn't taking any classes on how to be the proper wife, other than the premarital classes with our pastor. She is perfect for me just like she is."

"We're only trying to protect you from a future that will be wrought with—"

"Frankly, my dear mother, I don't give a—"

"Kevin!" I gasp.

He turns with me still in his arms, and we sweep out the door. Well, stagger is more like it. Kevin is beet-red by the time we get to the porch, and thoroughly winded. He sets me down.

"That's it? Rhett Butler took Scarlett to the top of that big staircase."

"That's because he knew what was waiting at the end of that staircase. We're not married yet, so I'm not as motivated."

I crack up and throw my arms around his neck. "I love you, Dr. Kevin Novak."

"Do you believe me now? That I love you more than anything? That I will leave my mother and cleave to you?"

Thinking about his mother's stunned expression, his sister's rage . . . "Yeah, I believe you now." We head for the car.

"Good, because a man can only take so much estrogen. Sheesh, I'm beginning to see why Seth had such an issue with commitment."

"Let's not forget he committed before you. He and Arin have already done the deed." I cross my arms in front of me.

"He settled. I didn't. Much less work involved when you settle. On the front end, that is." He winks at me and forces my skirt into the car before shutting the door.

W e drive for what seems an eternity. Kevin lets nary a word out without saying something about Philadelphia. Clearly, it was a mountaintop experience for him, with the satisfaction he found in the work there. Well, let's just say it tops having my name on a patent. We drive into Atherton's majestic tree-lined streets. Now Atherton is a town where residents consider the police their private security guards. Considering everything is hardwired with laser beams in the houses, the police keep themselves busy with speed traps in town.

"Don't speed through here," I warn.

"Ashley, they're going to pull us over anyway for driving a Dodge through here."

We both laugh. This used to be the town where Stanford doctors lived, but those days are mostly gone since high-tech stock options made cash for homes like Monopoly money. Soaring prices locked most doctors out of Atherton's price range. Often, these young yuppies will pay cash upwards of $6 million for a house. In other words, we're not exactly driving in our element.

"Where are we going?" I ask, knowing full well I'm probably not going to get an answer. But considering I'm dressed like Scarlett? The quieter the destination, the better.

"To the closest thing I could find to a Southern plantation in Silicon Valley."

Kevin pulls into a long brick driveway, and when the trees give way, I see a gargantuan Georgian estate. It is brick and stately on the grass mound of the property's center. Four white gables make me think of that book I hated in high school. A pristine white central door and window rise to the second floor in stately majesty. The entire lawn perimeter is surrounded by a short, cropped hedge, and every leaf seems to be in place. Kevin sets the emergency brake.

"What are we doing here? Your parents didn't buy this place for us, did they?" *Because if they did, I totally owe them the apology of my life.*

"You wish, Ashley. This is the chief of surgery's house. He's in Bermuda this week and offered it to me for what I needed to do. I borrowed it for this special occasion, so that we could be in our Southern element, of course, while we make some serious decisions."

Gulp. "What might those be?"

"Well, I had a lot of time to think in Philadelphia, believe it or not. You know, Ashley, this is the first time I realized what I wanted from my life. This is no longer about my dad or impressing him or being in the right job for my parents to brag about at the country club. Finally, this job is for me. This is what I love, having an impact on a child's future before God even brings that baby into the world. I've been giving my parents way too much power."

I have tears in my eyes as he explains, because once again, I see the man I fell in love with. "Philadelphia is calling," I state.

He nods. "I have to go, Ashley. I have to. I know I told you it was our decision, but, Ash, I need you to trust me to make this decision for us. I just know it's what is right for our future. I swept you off your feet to show you I'm done living for my parents. It's about us now."

"Kevin, how can I leave Gainnet now? They won't have anyone in legal. Except Tracy, and I think her low-cut blouses will do little to further patents."

"I'm asking you to come with me. I promised I wouldn't do that, but I can't alter this course, Ashley. I know this is where I'm supposed to be. If Holly, my little patient, had this operation in utero, she'd be healthy. She'd have her mother and her siblings. Maybe she never would have had the best family, but who does?"

"You got me there."

"I realized the love I felt for Holly as a patient. The responsibility. It was supposed to be there to lead me down the right path. Surgeons aren't supposed to be just like my father. That's not God's plan. The *secret* is to not allow your emotions to stop you from being effective."

I sewed beads back on my shoes while you were gone.

"You're leaving." Just like Seth. I feel my heart begin to pound. I focus on the silk leaves on my gown. Not only am I getting dumped, but I'm dressed for the high school play. The indignity!

Kevin gets out of the car and comes around for me. "I hope that *we're* leaving." He takes my hand, and we walk up the path to the great brick house.

Kevin unlocks the door, and we enter the most magnificent foyer I've ever seen. It's enormous, with soaring ceilings and a massive French window that reaches to the sky and brings the outside in. There's wainscoting at every level, and it's all painted a crisp white, making me feel as though I'm in a grand English estate.

"This is incredible."

"It's ten thousand square feet. We'll be lucky if our lot is ever that big."

"Point taken. I wouldn't want to clean all these bathrooms anyway."

"There are eight and a half of them. Doc is quite proud of that fact."

"Shut up!"

"I'm not kidding."

"You wouldn't even need to go to the gym, Kevin. You could just run around to the different bathrooms all day, and you'd be like a marathon runner. You just drink water, and on your mark, get set, go!"

"You really make me nervous sometimes."

Kevin leads me into the living room, which is decorated ad nauseam in baby blue: blue sofas, blue walls, blue sea paintings. Even with money available, there's no accounting for taste.

I sit down on the blue settee and drape my skirt around me dramatically. "I shall never decorate with one colah scheme again," I say, placing the back of my hand on my brow.

Kevin gets on his knee and takes my hand.

"What are you doing?"

"I want my grandmother's ring back." He looks at the ring and up at me again. "Do you mind?"

I get that sick feeling you get at the bottom of a roller-coaster ride. "Sure," I say as I yank it off. *Not getting this!* My stomach roils as I pull the ring off. *Another man packing a moving truck to escape me.* Okay, that's not really fair. Seth didn't take more than his video-game collection and a few pairs of khakis.

Kevin sees my turmoil and laughs with a tender smile. "Ashley, I brought you here to tell you that I want to carry you away if you'll let me." Suddenly, Kevin produces a brand-new ring. The diamond is amazing, and it sparkles and shows an array of rainbow colors under the light.

I clap my hands frantically. "Ooh, ooh, is that for me? I love presents! Especially diamond presents! See?" I pull my hair back. "I have my earrings on."

"Ashley Stockingdale, my grandmother was the meanest woman I ever knew. Your first engagement ring was her ring, and I can't let you wear it anymore in good conscience. I want to start fresh, not with my family's history attached to your finger and our marriage. Yes, my parents are still together, but only because neither one of them would admit to the failure of a divorce. So we're starting our own heritage, here and now. I'm marrying you and divorcing my family in a way."

"I get a new ring?" Trying not to seem too eager. After all, I loved the old ring, but seeing this one? *Gee, I'm just not nearly as loyal as I thought.*

"If you'll marry me, you do." He pulls the ring away.

"Wait a minute. I get to marry you, *and* I get a new ring? Something ain't right here." *If he's feeling this generous, maybe I can keep both.* Bad, bad Ashley!

"Ashley, if I get arthritis in my knees—"

"Okay, okay. Just one question. Philadelphia?"

"I'll resent it if I stay. I might resent you. That's the honest truth."

"I can't say yes just yet. It's not right to expect an answer while shining a diamond of that size in my face. It could be temporary blindness, and then where would I be? What if I resent you if we go to Philadelphia and I give up my job?"

Kevin stands up and lifts me off the couch. "A fair question. So I give you time to think about it. Come on out back." Kevin opens two French doors, and the sounds of a violin stream into earshot. He even arranged music for little ol' me!

"Kevin, it's perfect!"

He twirls me around and takes me into his arms. Looking into his eyes, I know as sure as I stand here that no job, no state, is worth giving him up for. I love this man with my whole heart. I want to replace his family heritage with a new one. We'll love our children if they're garbagemen. Or bus drivers.

"Okay. I've thought about it," I say nervously, feeling my breath catch in my throat. "Philadelphia, here we come."

Kevin slips the new platinum ring on my finger. "Let the party at Twelve Oaks begin!" Kevin shouts, and we break into wild laughter, while the poor violinist in sweltering gray wool accompanies us as we try an elegant reel.

"Did you know they put Clark Gable on a turning platform because he couldn't dance for that scene?"

"This is a fact-free zone, Ashley. Did I mention that? Let me revel in my moment. Right now, I have it all! The perfect job, the perfect spouse, the perfect life."

"Right back atcha, babe!"

33

"It's my wedding day! It's my wedding day! It's my wedding day!" I'm dancing around the room with my gown fluttering easily behind me. The last two months flew by, what with my settling all the patents I could before saying good-bye to everyone at Gainnet, packing boxes, and putting the finishing touches on the wedding day that I've always wanted. Yes, finally, the wedding day that *I've* always wanted.

"Yes, Ashley, it's your wedding day. Do you want to say something else now? You sound like you're stuck. I'd say like a broken record, but you probably don't remember what that is." Kay picks up the nylons I've strewn across my bed. "I didn't realize nylons were a big event for the day. What's to decide on?"

"I just can't believe I get to say it. I'm getting married today!" I sing. "Do you know how many times I lived this day through Barbies as a child? I mean, the Barbie Townhouse elevator was like, up and down wildly while Barbie prepared for her big day. Mom, you never would buy me the Ken tuxedo."

"Utter child abuse, Ashley," my mom deadpans. "Did you ever meet a more ungrateful child, Brea?"

Kay rolls her eyes. "Are you wearing any of these nylons you've got everywhere?"

I shake my head. "I'm going au naturel on the legs. Look, freshly waxed." I lift up my gown.

"Oversharing, thanks." Kay puts the stockings back into my drawer. Then she shakes her head. "No, on second thought, au naturel and you, just asking for trouble. You've had too many wardrobe malfunctions in your lifetime." She hands me the stockings, and I hang on to Brea while I try to slither into them.

My mom's taking pictures of everything. Even the discarded pantyhose. "Mom, we need photos of the nylons for what?"

"I just want to show that even on your wedding day, you were a complete slob. It will remind your father that now someone else is putting up with you, while we have our clean den."

"Amen!" Kay says. "And I won't trip over her four hundred pairs of shoes!"

"The limo should be here soon," Brea interrupts. "Your dress is perfect, Ashley! It's so elegant and flattering. Kevin's going to go nuts."

Speaking of Kevin, I can't believe I'm going to get to see him every day for the rest of my life, especially since I've hardly seen him at all since the Scarlett and Rhett Day. His new job is going well in Philadelphia, and I joined him on a couple of weekends to work on the new house. I even found a Starbucks with wireless Internet! Still searching for the roasting company, but God is good!

"You look lovely," my mom says. "The veil Mei Ling made you is the best part."

"It really is, Mei Ling. I just wish I knew where the dress came from," I say.

"Kay bought it," Brea says like I should know this.

"What? Kay?" I turn to Kay, who is busy organizing things. In my room, with boxes all around, on my wedding day, this is a hopeless cause.

Kay shrugs. "You waited your whole life for that dress. I even thought you might be desperate enough to marry Seth for it. I couldn't let you be without it because of *that woman*. I knew all the reasons you couldn't have the dress, and they were all reasons for others. You hide behind a shallow exterior, Ashley, but you'd give the

287

clothes off your back to someone else. It's just one of the secrets I've learned living with you. You'd tell someone living in denial for twenty years the truth when she needed to hear it." Kay grins, and we share our secret quietly.

I hug her tightly. "You are the best! What would I have done without you this last year?"

Seth, my beloved ex who can't seem to exit my life, needs more write-off with his new director position, not to mention his wife, so he's buying my share of the house. I can't say the situation surprises me. Considering how much time he's spent getting fed by Kay, it's probably a fair trade. The good news is that Kay will have her own place, and Seth will have his write-off while Arin tries to transform his bachelor pad into something livable. *Good luck with that.*

My stomach churns as I see the white limo drive up at the front of the curb.

"It's time," Brea says.

I grab Brea, Kay, Mei Ling, and my mom in a group hug. "I love you guys!"

Okay, no tears. The makeup is perfect.

"Enough blubber. We gotta go!" Brea announces. "I have to make sure John got Miles in his ring-bearer suit right. Let's go! Let's go!"

My mom fiddles with my veil as Kay and Brea take one last look in the mirror. "I like this boy, Ashley," Mom says. "You and Kevin will be very happy together. I hope you're as happy as I've been with your father."

Small thing, but please let me be happier than that, Lord!

After a giggle-fest in the car, we arrive at the church and take what feels like a million pictures. The truth is, I'm not all that photogenic, and I'm hoping for PhotoShop miracles here so I can remember myself as a young *Vogue* model when I'm in the rest home listening to the Dave Matthews Band. "Remember when we all looked like Angelina Jolie?" we'll say in our tired voices.

When the picture-taking finally comes to an end, I overhear

someone say that the groom isn't here, and it hits me with the force of a Florida hurricane. I can feel my heart in my throat as I wait. My hands are trembling, and I begin to have conversations without actually being present for them. People say something. I respond, but all I am really hearing is *Kevin's not here yet. Kevin's not here yet.* Something in the back of my mind fears he'll give me up for his heri-tage after all. What if I end up crying in the back pew—with Seth and his pregnant wife offering words of condolences? I hear Seth asking me if I'm okay, and by the way, does the house have any dry rot?

"He's here!" I hear Brea announce. My heart begins to beat again. "Get in the church before he sees you!" I scramble into the church's bride room, unable to wipe the huge smile from my face. *He's here. I am really getting married! I am really moving across the country with only Rhett to keep me company during the day. Today, I will become Mrs. Ashley Novak. I will leave behind General Counsel for General Manager of the home. How oddly Elaine Novak. The irony is not lost on me here.*

I pick up my bouquet and sniff the heather to remind me that dreams do come true. And I gaze upon the red tulips that remind me of my everlasting love. Gone are the hydrangeas and peonies that were Emily's idea. This is my dream. My day. My future.

After what feels like an eternity, and lots of people scrambling around me, the music starts and my dad stands beside me. Kay and Brea give me the thumbs-up sign. "It's time!" Kay says. "Listen to that, the bridal march for Ashley Stockingdale."

"Our baby is getting married!" Brea says.

"We did it!" Mei Ling says to my mother.

The bridesmaids are all satisfied in a dress that I hope they'll wear again. But all brides say that, and no one ever wears the dress again. The dress always makes you wonder, *Why am I friends with this girl, again? Do I even know this person who placed me in pink satin?* But I'm happy to report, they all look good. They're wearing a straight neckline across their collarbone and a bodice that hugs the waist. It's black, which I love the formality of, and it slims my already emaciated bridesmaid crew. At the waist, it's cinched before exploding into a full skirt in 1940s classic style. It was all created in amazing shantung silk that complements my gown, and with their black heels, they're amazing! All three of them look incredible, but more important, they *are* incredible. I wouldn't be here without any one of them.

Kay and Brea take their places beside the single doctors Kevin has standing up for him. The one he once tried to set me up with, and James, Kevin's best friend from childhood, who still lives in Atlanta. Apparently doctors like other doctors. Mei Ling will be meeting up with Dave, and Miles is my ring bearer. My family has no flower girls. We'll have to work on that.

My dad is fidgeting in his "monkey suit" and looking like he'd love to be nursing a beer about now. He lifts my veil and kisses my cheek. "You're a beautiful bride, but you were a beautiful single girl too. I'll miss my girl being around the house. You were always handy for the halftime beer," he jokes, but I see the tears in his eyes. I know he never thought he'd see this day.

Dad likes Kevin. Kevin understands sports, which is the universal male language, lost on many of the men in Silicon Valley. Certainly on Seth, and my dad never could trust a man who didn't know his football. "It's just not right," Dad would say. "Not natural for a man not to have a favorite football team."

"Mei Ling's a better daughter anyway," I quip to my dad. "She'll even frost your mug."

"No, Ashley." My dad has a sparkle in his eye. "I know we don't talk much, but that's because I figure you know what I think. You know I love you and that I couldn't be more proud of you. What else is there to say?" He shrugs.

"What indeed, Dad? I love you too." I kiss him on his cheek, and the flash nearly blinds me. The photographer is like paparazzi. *I love it! Colin Cowie's parties have nothing on an Ashley Stockingdale wedding!*

He puts the veil back in place, and we hear the "Wedding March" begin again.

"This is it," my dad says. "You sure you want to marry this no-good guy?"

"I'm sure. You're sure he's here?" I ask nervously.

"I saw him with my own eyes. He's here, and so is his family. Not many of their friends, though, so I had your brother seat people on both sides of the church."

"Here we go, Dad." He clutches my arm tightly and we start to step down the aisle.

My first look at Kevin is something right out of my dreams, and I can't stop my tears. I can't tear my eyes from his gaze either, and I don't see a soul sitting in the church. *Is there anyone here?* There's only Kevin in his black tuxedo and wide grin looking at me, beckoning me toward him with his love. I think about how when I met him, I had such illusions of grandeur about who he was. Now I've seen his love for his patients, his work, and me. He has so much love to give, and I don't feel worthy, but I am so grateful that God brought him to me. May I feel undeserving every day of my life. *Please, Lord.*

When I reach him, I see his own eyes glistening, which forces my tears down my cheeks. And I swallow over the lump in my throat. My makeup will be ruined. "Stop it," I whisper to him.

"I've never seen anyone more beautiful, Ash. I wish I could marry you every day," he whispers back.

I'm still clutching my dad's arm, but now he untangles himself and thrusts me toward Kevin. My fiancé smiles down on me, and for once in my life, I know all I need to know.

Pastor Craig, the man who discipled Kevin in Christian growth, starts the ceremony. "We are gathered here today to witness the Christian marriage and blessing of Dr. Kevin Novak and Ashley Stockingdale." He goes on, but my eyes are locked on Kevin's gaze, and my head is swimming in disbelief. *I* am standing up here. The pastor is talking to *me*! I have to look around and see Kay, Brea, and Mei Ling dressed in bridesmaid dresses. I look down and see, yes, it is me in white! How cool is this?

I'm leaving California. I'm leaving Gainnet. I'm leaving everything I know for the wild blue yonder of the unknown with a man I'm head over heels in love with. I can barely breathe at the thought of it. I should be scared to death, but I can't wait to jump. I can't wait to land in the warm, soft place that is my husband.

Kevin takes my ring and slides it down my finger. "I, Kevin Novak, take you, Ashley, to be my lawfully wedded wife. To love and cherish you as Christ loves His church. I pledge to be faithful to you and care for you as part of myself. May we grow together in His likeness and, come what may, weather the storms of life together."

The pastor looks at me, and I slide Kevin's ring on his ring finger.

"I, Ashley Stockingdale, take you, Kevin, to be my lawfully wedded husband. To love and honor you, to cherish you. To follow you through all life's experiences no matter what hills and valleys we may encounter. With this ring, I give you my love and respect. I choose to be your wife and to cherish you as long as we both shall live."

"By the power vested in me," the pastor booms, "I pronounce you man and wife. Kevin, you may kiss your bride."

I'm giggling as Kevin zeros in on my lips. *I'm a married woman!* It only took thirty-two years, three pathetic boyfriends, and a complete lack of faith on my part. Kevin turns me around, and I finally see the crowd.

"Let the games begin." Kevin winks and clutches my arm as we walk down the elegant aisle amid the gorgeous stained glass. Had I known I wouldn't even notice where I was, I would have spent less angst on the location.

I glide past Kevin's mom and sister. Elaine and Emily are applauding politely, but I fear their true emotions are painted on their expressions. I am not the bride of their dreams, and they think Kevin most definitely deserves better. Hey, he probably does. But *Read my lips, people. He's mine now!* Kevin's father looks resigned, pacified by the fact that we accepted a down payment for a house we chose, but still disgruntled that we refused the ugly gift house he already picked.

Reconciliation, I think to myself. It's my goal now, although made easier by the separation of several states.

I see Seth with a very pregnant Arin toward the back. The pregnancy shows even in her face. He smiles at me, and I smile back. He's happy for me, and I for him. It took a baby to make him act, and praise the Lord for that. He won't be alone. I see Sam sitting beside them, and I'm glad my marriage is starting out with just two people. Sacrifice in love is one thing. Looking at Seth, I'm reminded that ultimate surrender is quite another.

Matt Callaway is sitting in the last pew, fidgeting uncomfortably as he waits for Kay to finish her bridesmaid duties. They're dating seriously now, and while I can't approve, I can't do anything about it either, and I'm comfortable with that for now. I do not control the universe. Thankfully, that job belongs to Someone much more capable.

Kevin and I smile knowingly at each other. "We did it," he says.

I look down at the sparkling diamond on my left hand. We did do it. Confusion is part of God moving you out of a comfort zone. A comfort zone that should cease to exist. God's way is never the easy path, but it's by far the most exciting.

Kevin stops at the back of the church and looks at me intently. "Ashley Wilkes Stockingdale? I mean, Novak! Let's blow this popsicle stand!" He pulls me forward and we run out to the church foyer, only to be halted by a most disconcerting sight—or lack thereof. "Where's the limo?"

"Oh my goodness, I gave him directions to the reception hall and told him we'd be done about five."

Kevin starts to laugh out loud. "We don't have a way to get to our own reception?"

It's now that I see Emily running out with her Coach portfolio. "I thought something like this might happen. The limo driver's cell number is in here." Emily hands me the leather folder in a rare gesture of—could it be—kindness? "Welcome to the family, Ashley. You're a true Novak now."

293

At her words, I clutch the folder tightly to my chest and swallow hard. "I'm glad to be here, Emily."

Kevin dials the number for the limo, and the driver assures him he is just around the corner. I look at Kevin's startling green eyes and beautiful face in awe as he talks. Ashley Wilkes Stockingdale *Novak* is married! A Reason no more. Oh yeah, with this ring, I'm committed—not into an institution, but to a man who looks like Hugh Jackman on a good day. Is God good or what? I think I just might learn to trust the Lord a bit more now, lean on him instead of worrying so much. Yes, I'm sure of it.

Maybe.

Until we have children.

Children with those great green eyes and my sense of style. Oooh, children! A whole new fashion world to explore. Little, tiny Lilly Pulitzer dresses and—does Coach make diaper bags? I'm sure they must.

Wait a minute. What if they don't get my sense of style? What if they're born with a penchant for heavily sweetened iced tea, fried okra, and sweet potato pie? What if my daughter visits her favorite Aunt Emily and comes home wanting a parasol and calling me *Mothah?*

Help me, Lord!

I hear Kevin's voice, see the limo turning the corner, and suddenly realize that I've already fallen back into my worrying ways. *Sorry, Lord. I'm definitely a work in progress.*

"Ready, Mrs. Novak?" Kevin asks as I slide elegantly into the car. For once, a moment lives up to my expectation.

"Most definitely," I say. And I am. The question is, is the world ready for Mrs. Ashley Wilkes Stockingdale Novak? And how will I fit that name on my Visa card?

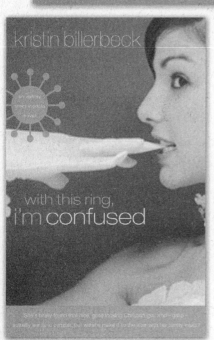

Don't miss any novels in the **Ashley Stockingdale** series!

Other novels by

Kristin Billerbeck

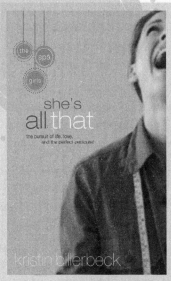